Forever After

Created by
Roger Zelazny

FOREVER AFTER

Copyright © 1995 by Bill Fawcett and Associates

A Baen Books Original.

Baen Publishing Enterprises
P.O. Box 1403
Riverdale, N.Y. 10471

ISBN: 0-671-87699-6

Cover art by David Mattingly

First printing, December 1995

Distributed by
SIMON & SCHUSTER
1230 Avenue of the Americas
New York, N.Y. 10020

Printed in the United States of America

I've been asked to dedicate
this book, Roger's final work,
to those who loved him,
and I do.

Jane Lindskold

ACKNOWLEDGEMENTS

There are many people who gave their strength and support during Roger's last days and during the sad, lonely days following his death. These include Kay McCauley, Kirby McCauley, Gerald and Lorry Hausman, George R.R. Martin, Parris, Melinda Snodgrass, Carl Keim, Sage Walker, Pati Nagel, Chris Krohn, Fred and Joan Saberhagen, Walter John Williams, David Weber, Mike Stackpole, Liz Danforth, Jay Haldeman, Steve Brust, and Neil Gaiman. To all of these people and to all of those who wrote letters, phoned, and otherwise offered help and sympathy, I offer my thanks and sincere affection.

Jane Lindskold

CONTENTS

*All preludes by Roger Zelazny

Prelude the First

Prince Rango stepped out onto the balcony and regarded the pair of comets hung in the night sky.

Pair?

He squinted at the strange, low patch of light in the west which had not been present the previous evening. It looked pretty much the way the others had but a few nights ago. Therefore, a third comet was probably on its way. Things such as this were supposed to presage the deaths of monarchs, changes in administration, social upheavals, natural disasters, the loss of price supports in industries run by one's relatives, bad weather, plagues, and losing lottery tickets. Rango smiled. He did not need signs in the heavens to tell him that change was in the air. He was part of it.

Abruptly, an ear-tormenting squeal filled the night. It was the sound of a stringed instrument played at at least a hundred times the volume of any stringed instrument ever heard in the area. Since last night, anyway. It had been occurring in the middle of the night, on and off, for about a week, and once it fell into a regular rhythm other amplified instruments joined it. Yes. There came some sort of bass. . . . And now a frantic drumbeat. Soon an invisible singer would begin shouting incomprehensible lyrics in an unknown language.

A tall, darkly handsome man, Rango raised his wine goblet and sipped from it as a ground-shaking thudding began somewhere to the east.

He sighed and turned his head in that direction. It had been strange enough, these past two months, living in a land that was not torn by civil war, a place that, for well over a decade, had been backdrop to assassinations, dark sorceries, skirmishes, quests, pursuits, escapes, vendettas, duels, betrayals, great acts of courage as well as treachery, all of them leading at last to a war in which the line was finally drawn and Good and Evil, Light and Dark, Order and Chaos, and all those other antonyms had faced off and had it out, steel against steel, spell against spell, dark gods and goddesses against their brighter relatives, toe to toe and hand to hand, the world red in tooth and claw and other combative appendages. When the dust settled, Good—in the person of himself and his followers—had just managed to squeak by.

Rango lowered his goblet and smiled. It had been touch and go there at the end, and, ultimately, nothing had gone according to the book, but he stood now in the imperial palace in Caltus, capital of the Faltane, with less than two months before the day of his wedding and coronation. Finally, with all of the perils laid to rest, he would be wed to his betrothed, the tall, dark-haired Rissa.

As the thudding sounds came more heavily out of the east—even the weird music could not completely smother them—he thought back over the years the respective adventures had taken, all rushing to culmination this past summer. . . .

Kalaran, demigod gone bad—Fallen Sunbird of high Vallada Tahana, home of the gods—had seemed to have everything going for him on the eve of the final battle. The four things which had tipped the balance against him had been the amulet, the ring, the sword, and the scroll—Anachron, Sombrisio, Mothganger, and Gwykander.

Gar Quithnick, the turncoat *hingu* master, had succeeded in recovering the lost amulet. Its protective, magic-dampening effect had saved the defenders from Kalaran's wrath. Sombrisio, the deadly ring of power, returned from the city of the dead, Anthurus, by Rissa and her big-boned blond companion, Jancy Gaine, had actually hurt Kalaran, reducing him to physical combat with the Prince. Even so, he would have faced no problem against a mortal hero no matter how well muscled, save that that muscular arm had wielded Mothganger—a godslayer of a weapon which he and his partner Spotty Gulick had brought back from *their* quest. And then there was the scroll of Gwykander—containing the words to the ancient rite of grand exorcism—delivered from the bottom of a monster-haunted lake, and rushed to the Faltane just in time. Along with the other magical tools, it was there when it was needed. Looking back, he reflected on all the coincidences, and just plain luck, involved in the four tools being conveyed to the proper place at the proper time within minutes of each other. The outcome had truly been balanced on the edge of a blade.

A white line traced itself slowly through the heavens, expanding in the wake of whatever emitted it. Shortly, there came a distant, muffled boom from overhead, followed by a growling sound.

He shook his head. While he could tell that it was neither meteor nor comet, he had no idea what the thing was. This disturbed him more than a little. He'd had enough of unknown variables tracking muddy footprints across his life's trail these past few years.

Yet, while he did not understand the nature of the disturbance, he had a fairly good idea as to what was causing it, even knew himself to be partly responsible for it. It was of a piece with the recent showers of blood, toads, rats, with the raucous parodies of music which filled the air, with the thing which shook the earth with its heavy, approaching footsteps. Indeed, it was also connected with the recent spate of unnatural births, of two-headed sheep and calves.

He sighed and smiled. It would be all dealt with. He would figure a way, as he had figured ways to deal with everything from minor annoyances to imminent doom in recent years. He had always been very fast on his mental feet.

With a sudden, silvery agitation, the small lake at the foot of one of the northern hills began to drain over its eastern edge, as if the land had suddenly been tipped. He nodded. That, too. Geography tended to rearrange itself periodically these days. Just where all that water was getting off to was not readily apparent. The site of the lake would be a muddy pit in the morning. Possibly, eventually, it would became a swamp. Or it might even be a lake again by tomorrow night. The interfaces between realities having grown somewhat thin in the neighborhood of Caltus, it was possible that a stream from some other place might be diverted to refill it.

There would be a meeting. Of course. With his chief advisers. In the morning. They would discuss the situation. He could see it all now, falling into place. Yes.

He waited out of misspent curiosity until the source of the approaching footsteps came into view—an enormous, heavy-footed, long-necked, long-tailed reptile—stomping its way slowly through the center of town, browsing leaves from various trees and thatching from peasant cottages along its course. He watched it make its way into the west, under the angled light of a rising piece of the moon. He finished his wine as it disappeared from sight, then turned and entered his apartments.

The following afternoon, as he inspected the new northern mud pit, viewing the long line of dinosaur tracks leading through it, Prince Rango was approached by the Princess Rissa along what had been the scenic lakeside trail.

"Rango, what the devil's going on?" she asked.

"Another bit of overstressed reality seems to have given way—" he began.

She glanced at the wet, brown declivity and shook her head.

"That is not what I mean," she said, jerking a quick gesture in that direction, a glowing silver ring flashing upon her hand. "I refer to this morning's meeting, to which I was not invited.

Rango winced and drew back.

"It was fairly technical," he responded. "I didn't think it would hold any interest for you at all."

"And I wouldn't even have heard about it if Jancy hadn't been involved," she said. "She just came by to say that you're taking away Sombrisio and sending it back to the ghouls."

As if in response to her latest angry gesture, there came a deep, throat-clearing gurgle at the pit's center. They both turned in that direction as a large circle of muck was sucked downward. A moment later, there came a brief rumble from underground. Then a streaming plume of liquid shot upward out of the hole, thirty, forty feet into the air.

The smell that followed was sulfurous.

"That is a part of the reason," he said. "Or, rather, a part of the effect—the reason for the meeting, and the effect we were discussing."

"She told me that you'd ordered her to take the ring back to Anthurus and secrete it there as best she might where we had found it."

"That is correct."

"And you're sending Gar Quithnick off to look for lost Gelfait to return the amulet, Anachron?"

"That, too."

". . . and Spotty north into the Penduggens, to dispose of Mothganger?"

"Right."

"And Domino Blaid is going to take the scroll of Gwykander back to the cursed lake that serves as its library?"

He nodded.

"Yes, that summarizes it. They're all tough, competent people—and probably more than a little bored now that peace has broken out. They're ideal choices for putting the instruments to rest in safe places, against any future need."

"I wasn't questioning their competence, Rango," she said, as a yellow cloud smelling of rotten eggs blew by them. "I'm wondering about the whole idea of putting the instruments out of reach at this point. I don't see how you could bear to be parted with Mothganger, the sword that saved our lives so many times. I find the idea of giving up Sombrisio and the power she wields extremely painful. Sombrisio saved us, too."

"I feel the same way you do," he said. "However, the situation is suddenly altered. Though they were a price-less benefit in the past, they have now become a grave peril."

"Are you sure that's true?" she asked, as the ground shook again and the geyser shot even higher.

They were forced to retreat suddenly to the right as a shift in the wind threw a shower of hot droplets over them.

"Reasonably sure," he said, offering her his handker-chief. "I had to rely on expert opinions, and the consen-sus among the best sorcerers we could consult was that having all four of the magical instruments in one place was rather too much of a good thing. That is to say, their combined forces have been building, and all of the strange and dangerous events which have begun to occur here are a direct result. They are damaging the fabric of reality and things can only get worse. The sorcerers say that this is the real reason such potent devices are nor-mally hidden in out-of-the-way places. Also, you'll not ordinarily find more than one stowed in the same spot. This is not just to make life difficult for people on quests. The things are so terribly potent that if you leave them in each other's vicinity for too long their combined forces place unnatural stresses on the area they occupy. We've got four of them here in Caltus, and the consensus is that their presence is the cause of all the magical disturbances we've been experiencing. And things will only get worse so long as they remain together."

"I don't know," she said, as the geyser belched at her back. "Supposing a few of Kalaran's nasties who survived the war were to show up, looking for trouble. For some of them, it would be very useful to have Mothganger or Sombrisio or Anachron handy. What I'm asking is, can we get a second opinion on this?"

Rango shook his head.

"I got the best I could find," he said, "and I told you there was a consensus. To delay longer while we hunted out a few more sages would be to court a real danger to no likely end. It's probable they'd all agree with their brothers and sisters in the Art. No, the sooner we ship the artifacts off to their resting places the sooner things will get back to normal here."

"You could probably keep one," she said. "Say, Mothganger or Sombrisio. There wouldn't be the same combination of powers then. None of them, off by itself, had worked the same sort of effects they're producing locally. Let's just send off two or three of the four and see if the situation stabilizes."

"This, too, was discussed," Rango said. "The reasoning is good and would probably work if we were just bringing a pair, say, of the instruments into a clear area. Unfortunately, some damage has already been done here. When the magical stresses have already occurred any object or operation of the Art may be likely to worsen things, or at least cause manifestations. So, yes, having one about would produce less stress than having all four. But it would still be taking a chance."

"In that case," she said, "couldn't you just move them out of town in four different directions until their effects are diminished to zero?"

Rango sighed and turned away, the fountain gurgling again at his back. One by one, a passing flock of birds began to fall, senseless, about them.

"Physically, what you are describing should work fine,"

he said at last. "However, there is the matter of security to be considered. If we stow them in too easily accessible places they may fall into the hands of enemies who could use them against us. This was doubtless the thinking of the ancients, as well, when they in their time secreted them. Their first consideration would have been to separate them to a great distance; their second, to make it risky for anyone who wanted to go after them. That's why there always have to be quests, and why they're always so damned difficult."

She moved nearer.

"It seems your experts did give it a lot of thought. . . ." she said slowly.

"I think that each generation has to rediscover these basic truths," he responded. "Once they've been realized, though, it explains the similarities in so much of high heroic literature. Moralists and literary critics have always been quick to point out that having heroes and heroines climb mountains, trudge through deserts, swim raging torrents, and face ferocious beasts or supernatural menaces has been a symbolic, external analogue of an inner, spiritual experience, intended to show a kind of initiation trial and ritual cleansing, making them worthy of the great boon they are about to bear back to their people. Now we see that this is just another example of the patriotic balderdash cultures use to glorify their values at the expense of the individual—not to mention other cultures. The real reason is a purely physical matter: It's dangerous to leave magical tools too close together for too long."

She stared at him through the yellow vapors. Then, "I never heard you talk so—so philosophically—before," she said, "back when we were on the road, and in war camps."

He smiled bleakly.

"I've had a lot of time for reflection since the conflict ended," he said, "time to examine my recent affairs and determine where I made my most serious mistakes. Time to think about all sorts of matters I hadn't the opportunity to dwell upon before."

She moved nearer yet to him.

"Perhaps you've been spending too much time thinking," she told him, placing her hand upon his arm. "All thought and no action is just as unbalanced a state of affairs as its opposite, dear."

Suddenly, she was very near, pressed up against him. His jaw muscles bunched, then relaxed. He put his arms about her, held her to him.

"You're right, of course," he said. "It's just that I want to have everything taken care of, everything in place, for us. I want life to be going smoothly here when we finally settle down to the happiness forever after business."

"Of course," she said. "I understand your concern."

She looked up into his eyes.

"For a while I thought that I had done something to offend you, or that you had changed," she said. "It seemed almost as if you were avoiding me. But I begin to understand all that you've had on your mind."

He nodded.

"It hasn't been easy," he said. "It almost seems the peace has been harder than the war in some ways. I'm sorry if I neglected you while I tried to deal with some of its problems. I intend to have everything in hand in time for our nuptials and the crowning. Soon, I promise."

"I can wait," she said. "Just so I know nothing's gone wrong between us. . . ."

"I'd have told you," he said, "if something had. No, it's the damned press of business that's been getting in the way."

Her lips parted slightly, so he leaned forward and kissed her. Moments later, another eruption occurred and more hot droplets fell upon them. He moved away, turned, and drew her after him.

"After life is safe from things like this, we can have more time for what we were doing," he said. "Unfortunately, it will probably keep me busy for a while yet."

"I appreciate that," she said, keeping up with his rapid

pace. "But even in a less than perfect world perhaps we could find a few hours to be together in some place that is not yet disturbed."

"Wish we could," he called above the growing rumble of the new eruption. "But I've got to be off to another meeting on just this matter. We'll have to get together later."

Rango sat in the back of the room, drinking a cup of tea. He was tired. The past several days in particular, this morning's meeting, the encounter with Rissa—all had been emotionally stressful, and he was physically tired. So he'd turned the briefing of the Bearers over to one of their own number, with whom he'd conferred quickly in advance. Colonel Dominik Blaid—no, damn it! General Domino Blaid—for whom he'd just signed the promotion papers a week or so back—had the full respect of her fellows and the experience of countless military briefings.

As if observing some exotic bird, he studied her. Up until fairly late in the war, everyone had assumed cavalry commander Dominik Blaid—son of the old General Kerman Blaid—was the most brilliant tactician in the field. Nor were they incorrect, save as to the Colonel's gender. Old Kerman had badly wanted a son to carry on the family tradition, but his late wife had not cooperated, leaving him with a single child of the female persuasion. Undaunted, he had decided to make the best of the material at hand, cross-dressing his daughter, calling her by the masculine version of her given name, and beginning her cavalry training as soon as she could stay on a horse's back. And something in her genes responded from the first.

As with six or seven generations of Blaids before her, she had the knack. And something extra. Emerging victorious in engagement after engagement, she quickly rose in her command, exhibiting more and more flashes of the family aptitude at its highest level.

It was somewhere in the final weeks of the war that

she had suffered a shoulder wound when enemy archers released clouds of arrows into her charge. Capturing the height she had stormed, she reeled then and slid from the saddle. Gar Quithnick, an unabashed admirer of the Colonel, was there immediately, tearing open the bloody shirt, ready to apply his *hingu* healing arts. When he realized that the man he most admired was a woman, Gar also realized that he had just fallen in love. But the lady did not share this sentiment. At least, not with him.

Rango smiled and sipped his tea as Domino began addressing the group. She still favored masculine garb, wore her hair short, and talked like a field commander. Hard to believe she'd fallen in love with a poet and scholar of ancient languages. But that is what the newly formed domestic intelligence service had told him. Jord Inder was the man's name.

Domino got along famously with Spotty Gulick, though there was nothing romantic there. As might be suspected with an infantry officer who had risen through the ranks and been involved in a number of the same campaigns, he had a lot in common with the Colonel. Besides, he seemed to favor petite blondes, and at five feet ten inches Domino was several inches taller than the husky captain.

On the other hand, Gar Quithnick was several inches taller than the lady. Slim, dark-haired, pale-eyed, he was graceful enough to be taken for a dancer rather than what he really was: one of the deadliest things on two feet. Trained from childhood in the killing arts of *hingu*, he had served in Kalaran's elite Guard until he learned of his master's part in his parents' deaths. Defecting then to Rango's standard, he had distinguished himself in the delaying action at Bardu Defile. The pass was narrow enough that only a pair of foot soldiers or a single mounted cavalryman could pass through at a time and led to the Plains of Paradath. There Rango's exhausted troops were encamped, not expecting an attack. One of six men volunteering to hold the Defile while word was carried to the encamped army below, Gar had waited, part of a sacrifice to gain five minutes—hopefully, ten.

The pass was held for the better part of an hour, the other five volunteers succumbing in less than half that time. The only reason Gar lived was that when he finally fell, so gashed, tattered, and covered with gore was he that no one cared to waste another swordstroke on an obvious dead man.

Still, hero though he was, Gar Quithnick had no real friends. There was a touch of fanaticism in that pale gaze, for he dwelled in the shadow of *hingu*'s death-aesthetic. Spotty, who had fought indoctrinated warriors of other persuasions in the past, had expressed a hope that peacetime might eventually turn Gar's mind to other affairs, and so humanize him. Gar's feeling toward the others, remained a mystery. He had never expressed himself, save in the case of Domino.

Rango finished his tea and listened for a time to Domino's presentation of the conference's conclusions concerning the magical instruments. There followed a series of questions, similar to those Rissa had asked him earlier. He poured himself more tea as Domino paced slapping her thigh and scratching her nose with her riding crop.

"And when are we to depart with the things?" Jancy Gaine asked.

Domino looked to Rango, who rose to his feet, nodded, and said, "Day after tomorrow. Everyone probably needs a day to settle current business and to get outfitted."

"Rissa was going to have some words with you about this."

"We've already had them."

He was about to reseat himself when he felt Gar Quithnick's gaze. He met it and raised his eyebrows.

"You've a question, Gar," he said.

"Yes," came that soft, level voice. "The only safe place for the amulet Anachron is its traditional home in a chapel in the mountain village of Gelfait. Unfortunately, the place only exists intermittently. It fades into and out of existence on no predictable schedule—years, sometimes decades or generations apart. I can cross the Waste of Rahoban and go to the place of the village, but I have no guarantee it will manifest when I get there."

Rango smiled.

"There is a secret tradition," he replied, "that the phenomenon will occur in response to the presence of the amulet. My consultants say there is every reason to believe this correct. Anachron and Gelfait seem to charge each other up in some fashion."

"I see," Gar said. "In that case, I will be ready to depart following this meeting if you will get me the amulet."

"Your party can prepare that quickly?"

"I was not accompanied in my travels when I fetched you the amulet," Gar replied. "I require no assistance in its return."

"I will address that matter after Domino's presentation," said Rango, seating himself and nodding to her to continue.

He glanced again at Jancy when he felt that she was glaring at him. Then she looked away. Just wanted to let him know her feelings, as if he wouldn't have known them in advance. A tough, husky blonde almost as tall as Domino and considerably heavier, she had been employed as a bouncer in the brothel to which the Princess had been taken after her purchase in the local slave market by the establishment's owner. Jancy had recognized Rissa as the last surviving member of the Royal House of Regaudia, recently destroyed by Kalaran. She had rescued Rissa and gotten her safely out of town. Their wanderings, for the better part of a year, had taken her, Rissa, and their elf companion Calla Mallanik through a long series of adventures resulting, among other things, in the discovery of the ring Sombrisio in lost Anthurus, city of the dead, and finally leading to a meeting with Prince Rango.

He frowned slightly. Jancy was totally devoted to the Princess. He did not doubt for a moment that she would lay her life down for her. She didn't get on well with men, however. Her feelings might have had to do with all she had seen and heard in the brothel. Or they might be something that ran deeper. She certainly didn't seem to trust him fully. He knew that she had referred to Gar Quithnick as "spooky." While she seemed to trust Spotty a little more than most men, if she had to talk with one of those present he knew that she would probably choose Domino, strictly because of gender.

He shrugged. Spotty and Domino were both aware of Jancy's quirks and were totally cordial to her. Even Gar had seemed kindly disposed toward the big woman, to the extent of having dined with her, though he later learned that the main thrust of Gar's conversation had involved an attempt to discover the death-aesthetic of the Northern totemic warriors—those fellows who wrapped themselves in animal skins and growled as they fought, occasionally gnawing the bodies of the slain in the aftermath of battle. In fact, now he reflected, it was after that dinner that she had begun referring to Gar as "spooky."

There was silence. Rango returned from his reverie as he realized that the last question had been answered, that Domino—raising her riding crop to her face and saluting him with it, with an outward-curved, downward gesture—was turning the meeting back over to him. He rose to his feet and nodded.

"Thank you, General Blaid," he said, moving forward. "Domino," he added then, "I just want to add a few things. First Stiller, Mothganger is in the vault at the palace and will be turned over to you, on the morning of your departure. Jancy, you can work out the terms of surrender on Sombrisio with Rissa—"

"We already have," she interrupted, "thank you."

"Good," Rango stated, smiling broadly at her. "The other two instruments—the amulet Anachron and the scroll of Gwykander—are technically out of my reach. That is to say, they are in the custody of the Temple. They seized them that final day, laying claim to them as religious items. I will refrain from commenting on any possible political motivation here, but I'm certainly not looking for an argument between the Crown and the

Church at this point. My experts are already seeking the Elders and the priests, to convince them of the danger involved in keeping the pieces. We hope to persuade them to turn the things loose the day after tomorrow. That, Gar, is why you will be unable to depart on your journey immediately after the meeting. I will let you and Domino—who will be Bearer of the Scroll—know immediately should we run into any problems with the negotiations. Any questions?"

He looked about the room. Finding no responses, he continued:

"I would like to introduce four gentlemen who will be accompanying you in your travels." He gestured toward a bench along the wall to his left at the room's rear where two bearded middle-aged men sat between a pair of beardless youths. One by one, they rose to their feet in order as he called their names. "Rolfus," he said of the first youth, "will accompany Stiller. Squill will go with Jancy. Piggon will join Domino's party. And Spido will keep company with Gar. All of these men are sorcellets— that is they have been trained in a single magical operation. They are communications specialists. They will keep me posted as to your progress and any problems. And they will advise me when your missions have been completed. It is essential that I have this information immediately rather than waiting upon your return, because I want all loose ends tied off before the coronation. I think it important that I come to power with all of the old business out of the way, and I want to be able to announce the settling of this matter as soon as possible."

Gar Quithnick raised his hand. When Rango nodded to him he said, "As I explained earlier, I travel faster when I travel alone."

Rango smiled.

"I am sure that this is generally true," he said, "but as *I* explained, the information is essential for preparing the proper opening to my reign. As to Spido's delaying you, you may be mistaken. He elected to join us when the Armbruss training center, south of Kalaran's capital, was liberated. He has had several years of *hingu* training, and he welcomes the opportunity of serving with you."

Spido bowed formally toward Gar, who responded with an elaborate hand gesture.

"You have satisfied my queries," he said to Rango.

"Are there any others?" Rango asked the group. When he saw that there were none, he concluded, "Then I thank you, and I wish you all good journeys."

When the midlevel priest, Lemml Touday, visited the palace that evening with a message for Prince Rango's ears alone, Rango told his steward to bring him to his quarters directly.

When they were alone he studied the stocky, middle-aged man.

"Do you bring bad news? Or should I offer you a glass of my favorite wine and celebrate with you?"

"I'd prefer the latter," Lemml said.

Rango gestured toward a cushioned couch and smiled as he filled a pair of goblets, placed them upon a tray, and brought them over.

Rango smiled when the other toasted him, then asked, "A problem with the release of the amulet and the scroll, I presume?"

"No," the priest replied. "In fact, the talks are going quite as you might have wished. They've been adjourned till tomorrow, but your experts on magical instruments and stresses are very persuasive, according to our experts. Off the record, I think they've won over everyone who matters."

"Oh?" Rango lowered his drink and stared. "I don't understand. There is, perhaps, something you'd like to have for a report of the Temple's private deliberations on this? Do you wish to let me know who my friends and my enemies are?"

The priest smiled.

"No, that wasn't what I had in mind at all. I was thinking of something likely worth a lot more."

"And what might that be?"

"I am the Keeper of the Skull."

Rango shook his head in puzzlement.

"I don't understand what that signifies," he said.

"The principle of evil, the fallen Sunbird, Lord Kalaran," Lemml said. "I am custodian of his skull."

"Oh," Rango remarked. "I wasn't aware that it had received special treatment."

The priest nodded.

"Yes, it was exposed on the Temple's main spire for a month, after which it was flensed of all flesh and other softnesses in a boiling vat of appropriate herbs. Our greatest artisan then installed the two small figures— Demon and Messenger of Light—within it. It is kept in a jeweled casket in a secret place in the Temple, and I am its custodian. I check it every day to see whether the bright spirit has emerged from the right eye socket or the dark one from the left."

Rango nodded.

"And what has the result been?" he asked.

"The light figure has been prominent ever since the artifact was created . . ."

"That is good."

". . . until this morning. When I checked today, I saw that the dark one had emerged."

"This is not good. If I understood you, this is to be interpreted as an ill omen, an indication of pending evil?"

"The skull was enchanted as such a warning system, yes."

"What have the Elders to say about this change, at this time?"

"Nothing. I haven't told them yet."

"Ah! I see. . . ."

"Yes. While it might be interpreted as indicating that the departure of the amulet and the scroll from the Temple would be a bad thing, it might also simply mean that the odd nightly phenomena in the area have finally reached the point of representing a danger—what with giant lizards stalking through town and all. With this interpretation, it would be a good thing to take your experts' advice and get rid of the instruments. Which interpretation do you think more likely?"

Rango rubbed his neck slowly. Politics!

"You are the interpreter as well as the custodian?"

"Yes, though a sufficiently high church official might take issue with my reading."

"Yes? . . ."

". . . and the phenomenon might be delayed in the reporting till the day *after* the Bearers depart—and then the latter interpretation would be more likely, in that it would be too late to do much about the former. You *do* have a preference?"

"Yes, I do. Have you a favorite charity?"

"Such things tend to begin at home, do they not?"

"This has always been my observation," said Rango, glancing at a pair of crossed swords which hung upon the wall to his right.

". . . and if anything were to happen to me," Lemml went on, "my successor would note the prognosticatory state of affairs tomorrow, probably read it incorrectly, and certainly report it immediately."

Rango took a large swallow of his wine, as did the priest.

"It is good that you came to me," Rango said. "Your visit is a thing both educational and patriotic. Yes, I've a mind to make a contribution. I assume you have the details with you?"

"Of course."

From beyond the balcony, through the opened window, they heard the frantic drumbeat commence, followed moments later by the shouted words none could understand. Shortly thereafter, the great thudding footfalls began. Then came a mournful saurian bellow which rattled their goblets on the tray.

Arts and Sciences:
The Gar Quithnick Story

I

It Starts at the End

Gar Quithnick fought the boredom of the ceremony by calculating the number of ways he could kill the Chief Priest of the Temple without using more than two major muscle groups. His count ended at two hundred fifty-three, which struck him as remarkable because the hand position of that number in *hingu*—Butterfly with Twin Fangs and Tail Spike—would have proved a challenge to employ. Piercing the gold-and-malachite pectoral the Chief Priest wore would be difficult and, worse yet, the ornament would interfere with the transference of enough lethal energy so that the blow would merely bruise the man's liver instead of rupturing it.

Before he could repeat his survey, expanding the parameters to include three muscle groups and immediately available blunt weapons of nonferrous metal, the Chief Priest turned from the tabernacle at the base of the solar deity's statue and held the amulet Anachron aloft. "Behold Anachron, the timeless amulet from far Gelfait. It has resided for a time in the sanctuary at the feet of Valnartha, He who watched over it while it remained in the Wastes of Rahoban. It is now again ready to journey. Bid the *hingist* approach."

Gar would have grimaced at the use of such a derogatory term to describe him, but it was the most polite term employed by his allies since their victory over Kalaran. Long and lean, he moved forward whisper-quiet and managed to leave the thick threads of incense smoke untouched by his passing. With Kalaran dead and his old master, Udan Kann, among the vanished, he knew he faced no serious threat in the Temple, yet caution born during years of training kept his gaze darting about. Gods, goddesses, and godlets all stared down at him from the Temple's sanctuary with their impassive stone faces.

Looking to his right, past Prince Rango and Princess Rissa, he saw Domino Blaid. He had hoped she would be looking at him, finally understanding the bond they shared. He knew they were meant for each other, as tightly linked as blood and life or death and pain or taxes and agonies, yet she refused to acknowledge how she must have felt about him. Jord Inder, the poet and linguist standing beside her, had stolen her heart.

Were he a thief, Gar could have stolen it back. Being an assassin without equal in Faltane, the tools at his disposal would have been effective for eliminating the competition, but killing Jord would not have transferred Domino's love to Gar. For the first time in his existence he had wanted something and it eluded him. He resigned himself to never being able to win her, and vowed to channel his unrequited love into his art.

The Chief Priest, an old man whose white hair and yellowed beard stank of old incense and young wine, bowed his head to the assassin. "Unto you we entrust this amulet for its safe return to Gelfait."

Gar brought his right hand up quickly and the Chief Priest leaped back a foot. "I will not accept the amulet from you." He looked over to the right again, but this time focused on the handsome Prince Rango. "My liege, Anachron passed to me from the leader of the Gelfaiti horde, and from me it passed to you. On your breast it saved us all from the frightful power of Kalaran's magick. It was taken from you by the Temple. As I will return it to Gelfait, I wish it to pass from your hands to mine, so the circuit may again be complete."

His request appeared to take Rango by surprise, but the Prince had always reacted well when faced with the unexpected. "I understand, *hingu-Grashanshao*, and I am pleased to make things right."

Gar allowed the hint of a smile on his lips as the Prince respectfully pronounced the title which Quithnick had inherited when Udan Kann fled from Kalaran's side. He let the smile linger as Rango calmed Rissa with a quick squeeze of her hand, then closed to within striking distance. The Chief Priest appeared annoyed at being upstaged, but he transferred the amulet to the Prince's hands without hesitation, and Rango settled the chain around Gar's neck.

The assassin marveled at how little the amulet and chain actually weighed. Sandcast in gold, with a starburst of diamonds at the heart of an ancient sunburst design, its weight should have been enough to discomfit him. Instead it seemed barely more noticeable than a lover's caress, or the force used in the Velvet Palm Strike when it spalled splinters from the insides of the ribs and impaled the heart.

The Chief Priest frowned mightily, as if he could read Gar's mind, and again raised his hands. "May the Way be Clear, the Heart be Pure and the Mind filled with Loving Thoughts."

"This I believe," breathed Gar as he erased the smile from his face.

"There you are, Gar. You have the amulet." Rango, having retreated to Rissa's side, spoke cordially, as if no distance separated them. "You are determined to be off immediately?"

"The value of immediacy has fallen of recent, my lord.

Were it not for this ceremony, I would already be in the heart of the Wastes, on my way to Gelfait. Spido has been kind enough to gather horses and supplies, but were he not with me, I would need neither. If you will permit me to leave him behind, I can be there and back again to report to you myself on the success of my quest."

Rango shook his head ruefully. "Did not the demands of rulership prevent me from granting your request, you would be unfettered in an instant. Alas, I am trapped, for Spotty and Jancy have already embarked with their sorcellets accompanying them. Were I to permit you or Domino to travel without them, our other companions would wonder why we doubted their ability to complete their quests unmonitored. And you especially, my friend, should appreciate the suspicions and protests I have already fought in entrusting Anachron to you."

"I know—a leopard cannot change his spots." Gar glanced at Domino, wondering at the omen of her name and what it might stand for. "I shall protest no more, my lord, and only did so in the hopes of serving you more efficiently."

"I shall settle for faithful service, Gar, as faithful service as you rendered me at Bardu Defile."

Gar shivered, a barely perceptible tremor that would not have raised ripples in a goblet of wine, were he holding one, but a shiver nonetheless. Lying in the Defile, beneath men he had slain, beside comrades he could not save, he had at last been prepared to go from being Death's agent to Death's client. Yet, before he could succumb, Rango had appeared and tapped the healing power of Anachron. At that point, with searing sunbeams sealing his wounds, Gar Quithnick was reborn from sworn enemy of Lord Kalaran to being a servant to Prince Rango.

"Even if this mission demands the sacrifice of my life, it will be done." Gar bowed to his Prince and the Princess, then tossed Domino a salute and walked away from those he considered friends. As he left the Temple he glanced once at the dark opening to the crypt in which

Kalaran's skull lay, and for a second he thought it would be better to carry the skull away than Anachron. But his mission called, and that thought vanished into the long, deep dark of his soul where it would haunt him for the rest of his life.

II

Thy Midwife: Deception

Gar narrowed his eyes as he stepped from the Temple into sunlight. He felt the heat of the day immediately against his somber black clothing. It might have warmed another, but Gar had already begun to steel himself against the hellish heats of the waste, so it went unnoticed. Instead he concentrated on the silhouette of a rider leading three other horses, and of the two men malevolently staring in his own direction.

"Spido, remain there." Gar looked away from his mounted aide and nodded first to one of the men, and then to the other. "Nothing you have been paid is worth your trying to kill me."

The two of them looked enough alike to have been father and son. "You paid us," shouted the younger of them. "My uncle and I are all that remains of families you slew, traitor! You have deprived us of our lives, now we will destroy you."

"Obliged to be a completist." Gar leaped from the Temple's steps to the flat of the courtyard. He landed heavily and loudly on his feet, but neither of the two farmers rushing in at him realized he had Dragon Stomped their long shadows. Letting his leap flow into a crouch, he slid forward into the Grand Monitor form. He posted the uncle up on his left elbow, then snapped his forearm up to let the Velvet Palm Strike reunite the man with his family.

Jumping up and tucking himself into a double backflip, Gar spun safely above the nephew's backhanded sword slash. Lighting on the ground as delicately as a rose petal falling from a blossom, Gar flicked his right hand out. His index finger darted in and out, twice and twice again, in the Dragonfly Pulse Strike. Hitting once over each carotid artery and jugular vein, it created a pressure wave that ruptured the boy's cranial capillary system.

At Spido's side before the boy staggered out his last step and collapsed, Gar looked up at his sorcellet. The youth's gape-jawed look of astonishment confirmed something the assassin had assumed about his aide, but he did not give voice to his suspicion. Instead he swung himself up into the saddle and nodded slightly. "Is there something you wish to comment, Spido?"

"You killed them just like that!" The youth snapped his fingers and shook his head. "Bip, bip, just like that."

"That *is* what an assassin does, you know."

"Well, yes, of course I know that. I was at Armbruss, wasn't I? But I mean, tap, tap, and they're dead."

Gar reined his horse around, loathing the surrender of his mobility to the bloated, heavy-hooved beast between his legs. "They knew what they were about."

Spido rode up beside Gar, with the two mightily laden packhorses falling in line behind. "I'm not sure they did know what they were doing, sir. They'd have been more evenly matched against a stalk of wheat than you."

"Pity the farmer who mistakes me for a stalk of wheat then. At least they are with their families." Gar turned quickly toward Spido but the youth, who had turned to stare back at the bodies, did not notice. "Spido, what of your family?"

"Not so much different than them, I reckon." The chunky youth shrugged as they rode toward Caltus's west gate. "My dad ran off and we think he died in the war, of course, though you didn't kill him. My mum and my uncle still live in Torfay, up in the mountains, a bit south of where Gelfait is supposed to be."

Gar nodded as a crossbowman stepped from an alley farther down the road. The man triggered his bow and Gar snatched the poorly aimed missile from the air, for fear it would hit any of a number of people who were peeking at him through drawn curtains or shuttered windows. The assassin hurled it back at his assailant, with all of the disdain of a professional for the efforts of an amateur, ensuring that though the man would limp for the rest of his life, he would not breed.

Spido blanched a bit at the soprano curses echoing from the alley. "Being a master of *hingu* is dangerous, eh?"

"The *hingu-shanshao* lives in Death's Shadow, so he learns to take comfort there." Gar yawned. "Surely you remember the Third Precept."

"Of course, but things in practice are so much more, ah, real, than in theory, eh?"

"Ah, you rebuke me with the Fourth of the Thirteen Truths." Gar arched an eyebrow at Spido, which made the younger man blush and convinced a swordsman to remain in the shadows beyond him. "You learned much at Armbruss. I trust you enjoyed your time there?"

"Very much, sir."

Their conversation lapsed as they reached Westgate. Rango's soldiers hurried to clear the way for Gar. Their shouting spooked one horse, which would not have been bad were it not attached to a cart filled with pickle casks. Green gherkins bounced up off dark cobblestones like tubular frogs, while dill spears fell in a phallic avalanche over bystanders.

Emulating the elan with which Gar had plucked the quarrel from the air, Spido arrested a large sweet pickle in midflight. He held it aloft triumphantly, but the gesture's majesty failed as two more pickles pummeled him and nearly unhorsed him. In revenge, Spido bit the head off his captive and crunched it with great gusto.

Gar said nothing as they rode from Caltus. He knew well the route they would take and imagined the journey would only suffer because of his companion. From Caltus they would head north until they reached the Failles of Dunn. From there the trek would take them west by northwest, up to the rim country where they would cross the Wastes of Rahoban. On the other side of that lay the mountains and, in a deep mountain valley, the village of Gelfait.

Gar's single misgiving about his mission—aside from Spido—concerned Gelfait itself. The village, as nearly as could be determined by legend, had no anchor in time. It appeared outside any discernible cycle, and no one could remember having seen it in the last century. Even he had never been there and while he did not doubt its existence in the past, he wondered if it would again manifest itself.

His fear that it would not had been born out of his success at obtaining Anachron in the first place. On his original quest, on a night in the middle of the wastes, a howling storm had arisen around him. Dust and the dry bones of the meager plants living on the arid plateau swirled about him. The red dust became a bloody cyclone shot through with lightning black and gold. Pressure built, surrounding him, while debris tugged at his clothing and grit choked him.

Suddenly, in confirmation of the storm's unnatural origins, argent and ivory men clad in ancient armor stepped through the seething stormwall and confronted him. Their leader, the legendary Belamon, who had sought to bring the amulet Anachron to the Failles of Dunn to end the threat of a proto-Kalaranian despot, challenged Gar. The Gelfaiti warrior had sensed in him a desire for Anachron and took him to be an agent of evil meant to stop them. Though Gar tried to explain the situation, Belamon refused to believe they had been lost in their travels for tens of centuries, and decided only combat could resolve the conflict between them.

The threat of a smile tugged at Gar's lips as he remembered that battle. In the midst of the howling storm, a silvery giant in a place out of time battled an assassin willfully divorced from his own past. Blows struck by Belamon that night had the force sufficient to split mountains and recourse rivers, yet Gar had proved a most elusive target. Conversely Belamon withstood the Rabid Lemur Punch, the Lethal Orchid Caress and even the

Hammerstrike with Wedge and Awl. Gar remained awed by the stamina and skill the Gelfaiti displayed, and the Gelfaiti company repeatedly cried out in admiration of how Gar handled their Champion.

Finally, simultaneously, the two men called "Hold!" Belamon dropped to one knee and held his spear like a staff to support himself. "Though your story of time passing speaks of deception to me, the heart you display in battle could harbor no deceit. To you I yield."

Gar, his chest heaving with exertion and his heart racing with exhilaration, shook his head. "Nay, it is I who must yield to you. In you I have confirmation of what I have known: the nobility and martial skills we possess today are but degraded forms of what you know. You are my superior, and to you I yield."

A great cry rose up from the Gelfaiti horde and Gar saw Belamon was smiling. "You have bested me, Gar Quithnick, for it is told that Anachron cannot be taken by force, but must be given freely. Upon the death of the Bearer, it will return to the one who gave it, or from whom it was taken. By passing it among us, we have guaranteed we would not lose it, yet we have failed to deliver it in time. To you, we entrust Anachron, and pray you will remember us with the honor you have shown us here. Our mission is done, so now we shall return home."

Gar accepted Anachron from Belamon, then watched as the horde moved back off to the west. As they faded from sight, so did the storm die. He wondered if Gelfait would have faded for all time with them or if, as Rango suggested, bringing Anachron again to its home would summon the village from whatever limbo claimed it. Only finding the city, which was said to appear at dawn and disappear with the sun—prompting some to consider it a solar illusion—would allow him to complete his mission.

If the presence of Anachron did not bring the village back, he reasoned, he had two choices open to him. One was to wait in the mountains against a time when it would appear. While his self-imposed exile would doubtlessly please many in the court at Caltus—and spare many a revenge-minded farmer from death—it would deprive him of access to ancient tomes of lore and similar records of the time of the Gelfaitis and even before.

It would also forever remove him from Domino Blaid. Were his mission a failure, he considered returning to Caltus. He knew he would do so under the blind of seeking new orders. That he would bring Anachron with him presented him no worry because having *one* of the artifacts back in the capital certainly would be no problem.

Even with that rationale, he knew if he went back he would be going to see Domino. As he thought of her, a pang of regret tightened his chest. He marveled at the sensation because it was so alien to his emotionless upbringing within the *shenkai* at Armbruss. There Udan Kann had taught him and the other *hingu-kun* all the myriad ways to inflict death, and praised those who were able to do so without squeamishness or emotion.

A harsh rolling burp from Spido brought Gar out of his brooding. The sorcellet smiled sheepishly and pounded his chest with a fist. "Sorry. Sweet pickles do that to me."

Gar shrugged. "Burping is hardly a crime, Spido." The assassin gave him half a smile. "But impersonating a *hingu-kun* is."

All color drained from Spido's face. "I'm not impersonating anyone."

"True, for no one could recognize in you a student of *hingu*." Gar reined his horse in closer to Spido. "Why did you lie about being at Armbruss?"

"I didn't. I was there." Spido brought his head up and thrust his chin out. "I was there, really."

Gar slowly shook his head. "Spido, at Armbruss they train children, children that have no families. You have admitted to having a mother and uncle in a mountain village. Clearly you are deceiving me, or trying to."

"No, yes, wait." He held both of his hands up to forestall a blow, but raised them so slowly that even a broken-spined *hingu-dan* could have killed him with a casual effort. "I *infiltrated* Armbruss four years ago. I had to. It was my destiny, you see."

Gar frowned. "So you entered Armbruss as an adult? What did you learn there, Spido?"

The aide swallowed hard. "Well, my first year was a lot of sweeping up, see. And putting wax on things and taking it off again. But I did right good, and they let me move on. And in my second year I did lots better at learning."

"Excellent, then our meals on the journey shall be acceptable." The assassin watched his aide closely. "And in your third year? Did you learn anything of *hingu?*"

Spido nodded proudly. "I learned a strike."

"Show me."

Spido clapped his hands.

"Again."

The urgency in Gar's voice made Spido clap faster. "My master, he said I had the speed necessary to get flies and mosquitoes and such. He was proud of me."

"A keen observer, your *shanshao.*"

"He was that, sir. He was Nindal Gor. Did you know him?"

"I did." Gar nodded carefully. "At Bardu I shattered his fifth, seventeenth and twenty-first vertebrae, then broke his legs and punctured his lungs. Then, of course, I killed him."

Spido's eyes bugged out farther than if he'd tasted of Lotus Tincture number five. "You did that to him?"

"Only because he was a friend." Gar looked away. "Growing up he said he hoped he would die of a cerebral hemorrhage while entertaining amorous triplets. I thought he would appreciate the irony."

"I can see that, sir. Great one for irony he was."

Such as the irony of watching a little lardbutt laborer become an assassin. The *hingu-Grashanshao* looked again at Spido. "So, you did spend time at Armbruss. I gather, however, you overstated the extent of your instruction in order to be appointed my sorcellet. Why did you want to accompany me?"

"Well, sir, it's a long story . . ."

". . . which you will abbreviate succinctly . . ."

". . . but putting it into a succinctly abbreviated form, it's my destiny, you see, sir."

"Ah, your destiny. Let us try it again, not quite so sparing on the words this time, shall we?"

"Yes, sir. See, sir, I'm from Torfay and we're just a little village. And most all of the menfolk, they went off to fight under Prince Rango's banner, but with them gone, a man calling himself Dolonicus the Magnanimous has come in and set himself up as the Mayor, which he isn't, since the last Mayor went off to the war and his ceremonial sword hasn't been returned so there's not been a new Mayor since then even though the old one is dead, you see, sir."

"Do all of the Torfay speak as you do?"

"Only thems of us what has some education, sir. Now this Dolonicus, according to my mum, who writes me regular—well, she doesn't write but gets someone else to write it for her, see—used to fight for Kalaran. Now he's saying that he's the Lord of Torfay and it's my destiny to defeat him and drive him from our town."

The assassin raised an eyebrow. "You use the term 'destiny' as if it is synonymous with 'intent' or 'desire.' "

"Begging your pardon, sir, but it is my *destiny*. I've heard a prophecy, see, sir, and I know it pertains to me. So I need to make sure I do it right so everything will work right and proper. 'With wings of death/Swiftly he comes swooping/Laying low the mighty/For the fallen stooping.' "

"*That* is your prophecy?"

"Well, not the whole thing, sir, but the part about you, it is, sir."

"About me?"

Spido nodded confidently. "Figured it out myself, sir. See, wings sort of rhymes with *hingu*, sir, so I'll be coming to Torfay with you, being the *hingu* of death."

"*Hingu* means death in Ancient Thermaean, you know."

"No, sir, but thank you, sir, for you're certainly the one who could be the death of Death, if you don't mind me saying so, sir." Spido rubbed his hands together. "Now to put the rest of it together. A verse I've not figured out is: The flower of Life/nurtured in love fey/ Form of goddess-wife/Will win him the day."

"That, too, is part of your prophecy?"

"It is, sir." Spido smiled proudly. "I've been trying to figure out which goddess I'll have to bed, see, sir."

"A difficult business being a hero."

"I expect so, sir."

Especially when your prophecy is a product of pro-Rango propaganda. In keeping with the *hingu* precepts he had learned since he was weaned, Gar had sought out all information he could find about Jord Inder. Normally the information he gathered would have been employed to provide the victim with a suitable death, but Gar merely wanted to understand what Domino saw in the slender, blond poet.

Until he had begun his lorestalking of Jord, Gar had never studied poetry. Even after his researches he was uncertain what constituted art, but he knew what he liked. While a few doyens of society had reviewed some of Jord's performances—and assassinated his work with the skill of a hingu-dan—Gar had found a resonance and peace in the poems that surprised him. Jord's words related emotions and spun stories with feelings. They stirred the soul and, during the rebellion against Kalaran, had inflamed the people so they flocked to Rango's banner.

The poem Spido quoted had been one of the more obscure and obtuse ones credited to Jord. Supposedly uttered by him, bit by bit, day by day, while he was locked in the throes of fever delirium in one of Kalaran's prisons, "Warrior Day" had taken on prophetic import. The different verses had been assigned to those who came to aid Rango, and Spido had correctly identified the verse often linked to Gar himself.

The second verse the sorcellet had quoted had generally

been thought to be an allusion to the love of Rissa for Rango. It also applied, in part, to another encounter Gar had experienced on his way to Bardu with Anachron, but Jord could not have known of it because it had happened long after the poem had spread throughout the land. Gar doubted the fever had given Jord a second sight—and the poem was obscure enough that anyone could characterize any part of it as anything, as had Spido—but some of the verses made him uneasy when he speculated on what they might mean for him.

Gar started to explain to Spido his error, but the confidence and happiness in the man's eyes stopped him. Before the war, when he still served Kalaran and Udan Kann, he would have gladly crushed Spido's spirit, but he could not, now. Before he would have scorned the young man for his failure to become a hingu-dan, but now he could respect the courage it took for a pudgy youth to leave the mountains and enter Armbruss. That courage demanded reward, or at least not to be broken.

"Spido, if I may, I would inquire what your plan is for liberating Torfay."

The man's smile dwindled and he almost cringed. "I was thinking, sir, that we might divert from the edge of the Wastes and swing around through the mountains to Torfay, then go to Gelfait."

"Impossible, we have a mission."

"I know that, sir, see, but I was thinking . . ."

"Were you?" Gar settled an impassive mask over his face. "I have told Rango we will go to Gelfait without delay. I cannot be swayed from my course."

"But sir, there are stories of bandits all over the north country here, and up into the Lake District."

"There are ways to dispose of bandits."

"I know, sir, but I didn't bring that much rope."

"Think like a *hingu-kun*, Spido. I do not need rope."

"Begging your pardon, but you can't hang them if you don't have rope."

Gar shook his head. "What does hanging do?"

"Kills them, sir."

"Can you be more specific?"

"Ah, kills them dead, sir?"

"We are talking methodology, not philosophy, Spido. What does hanging do to their bodies?"

"Well now, 'cepting the tall ones what can touch the ground, they break their necks."

"Good, Spido." Gar stabbed out with his left index finger in a Iron Spike Stab, snapping a meandering dragon fly in half. "A *hingu-Grashanshao* knows three hundred and twenty-three ways to break a man's neck, excluding those methods that require siege machinery or thirty-year-old brandy and a pipette of boiled egg albumin."

"You're saying, sir, the bandits will be no trouble."

"Exactly. And, in keeping with my pledges as a liege-man of Prince Rango, I am duty bound to kill bandits."

Spido retreated within himself for a second, then nodded. "Well, sir, begging your pardon, but isn't it likely that any of your enemies are going to know that you'll be going from the Failles of Dunn to the Wastes of Rahoban and on to Gelfait, so they'll be waiting to waylay you on the route?"

"As the farmers were waiting for me?"

Spido frowned. "Your point is well taken, sir, but, as you was saying about the fourth of them thirteen precepts—"

"Thirteen Truths."

"Right you are, sir, with the theory and reality and all, wouldn't it make sense to take another route to avoid possible trouble?"

Gar thought for a moment, and some of the unease that had begun to gnaw on him during the preparation for the trek bit down hard. "While your suggestion has merit, you present me a problem in that respect."

A pale Spido shook his head. "I'll be no trouble at all, sir."

"Ah, but are you not to report to Prince Rango on our progress?"

"Yes, sir, but . . ."

"But? . . ."

"Well, sir, being brutally honest, I played poker with

Squill and Rolfus and Piggon the night before we were all introduced to you and if the three of them had a brain between them, I'd have won it fair early on that evening. I was thinking, sir, that I would lie to them about where we were."

"But you could not fool Rango."

"Begging your pardon, sir, but I *am* here and he's back there believing I'm a *hingu-kun*."

"Point taken."

"So you see, sir, we could divert and I could give them reports that put us on course and on track. And you have to admit it would surprise anyone waiting to waylay you. Take a bit more time, of course, but would be well worth it."

Gar felt his stomach clench. *More time I cannot afford.* More time meant he would be separated from Domino that much longer. While he knew she would never love him while Jord lived, she had provided a spark that kindled emotions within him. Had he not learned how to respect another by respecting her feats despite her gender, he could never have respected Spido's courage. Being apart from her, no matter how much it hurt to be near her, was something he would never accept. Nothing, not ease of passage or avoidance of enemies, would keep them apart.

"No, Spido, we go on as planned."

The sorcellet shook his head. "Pity, sir, but I understand. Still, to leave Dolonicus's killing machines ravaging the land . . ."

Gar's head came up. "Killing machines?"

"Well, beasts really, sir. He has three of them, according to my mum, who can count as long as it's not more than four and a half since she had that accident with the butcher knife. She calls 'em 'TerribleClaw FastHunters'. . . ."

"Your mother has an imagination. . . . Is Spido your real name?"

The sorcellet groaned. "You don't want to know, sir. Anyway, these things are fast and have this terrible, sickle-shaped claw, one on each of the two hind legs.

And they're covered with brilliant feathers and have lots
of teeth. Dolonicus uses them to hunt deer and mooses
and they can outrun horses and they work like a pack
and call to each other. They've long tails that balance
them, and small arms up front, kind of like some of them
big lizards what have been around the mud lakes that
have come up in Faltane, sir."

"These things are very deadly?"

"The deadliest, sir." Spido nodded solemnly. "My
uncle Gordo calls 'em dinner-sores cause of the way they
rip long wounds into what they take for prey."

"And there are three of them?"

"Three and they hunts together."

"And they are a threat to loyal citizens of Faltane?"

"The most loyal, sir. These clawthings are a clear
threat to Prince Rango's realm."

Gar nodded solemnly. "More of a threat than bandits,
I believe."

"I thought you'd think so, sir. So we divert and go
after them?"

"I would be derelict in my duty if we did not."

"My thinking exactly, sir."

"Spido, I guess you *did* learn something at Armbruss."

"Ironic, eh, sir?"

"Indeed. If you're lying, you'll learn something else."

"On my honor, I'd die before I'd lie to you, sir."

"Or certainly afterward, Spido."

III

Visitations and Revelations

Gar opted to let Spido choose their path for two main
reasons. The first was that Spido, having grown up in
Torfay, but having made two round trips to Caltus before
he ran away to Armbruss, knew the best route and likely
places they could camp out or lodge themselves for the
night. The accommodations Spido chose were pleasant

and yet not expensive enough for anyone to believe that he, Gar Quithnick, Rango's loyal *hingu-Grashanshao*, would be staying there.

The second and more cogent reason he let Spido lead was because he felt certain any old enemy trying to out-guess Gar Quithnick would be utterly unable to predict any of Spido's actions. While the route they took lacked beeline precision, it did have an aesthetic quality that Gar had previously ignored concerning the Faltane coun-tryside. As they traveled through the Vales of Dorn, well west and south of the Failles of Dunn, Gar recalled one of Jord Inder's poems, "Vales and Failles," in which Dorn had been described in terms of a silken tapestry allowed to fall crinkled to the earth by the gods. While some of the metaphors included in the poem related to the female anatomy—and Gar easily translated that into an image of Domino—the assassin worked beyond the pain the words brought to him and mentally congratu-lated the poet on capturing the essence of Dorn in his work.

Gar turned to Spido as they rode along. "Do you see a woman in these hills, Spido?"

"I'm not sure that I do, sir. Should I?"

"The fecundity of the vales, the hills, the hollows?"

"Would this be one of those 'troptical allusions,' sir, what a man sees when he's got thirst-fever or his brain's been sunbaked? I have a spare hat here, sir."

"Thank you, Spido, I am fine. Merely remembering some things."

"Oh, like someone you were sweet on?" When Gar frowned, Spido added, "That is, 'sweet on' in a *hingu-Grashanshao* sort of way, sir."

"I understand, Spido." Gar considered the question for a moment, then nodded. "Love is an alien and power-ful force, isn't it?"

"It is, sir. Prince Rango killed off old Kalaran for the love of his nation and Princess Rissa, didn't he, sir?" Spido smiled. "And I loves me mum, which is why I writes to her—well, not to her but to someone who can read it to her—with news of my life and quest to destroy Dolonicus . . . and his killing clawthings."

"I was thinking of love for another, not a relative."

"Oh, yes, sir, I can see that, sir. . . ."

Spido's voice trailed off wispily, which caught Gar's attention. "Do you have someone you love back in Torfay?"

Spido blushed and nodded. "Now you've caught me out, sir. The fair Squashblossom is the one I love."

"Squashblossom?"

"Well, sir, she's the twelfth daughter, and the others were all named for flowers like Dahlia and Daffodil and Rose and . . ."

"And your mother, with her imagination, helped come up with Squashblossom, did she?"

"How did you know, sir?"

"There are many things a *hingu-Grashanshao* knows, Spido."

"Yes, sir, I see that, sir. In any event, Dolonicus is a threat to my Squashblossom."

"He intends to make her his wife?"

"Not exactly, sir. He intends to feed her to the clawthings." Spido shook his head. "He had intended to wed her, but she wouldn't have him and spilled hot soup in his lap—of course, she was always a bit clumsy . . ."

"But of fine character and good virtue."

"You speak as though you know her, sir. Anyway, being as how the bedsheet only covered part of Dolonicus at the time, he was a bit scalded and ornery until he healed up. Squashblossom has been in hiding since then, taking lodgings with those that will have her. . . ."

Gar's eyes narrowed.

"Mostly bachelors because Dolonicus would never think of looking for Squashblossom in the homes of single men, where a woman of her virtue would never consider hiding."

"A *hingu-Grashanshao* must have second sight, that's for certain, sir. It's like you've been reading my mum's letters—well, not *her*—"

"You've explained the procedure to me, at least four and a half times, Spido."

"Right you are, sir. So Squashblossom is the reason why we have to go to Torfay and kill Dolonicus, and therefore she is the reason I need you to complete my training as a *hingu-shanshao* so's I can slay him."

"Before I can do that, Spido, I need to determine what you know of *hingu*. You didn't know enough of it to know the Thirteen Truths or the Nine Precepts don't exist."

"No, sir."

"But they *do* exist, Spido."

His aide looked more confused than usual. "Yes, sir, I mean, no, sir, I think." Spido's shoulders slumped forward. "I have a lot to learn, yes?"

"You and every other *hingu-kun*." Gar refrained from giving Spido a smile and scaring him further. "You see, Spido, the science of *hingu* itself is but a degraded and diminished form of a much older *art* known as *Tian-shi-sheqi*. *Hingu* means death, but *Tian-shi-sheqi* is harder to translate from ancient Thermaean. The closest we can get now is 'cycle of life' but that lacks the inclusiveness of the art. If you will, *Tian-shi-sheqi* is the philosophy for which *hingu* is the practical operation."

"If you say so, sir."

"*Tian-shi-sheqi* demands that death not be a cessation of life, but a summing up of all life experience. The idea that, in the face of impending death, one's life flashes before one's eyes is merely a poor layman's understanding of the soul of the art, you see. If you will, a practitioner of *Tian-shi-sheqi* becomes a poet working in the fabric of life to perform his art."

Spido's confusion began to clear. "Poetry I understand, sir. I even have tried my hand at it. I have a bit about you."

Ah, Domino, your lover may not be the only poet in Faltane! "You do? Please, tell me."

"Oh, no, sir, I don't think so."

"Spido, you *do* wish me to hear it."

"So I do, sir, you can put your hand down now." Spido

swallowed hard, then ducked his head sheepishly. "Here goes: When his mind is idle/He thinks homicidal."

Gar smiled and Spido cringed reflexively. "Spido, that *is* special."

"It is?"

"Yes, yes indeed. You may not have learned much at Armbruss, but this may be a help, not a hindrance. In that couplet you have captured me perfectly."

"I have?"

"Indeed, yes, you have distilled me to the essence of my being." Gar nodded solemnly, for the first time not regretting the presence of his traveling companion. "This ability you have exhibited suggests to me that you might have an innate grasp of some tenets of *Tian-shi-sheqi*. I might be able to teach you things, wonderful things."

"Could you, sir?"

"Yes, oh, yes." Gar's pale eyes flashed as he looked at his aide. "Do you remember hearing of the battle at Stone Crossing?"

"Where Kalaran's Dread Legion of Implacable Retribution fell dead when they heard Rango's trumpeters sound a charge?"

"The very same. Do you know why they died like that?"

Spido shrugged warily. "I'd have to be guessing *Tian-shi-sheqi*, sir."

"And right you would be. What do you think is the core of any soldier's life?"

"Fear, sir?"

"Exactly. What I did, the night before the battle, was to steal into Kalaran's camp and travel among the sleeping Legionnaires. Using *kuo-tak*, a special *Tian-shi* technique, I was able to lay them low with a touch."

Spido raised an eyebrow. "But they died all at once, on the field, and, begging your pardon, sir, but you might be fast as Spotty Gulick sniffing out a poker game, but you're still not fast enough to touch each of them so they dies that quick."

"No, no, you misunderstand. With *kuo-tak*, a touch

kills, but the death is delayed and can even be triggered by a sight or a sound or a scent. The key is to distill the victim's life down to one event, one sensation, then to work off it and back to where the trigger brings death." Gar stared off distantly. "I knew, for those men, that when they heard our side sound a charge, no matter their confidence, there would be a moment of self-doubt, of fear. When the unknown yawned before them, as the battle joined, I knew that moment would be there. It was a moment, a thought that had occurred in every battle to every warrior ever, and that was the moment I chose to define them and their existence as soldiers. And in that moment, when they heard the trumpets, they were slain by *kuo-tak* and the touch I had given each of them while they slept the night before."

Spido's horse sidled away from Gar. "Fascinating, sir, really. And you learned this from Udan Kann?"

"That fool? No. He thinks of killing as a science. *Hingu* is all formulae and techniques to him. Things are learned by rote and become mechanical in execution. The other *hingu-shanshao* I fought in the war were stiff and slow when seen through eyes colored with the artistry of *Tian-shi-sheqi*. As with your *shanshao*, I had no trouble slaying them."

"And you'd destroy Udan Kann if we ran into him?"

Gar nodded solemnly. "He was the master, but this student has gone beyond him. I may not know all he knew, but I understand more than he will ever comprehend."

They rode in silence for a couple more miles until Spido suggested they camp in a grove of trees beside a crystal-clear stream. Gar agreed and left Spido to make up the camp and prepare the evening meal while he wandered off through the long grasses of the nearby meadow and worked through two hours of martial exercises.

By the time he finished, the sun had set and Spido called him to supper. His exercises—a regimen he had created specifically to increase his stamina so he could last longer than the half hour during which he had defended Bardu Defile—had helped him burn off the anger he felt at the memory of Udan Kann. The *hingu-Grashanshao* had been like a father to Gar and the other orphans being trained at Armbruss. Gar had spent his life believing his parents had died accidentally, but when he learned the truth—that Udan Kann had murdered them at Kalaran's order—his rebellion and defection had been the only options open to him.

Spido put his bowl down after finishing his second helping of gruel and patted his stomach. "My cooking is not bad, but nothing like me mum's cooking."

"You wear evidence of her skills around your middle, Spido."

"She'll fatten you up, too, sir, in a week or less." Spido thought for a second, then nodded with a smile. "She'll let you stay with us, I'm thinking, sir, given that you're dark haired and all. The eyes might bother her—she's not much on Northerners like that Jancy Gaine, though I'd have been much on her would she have given me so much as a wink and a nod, eh, sir? Not much of a chance of that, given how stingy she is with smiles, of course."

Gar frowned. "Jancy seems quite affable to me."

"Beg pardon, sir, but compared to you, there's rocks what are fair lunatic with laughter and smiles."

"So you fancied Jancy, did you?" Gar looked slyly at his aide. "Wouldn't such a dalliance play hob with your relationship with the fair Squashblossom?"

"Well, as me mum says, men are meant to hunt treasure, if you catch my drift, and you can't fault us for our nature. Still and all," his voice lowered a bit, "I'd only entertain a lass if she were meant for me 'cuz of the prophecy."

"The one about the goddess?"

"Yes, sir."

"While Jancy fights with the heart and skill that can only be a divine gift, I'm not certain she is a goddess."

"I was allowing for allegory in the poem, sir."

"Ah, a wise idea." Gar looked up and out beyond the

perimeter of the firelight. "Do you see a woman out there?"

"Is this another of them 'allusions' of yours, sir?"

"No, Spido, the glowing, lavender woman out there."

"Now that you mention it, I do see someone." Spido stood and stared for a moment. "She's glowing, sir. Maybe she's my goddess. Do you think, sir?"

"I don't know, Spido. Perhaps I should go check it out."

"I can go, sir, no trouble at all."

"And bring her back to a camp that has dirty bowls and the like scattered about? This is a goddess, Spido."

"Right, sir. Shall I call out to you when things are clear?"

"Very good, Spido."

Gar left his aide scurrying around the camp and strode out to where the glowing woman stood. The purple-white light she gave off had prompted some of the wildflowers in the vicinity to blossom. Behind her Gar saw faint flashes of gold as a remarkable doe cropped grass as if out grazing on a lazy spring afternoon.

Gar granted the glowing woman a generous smile and she did not shy from it. He bowed and kept his voice respectfully low. "I am honored by your presence, Osina of the Flowers. To what do I owe this visit?"

A rosy glow came to Osina's cheeks and her flaxen hair drifted as the night breeze caressed it gently. "I have heard much of you lately and felt compelled to seek you out." The demigoddess opened her arms and revealed herself in all her naked glory. "The only mortal to refuse my charms is a mortal about whom I am curious. And of whom I have learned much."

"I am honored by your attention, Osina."

"And will you accept me now, or is your orientation still in question?"

She laughed and Gar blushed. "My orientation was never in question."

"There was some confusion, though, last time we

spoke. As I recall you had feelings for Colonel Dominik Blaid. He was one of your comrades in arms."

"Yes, but he was a *she*."

"But you did not know that at the time."

"True, but I had sensed it."

"And what do you sense from her now?"

"That she has given her heart to someone else."

Osina reached a supple arm out and stroked Gar's cheek with her hand. "I sense this of you, as well. You will resist me again, will you not?"

"As long as we both live, I will always harbor hope that Domino will return my feelings."

"Then I do have a chance."

Gar stiffened. "Do not think to harm her, Osina."

The willowy goddess held her hands up. "Calm yourself, *Grashanshao-tian-shi*, my half brother Kalaran inherited the family's sociopathic tendencies. I am merely one who blossoms in your presence."

"There must be others for whom you blossom."

"Not really. Good stamen are hard to find."

"Sir, oh, sir, everything is ready, sir."

Osina looked past Gar toward the camp. "Who is that bulbous, naked man bouncing from foot to foot in your camp?"

"That is Spido. He is a great hero who has deciphered a prophecy that will lead to the liberation of his village from the forces of evil. He is in love with Squashblossom, but he believes the prophecy indicates he will have a liaison with a goddess."

The goddess frowned. "Squashblossom of Torfay?"

"You know of her?"

"I keep a watch over my flower-children. Quite the pistil, that one."

"You know that, and I know that, but Spido doesn't have a clue. I intend to find a way to let him down easy."

Osina squinted at the camp. "At the moment, letting Spido down is not going to be easy." She smiled as Gar winced. "I think, though, I can do something."

The demigoddess of flowers turned and gestured

toward the golden deer. Lavender and lilac lights played over the beast, which slowly transformed itself into a naked woman with closely cropped golden hair, big brown doe eyes, and ears slightly more pointed than most humans. She reached down and plucked a daisy, then scampered off toward the camp as she nibbled the flower.

"Nice trick with the hind."

Osina half closed her eyes of violet. "The trick was in undoing magicks my brother, the Horned One, worked a century or two ago. He saw Elise and fell in love with her. He transformed her into a doe and, well, she was just another point on his rack. Come autumn he got the hots for some swan and flew south. Elise was hart-broken, so I've taken care of her."

"Still, it's nice of you to have done that for Spido."

"No problem. Elise was eating some of my cousins there anyway."

Gar looked down at the flowers. "Your cousins? Were they how you found me?"

"No, you have to torture daisies before they'll talk." Osina slowly seated herself and patted a spot beside her. "The etheric winds have been carrying your name. Rango's sorcellets bandy it about amongst themselves. They've cut your Spido out of many conversations, and consider him an idiot as far as geography is concerned."

Gar sat down facing her instead of beside her. "Part of the prophecy business. Spido is misreporting our location."

"Just as well. I was misled and visited some of those spots. Quite crowded, they were."

The assassin's head came up. "Oh? Your brother's minions?"

"They were. Wanted to deflower me." She laughed. "They're all mulch now. In fact, you should thank me."

"Yes?"

"I have been effective enough in eliminating the groups who flock to where Spido reports you to be, that it is assumed you *are* there killing them off."

Gar took her hand and kissed her petal-soft flesh. "I am in your debt. Not only have you helped safeguard me, but you have told me that there is a traitor among the sorcellets."

"Not necessarily. Someone could be eavesdropping, much as I have."

"Kalaran?"

"He is otherwise occupied."

"Death will do that."

"Indeed. No, actually, listening in to the conversations would be relatively easy because your sorcellets are flowers with only one blossom. They only understand how to work their communication magick, and they are sending their messages out to specific individuals, but people they do not know well. In fact, the link to them only comes through names. If an enemy were to undertake a baptism or naming ritual and claim the same name, he would get the messages being sent to that person."

"And if he were a sorcellet himself, he could order the movement of troops to waylay me." Gar scowled at a daisy and it began to wilt. "Rango's communications network is compromised, but the only way to get a warning to Spotty, Jancy, and Domino is by using that network. Unless *you* would take them a message for me."

Osina reached out, touched the wilted flower and it immediately came back to life. "I could, but I will not. It is not my place to interfere in the affairs of mortals."

"But telling me this much is interference isn't it?"

The demigoddess shook her head slowly. "I am merely fulfilling my part in the unfolding drama. That amulet you wear, Anachron, has a past and a future. You and I are custodians to ensure it passes from one into the other." A silence fell heavy between them, but giggles and moans from the camp shattered it. Osina stood and smiled down at the assassin. "Fare thee well, Gar Quithnick. Remember that I am in every flower you smell and that the long grasses that caress your legs are my fingers."

IV

By Any Other Name

Spido hid a yawn behind his hand as they rode along the next morning. "Sorry, sir, for not being up at the crack of dawn and having everything ready. Sorry to keep you waiting."

Gar shrugged. "I have no trouble killing time, Spido." His aide looked strangely at him, so the assassin added, "That was a joke, Spido."

"Right, sir." He forced a laugh, but it ended in a yawn.

"Dead tired, are you?"

"Yes, sir." Spido glanced back along the road. When Gar turned in the same direction he caught a flash of gold from the treeline. "Can I ask you a question, sir?"

"By all means."

"I'm thinking, sir, about changing my name. Do you think Buck suits me?"

Gar shook his head. "Buck is out, Spido. *Hingu* and *Tian-shi-sheqi* do not often bestow nicknames on their practitioners."

"So you've never had one, sir?"

"No, I have not. At least not formally, for all I am referred to by other names among Prince Rango's forces."

"I know, sir, I've heard many of them. You're called Death Machine, the Lethal Legate, the Murderous Missionary, the Son of a—"

"I don't need a recital." Gar smiled quixotically. "Actually, Udan Kann has renamed me. I suppose that counts as a nickname of sorts."

"Likely does, sir." Spido nodded confidently. "What does he call you?"

"With my defection to Rango's side, Udan Kann forbade any other *hingu-kun* to speak my name in his hearing. To him I am known only as the Pariah."

"Sounds as if he took your departure fair personal."

"Oh, I'm certain he did, but it was unavoidable." Gar shook his head. "You see, I learned that Udan Kann had murdered my parents and my sister. Strangled them and made me an orphan."

"Strangled them, sir? I can understand your upset."

"I daresay you can. You see, my father was a learned man and he had a vision for the future of Faltane. He had opposed Kalaran's ascension to power." Anger seethed through Gar's voice. "Udan Kann tore them from our manor house and choked the life out of them. And he described their murder to me in exquisite detail, as if he could remember their pulses getting thready beneath his hands, their faces turning purple, and their life flowing out of them. He was proud and I was disgusted."

"With good cause, sir. That'd have riled me some. If he'd done my mum like that . . ."

"Indeed, you do understand, Spido. Strangling your mother would be wrong."

"It would that, sir."

"Yes. From all you have said of her, she should die in her kitchen, baking something that she expects to serve to you and Squashblossom. It should be a new invention, something upon which she used her imagination. And right at the moment of inspiration, when the perfect name comes to her, that is when she should die."

Spido winced as the blood drained from his face. "But then she would be dead, sir."

"Yes, but she would have been transformed by *Tian-shi-sheqi*, Spido. My parents and sister deserved that sort of death."

"In me mum's kitchen, sir?"

"No, Spido, they deserved deaths that encapsulated their lives. My father should have died overreaching himself like the visionary he was, not strangled and choked and smothered. There was nothing choking or strangling about the man. And my mother, she was from a noble house. She should have died listening to music or walking in a garden. And my sister, she was but a child. She should have died in a fantasy world of faery stories and sweets."

"Well, I think you have a reason to hate him, killing your kin like that."

"No, Spido, Udan Kann did not kill my parents, he slaughtered them. Had he slain them in appropriate ways, I would not be his enemy. His callousness toward them forever drove us apart. Mark me, Spido, I will slay Udan Kann when next we meet."

"My money will be on you, sir." Spido spurred his horse on, but in doing so he drifted toward the far side of the road. "Can I ask you another question, sir?"

"You may."

"Has anyone ever told you that you can be a bit spooky?"

Gar decided, and Spido agreed, that his training should begin in earnest immediately. Over the next three weeks on the road, in addition to pitching and tearing down camp and preparing all the meals, Spido spent a fair amount of time trotting along behind the horses in an effort to improve his wind. In the evening and again in the morning Spido went through a series of exercises designed to improve his speed and reaction time. After dinner he often chased after the golden hind, honing his agility and, when he caught her and she transformed into Elise, picking his spirits up.

The exercise did him a world of good, especially after Gar cut his rations. Spido thinned down a bit and built up some muscle. Using swords that Spido had packed for the journey, Gar was able to instruct him in the rudiments of swordfighting, but he found Spido had a natural affinity for wrestling and punching when he got in close. This presented something of a problem as that sort of attack brings the fighter in closer than most want to be to their foes.

The last day before their entry in the Torfay valley, Gar bid Spido pay special attention. "You are a promising *Tian-shi-kun*, Spido, but we do not have the time we need to complete your training before you may need to avail yourself of martial skills. As a result I will show you something no one else knows. It is called *wan-tej*." Gar pulled his fingers down into a fist, but thrust his thumb up between the index and middle fingers. "It is a very special thumb thrust. When you hit Dolonicus with it, shout his name and you will kill him."

Spido looked at his hand. "Really? Just bip, 'Dolonicus,' and he'll be down?"

"I will guarantee it." Gar bowed to his pupil, who returned the bow with deep respect. "Tomorrow we will enter Torfay. I will slay these dinner-sores and you will kill Dolonicus. Before two days have passed, you will be a hero and Torfay will be free."

V

The Four Labors of Gar Quithnick

The valley in which Torfay lay had steep mountain walls that rose to the clouds. Though it lay on a northwest-southeast angle, at either end it broke north and south for just under a mile in length. Thick bamboo forests and virgin underbrush covered the mountains in green, but down near the river that ran through the valley, the native growth had been cut away and terraces had been built up. Orderly rows of plantings covered the dark soil and split-bamboo aqueducts and waterwheels gave mute evidence to the care which the farmers lavished upon their fields.

Crouched at the bamboo line, Gar studied the tight little entrance valley. Two stone crofts stood up and away from the river and appeared to have been half dug into the mountain itself. Both had been built on a level equal to that of the middle terraces, and each had a corral and a series of henhouses near it. While the whole spectacle did not speak of prosperity, it seemed clear to Gar that the crofters were able to make a comfortable living from their holdings.

The screams coming from the people standing on the roof of the croft on the east side of the river contrasted sharply with the picture of idyllic beauty. Two goats lay in the mud of the corral. Their bright blood had not yet begun to turn brown, marking the kills as very recent. A third goat bleated pitifully as it ran pell-mell across the middle terrace.

Chasing after came a dinner-sore.

"What do you think, sir?"

"I think it's beautiful, Spido, absolutely beautiful."

Roughly twice as long as Gar was tall, the sorian held its little foreclaws tight to its chest as it ran on its powerful hind legs. It used its long, rigid tail to balance its body, and at the shoulder it would have been no taller than Gar himself. At one point, as it cut across the goat's path, Gar saw its narrow silhouette and the way both eyes looked forward.

Gorgeous blue and green plumage covered the creature and rose to a bluejay crest above its head. It ran with a long bouncing stride and occasionally hopped as if it could not control itself. For a short time it paralleled the goat, then darted ahead in a burst of speed and herded the creature back toward the paddock where its slain companions lay, all the while savagely scolding the goat with loud cries.

The creature's motion and economy sent a thrill through Gar. The sorian moved with a fluid grace that belied the power in its muscles. By coursing and herding the goat and calling out in various songs, it displayed intelligence and malicious ferocity. Gar found it almost catlike in its desire to control its prey before it killed it. The creature hunting below him possessed an artistry and focus that made it the most naturally lethal organism Gar had ever seen.

The goat leaped down from the middle terrace and took the six-foot drop without harm. It turned and ran along the wall and the dinner-sore landed behind it without breaking stride. The creature shot off on a course at the right angles to the goat's route, its melodic voice chortling out an excited song. The sorian turned and paralleled the goat before angling in for the kill.

"Yes, yes, of course."

"What, sir?"

Gar pointed at the sorian. "The profile provides a bigger target. It took the others from the side, and will get this one that way."

The TerribleClaw FastHunter raced in at the goat, then leaped out with a sharp scream of triumph. The huge, sickle-shaped claw on the left foot struck first and sliced through the goat's spine just in back of the shoulders. It cut down through viscera and came away bloody. The right claw slashed the goat's rear haunch with what would have only been a flesh wound.

The goat tumbled away and slammed into the stone restraining wall for the upper terrace. It rebounded hard and flew up into the air. Internal organs began to spray out, and Spido reeled away with his hand over his mouth. Gar watched in fascination as dirt clods flew from where the goat's hooves dug into the rich loam, then he turned away as Spido's retching noises drowned out the renewed screams from below.

His aide looked back up at him, wiping spittle and vomitus from his mouth. "How can you consider that beautiful?"

Gar's eyes narrowed. "In the hunt it was poetry, Spido. That creature, in the way it moves and the weaponry nature gave it, embodies *Tian-shi-sheqi*. What men have had to learn, it has by nature. In its own place, that creature would be magnificent."

The assassin took in a deep breath. "Clearly it is not of this world. Anachron and the other items of power were what caused that beast and its kin to appear here. Their transportation here corrupted them. They went from being artists to mechanical creatures. They are now things of *hingu*."

Spido retched again, then squeaked out. "What in hell are you saying?"

"Before I *wanted* to kill these creatures." Gar drew

Spido's machete and sliced off a slender bamboo pole. "Now I *must* kill them, to redeem them. I will slay them in keeping with *Tian-shi-sheqi.*"

"How's that?"

Gar smiled coldly. "Hunting defines them. Hunting they will die."

Using the machete, Gar trimmed foliage from a twelve-foot length of the pole, then cut the pole down to ten feet. From his boot he drew a dagger and jammed the hilt down into the open cylinder at one end. It fit snugly and the assassin tested the newly formed spear for balance. It was not quite what he wanted, but it would be sufficient.

Spido stood up. He looked pale and sweat covered him. He spat, then looked down at the village. "It's feeding."

Before Gar could acknowledge that information, a harsh, brassy horn call echoed through the valley. Gar glanced at the dinner-sore and saw its head come up. The beast returned to feeding immediately, but a second horn call caught its attention again. It took a step toward the sound of the horn then, straddling the goat, it tore a mouthful of flesh from it and gulped it down.

"Did your mother say anything about Dolonicus having the beasts trained to come to a call?"

"I don't recall that, but she's a bit deaf, so she might not have noticed."

Gar nodded once, then stepped out of the bamboo and started walking down the hillside toward the croft. The people on the roof saw him immediately and started to shout at him to run, but their cries attracted the bloody-faced sorian's attention, so they fell silent and just tried to wave him away.

Brandishing the makeshift spear in his right fist, Gar voiced an inhuman call. The undulating sound came to him, building note after note based on what he recognized through *Tian-shi-sheqi* as a challenge to the beast. As much as the horn had attracted the beast's attention, this call riveted it on Gar, and the assassin used the same scolding tones the sorian had used on the goat to goad the beast into action.

Red blood splashing back from its facial plumage, the sorian galloped toward him. Gar read cold brutality in the golden eyes. The beast held its jaw agape, giving him a clear view of the shreds of meat trapped between its slicing teeth. The little forearms with their nasty claws made little grasping motions at him as the sorian came on. It screamed at him, defiantly, then confidently as it leaned into its run and brought itself to full spring speed.

Gar brought the spear back. His pale eyes half closed, then he nodded a salute to the sorian. He knew it would not understand that gesture, but he made it because *Tian-shi-sheqi* demanded it. Then he threw the spear.

It sped from his hand and caught the sorian in the throat, strangling the beast's cry. The little forearms clawed at the shaft and clutched it, but only succeeded in dragging it down so it caught on the ground. The bamboo shaft dug in, then bowed, but refused to break. The sorian started to vault up and over as the force drove the spear out through the other side of the neck. The sorian landed on the point of its chin, then the rest of its body slammed down, mashing the feathery crest and snapping the beast's neck.

It thrashed a bit, and its sickle claw deftly sliced a fat watermelon in half in the process, then it lay still. Gar walked down to it and squatted ten feet away, studying both the beast and the wound his spear had inflicted. His cast had not been perfect, but he accepted the blame for that instead of attributing it to the slight balance problem with the bamboo spear.

Spido came trotting up beside him. "Well, sir, you got it. That was amazing."

"No, Spido, it was disgusting."

"I was referring to your throw, sir, not the beast."

"As was I, Spido."

"Excuse me, sir."

Gar looked up at his aide. "I wanted to kill it in keeping with *Tian-shi-sheqi*."

"And you did, sir. You killed it while it was hunting."

"Yes, but I killed it at long distance. I could see in its eyes it had not reached the defining moment of its existence, yet. When it leaps, I think it will be then. I *know* it will be then."

"Begging your pardon, sir, but that means you have to be close enough for it to leap at you."

"Art requires sacrifice, Spido."

"If you say so, sir." Spido picked up a feather and twirled it between his fingers. "Does art say what we should do with it now?"

Gar frowned. "No, but I think it should be in keeping with *Tian-shi-sheqi*."

"Defining moment and all that, eh, sir?"

"Yes, Spido. Have you an idea?"

"Well, sir, to leave the carcass here would be to get these crofters—cousins of mine they are, sir—in trouble. We have to get rid of it and, given what I've seen defining this beastie, sir, I think I know how we should do it." Spido smiled carefully. "I think we should eat it."

"Eat it?" Gar stood slowly. "Eating does seem to define these sorians. Do you think we can eat it?"

"Well, sir, I've not known of much what eats what we eat that we couldn't eat, if you catch my drift, sir." Spido smoothed the feather out, then tucked it through a button hole on his tunic. "In fact, sir, unless I miss my guess, I think this beastie will taste a lot like chicken."

The crofters gladly lent Spido an ax for the butchering of the sorian once he managed to convince them that, despite his reduced belly, he truly was Spido. At Gar's urging, he cautioned his cousins not to say anything about his return, else more of the sorians would be let run loose in the Torfay valley. That, and three quarters of the meat from the beast, bought their silence.

The village of Torfay itself lay in the middle of the valley. Spido led Gar around it on a narrow woodsman's track that circumvented the village but still provided an occasional glimpse of it below. Spido remarked that it had grown a bit since he had left and indeed Gar saw a settlement he would have characterized as larger than a village.

Torfay had been organized around a fairly small town square that appeared to be covered in grass except where a muddy road ringed and quartered it. Arranged around that were some large buildings of stone, with thatched roofs. Only one rose to two full stories, the rest were more squat. Ringing them in a labyrinth of narrow alleys, single dwellings with small fenced yards predominated—though fairly often one home leaned against another for mutual support.

Spido pointed to the largest building at the city square. "That would be the Prince's Haven. It used to be Kalaran's Throne, but me mum says it was changed. Dolonicus calls it the Prince's Craven and says the tavern should have your picture on the sign." He winced as he reported that fact, then brought this head up and added, "I figured I'd kill him for that alone."

Gar nodded solemnly. "Kill him to save your village. Make him suffer to avenge me."

"Ah, yes, sir." Spido stumbled on uphill, the sorian haunch swinging precariously over his shoulder before he recovered himself. "Dolonicus has a room there and uses the stable in the back to keep his dinner-sores. I reckon he has them trained to come at the horn."

"So I gathered."

"No one else has opposed them, 'cept One-Armed Horrigan."

"Lost an arm to the sorians?"

"No, sir." Spido frowned. "All they found to bury of him was one arm."

"I see." Gar heard something in Spido's voice he had a hard time identifying. "This prophecy you follow, it says nothing about you fighting any of these creatures, does it?"

Fear spilled over into Spido's voice. "No, sir, I can't see as how it does."

Gar forced a sigh. "Good."

"Good, sir?"

"Yes, Spido, I was afraid you were going to claim the remaining sorians for yourself."

"Not if you want them, sir."

"If you don't mind, I would like them."

"Don't let me stand in your way, sir."

"You are most generous." Gar's eyes narrowed. "I've taken one with a spear, but that was unfair. These beasts use their claws, and their claws are equivalent to a sickle or a sword. I will use a sword to take the next one."

"Doom on that one, then."

"Indeed."

Spido led the way on along the track, then cut off on a side trail that wound back and around and on down into a valley thick with lush growth. They broke from the woods and found a croft similar to the two they had seen before. The ramshackle stone building had a crooked chimney from which rose white smoke; chickens and goats wandered around in the front yard. A small stream trickled down, heading toward the river that split the main valley, and small patches of cultivated ground blossomed with corn, squash, pumpkins and a seemingly endless variety of beans.

Spido looked back at Gar with a bigger smile on his face than a night with Elise had generated. "Welcome to me home, Grashanshao."

Apparently his voice carried because the front door of the croft flew open and a small, stocky battle-ax of a woman boiled out with an ax in her hands. In her hooked nose and sharp chin Gar saw some of Spido, but the way she piled her gray hair up on top of her head and the unsteady, lock-kneed gait she used swallowed all other similarities.

"I don't care who you are, you're not getting nothing more from this farm, and I brook no opposition in that!"

"Ma? It's me."

She stopped, her head coming forward beneath the upraised ax, and she squinted. "Who are you?"

"You only have one son, Ma."

"And he doesn't look like you, does he?"

"Ma, it's me. The war and all, I've lost some pounds."

Her fierce visage softened. "Malveysean *Aloysius* Kentigern Blott the Fourth?"

Spido winced, but nodded. "It's me, Ma."

Gar frowned. "How do you get Spido out of that?"

As his mother scurried forward toward them, Spido dropped his voice to a whisper. "My father's nickname was Longlegs, and he was my daddy, so I became Spido. The alternatives were worse." He shivered.

"I find that hard to believe."

"Mallo, give your mum a kiss, there's a good boy." Close up the old woman looked as if hard times had plowed deeper furrows into her face than in the fields below. "Who did my little Wishie-wishy bring home with him? Is this one of your little friends from the war?"

"Mother, this is Gar Quithnick."

"Pleased to meet you, Mr. Hiccup."

Spido's eyes grew white with terror. "Quithnick, Mother."

"I heard you the first time, Gernie." She smiled graciously at Gar. "And how do you know my little Mallo, Mr. Quiknik?"

"Spido and I have been assigned a mission."

"Ooooh, I hate that name." She grabbed Spido's right ear and gave it a twist. "You didn't tell them that was your name, did you?"

"I wouldn't do that, would I, Mum?" Spido winced, but did not free himself from her grasp. "I, ah, I . . ."

"He earned it, Goodwife Blott." Gar smiled, noting to himself that a three-point Firetalon Touch on her left scapular region would likely free Spido and sink her into unbearable agonies. "He is linked into a weblike communications network of sorcellets. The sobriquet was natural."

"I hope indeed he has been sober, I tell you, not like Gordo."

Spido's face brightened. "Is Uncle Gordo here?"

"As if he would have moved since you left?" She

released Spido, then looked at Gar carefully, giving the assassin the impression that he might not be the most dangerous predator in the valley at the moment. "And you are aiding my son on a mission?"

"We are companions, yes."

"Ma, we can't talk about it." Tugging on her arm, Spido looked up at Gar with an expression that implored the assassin not to kill his mother. "We've come all this way because I, wanted to see you and we wanted a home-cooked meal."

She pinched the flesh over her son's flat belly. "I can see you need a meal, that's for evident plain. You shouldn't let your aide do your cooking for you, Mallo, for he's not got an idea what a strapping boy like you needs."

She turned back toward Gar as they walked down toward the croft. "My son's quite the trencherman, he is. When the valley harvest fair came around there wasn't no one who could beat Mallo at pie eating or milk drinking."

"Uncle Gordo could have."

"Only if they brought the fair here and channeled a trough to his mouth." Again she turned toward Gar. "You being malnourished and all, you'd not be knowing about the pride we takes in a healthy appetite."

Gar smiled politely. "Your son has been extolling the virtues of your culinary skill throughout our journey."

"Well he should, for the boy does love his mother's cooking."

"Ma!"

"Am I lying, Mallo?"

"No, Ma, but this is Gar Quithnick. He's a hero. We're on a mission for the Prince."

"Well, then, counting your uncle, we'll have two heroes at the table tonight, won't we? Mr. Quiknik, did your mum like to feed you?"

"Ma!"

Gar shook his head. "She died when I was very young, so I do not remember."

"Pity. Now, if you'd had a proper upbringing like my boy, you'd know the qualities that the Prince saw in him to give him this dangerous and important mission."

Spido raised the sorian haunch and almost made to bash his mother with it, then lowered it. "Ma, this man is not my aide, I'm *his* aide. The Prince gave him the mission and I'm just going along to go along."

"False modesty is a foul thing, Mallo."

"Ma! Listen to me. This is Gar Quithnick, the world's greatest assassin!"

"How great can he be if his mother wouldn't cook for him?"

An inarticulate scream both preceded and punctuated Spido's next cry of "Ma!"

Gar gestured toward the haunch. "Goodwife Blott, your son and I procured this fine haunch in hopes you would work your culinary magick on it."

Spido's mother dropped her ax and hefted the sorian leg. "Big chicken this came from, and ugly, too." She tucked it under her arm, and glanced sidelong at Gar. "Well, Mr. Quiknik, being as how your mum never cooked for you, and you doubt my son's appetite, and you've never been at a harvest fair, and my son brought me this fine gift of meat all the way from Prince Rango himself, I'll be fixing you up a meal you'll never forget."

She marched on in through the door, leaving Spido and Gar alone. "Please, sir, don't take offense at her."

"Never, Spido, she is just proud of you." Gar looked at the valley and then into the croft's dark interior. "She does live in her own world, doesn't she?"

"Her world, her rules." Spido shrugged. "Not so bad, really, 'cept for one thing."

"And that is?"

"It's not that she won't take no for an answer, sir, it's just that she never even hears it."

"Understood, Spido."

"Very good, sir. And one more thing."

"Yes?"

"Loosen your belt now, sir, saves time later."

*   *   *

Once they had watered, brushed and fed the horses, Spido and Gar repaired to the Blott homestead. Gar had to stoop to get through the door, and the dim light from oil lamps combined with smoke from the leaky chimney to leave the home in a state of perpetual dusk. Some curtains separated a back corner of the only room off from what was kitchen. In fact, from stove and storage bins to the chairs and solid table, the whole of the croft was kitchen.

Sitting equidistant between the fireplace and the cider keg in the corner, Gar saw a hirsute slag heap of a man swathed in a bedspread with a hole cut in the center of it. Dark stains formed a cone from where his beard left off to the hem of the garment. One arm ended in a book and the other in a tankard, and eyes stared out at him like dark water in the bottom of a deep, deep well.

"This is me uncle Gordo. Gordo Blott, this is Gar Quithnick."

" 'Scuse me if I don't get up."

"That's a laugh," sniped Goodwife Blott.

Gar marveled as the book became tucked beneath a wave of fat and the free hand was offered to him. Gar took it, barely able to feel bones beneath the puffy flesh, and shook it. He watched as the fat rippled up and down the arm and wondered how such an abundance of adipose tissue would serve to dissipate the force of a Butterfly with Twin Fangs and Tail Spike Blow.

Gordo shifted his head up, giving Gar the impression that the man's skull had tipped up within its fleshy shroud without affecting anything else. "You're the Prince's assassin, the one they call Pariah, eh?"

"I am."

"I was a fair killer in my youth, I was, eh, Fannie?"

"Killed a fair number of pies and kegs and tavern stools, you did, you lump."

"Women, they can't remember nothing. Killed me a dragon, I did. Schmirnov was its name. Killed it dead."

"Breathed on it, did you, Gordo?"

"Painted him a picture of you, Fannie." Gordo flashed a smile, giving Gar a glimpse of teeth that looked like tree stumps after a forest fire. "What does she know. You believe me, don't you, boy?"

"Of course, sir."

"There's a good lad." Gordo's face flowed in Gar's direction. "If you'll be wanting a workout, I'll give it to you. Not as spry as I was in my youth, mind you."

"I'd not take advantage, sir." Gar gestured toward the tankard. "Can I refill that for you?"

"Please. Thirsty work, remembering."

"I can imagine. Here you are."

"Thank you kindly. See, Fannie, your boy did show them capital folks some manners."

Spido's mother answered with a growl and menacing clatter of pots and pans. Spido, anticipating his mother, went to fetch water and harvest turnips, leaving Gar in the company of Uncle Gordo. As Gordo went on to describe the time he almost killed Udan Kann, after having been ambushed by a dozen *hingists* that he slew even though he felt sorry for them and all, Gar searched his mind for *Tian-shi-sheqi* treatises on hastening the inevitable in cases of morbid obesity.

As afternoon passed into evening, and Gordo's exploits took him north to Jancy Gaine's homeland and beyond, the scents of things boiling, broiling and baking did lure Gar from his own remembrances. They even deflected Gordo into adding a description of a feast in the middle of a raging battle and started him drooling like a starving hound dog standing downwind of a well-cooked roast.

Spido's mother sent Gar and her son down to the stream to wash up and fetch water, and Spido looked pitiful. "Please, sir, I don't know what you must think of my family."

"I find them quite intriguing. You spoke of your mother living in her own world. . . ."

"Yes, sir."

"Your uncle sublets a goodly portion of it."

"He does, sir. Never know what he's going to say."

"Or how much of it to believe."

Spido arched an eyebrow at the assassin. "Sir, I think you know exactly how much of it to believe."

"Point taken."

Spido shook the water from his hands. "If Uncle Gordo's not talking about the village or events happening in it, his information is twenty years old."

"Except for what you told him in your letters."

"Which mentioned you in passing, sir, before I knew about this mission and all."

"I will bear this in mind, Spido. Thank you."

By the time they returned to the house, Gordo had moved from the space by the wall to the head of the table. Gar noted that there was no bench or stool along the wall where the man had been sitting. Beneath the bedspread he thought he caught a glimpse of a tree stump, but he could not be certain because Gordo perched on it as if some strange man-mushroom hybrid.

Goodwife Blott settled Spido at her right hand and Gar on her left, then smacked the top of the oaken table with a wooden serving spoon. The sharp report stopped Gordo's account of his adventure in the Tower of the Nuns of Our Lady of a Racing Heart, and Goodwife Blott started talking before Gordo could continue. "All right, what we have here, in honor of the return of my son the hero to Torfay, is what we calls a formal banquet. It'll be served in four and a half courses and some. First, the soup."

She marched back over to the stove and returned with a huge cauldron and four bowls the size of steel helmets. She ladled thick, brown goop with oddly shaped lumps into the bowls, then set one each in front of her guests. "Go on, eat it, eat it all!"

Gordo and Spido hefted the bowls and started to drink, so Gar followed suit instead of waiting for a spoon. The aroma hit his nose like a punch—not painful, but powerful—and the first taste sent a thrill through him. The thick, spicy broth tasted delicious and the little vegetable lumps exploded on his tongue like surprise packages of flavor.

Bits of ham melted in his mouth and morsels of a slightly tough meat—which tasted a lot like chicken—brought an exotic difference to the dish. Before he knew it he had drained his bowl, as did Spido across from him, and extended it toward Goodwife Blott. "More, please."

With a broad smile on her face, Goodwife Blott split the remainder between Gar and Spido, freezing Gordo out. That appeared to affront Gordo, but he quickly realized that if he couldn't fill his mouth with food, he could fill the air with words, and he resumed his story about the nuns.

The soup was good enough that Gar felt the story had improved incredibly since the start of the meal, and he even found himself disinclined to provide for Spido the sort of service Udan Kann had done for him.

The second course came in the form of three little oval puff pastries placed on a plate in a shamrock pattern, drizzled with an egg-yolk-yellow sauce and garnished with a sprig of fresh peppermint. For this Gar got a fork, though with his first bite he considered it a probable violation of *Tian-shi-sheqi* to use the fork on the light, fluffy bits of dough. The sauce proved both sweet and tangy, and complemented the heavily spiced meat mixture at the heart of each pastry.

Gar and Spido each requested another serving, which Goodwife Blott supplied, but she clearly did not like the fact that the skinny Gar was matching her son bite for bite.

Gordo noticed her discomfort immediately. "Oh, Fannie, your boy has met his match. I'll just let the two of them fight it out."

"You'll do that because you won't be getting no more, you behemouth!" She smiled sweetly at Gar and Spido. "Does me heart good to see you eat, boys. We'll put some meat on your ribs, we will indeed."

She returned to her stove, turning her back on the table, but still remaining in the conversation as Gordo prattled on. "Oh, you should have seen it, boys, there I was in the Tower, eating what I could to keep my

strength up, you see, because them nuns were in a powerful fit of need. And a lot of them were Northerners,
and you know what that means, eh? No one quite so
passionate as Northerners, you know."

"Pish and tosh, Gordo Gourdo." Goodwife Blott
wheeled around brandishing a meat-ax. "Nothing wrong
with a good Faltane girl. You want exotic, but you can't
get no pleasure from that, can you, Mallo?"

"Well, Ma, how would I know?"

She looked at him sidelong, then gave him the hint of
a smile. "You'd not be trying to convince your mum that
you've not become more worldly-wise since you've
been gone."

Spido blushed and stammered a bit. "Well, perhaps I
have sought, on the eve of a battle when I didn't know
if I'd live or die the next day, some companionship."

"I knew it! I knew it! Catting about in the capital.
Probably sleeping with that Fancy Jane, the brothel
keeper."

"She's Jancy Gaine, Ma, and was a guard at a brothel."

"If you work at a brothel, you work at a brothel." The
meat ax *ka-choonk*ed through a piece of pink meat on
the cutting board. "Ladies of breeding are not found
in brothels."

"Ma, Princess Rissa was in the brothel that Jancy
Gaine guarded."

"Oh, and you'll be telling me this Northern floozy of
yours, Fancy What's-her-name, rescued Rissa and took
her away from there."

"Well, yes."

"And *you* believe it?" Goodwife Blott groaned and
diced meat. "You Blott men. A wink, a smile, a whistle
and you'd believe anything. Weakness it is for the blond
hair. I hope that Fancy Jain was worth breaking your
mother's heart."

"Ma!"

"Goodwife Blott, I can assure you that your son is of
fine, upstanding moral character." Gar smiled disarmingly
at her. "Prince Rango personally chose him to accompany

me on a mission of incredible danger, that only the most virtuous and valiant of men could hope to survive."

Spido's mother turned around. "Really?"

"Quite so, goodwife. In fact, your son was selected specifically because, in addition to being a moral stalwart, he so loves you and reveres you, that his feelings for you more than compensate for the lack of feeling I have for my mother, because I did not have the opportunity to get to know her." Gar frowned, realizing he had begun to string sentences together as Spido had, but recognizing that doing that was the only way to compete in the Blott household.

"He's a good boy, my son. Wouldn't see anything in a Northern girl."

"No, Mum, never."

"Good, 'cuz there's no Northern girl good enough for you."

"Speaking of which, where is Squashblossom?"

Gar caught the scowl as it flashed over Goodwife Blott's face, but she turned from her son and Gar knew Spido had missed it. "More time to talk about that later, Mallo. Third course coming up."

Had Spido not been used to his uncle's prattling, he might have caught news of Squashblossom in the way a particularly frisky nun was described as bestowing a blessing on everyone in the company that had somehow appeared to join Gordo's adventure. As it was, Goodwife Blott's return to the table with the next dish precluded anything beyond understanding how mouth-hunger can convince the belly that it's not nearly as full as it thought it was.

A curtain of aromatic steam parted before Gar as he looked down at his plate. The plate itself had been covered with a bed of brown rice that had been raked with a fork into concentric circles emanating out from around three broccoli tips that had been arrayed symmetrically on the plate. Strips of sorian meat, cut long and thin and glazed with a spicy but sweet sauce, trifurcated the rice ocean and isolated each of the green broccoli islands.

Little slivers of red and green pepper braved the brown ocean between the meaty continent and the lush islands, rising on the crest of a rice-wave or plunging into the trough between them.

The half course, consisting of a heavy potato bread slathered with butter followed, then Goodwife Blott delivered breaded and deep-fried sorian steaks awash in brown gravy. Mountains of whipped potatoes surrounded them, with melted butter pouring down the sides like lava from a volcano. Peas and pearl onions provided color for the dish and the potatoes slowed the peas down enough that Gar could deftly scoop them up on his fork.

Both Spido and Gar went for seconds on the bread and the fried sorian, then asked for bread again to sop up the gravy. The two of them smiled at each other, enjoying the contest and the look of consternation on Goodwife Blott's face. For Gar, who had never had a family and never knew what a family was like, found the good-natured competition enjoyable. At Armbruss, internecine squabbling proved lethal and though Spido's family might hammer each other verbally, woe be to any outsider who tried to get away with the sort of abuse they heaped on each other as a matter of course.

Goodwife Blott fed both of them apple tarts and custard, then went back to work at the stove when she saw the contest, which stood at even after four and a half courses and some and some more, would not be decided over dessert. As she worked she asked Spido about his time away from Torfay, and kept Gar involved in the conversation by asking him to confirm or deny something Spido had said.

Gar answered in accord with the facial expressions Spido wore and the subtle tones woven through Goodwife Blott's questions. Clearly she had been given some impressions of Spido's time in Caltus that did not correspond with any reality Gar knew, but he figured any one part brag by Spido had been blown into one hundred parts truth in her imagination. Still, he could feel her shifting the conversation around like a spider in a web, angling toward some information about her son.

"Now, Mallo, Mr. Quiknik says you are a fine upstanding boy."

Gar nodded. "A credit to Torfay and an inspiration to us all."

Spido rolled his eyes.

"And, of course, you'd be keeping yourself faithful to vows you made here, excepting when you were prepared to go off to battle, as you said before."

"That's true, Mum, and I only was comforted once or twice."

"That's a good boy. Now I was wondering if, in Caltus, given that you are so upstanding, if there might not have been someone to eclipse Squashblossom in your heart."

Gar caught the hopeful tone in Goodwife Blott's voice, but her son missed. "Not me, Mum. My heart is still with Squashblossom."

"You'd not be trying to protect me, would you, Mallo? As much as it might pain me to think of you two apart, dear, I would endure it for your happiness."

"No, Mother, she's still the one for me."

"Are you sure, dear? You've not seen her for a while. She's changed."

"I still love her, Mum."

"There's been some *big* changes, Mallo."

"Same with me, Mum."

"Not hardly, dear."

Gar intervened. "Your son *is* trying to protect you, goodwife. He has many lady admirers, and has been seeing one recently."

Goodwife Blott's face brightened and Spido looked confused. "Have you, Mallo? Is she pretty?"

"Ah, well, she is, Mother."

"Where did you meet her, dear?"

Spido looked at Gar.

The assassin smiled. "She is in service to a goddess, goodwife. She is a cleric and has ministered to your son's spiritual needs. He has spent much time in consummation, er, communion with her."

"Oh, good." She glanced at an hourglass as the last of the sand ran out of it. "Well, then, it is time to decide this eating contest." She stooped at the oven and pulled out a pie. "You may have matched Mallo bite for bite before, but no more. This is his favorite and he'll eat this up right quick."

She cut a steaming slice of the meat pie and set it down before her son, then matched it with another in front of Gar. Each of the men sat with his fork poised, then dug in. Goodwife Blott clapped as they swallowed their first mouthfuls. "Nothing my Mallo likes more than a good venison and kidney pie."

Spido turned white and clapped his hand over his mouth. His chair rocketed back as he stood and ran for the door. Yanking it open, he ran out into the night.

His mother watched him, then shook her head. "What's gotten into him?"

"While on the road, he's had quite a bit of venison, goodwife."

"That wouldn't keep him from my pie, no, sir." She thought for a second, then smiled. "Of course, that's my boy."

"Beg pardon?"

"That's my Mallo. Always the polite one." She smiled and took a forkful of his pie. "You being a guest means only by faking sick could he be polite and let you win the contest, eh, Mr. Quiknik?"

Gar would have replied, but, being polite, he didn't speak with his mouth full.

Gar was awake and away from the Blott croft well before the sun came up and the morning hunting horn was blown. As Gordo had explained, Dolonicus let his sorians out in the morning and before dusk to hunt, and woe unto those who found themselves or their livestock out and about during the time between trumpet calls. After the beasts had fed and had been recalled, Dolonicus would emerge from the Prince's Haven and inform the assembled multitude of whatever brilliant, leaderlike decisions he had made during the night.

Spido had agreed with Gar's suggestion to wait with his mother instead of following the assassin into town to deal with the sorians. Spido had actually offered to accompany Gar, and the assassin realized Spido had been serious. The assassin gave Spido one of his carefully hoarded smiles for his bravery, but indicated he wanted Spido to remain behind so someone could deal with Dolonicus in case Gar died in his battle with the sorians.

Armed with a single-edged, slightly curved *tatiq* sword, the world's only *Grashanshao* of *Tian-shi-sheqi* drifted through the sleeping hamlet of Torfay. Striding smoothly into the hunting grounds of a pair of monsters, he felt very much at home. *I have slain one of you. I have eaten of your flesh. I know you, and I will give your life definition in your death!* He paused and studied the parallel sorian tracks. *When hunters hunt hunters, only Death is sated.*

Gar shifted his sword so he gripped the hilt in his right hand, with the pommel cap projecting out between his thumb and forefinger. The blade itself ran along the dorsal side of his right arm. The dawn sun glinted from the razored edge, its silver contrasting sharply with the loose, black clothing the assassin wore.

Unopposed, Gar moved to the center of the village square, then caught movements to his left. He turned to face it and saw one of the sorians standing twenty yards away, between two houses. It lowered its muzzle toward the ground, then brought it up in a smooth motion counterbalanced by the stiff tail. Again it sniffed the air and took a half step toward him.

The intelligence in its eyes—a feral cunning the other sorian had lacked—betrayed it. The breeze it feigned sniffing blew from left to right, carrying his scent well away from it. *Which means . . .*

Gar threw himself to the left in a shoulder roll that took him down and away from where he had been standing.

The second sorian, claws rending the air with furious cuts, flew past him and cried out in frustration. Pain bled into that cry as Gar's blade flicked out and slashed the sailing beast across its feathered belly. Coming up as the beast tried to turn and stumbled, Gar whipped the blade down in an overhand strike that beheaded it.

Frustration and disgust swallowed Gar's momentary elation. He'd killed it as it hunted, as it leaped at him. His training and reflexes, his intelligence and his species' toolmaking legacy had granted him victory over a creature that should have been faster and more deadly than anything he had ever faced before. His triumph was one of mankind over the sorts of beasts that had stalked men in times best forgotten.

That same intelligence forced him to reject any pride he felt in the kill. He had timed his action correctly—the evidence of that lay in two pieces at his feet. Any man could have been ecstatic with what he had done, but Gar was not *any* man. He had chosen to define his life through *Tian-shi-sheqi* and his discipline identified for him where he had failed. It pointed out how he had betrayed the beast and himself and *Tian-shi-sheqi*.

Shaking his head ruefully, he tossed the bloodied *tatiq* on the body of the beast it had slain. "I used a tool when you only used what nature has given you. I cheated."

It was not the whisper of footfalls that prompted him to move, but the crunch of gravel and the cessation of footsteps that told him the remaining sorian had launched itself at him. He cartwheeled off to the right and felt a tug on his tunic as a razor talon sliced through it and scored the flesh over his ribs. On his feet again in an instant, he sidestepped toward where he knew the beast would turn and snapped a kick out at it.

The kick missed because the sorian had let momentum carry it a step farther than he anticipated. Though his foot flashed in and out in an eyeblink, the sorian lunged forward and jagged teeth came away with cloth shreds from his trousers. The sorian shook its head like a terrier dispatching a rat, then spat out the cloth. It looked at him, then bobbed its head and let go a bloodcurdling scream.

Gar grinned from ear to ear and set himself. The sorian feinted once, then turned and trotted off on a long, looping course that allowed it to pick up speed. Gar nodded, recognizing the intelligence of the beast. It already knew that he was fast, but that it was faster. With enough velocity built up it could slice him or bowl him over or just nip at him as it ran by. It had him, and they both knew it.

It had him as easily as a hound would have a hare.

If, of course, the hare decided to stand in one place.

While *Tian-shi-sheqi* allowed Gar to sympathize with a suicidal lagomorph, he rejected the impulse to emulate one. He, too, was a predator. This creature circled to hunt him, and in doing so it defined itself. *Tian-shi-sheqi* demanded that it do so, so its death would be perfect.

And *Tian-shi-sheqi* demanded Gar give it the death it deserved.

As the sorian circled, Gar sprinted forward toward an alley. He heard the sorian scream at him, and he returned an equally challenging and bestial call. Running full out the assassin dashed into the alley. He would have risked a look back to see how close the sorian had gotten, but its cry echoed from the alley's tight walls, telling him it had closed faster than he had thought it could.

Gar leaped over a small crate that the sorian smashed to splinters a couple of seconds later. Ahead of them, barely twenty feet from where the crate had died, an eight-foot-tall wooden wall blocked the alley, which gave neither hunter a choice. *It has to be now!*

Gar threw himself forward into a somersault as the sorian leaped at his back. A claw hit his left shoulder, tearing cloth and muscle, but the assassin forced away any thought of pain. Tucking tightly, he rolled quickly and extended both legs as he came around and over. Pushing off with his hands, he launched himself upward, feet first.

His feet caught the sorian where hip joined tail and

boosted the beast's pelvis higher into the air. Screaming out in surprise and terror, the fletched sorian sailed through the air, his foreclaws scrabbling like an ugly chick fallen from the nest before its wings worked. It smacked into the wooden fence face first and destroyed the structure as effectively as it had stomped the crate into splinters.

Gar's maneuver landed him on his feet and he dashed forward. The sorian tried to turn toward him, but its stiff tail slapped against the alley wall. The assassin leaped above the tail's return sweep and landed with his knees on the beast's shoulders. Before it could twist to throw him off, Gar jabbed a stiff-fingered Spearpoint Blow down where the sorian's jaw joined its skull. The strike found a nerve center and the sorian collapsed.

As he reached down to grab its muzzle and twist its head off, doubt again assailed him. He acknowledged that he had met the beast fairly and had defeated it. *Tian-shi-sheqi* allowed him to use environment against the beast, and the sorian had hunted in the village before. Moreover, had Gar chosen to run into the surrounding forests, the stands of bamboo would have served just as effectively to limit the sorian's mobility. He had won fairly, and he had paid in blood for his victory.

Even so, this was a beast out of time and place. Any death he could visit upon it, because it came from a world to which this beast was not native, would be unnatural. Perhaps where it came from, it had exterminated all men. Were that true, its death at Gar's hands would be the ultimate display of disrespect possible for it.

Tian-shi-sheqi offered Gar a way out of his dilemma. He rose above the fallen beast and studied it for a second, then nodded. Centering himself, Gar touched the beast at the back of its skull and where pelvis joined its spine. As he did so, using *kuo-tak* techniques, he felt the creature's life-energy flowing up and down the spine, and he felt the course eddy and whirl around the minute obstructions he had introduced.

Nodding grimly, Gar retraced his steps to the alley

mouth. A small knot of people, including Spido and his mother, stood over the dead sorian's body. Spido's head came up and concern flashed over his face, but Gar shook his head. He did gently probe the hole in his shoulder, and clenched his jaw against the pain. He contemplated using Anachron to heal himself, but he rejected that idea out of respect for the beast that had inflicted the wounds on him.

The door to the Prince's Haven opened and a large man stood in the doorway for a moment. Hitching his pants up, he walked out into the central square and, as if he had been a cork pulled from a bottle, a number of young toughs poured from the tavern and pooled behind him. A number of them blanched when they saw the dead sorian, but others let their youth cloak them in invincibility.

Dolonicus said nothing until Gar had reached Spido's side. "So, the Pariah has come to Torfay. I should be honored that Prince Rango has deemed me worthy of your attention."

Gar shook his head. "Your attention? I believe you are mistaken. I came to the mountains to do a little hunting. And to watch my companion here kill you."

"Him? A gobbet from that suetball Gordo?"

Spido stuck his chin out. "I'm a neph-gobbet, I am."

Dolonicus looked at Gar. "You may be mad, Pariah, but even you cannot imagine this one will be able to defeat me."

"No?" Gar darted forward and clapped his hands on Dolonicus's breastbone and spine, prompting a cough from the larger man. "You're terribly slow. I shouldn't think Spido will have much difficulty with you."

Dolonicus waded back into his henchmen. "He has to kill them first."

"Gar?"

"Don't worry, Spido." Gar yawned casually. "They won't even lay a hand on you."

Tension filled the square as the dozen toughs tried to stare Spido down. They might have succeeded except for a wheezy trumpet blast from atop a hill to the east of Torfay. All eyes turned toward the sound and, centered on the road leading down the hill into the town, they saw a man whose silhouette eclipsed the rising sun. A horn again sounded, then the figure moved forward and its spherical outline quivered up and down with each step.

"Uncle Gordo?"

With battered horn in one hand, and a knobby club in the other, Uncle Gordo pumped his arms as he trotted down the hill. "For Prince and Family," he wheezed at the top of his lungs. Each footfall sent tremors through the man's bulk and increased his speed. A human juggernaut, he thundered down the road and the crowd parted before him.

Everyone watched him, and every *thing* as well. Looping out along the hillside, the last sorian shook its head and raced in at the running man. Back, belly and flank offered equally inviting targets, but the sunlight glinting from the bronze war horn appeared to decide it for the beast. Voicing a cry that made knees go weak, it closed from Gordo's right and leaped.

As it left the ground, its heart stopped and its muscles locked up, freezing it into the perfect portrait of a hunter's hunter in mid strike. Gar laughed aloud with satisfaction as the *kuo-tak* strike slew it at the height of its power. Gordo's presence, though unanticipated, made things even more perfect, for such ample and succulent prey the creature doubtless had never hunted before.

Because of his contribution to the sorian's rapture before death, Gar forgave Gordo the last-minute twist to the right. The horn smacked the sorian in the head, sparking a wondrous cry from the villagers. As the sorian fell, so did Gordo. Tripped up by his own momentum, Gordo tumbled and flipped into the central square. He bowled over a half dozen of the toughs, scattering them like tenpins.

Gordo's explosive entry into the square broke the tension and the remaining toughs leaped at Spido. One brushed past Gar, nudging the wound in his flank. The pain eroded his control, or so Gar told himself, which was why his right hand flicked out in a Whipcrack Strike that drove one of the man's spinal disks through his aorta.

Another tough ran afoul of Spido's mother. Goodwife Blott, Gar noticed with satisfaction, employed a rather crude, unschooled Kneejerk to the groin, then followed it with a Unicorn Strike to the man's face. Both assailant and victim staggered away from the collision of heads, but the tough went down and Goodwife Blott managed to stay up.

Spido acquitted himself better than Gar would have imagined possible. He ducked beneath a roundhouse right and sent that fighter to the dirt with a Carat-cracker Blow. Because he remained low, another man kicked at him, but he parried the blow with a forearm, then pumped a Fleshmace Punch through the man's knee. Leaping up, Spido finished him with a Springbok Kick, then came down and rolled away from a jab at his heart. Stumbling on for one more step in the Wounded-Bird-Protecting-Nest Kata, Spido threw his attacker in, then posted him up on a Stallion Kick to the midsection.

Unfortunately, as he had moved to draw that assailant in, Spido lost track of his final foe. Steel rasped against scabbard as the last man drew a wickedly curved dagger and rushed at Spido's back. Spido, straightening up from the kick, started to spin toward his attacker and though Gar knew a dozen dozen parries and ripostes to that attack, he also knew Spido had no chance to stave death off.

The attacker came to that same realization, and a smile blossomed on his face for a second, then died as a golden hind came bounding through the square and boosted the man into the air with a head butt. The tough flew back and caught his heels on Gordo's stomach. His feet went up and his head went down to slam into the ground hard. Even as the man bounced back up, Spido's leap carried him well above his uncle's bulk and his Flying Dragon Kick snapped the man's head back.

Spido landed on cat's feet as his last foe's body flopped in the dust. He nodded at Gar, then stared at Dolonicus. "I am come to liberate Torfay from you." Spido held his right fist up and thrust his thumb out between his first and second fingers. "Look upon this and tremble. This is your death."

Dolonicus balled his fists. "That? You don't even know how to make a proper fist! Teaching you the error of your ways will be a pleasure."

The village headman rushed forward and hammered Spido with a roundhouse right that whipped Spido's head around. Spido took one step, then dropped to his knees. He started to waver and pitch forward, but something stopped him from falling flat on his face.

Spido sat back, shaking his head, and wiped blood from his nose on the back of his left hand. "A real man from Torfay could hit harder than that."

Dolonicus looked down at Spido, then over at Gar. "Your student is a fool, Pariah."

"Fool or not, he is correct."

"Is he?" Dolonicus looked down again and patted his midsection. "Come on, Spido, show me how hard you can punch."

"As you wish, *Dolonicus!*" Shouting his foe's name, Spido drove his right hand upward.

Dolonicus twisted to the left and cried out in triumph as the strike missed.

Exhausted, hurt and broken, Spido fell forward.

His right fist bounced off Dolonicus's booted foot.

Dolonicus looked over at Gar, then his eyes rolled up in his head and he pitched backward all boneless and flaccid.

The assassin crouched beside Dolonicus and felt his throat for a pulse. "Dead."

Spido looked up, dust coating half his face. "Dead?"

Gar nodded.

Gordo rolled himself over to his nephew and patted him on the back. "Of course he's dead. You used the dreaded *hingu* Bunion Strike on him."

"Executed with cleaner technique than I've seen ever come out of Armbruss." Gar nodded and straightened up, then helped Spido to his feet. "People of Torfay, this is Spido Blott, sent by Prince Rango to liberate your village from the last taint of Kalaran!"

A great cry went up from the villagers, but one piercing voice broke through the din. The crowd parted as quickly as it had before Gordo and a woman launched herself at Spido. He caught her in his arms and gave her an awkward hug, then held her out at arm's length—a move that still had them touching belly to belly.

"Squashblossom?"

The dark-haired woman nodded. "It's me. I've missed you so much."

"Ha!" snapped Goodwife Blott.

"Crone!"

"Slut!"

"Witch!"

"Wait!" Spido's shout cut off his mother's rhymed riposte. "Squashblossom, I, ah, er, um . . ."

"You were gone so long, Spido, and I feared you might be dead. I sought solace in the arms of another. . . ."

"Dozen dozen," his mother amended.

"Can you ever forgive me?"

"Over my dead body," mumbled Goodwife Blott, and had Squashblossom been an adept at *Tian-shi-sheqi*, the glare she gave Fannie Blott might have accomplished that end.

Spido shivered and frowned. "I could forgive the woman I love anything, Squashblossom."

"Good. You'll be a great father for my children."

"Children?"

"I'm too young to be a grandmother."

Squashblossom blushed. "I have a few children, Spido, though in my heart you fathered them all."

Spido looked at Gar, but the assassin only shrugged. "I, ah, appreciate the thought, Squashblossom, but, I, ah, love another."

"Thank the gods!" Goodwife Blott glanced at Gar. "It's

not you, is it, Mr. Quiknik? I don't know if I could take that."

"Nor I, goodwife." Gar nodded toward the golden hind. "He refers to Elise."

Goodwife Blott looked from the deer to the assassin and back again. "Are you *sure* it's not you, Quiknik? I might have been hasty."

As Spido held his hand out to her, Elise shimmered and flowed from her cervoid form into the beautiful woman Gar had grown used to hearing giggle around their camp. "Mother, this is Elise. She will be my wife."

"Over my dead body! No mixed marriages in my family!"

"I assure you, Goodwife Blott, she is quite human."

"Not that, Mr. Quiknik, look at her."

"I am." Gar frowned. "I don't understand."

"Are you daft? She's blond!" Goodwife Blott scowled at Elise. "I'll not have my son marrying a Northern woman. Away with you, witch!"

Spido interposed his body between Elise and his mother. "No! I love her. We are meant to be together!"

From somewhere back in the crowd, someone threw an overripe tomato. It exploded on Spido's chest, spraying seeds and pulp over him and the ground. Before he could sputter a protest, one of the seeds germinated and sprang up thick and full and lush. Yellow blossoms appeared, then withered as tomatoes grew and ripened. As they shifted around, the leafy plant molded itself into the shape of a beautiful verdant woman with magnificent foliage.

Gar dropped to one knee. "Torfay is honored by your presence, Osina of the Flowers!"

"I have no doubt at least three of you hold me in the proper amount of respect." Osina gestured in a way that included Spido and Elise with Gar, but managed to exclude everyone else. She looked at Goodwife Blott. "You oppose this marriage of my handmaid Elise and your son?"

"Well, she's a Northerner."

"And if I told you that her people would protest your son because he is a Southerner?"

"There's nothing wrong with my son!"

"Exactly."

Gar caught the message Osina tried to send, but the people of Torfay did not. Northern rejection of Spido did not strike them as a mirror of their own prejudice, but justification for it. The assassin looked up at Osina and, had she given the word, he would have turned Torfay into a large composting heap.

Osina shook her head, then looked at Spido and Elise standing together. "You would grow together instead of growing apart, yes?"

"We would."

"If you both wish it, I will see to it that you need never be apart."

The two lovers looked at each other, then nodded. "Please, goddess."

With a wave of her hand, Osina turned Elise back into the golden hind, then transformed Spido into a magnificent stag. His rack had many points, each of which sparkled with a jewel. Her tail wagging, Elise ran off and Spido bounded from the square after her.

Gar frowned and whispered to Osina, "I thought you didn't do transformations, just untransformations."

"My brother, the Horned One, sometimes travels among mortals for his amusement. He calls himself Longlegs when he does so."

Gar raised an eyebrow at Goodwife Blott and she blushed.

Osina doubled her size so she towered over the people of Torfay. "Before you go home with dreams of venison, mark me. You are farmers. Your crops blossom by my will. Let one of you harm a golden deer in this valley, let one of you deny them any food, and so shall you be denied."

Gar looked up and saw Spido on the crest of the hill his uncle had descended. The sunlight sparked fire in his rack. The assassin waved before he could catch himself, then smiled. He metamorphed that smile into a cruel grin and nodded. "Tell any hunters who think to prove their prowess by hunting the golden stag that I also hunt. I seek stupid prey that does not heed the words of Osina and who would seek to kill the blessed deer of Torfay."

Squashblossom fingered Gar's tunic. "Does that mean you'll be settling down here, handsome?"

Gar answered her with a Firetalon Touch to the shoulder that induced instant labor, and dragged Dolonicus's body off during the ensuing chaos.

VI

It Ends at the Start

Dolonicus opened his eyes as the golden glow from Anachron faded over him. He looked down at his foot, then shivered. "I was dead. What happened? Did Anachron bring me back to life?"

Gar shook his head. "No, it did not. It healed you."

"What?"

The assassin tucked the amulet back in his tunic. "You addressed me as Pariah. This term has some significance to me. I had intended to let Spido kill you, but the need for information superseded the need for your death. When I touched you I used a *kuo-tak* technique that rendered you unconscious with Spido's strike. Had I not revived you, you would have come awake in three days, by which time the people of Torfay would have buried you."

"Yuck."

"Of course, as I had things set up, had they decided to cremate you, you would have awakened——"

"I get the picture."

"Do you? It is rude to interrupt."

"Sorry."

"I doubt it."

"I really am sorry, really," Dolonicus moved his left foot around. "So, now what?"

"You will tell me where Udan Kann is."

"I don't know what you're—*ouch*!"

"Believe me, I have no great love of inflicting unnecessary pain on someone, but I do have ample facility in doing it. *And* your willingness to lie is making this quite necessary." Gar poised two fingers above Dolonicus's kneecap. "Do you fancy the nickname Gimpy?"

"Udan Kann will kill me if I tell."

"Had he not wanted me to have the information, he would have already killed you." Gar's two fingers drifted lower toward the nerve center in Dolonicus's leg. "You would not have called me Pariah had he not told you he did not tolerate having my name spoken in his presence. In addition, Spido said his uncle's knowledge of current events outside Torfay were limited to things twenty years in the past. Twenty years ago, Udan Kann labored in obscurity at Armbruss, yet Gordo knew his name and my nickname! You or your henchmen let word slip. And for *that* Udan Kann would have you killed."

"You win, you win." Dolonicus shook his head. "Udan Kann said you would come. He waited for you to the north. He waits for you at Gelfait."

"Gelfait?" Gar's finger's twitched and he almost treated Dolonicus to the Twelve Agonies, but he knew the man was not lying. *Either Udan Kann seeks Gelfait because he believes that he can escape me when the city fades or . . .*" Gar shivered with the alternative. "That can't be."

"Oh, it is. He is waiting for you." Dolonicus drew his legs up and clutched them to his chest. "There, I have told you. You should reward me."

Gar shrugged. "I have."

Dolonicus stood and stepped back. "You're going to let me live?"

"No."

"Death is not much of a reward."

"You're not much of a person, but that's not what I awarded in you." Gar pointed back down the mountainside toward Torfay. "You terrorized those people. You made their lives hell, and in doing so you have defined yourself. I have slain you, but you will only die when you imagine yourself superior and invincible. Modesty and humility will allow you to live a long life. Your old way will kill you."

Dolonicus sat down hard. "You ... how could you ... that's not fair."

"It is justice."

"It's torture."

"Torture would be rendering you paralyzed except for the two hours directly after you listened to Gordo tell a story of his fabled career." Gar patted Dolonicus on the shoulder. "I'll extend to Udan Kann your humble regrets at missing his death."

The trek to Gelfait passed quickly for Gar, yet each step became torture for him. He tried to focus on the pain of his shoulder and side, but that could not deflect him from the dark ruminations spawned by Udan Kann's choice of hiding place. Choosing a city renowned for its warrior tradition might make sense, especially when the city seemed to travel in time and could afford escape from temporally hostile political circumstances. Udan Kann was capable of making that choice, and Gar would have believed it except for one thing.

Udan Kann had never run from a fight in his career. His disappearance had bothered Gar Quithnick but not for the reason many had supposed. Gar had begun to accept that he had been upset at not being able to avenge the sloppy death of his parents, and even he had failed to identify the true source of his discomfort. Then, slipping through the forests to Gelfait, the true reason revealed itself to him.

Udan Kann had not been present at Kalaran's defeat. The reason for that could only have been orders from the demigod to absent himself. Kalaran could only have given those orders if he had a plan. While it was possible Kalaran's plan had not accounted for his death, Gar did not believe it. Having served Kalaran, Gar knew of the tyrant's prescience, and he respected it. Kalaran had anticipated his defeat, and had worked to circumvent it.

Osina's information concerning the people waiting along the course Spido had reported them taking dovetailed with his knowledge that Udan Kann was coordinating the effort against him. The assaults in the desert meant only one thing: Udan Kann wanted Anachron.

And if Udan Kann wanted Anachron, that meant Kalaran wanted Anachron.

I have to deny it to him. Kalaran, or his skull, was in Caltus. That meant the best place for the amulet was in Gelfait. Getting it there was Gar's mission, and one he would accomplish. "First things first. Take care of the amulet, then find a way to warn the others about Kalaran's plan."

Gar cut up and over a ridgeline and in the valley below saw the shimmering village of Gelfait. It had been laid out much akin to Torfay, but the narrowness of the valley stretched and contracted the village into more of a lozenge shape. What had been whitewashed wattle and daub in Torfay became polished opalescent stone in Gelfait. Straw thatching in Torfay gave way to amethyst tiles and vast roof gardens laden with legions of rainbow blossoms.

Central to it all lay the Chapel of Anachron. It seemed more substantial than the rest of the village, and it had fallen into disrepair. The main dome had collapsed and had taken one of the opal walls with it. As Gar came down the mountain, he caught glimpses of the chapel's interior through gaps in the trees. Were the stone not so elegant, it would have appeared like the many sand-smothered buildings the desert winds dug up and buried from time to time.

Gelfait itself, as he entered the village, appeared to be covered in a light fog. As he strode down the streets, the fog cleared in an area roughly twenty feet in diameter surrounding him. Where it did cling to something, it outlined men, women, children and animals. They appeared perfectly animated and almost ghostly in their aspects. He realized, as he first recognized one man and then another, that he was seeing the people who lived in Ccifait and that the warriors who had borne Anachron had all come home.

As have I. That thought startled him, yet crystallized thoughts into action. Gar felt within himself a peace he had never known before. He decided it was the same peace that death through *Tian-shi-sheqi* conferred, and while it did not necessarily herald his death, it did leave him ready for it. *And ready for what I must do here to earn it.*

Gar entered the shattered temple and bowed to the man standing across the open apse. "Udan Kann, thus I face the spider in the heart of its web."

The older man, whose long, gray hair had been gathered back into a ponytail, did not return the bow. "Pariah, you have perverted the gift I gave you. It is now time for your transgressions to be punished. I demand *hingu-cor.*"

Gar raised an eyebrow. "Only *hingu-cor*? I have acknowledged the title *hingu-Grashanshao*. We should engage in *hingu-Gracor*."

Udan Kann shook his head. "Technically speaking we cannot because *hingu-Gracor* is to death."

"Afraid I will kill you?"

"Hardly." Udan Kann pointed at him. "You wear Anachron, and I mean to have it. I know that if its bearer is slain, the amulet vanishes and passes into the hands of the previous bearer."

"Prince Rango."

"Indeed. This I wish to avoid."

"You mean Kalaran wishes to avoid Rango having the amulet."

"You merely need to know that I desire it."

Gar brought the amulet out from within his tunic. "Then here, I will give it to you."

"Your offer is most kind, but I prefer to win it through combat. I take pride in my work." Udan Kann stretched his arms out wide and flexed his fingers. "This *hingu-cor* will remind the world who is the true *hingu-Grashanshao*."

"That title is yours, Udan Kann." Gar shrugged, "But that fact will not stop me from killing you."

"Never thought it would, but this will." The older man smiled with the cold cruelty Gar had long ago come to think of as more affected than real. "If I die in this fight, or you delay me enough that I vanish with Gelfait, my henchmen will destroy all the little farming villages like Torfay throughout this district."

Gar stiffened. "Destroy? Do you care to be more specific?"

Udan Kann hesitated for a second, then frowned. "Fire, slaughter, midnight raids, and the like. The usual stuff."

"Not locusts or famine or an overabundant harvest that produces so much that laborers die in the fields bringing more grain to silos that burst as do their hearts?"

"I hadn't thought to make it that much of a production, really."

Gar shook his head. *Had you only seen the true way to destroy them . . .* "*Hingu* is a perversion, and you perpetuate it. You give me no choice but to kill you."

"The dreams of the young so often go unfulfilled."

"And the illusions of the ancients sour into mortification."

Slowly the two men began to circle each other. Udan Kann slithered into the Viper form and Gar held himself back in the Mongoose defense. Both knew they were posturing, yet both acknowledged the lethal capability of the other. Tiger and Wolf, Eagle and Wasp, Ant and Aardvark, they slid through the most basic animal forms as if reassuring each other that they had not forgotten their training.

As Udan Kann shifted from Ant to Antlion—the proper wrist rotations and four-part posture adjustment being a work of art requiring a decade of study—Gar darted forward and caught Udan Kann in the breastbone with a Spearpoint Blow. The posture adjustments rendered the strike feather light, and Udan Kann parried him high. Bringing his fingers together into a Firetalon Touch, he let his fingertips ricochet from Udan Kann's forehead, then he bounced back and assumed the Tarantula Wasp counter to Udan Kann's Antlion.

The older man staggered back for a moment, then blinked his eyes. "You broke form, Pariah."

"Yes, but I got you."

"Touches are for *hingu-cor* among children." Gar's old master snarled, then brought his elbows in toward his ribs, perfecting his Antlion. "Of course, you have ever been the child, Pariah. Had you applied yourself, had you truly learned what I had to offer, that blow could have killed me instantly."

"And most crudely and grotesquely, too, I imagine."

"Of course."

"Not my style, that." Gar slowly smiled. "There is more to the world than what you have to teach, Udan Kann."

"And much you have yet to learn, Pariah." Udan Kann swept in, contorting his body into the King Crab position. His right hand shot out and delivered a nasty pinch to Gar's left thigh. "My faithful students know you must make every touch count."

Gar jumped back and tested his leg as the wave of pain faded into numbness. "Pain for pain I can give." Gar launched his left foot into a Gouge-kick, but all he caught was Udan Kann's ponytail. The elder fighter ducked below the strike and countered with a two-fingered Agony-needle to the inside of Gar's thigh.

Gar fought the pain, but his weakened right leg slowed his retreat. Udan Kann swept in and pounded a Steelhammer Punch into the sorian cut over Gar's ribs. A Cleaver-chop came down on the torn shoulder and the twin waves of pain collided in the center of Gar's chest.

Gar should have retreated, but he stood his ground and smashed a Hand-lance Blow to Udan Kann's ribs. Flicking his right hand up, Gar snapped a finger against the tip of Udan Kann's nose, then stabbed Fork-fingers at the elder man's eyes. Udan Kann countered with a Handwidth Parry that stopped the Eye-gouge but irritated his tweaked nose. Snarling angrily, he brought his right hand up in a Spearpoint Blow aimed at Gar's midsection.

Gar saw the blow and had time to move from it, but did nothing. He felt the pressure build against his flesh. Blood vessels ruptured in the skin and bruises spread to his taut abdominal muscles. Udan Kann's fingernails pierced his tunic and his skin. With the speed and experience the older man possessed, he could have pushed on through and ripped a handful of Gar's liver out before the pain even began.

Udan Kann spun away and screamed in frustration as he flicked blood off his fingers. "Foul!"

Gar staggered back as sweat boiled into the open wounds on his body. "You want to kill me. Do it."

"Yes, I want to kill you, but later. After I have Anachron. After I do what I must. I will come back for you." He glanced over his shoulder toward the west and the setting sun. "I will not be trapped here for all time, Pariah. I will have the amulet and be away from here. Later I will return with it and kill you."

"Or die trying."

"Enough. You are done" Udan Kann came in full force, employing the Most Dread Tsunami series of attacks. As his former master came in, his limbs blurring through a flurry of feints and strikes, Gar realized that as a student the attack would have destroyed him. *Tian-shi-sheqi* allowed him to see the cycle of the forms and to detect the rhythms in it. Had his limbs all been working, he could have dismantled it and Udan Kann in the process.

But *Tian-shi-sheqi* also told him it was unnecessary to do so.

Fireneedle Strikes injected pain into his shoulders and elbows. Foot-saber Kicks cut his legs out from under him. Abbreviated Velvet Palm Strikes cracked ribs 'and an Elbow-spear broke his right cheekbone. And then, after he hit the ground, more assaults bruised and battered him. Parts of his body that were not numb howled with pain and it appeared to him, as Udan Kann hauled him into a sitting position and leaned him against a cool wall, that the only part of his body that worked correctly was his pain-reporting nervous system.

Udan Kann slipped Anachron from around Gar's neck. "Forgive my hasty departure, but I have things to do, tyrants to see and all that. I will let your friends know what happened to you. Perhaps they will even give me a reward."

"Perhaps you'll get what you deserve."

Udan Kann shook his head. "You were my most promising student, and I thought that you would be the one to supplant me. Perhaps, when I return, I will have Anachron make you whole again and we will see if I was right."

"You were."

"That is to be decided at another time, Pariah."

Gar nodded as Udan Kann strode from the chapel and was lost in the mists of Gelfait. Gar clenched his teeth against the pain, then sought to clear his mind so he could limit his discomfort. As he did so he caught words and images, all quick and incomplete. He saw Domino's face flash past, then he smiled. "Wedding . . . surprise? I certainly hope so."

A last image of Jord burst through his brain, and in its wake came a memory of the last stanza of the poem Spido had taken as prophecy:

> Born out of time
>   to right an ancient wrong
> I enter my father's future
>   familiar distant dawn.
> My present become past
>   fading with the sky
> Never to see her again
>   dead man pass by.

Gar Quithnick, the last *Tian-shi-Grashanshao*, did not know why those words came to him, or what they meant. He did not know if they were good poetry or bad, but he knew he liked them. As the sun set, and Gelfait faded from the world, he considered Jord's words and reclaimed the peace of *Tian-shi-sheqi*.

Prelude the Second

Princess Rissa stood on the balcony outside of her room, staring mournfully at the geyser of mud and sulphur that had replaced the clear lake behind the castle, reflecting that sometimes reality was a bit more symbolic than was polite. Perhaps she should have gone with Jancy to return Sombrisio. They would be out in the wastes together, listening to the gripes of the mercenaries and trading dreams about what they would do after everything was right again. Calla Mallanik might tell some tale of elven valor designed to make humans feel subtly inferior and Sombrisio would—

She grimaced as the lake farted mud and filthy water. Sombrisio would love to pull something like that.

"Your Royal Highness!" twittered a voice from behind her. "The dressmaker is here to fit your wedding gown!"

Rissa came indoors with a final wistful look toward the distant Desolation and stepped into her bedchamber.

In the parlor, Daisy, her maid since her return from slavery and adventure, conversed with the seamstress, a slim, angular woman with a pronounced squint. Silvery-haired Daisy was buxom and plump. Together, they reminded the Princess of a needle and pincushion.

As she stripped down to her shift, the Princess eavesdropped on their conversation.

"You don't say!" Daisy said. "Giant snakes! Winged! Flying!"

"I do say," the seamstress said. "They've been harrying the cattle market two hours since. The Prince's archers brought one down. It had lovely scales once you could stop worrying about it swallowing you whole without so much as a by-your-leave."

The Princess stepped into the room and the servants curtsied deeply. Rissa accepted their homage graciously. Part of being a princess, Mama had always said, was being poised even in your underwear.

The seamstress began unwrapping the parcels her assistant carried. There were yards and yards of ivory silk, lengths of hand-tatted lace, and a rattling box of pearls. When the seamstress and Daisy shook the fabric out, Rissa could see that it had begun to take on the form of a elegant, long-trained wedding gown. Her earlier bleak mood gave way to excitement.

When the fitting was finished and the seamstress sent on her way, Rissa put on riding clothes, picked up the elven bow and arrows that Calla had made her, and went looking for Rango. The guards said that the Prince was alone in his privy council chambers and she bustled down, still full of her excitement about the wedding.

"Rango, darling," she said, sweeping in with a *pro forma* rap on the door, "come hunting with me!"

The Prince looked up from a heap of papers, the flicker of annoyance on his handsome features changing into something warmer, but not precisely welcoming. He rose and kissed her hand.

"Rissa, dearest," he said. "Hunting? Now, with our coronation and wedding to plan and our country in peril?"

"That peril was what I thought to hunt," she said, somewhat tartly. "Report is that winged serpents are harrying the cattle merchants. I thought that we could go and bag ourselves one. The skin would make us fine matching boots and belts."

"Boot and belts are far from my concern now," he said, relinquishing his grasp on her hand.

"Then what about the morale of our citizens?" she asked. "They await a warrior prince to ascend the throne, but you seem transformed into a clerk!"

"Perhaps a clerk is what peacetime needs, precious," he said. "If they need martial succor, I shall send one of the Guard units down. They will deal with the serpents."

Rissa pouted, hating herself for it, but unable to stop. Rango spoke rightly. Her own parents had reigned more with law book and example than with martial valor, but she had not expected Rango to settle down so quickly. When she and Jancy had met him after their departure from Anthurus . . .

She might have said more, but there was a rap on the council chamber door.

"My next meeting, Rissa," the Prince said, his expression neutral. "I will send a division of the Guard out after the winged serpents."

Rissa knew a dismissal when she heard one. She left the chamber, barely sparing a glance for the wiry man in priest's robes who was waiting to enter.

Lemml Touday looked after the Princess as she departed.

"The Princess seems less than happy," he observed to Prince Rango.

"The Princess will be more settled after the wedding and coronation," the Prince replied. "Right now she is still adjusting to her new duties after a trouble-free life of adventure."

"I heard that the Princess was taken as slave, sold into a brothel, and escaped only by daring a journey across the ghoul-haunted Desolation to the very gates of Anthurus, City of the Dead," Lemml commented.

"Precisely," the Prince said. "Days without responsibility except to oneself. Days of immediate gratification and glory. Days without ritual, pomp, or protocol. She will settle down when the weight of her new position comes home to her."

"As it has to you, Your Highness?"

"Indeed. You have a report for me?" The Prince smiled suddenly. "Forgive me, Lemml. I have not yet offered you hospitality. My little interview with Rissa unsettled me. Take a seat by the fire and let me fetch some wine."

When the Prince uncorked the wine, the liquid frothed in a fashion quite unlike champagne or beer and spilled thick and brown into the goblets. Brow wrinkled, the Prince sniffed the liqueur.

"It is not beer. In fact, it smells curiously sweet."

Carefully, he sipped, then took a larger swallow.

"Not bad at all. Lemml, I believe that the magical anomalies have spread to my wine cellar. Will you drink? This is certainly a rare beverage."

"Whatever you drink, my Prince, is fine with me," the priest replied, tasting the odd brew.

"Shall we get to business?" Prince Rango prompted gently.

"As you wish, sire. I come to report that the Demon of Darkness continues to emerge from the skull of Kalaran. I have interpreted the portent as soothingly as I can, but the High Priest is becoming concerned that we should not have permitted the scroll and the amulet to be taken from Caltus."

The Prince smiled and sipped his dark, sticky brew.

"What do they expect me to do?" he asked. "They acceded to my councilor's requests and now the artifacts are gone to their resting places."

"Some recall that you had communication sorcellets sent with each of the heroes," Lemml Touday replied, feigning unhappiness at his news. "There is talk of having you recall General Blaid and Gar Quithnick before they can complete their quests."

"Damn the impertinence!" the Prince snarled. "Do they not see that larger things are at stake than a few portents from an enchanted skull? I would not put it past the wickedness of Kalaran to permeate his skull so that it would give us misleading portents!"

Lemml smiled, "Why, that's rather nice, Your Highness. I could do something with that, if protest becomes too strong. Of course, I would need to plant my hints very carefully . . ."

The Prince opened a drawer and pulled out a small, jingling pouch. He handed it to the priest.

"I have been collecting for your favorite charity," he said, "and have come up with some extra donations. I do not think I can raise extra funds easily again before the coronation. Of course, after the coronation, I will have access to all the treasury. However, if the amulet and scroll are returned, the coronation may be greatly delayed."

Lemml swallowed the rest of his drink, rose from his chair, and bowed deeply. The pouch vanished into the sleeve of his robe.

"I understand, Your Highness. I will do my best for you."

"Do," the Prince said, watching him depart, "do."

A Very Offensive Weapon

The sun rising behind the walls and towers of Caltus reddened the armor of Jancy Gaine and her companions as they looked back from the mound west of the city. Squill, the sorcellet, knelt apart from the others, busied with the customs of his art.

The packhorses whickered, looking discontentedly for foliage to browse during the brief halt. There would be still less forage for them when the party entered the Desolation of Thaumidor; much of the pack train's burden consisted of its own fodder.

The horses were under the control of ten hard-bitten mercenaries—five humans, the rest elves. These retainers were scarred, dour folk every one. They had seen death in a hundred fashions already, and their hearts were prepared to face him yet again.

Calla Mallanik, Jancy's faithful elf companion, stood at her side with a grim look on his aristocratic visage. He held his silver-strung bow. Its arrows of fiery, elf-wrought gold never failed to find the life of the evildoers at whom they were shot.

Jancy Gaine wore her horned helmet and a leathern jackshirt to which were riveted iron medallions cast in the image of terrible gods. Her small buckler, steel rimmed and its boss spiked with steel, hung at her left hip. There it balanced the right-side weight of her bearded ax Castrator.

A distorted female image circled the middle finger of Jancy's right hand: the massive ring Sombrisio, hammered by demigods from native silver torn out of a glowing meteor. The fire that winked in Sombrisio's eyes was only partly reflected from the sunrise, for the ring was as surely alive as Jancy herself.

Some lanterns still scuttled through the streets of Caltus. A few windows were lighted, but not those of the tower suite in which Princess Rissa would dwell until her marriage to Prince Rango. Rissa, whom Jancy had rescued, and who with Jancy had fought through scores of perils, each more dangerous than the last, to take her place in triumph at the side of the Prince...

Heat lightning flickered among the clouds to the west. The air on the top of the mound was as still as the faces of the heroes turned toward the homes many of them might never see again.

Sombrisio farted.

"I had the royal lottery on *ice*," Calla said in a voice like stones grinding. "No way any ball was going to get out of the trap but good old one million, seven hundred ninety-two thousand, five hundred thirty-nine. I had the tolerances down closer than flea whiskers! Not another elf craftsman in—"

A cry of horrible, hollow pain filled the air. Jancy turned her head. "Squill!" she said. "What in Sif's name are you doing?"

Squill grimaced and shook his head. He held his left arm crooked; his fingers were bunched near his ear in the mysterious handset which was part of his magic. Above the squatting sorcellet waved the wand of his specialist profession, a twelve-foot whip of thin steel. Its base was screwed into Squill's knapsack.

Instead of answering Jancy, Squill repeated, "Knowed Wyvern Two to Knowed Wyvern Base. Communications check. Over."

Squill unclenched the fingers of his left hand. The hideous moan sounded again. Squill shook his head and muttered uncomfortably, "Sorry, sorry, I guess I'll have to change crystals. Too many lost souls drifting in the part of the ether where this crystal resonates."

"Oh, right," cried the ring Sombrisio in a shrill, unpleasant voice. "Blame your equipment, sure. The trouble couldn't be because you're a half-trained boob sent out with a bunch of losers, no."

"Don't mind her, sorcellet," Jancy snapped, covering Sombrisio with her callused left palm. "Just get on with your work. I don't want to spend the rest of my life here on the municipal garbage dump."

Squill shrugged off his backpack. He rummaged in its side fittings, removing a chip of malachite and replacing it with a block of green tourmaline from his belt pouch. The wand that intensified his spells waggled above him.

"There was no way any other ball could've come out of the tumbler after I'd worked over the machinery in the basement of the palace," Calla resumed grimly. His face was turned toward the towers of the capital, but his mind was focused solely on the injustice done him and his skill.

Last week's royal lottery had been held to defray expenses incurred in the Triumph of Good and Return of the True King. Faithful elf companions had incurred plenty of expenses, too; Calla would tell the *world* he had! And it'd seemed so simple—to an elf of Calla Mallanik's unique skill and craftsmanship—to jigger the result in a completely undetectable fashion.

"Naw," one of Jancy's stalwart human retainers said to the slimmer (but otherwise equally stalwart) elf beside him. "There'll never be an equal to Hormazd the Centurion. Seventy-eight wounds to the body, *seventy*-eight."

The elf pursed his lips. "I heard that was body and limbs combined," he replied. The horse he held pawed rotting garbage in a desultory attempt to find something edible.

"No way!" said the human. "Body alone. Well, body

and head, but that's only counting ones that broke the skin, not what was sticking in his armor."

Sombrisio managed a prolonged burst of flatulence. Jancy lifted her left hand and waved it; not that it made a lot of difference, what with the pong of the rubbish tip.

Squill snapped the side fitting over the new crystal. Instead of hitching the knapsack onto his back again, he knelt over it and formed the handset. He began to speak earnestly to unseen listeners.

"*No* ball but one million, seven hundred ninety-two thousand, five hundred thirty-nine could come down the chute," Calla said in the stark tones of the deeply wronged. "So what happens? Balloons float up, hautboys hoot and gonfalons flutter, and Princess Rissa announces the winner is nine million, three hundred fifty-two thousand, nine hundred seventy-one. There shouldn't have *been* a number that high!"

"Look, I'm not taking anything away from Hormazd," said another of the elves, "but seventy-eight, a hundred seventy-eight—I don't see where the *art* is in that."

Squill relaxed his handset. This time clipped voices sounded faintly through the keening spirits of the atmosphere.

"And not only that," Calla said. The others no longer listened to him. The story's constant repetition over the past week had worn grooves in the surface of their hearing. The elf's words rolled along without leaving a trace in the others' consciousness. "The guy who wins is a stranger to Caltus who bought a chance ten minutes before the drawing. And he's the *ugliest* pipsqueak I've ever seen in my life, more like a gander than a human!"

"Art!" said the leading human retainer. "Art, schmart! We're talking about craftsmanship here, boy, a man who took *pride* in his death!"

"Roger, five by five," said Squill. "Knowed Wyvern Two, out." He broke the handset completely and rose, hefting the backpack with him.

"Are you done, then, sorcellet?" Jancy asked sourly. Fifteen fucking minutes marking time on a garbage heap.

Mind you, the Desolation of Thaumidor wasn't the Garden Spot of the Universe either. More like the fucking asshole, it was.

"I've established communication with our base, if that's what you mean," Squill replied, flushing. He'd recovered his sense of self-importance now that he'd finally managed to do his job. "I wish you wouldn't call me that, though."

"Sorcellet?" said Jancy with a frown. "You *are* a sorcellet."

She didn't have a lot of use for men who thought the ability to call spirits from the vasty deep made them something special. To tell the truth, she didn't have a lot of use for men, period.

Calla awakened enough from his bleak revery to help Squill fit his arms through the straps of his knapsack. "A sorcellet," Squill said tightly, "is a wizard in training with a limited number of skills. *I* am a comspec, a specialist in the communicatory arts. An artio, to use the term of, well, art."

Sombrisio let out what was either a raspberry or another fart. "You're a one-trick pony," the ring shrilled. "A loser in a dead-end job. And if you want to know how dead a loser you are, just take a look at the turkeys you've been sent along with!"

"Move 'em out!" Jancy ordered. "And Sombrisio, shut up. It's going to be a long enough trip without you going on about it."

The party started forward. Every finger's breadth the sun rose above the horizon boiled new levels of reeking effluvium from the garbage. Honey wagons were already wending their way from the west gate of Caltus with the night's further increment to the surroundings.

"You think this is a good time for me?" Sombrisio demanded. "Traipsing along with the Company of Intellectually Challenged Adventurers? And for what? So I can spend the rest of eternity in the Lost City of Anthurus, that's what!"

"I said," Jancy said in a voice so quiet that hair pricked

at the back of the neck of everybody who heard it, "shut up."

Of course Rissa wasn't watching. What would a princess want to look out over the municipal garbage dump for, anyway? Besides, Rissa probably had lots of important things to talk over with her fiancé, the Prince.

Got a quest for a city lost in the Desolation of Thaumidor? Well, jeepers, the only road in *that* direction leads out through the garbage dump. Let's send Jancy, shall we? After all, she's only saved our life and honor about twenty dozen times.

"The only ball that could get through the trap . . ." Calla murmured.

"Gobble-gobble-gobble," Sombrisio said in a piercing whisper.

It was hard to tell where the sun was. The sky was bright, but the landscape itself was gloomy and shadowed. The sparse vegetation had a grayish tinge, and sometimes a shrub collapsed in a cloud of bitter dust when one of the party brushed it.

They'd reached the Desolation of Thaumidor, all right.

"Is that—" Calla said. "Yeah, that's it. That's got to be the hermit. Who else would live in a bone hut?"

"Now, I'll tell you what was a first-class death," said one of the stalwart elf retainers. "When Brightlock, Prince of the Windward Elves, fought Sokitoomi, the Crystal Giant—"

"Sif, what a desolate place," muttered Jancy Gaine.

"Hey, what a surprise!" said Sombrisio. "You go to a desolation and it's *desolate*. Did your schooling get to the part about not sticking your hand in the fire? Or is fire itself too advanced a concept for northern bumpkins?"

Jancy twisted the ring so that Sombrisio faced palmward, but by now the sniping didn't really bother her. No more than everything else, at any rate.

Thaumidor was a waste of ill-watered dust, not sand. The soil was light and yellow-gray: loess, a concretion of windblown particles, though there hadn't been any wind in the few minutes since the party had entered the Desolation. The border between Thaumidor and the unpeopled but ordinary barrens they'd crossed to reach it was as sharp as a fenceline.

"—when the lance hit Sokitoomi at the cleave point," the elf was saying, "the Crystal Giant broke into shards that rained down on Brightlock's retainers, the warrior-sisters Everill and Worrell. They—"

The agatized femurs of monsters of a bygone day formed the main structure of the hut's walls. The interstices between these great bones were filled with parts of lesser skeletons in a puzzle of immense complexity. Rabbit tibiae bound bear clavicles and were wedged in turn by the ulnae of sparrows, themselves associated with still finer ossicles. The gill rakers of an enormous shark formed the roof beams, though no sea had penetrated within a hundred miles of Thaumidor during the present Fourth Age of Man.

"Hail, hermit!" Jancy called, twenty feet from the door. "A party of noble travelers comes, seeking your assistance on a dangerous quest."

A jewel-eyed viper sunning itself on the hut's roof slid back within the thatching of mouse ribs. The snake's eyes were literally jewels—yellow topaz, Jancy thought. They had no lids or pupils.

"—cut Everill and Worrell into slices thin enough to see through if you put them between glass plates," the elf said, continuing his story. "Which is about how it happened, after all. We raised a joint monument over them, because sorting them into separate coffins would've been harder than putting two salamis back together after you dropped the slices."

"Are you going to stand here forever?" Sombrisio demanded in a muffled voice. "That's all right with me, I'm the one who's going to be buried for the rest of eternity, but—"

"Hermit!" Jancy bellowed. "Get your sanctified ass out here!"

"Bet it wasn't seventy-eight slices, though," said a

human retainer. "Not even seventy-eight between the two of them."

A crabbed little man scuttled out of the hut. His sclera were almost as yellow as those of the viper. The diet of hermits in the Desolation of Thaumidor couldn't be a very healthy one.

"Well, well," the hermit said. "Decided to stop by and say hello to the fellow who's devoted decades to learning the life and lore of the Desolation, have you? Hello, then! Now go away and leave me alone."

"Hey, wait a minute!" Calla demanded.

The hermit had ducked beneath his lintel of buffalo humerus. He turned again and cried, "I have more important things to do than be gaped at by scabs on a second-rate quest! Like watching my fingernails grow!"

Sombrisio giggled. "Well, he's got you lot pegged," she noted.

"Wait a darn minute," said Jancy. "What do you mean, 'scabs'? We're here on a bona fide quest, requesting—"

"Requesting now, that you are," the hermit said, stepping closer and waggling his gnarled index finger toward Jancy's face. "But let me ask you, Little Miss Venturer, just which member of the Guild of Licensed Cicerones did you employ on your first journey through the Desolation? On a real quest!"

"Ah," said Jancy. "Ah. Well. You see, the Princess and I were fleeing from minions of the Ghoul-Lord of Otchbacko and we didn't have a lot of time shop around for guides, so we—"

"Hired scabs!" the hermit snapped. "Well, you can just go—"

"We didn't hire anybody!" Jancy shouted. Rows of lizard sternums pinning the thatch to the roof beams jounced when she bellowed. "We didn't have time to hire anybody!"

"Right, right!" the hermit crowed in triumph. "Well, you're not going to hire anybody now either, because the regulations of the guild forbid members to accept employment from those who've previously used scabs. So there!"

He stuck his thumbs in his hairy ears and wriggled his fingers at Jancy.

"Look—" said Jancy.

The hermit lowered his hands and flowered. "Do you know how dangerous the Desolation of Thaumidor is?" he asked. "Three centuries ago, King Voroshek the Extremely Ill-Tempered the Fourth refused to employ guild members when he marched into the Desolation on his way to attack Faltane. He and his army are still there, girlie! And so will you and elfikins here be, three centuries hence!"

"That's telling them, hermit!" said Sombrisio. "Of course, if you really knew jack shit about this place, you'd have found me yourself, wouldn't you?"

"That's it," Jancy said in her quiet voice. "That's all of this we're going to hear."

She twisted Sombrisio outward and thrust her clenched fist toward the hermit so that he got a good look at the massive ring. "Now," Jancy said, "you're going to guide us on our quest. And no smart remarks about second rate or losers or turkeys, do you understand? Or I'm going to use the power of Sombrisio here to turn you into a lobster."

"And I," said Calla Mallanik, leaning forward to call attention to himself, "will eat you in cream sauce."

Jancy blinked. "Well, you know," she said to her faithful companion, "he won't really be a lobster, he'll just think he is."

The elf shrugged. "So what?" he said. "It's not cannibalism so long as it's out of species. And I'll guarantee he'll taste better than the can of ham and lima beans I had last night. Where on Middle Earth did the royal commissary get sea rations, anyway? Faltane doesn't have a navy."

Jancy returned her attention to the hermit. "Well, anyway," she said. "If you don't guide us, it'll be the worse for you. Do you understand?"

"Oh, sure," said the hermit bitterly. "Well, my guild's going to hear about it, though. Wait till the wave of sympathy strikes hits your employers! What kind of a wedding do you suppose it's going to be when the flower girls down tools, hey? And the Worshipful Company of Rice Sellers bans their products from crossing a picket line!"

Jancy sighed. "All you need to know," she said, "is that if you're not packed and ready to guide us in fifteen minutes, I'm going to help Calla here look for a cow for the cream sauce."

The hermit reentered his hut, muttering about strong-arm bully-girls. After that, the only sound for a time was the squeal of Squill's apparatus. The artio was reporting to base on the progress of the quest.

Though the sun even at zenith was wan, its heat hammered the landscape. The rock basin was rimmed by three distinct margins of differing color: yellow, orange, and a virid hue close to that of copper acetoarsenite. The fluid (it certainly wasn't water) in the center of the pool quivered; Jancy thought she felt microshocks through the soles of her boots as well.

"Are there earthquakes here?" she asked.

The hermit shrugged. His expression wavered. An expert's natural urge to pontificate warred with his personal desire in this case to be as obstructive as possible. The former won out, perhaps aided by the way Calla Mallanik fished from his wallet a miracle of elf craftsmanship—a nested nine-piece flatware set, including cracking tongs and a miniature mallet.

"Well, it's not so much earth tremors as it is a dog scratching itself in its sleep," the hermit explained. "The Desolation is a living entity." He pursed his lips, then added, "A thoroughly grumpy and ill-tempered one, too."

A small armadillo charged from its burrow and began to urinate on Calla's right boot. The elf kicked the little creature through the center of a squamous-looking cactus which collapsed with a sucking sound.

"Seems to attract dwellers of similar temperament," Calla said with a significant glance toward the hermit.

"I know what you're hinting at!" the hermit cried, as if anybody with brains enough to breathe wouldn't have known. "The reason *I* inhabit the Desolation is that it frees me from the cares of the world, so that I can immerse my mind in holy contemplation."

"You bet," said Sombrisio. Either the ring had been dozing for most of the morning, or she'd waited like a true artist for the right opening. "Cares like the string of bad debts you've left behind you, starting when you did a midnight flit from the seminary in Quiberon."

The hermit turned his head with an expression whose horror melted into rage before settling on injured innocence. "Silence, demon, in the name of the Twelve Beneficent Aspects of God!" he said in a piping attempt at thunder.

"Not to mention," Sombrisio continued with lip-smacking enthusiasm, "that your wife's new boyfriend said he'd pull your face *off* if he ever saw it again in Caltus. Those the cares you had in mind?"

"I won't dignify that with a response," the hermit muttered. Rather, he mouthed the comment. He'd already demonstrated a capacity for knowing when to cut his losses.

The party topped a rise. What Jancy had thought was the keening of the wind resolved itself into desperate, fluting screams coming from just off the trail.

"Unhand her, you brute!" Jancy shouted as she lifted her ax from its belt loops. She leaped into the brush without waiting to free her shield from the slip knot holding it to her left hip. It was going to be embarrassing if the screams were from a rabbit; or worse, from a man rather than the woman she'd assumed.

It was a woman, all right, buried to the waist beneath a thorn tree. Her marble bosom was bare; her alabaster arms were raised to fend off unseen horror.

Jancy grasped the woman's right hand and realized her

mistake. The arms, like the bosom, were marble. The screams came from the open throat of a statue.

Calla Mallanik eeled into the small clearing. Behind him galumphed the retainers, bellowing their war cry: "Death and glory!"

The screams stopped abruptly. The retainers looked in disappointment at the dismal but harmless surroundings.

Jancy straightened. "What in blazes?" she said as the hermit joined them with a smirk on his visage. "She stopped screaming."

"Union rules," the hermit explained. "She gets five minutes off in every two-hour period."

"Well ..." Jancy said. She stared at Castrator as if wondering how the ax had come to be in her hand.

"She doesn't need to be rescued, then?" said Calla Mallanik.

"Rescued from what, dummy?" Sombrisio said. "It's a statue. Rescued from being a chunk of rock lying in the ground? Boy, I've heard elves were dumb, but I'm beginning to think communing with the earthworms in Anthurus is going to be an improvement over you guys."

Jancy rehung Castrator as furtively as you can hang an ax with a hooked, sixteen-inch cutting edge. She cleared her throat. "Best be getting on," she said. "I want to march at least another couple of miles before we camp for the night."

"And if any of you lot is wondering just how stupid your leader is," Sombrisio continued in a voice that carried like brakes squealing, "*she's* wondering if the Princess Rissa might just be in love with her after all."

"I am not!" Jancy shouted. "Why, the Princess wouldn't even *think* of such a thing!"

"You got that one right, boss-lady," the ring agreed gleefully. "Rissa doesn't even know that sort of thing happens. Boy, it'd really turn her stomach if she knew her sturdy defender here dreamed about—"

That was as far as Sombrisio got before Jancy wadded a handful of friable soil around the ring and spat on it. She kneaded the wad into a blanket of clay. The casing smothered Sombrisio's complaints to a sound as faint as the buzz of a fly's wings on the other side of a closed window.

Jancy stuck the ball of clay onto the spike of her shield boss, where it would dry rock hard in the sunlight. Dusting her palms against one another, she glowered at Calla Mallanik and said, "Any comment you want to make?"

"Do I look like I want to say anything?" the elf protested. "No, not me. Not a word."

"Good," Jancy said. She tramped back out to the trail, deliberately kicking the shrubbery to bits. A bush with thorns and dirty pink flowers squeaked as it trotted out of the way, its taproot twitching behind it.

"What I figure," Calla continued, "is that anything adult humans want to do within the privacy of their own bedrooms is going to be unspeakably disgusting. So there's no point in drawing distinctions between one revolting act and another."

The statue was screaming again. It struck Jancy as a pretty reasonable way to pass the time around here.

"If we're headed toward the city of Anthurus," said Calla Mallanik in a tone so coolly reasonable that it was twice as threatening as a shout, "then why is the sun setting to our left, hermit?"

"Look, do you want to take over the guiding?" the hermit said. "I didn't ask to come with you, you know! Fine, I'll just go back to—"

Jancy grabbed a handful of the hermit's long, scraggly hair and lifted. She didn't have quite the strength in her shoulder muscles to raise the hermit completely off the ground, but the pain brought him instantly up on his tiptoes.

"I think," Jancy said, "that we'd all be more comfortable if you just answered the question. Especially you'd be more comfortable."

She let him go. The hermit's mouth twisted, showing that he was swallowing a spate of shrill complaints; but he did swallow them.

"Directions aren't fixed in the usual fashion in the Desolation of Thaumidor," he explained in a chastened tone as he massaged his scalp with both bony hands. "That's why it's so important to employ a licensed practitioner, a god-guided soul whose wisdom penetrates demonic illusion."

Sombrisio responded with a high-pitched whine. The ball of dried clay smothered the ring's comment to unintelligibility.

"It's about time we think about camping," Jancy said. The sun, which had remained motionless for what seemed like hours, now settled as though somebody was pulling a shade down over the sky.

"Yes," said the hermit, pointing to a hill to the right of the road. At the top of the moderate slope was a small ruined building with a spire. "We'll shelter there, in the Little Brown Church in the Vale. It will protect us from the spirits which meep and gibber in the darkness."

"The little brown church in the *what?*" Calla said.

"I don't name them!" the hermit snapped. "If it comes to that, the boards are weathered pretty much gray by now, too."

Jancy didn't speak; but she looked at the hermit, and she hadn't looked warmly at any damn thing since she'd got this assignment. In a more cautious voice the hermit added, "I suppose it was in a vale, once. I told you, things change around here."

"I don't remember the sun going wonky the other time we were here," Jancy said to Calla Mallanik.

The elf shrugged. "What I do remember about that trip," he said, "is we were being chased by thirty thousand Ghoul Myrmidons. Put them behind us again, and I don't expect I'd notice where the sun was this time either."

He looked over his shoulder. A huge, misshapen shadow fell across the party from behind The creature casting the shadow was invisible; but then, so was the light source that the creature's body blocked.

"Run for the church!" the hermit screamed. Everybody, including the terrified packhorses, was already doing that.

Jancy charged up the slope, the fatigue of a few moments before forgotten. Castrator swung on its loops. Brandishing an ax against the oncoming invisible giant was obviously a waste of time that could be better spent in flight.

The ring, though . . .

Jancy plucked the wad off the shield boss and tried to crush the clay between her palms. It was hard as a rock. Hard as her own damned head for hiding the magical weapon while they were in the Desolation of Thaumidor.

The party had been marching in a straggling line. Jancy, Calla and the hermit led, with Squill a few steps back with his apparatus. The packhorses broke free of the retainers leading them and streamed forward across a broad front. Their panniers strewed bags of oats, skins of water, and the ugly green cans of sea rations that rolled in broad arcs when they hit the ground.

One of the retainers kept hold of the lead strap for some time. His boots raised a spectacular plume from the light soil, but there weren't enough rocks or thorns— for a wonder—on the hillside to drag him to death properly. When the strap broke, the retainer bounced a couple times, then rose and limped toward the hallowed ground on his own.

Jancy slammed the ball of clay against the rim of her buckler. The metal bonged. Bits flaked from the clay, but the mass didn't break apart as she'd hoped. She was at least halfway to what they hoped was safety, but the curve of the slope now hid all but the tip of the church's spire.

Calla Mallanik's long legs had carried him some way ahead of his leader. The hermit was showing a remarkable turn of speed for somebody so old and apparently infirm, staying alongside Jancy even though he took four steps to her three.

It was hard to tell how tall the giant stood, since the question depended on the position of the equally unseen

light source casting his shadow. At least the giant's sex
wasn't in doubt, unless that was a second spike-headed
club swinging between his bandy legs.

Jancy had a moment to wonder what the giant's girl-
friends must look like the next morning. The chill the
thought shot down her spine should have been pleasant
relief from the sweaty overload of her uphill run, but
it wasn't.

Calla Mallanik flung himself through the sagging doorway of the Little Brown Church at One Time in a Vale.
The packhorses were already inside, frothing from their
unexpected run. Jancy lost a half step to the hermit when
she shifted her weight to rap the ball containing Sombrisio on Castrator's upper tip. The clay finally
disintegrated.

Sif's Hair! If the stuff was that tough when air dried,
somebody ought to be mining the Desolation for the raw
material of unbreakable dinnerware.

Jancy halted beside the church doorway. She tried to
fit Sombrisio onto her middle finger. The finger hole was
still packed with clay. Jancy reamed it desperately on
Castrator's point.

"Ooh, do that again!" Sombrisio cried. "So nice of you
to provide me with a little recreation now that everything's quiet."

Retainers dived one by one through the doorway like
pinballs falling out of play. Squill crouched by a sidewall;
he'd formed his handset. Most of the chapel's roof was
missing, so the tip of artio's wand wobbled between
bare beams.

The packhorses at the front of the nave neighed con-
gratulations to one another. A gelding snuffled the tattered altar cloth in vain hopes of a snack.

Calla stood at one of the Norman windows in a litter
of stained glass and lead strips. He drew an arrow to its
gold-glittering head and loosed it.

The elf-forged arrow sped like a jet of noonday sun,
over the helmets of the struggling retainers and toward
the distant horizon. The missile's course was straight for

as far as the eye could follow. Unaffected, the shadow continued to lurch up the slope toward the party.

"There's nothing there!" shouted Calla Mallanik. "We're running from nothing, because my arrow would have slain it unerringly if—"

The shadow club lengthened and shrank, as if the invisible reality casting it had been swung in a high arc. Arc and foreshortened shadow ended on the last of the retainers, a human. The ground dimpled into a cavity ten feet across. For the most part, the retainer remained on the bottom of the basin, but some of him spattered as far as the ruined church.

"Well, you know, maybe there's something there after all," Calla said, examining the point of another golden arrow with an expression of puzzled concern.

"Who needs Sombrisio?" the ring said as Jancy tried to work her finger through the hole again. "We're such all-knowing heroes ourselves that we don't need *her* help!"

The now hindermost retainer was an elf. The shadow bunched as the giant that cast it bent over. The retainer turned, swinging the leaf-shaped blade of his elven sword in a shimmering arc.

The edge, keen enough to cut a moonbeam, touched nothing. Only the elf's innate grace permitted him to pirouette instead of falling on his face the way a human would probably have done.

The elf suddenly rose a hundred feet in the air, dancing helplessly in the grip of something invisible.

"Well, I don't know," muttered Calla Mallanik. "I'm sure I was all right for azimuth, but maybe I wasn't allowing enough elevation."

His silver bow twanged. The arrow, blazing with right, justice and the elven way, shrieked through empty air on an apparent track to lunar orbit.

The eighth retainer wheeled and blew his way through the chapel's doorway. The interior of the fane took on a pearly glow. Music as soothing as a bath in warm syrup whispered on the night air.

The elf hanging in the air spun a little higher, tossed by the invisible hand. The shadow shook itself in the two-dimensional projection of an unintelligible three-dimensional reality.

Invisible club met visible retainer in a loud *whock*! that sent the elf in a screaming drive toward the sunset. Bits of equipment and, well, other things, dribbled along the route of passage the way a meteor fragments on hitting the atmosphere.

"Are you ready, ring?" Jancy demanded. She raised her right fist toward the air above the base of the shadow.

"Me?" Sombrisio said. "I've been ready all bloody day, haven't I? It's you who haven't—"

"By the power of this ring!" Jancy shouted. "Thou art a rabbit!"

The invisible giant had paused just outside the glow of the ruined church, though Jancy for one wouldn't have bet he was going to stay there. For a moment, the looming shadow froze. Then it turned, hunched, jumped back in the direction from which it had come.

Dirt exploded at the base of the slope where the creature touched down. He leaped again, then again. The line of dust geysers continued into the fallen night, each impact a good hundred yards from the previous one.

"Sif," Jancy muttered.

"Not bad, if I do say so myself," said Sombrisio. "And not before time, I might add."

"Don't expect an argument from me," said Jancy.

They'd wait till morning to gather the supplies strewn up the hillslope, but there ought to be something in the horses' loads. Jancy figured food right now to settle her stomach might be a good idea.

Brushwood gathered from the hillside blazed hot and cleanly on the bonfire in front of the ruined chapel. The lack of wind meant that the smoke, which smelled as if sulphur was being cooked on a bed of cat turds, wasn't generally a problem to those sitting around the fire.

The surviving retainers were going to be pretty busy

feeding the blaze. The hair-fine thorns on many of the plants around here burned like the coals themselves, but that wasn't one of Jancy's problems. Rank hath its privileges.

Jancy's most pressing problem was that she very clearly saw figures in the flame. Including the figure of the Princess Rissa. Rissa wasn't being tortured—quite the contrary; but the glimpses Jancy got when she forgot and looked into the fire were torture for her.

Jancy was sure the images were demonic sendings, not a real view of what was going on in the Princess's suite in Caltus. She didn't even consider asking anybody else what they saw in the flames. Sombrisio had already had a field day with Jancy's daydreams: Jancy wasn't about to reopen the subject.

Calla Mallanik stared grimly at the contents of the can he'd just opened. "This is supposed to be pound cake," he said. "I think I really could pound nails with it. If the Commissary Service is so determined to punish us, couldn't they just have arranged for a plague of boils? Meals were always a happy occasion for me in the past."

"I'm not going to say Athos let down the side . . ." a human retainer remarked morosely. He was carrying toward the fire a bush which thrashed feebly and called for its mother. "But the truth is, I was hoping for a more inspired performance than he gave us."

"Well, I don't know," said one of the elves dragging a matronly shrub which was, in fact, the mother of the other one. "I rather liked the splash. Sometimes the simplest effects are the most memorable."

"Give Athos his due, Aramis," said a human across the fire from Jancy. "The giant didn't give him a lot to work with. You can't make a silk purse out of a sow's ear."

"Why not?" said an elf retainer in surprise. "It's a pretty simple protein conversion. If it was me, I'd start with the collagen and . . ."

The conversation drifted off into technicalities. A retainer tossed the small bush on the fire. The crackle with which it flared up drew Jancy's reflexive attention.

She looked down hurriedly. She was *absolutely* sure that the Princess Rissa wasn't on such affectionate terms with an aardvark.

Squill was in the spire of the church. The ladder didn't look safe or even possible, but the artio had finally managed to clamber up when he found he couldn't reach Caltus from anywhere else on the hilltop.

He must have finally gotten through, because Jancy heard in intervals between the howls of atmospherics the words, "... figures two KIA but hostile forces beaten off ..."

Maybe this church really was in a vale. It'd sure seemed like a hill when Jancy was trying to reach the church before the giant reached *her*.

A shimmering image caught Jancy's eye again. She deliberately got up and walked to the other side of the fire. She seated herself with her back to the flames, looking out into the night.

Something sparkled in the distant darkness. She couldn't tell whether it was on the horizon or closer, since the moon and stars had vanished behind a cloudbank as black as the ground beneath.

The soil trembled, though of course it usually did here.

"Now, I don't expect aspic-preserved duck à l'orange in the field," Calla Mallanik said to the round of pound cake. It was probably as interested in his comments as the rest of the party was. "Not from humans, at any rate. But I don't see any reason chicken Marengo couldn't be supplied. Chicken Marengo was *developed* as a field collation, for pity's sake!"

Jancy saw the sparkles again. As a matter of fact, when she squinted she realized that the slowly moving effect dimmed and brightened, but never completely vanished.

"Hermit!" Jancy called.

"I think he dossed down inside," one of the retainers offered.

"Well, bring him out here," Jancy said.

"Your boy did pretty well," a human retainer said to the elf beside him.

"Melaril?" the elf said. "Yeah, that was a nice job, wasn't it, especially for a kid who'd just turned seven hundred last Thursday."

"Mind you," said another elf, "for a real disintegrating arc, there was Count Diamondbringer the Undaunted, when love of the nymph Arachneida caused him to hurl himself into the vent of the volcano Earthsfire."

"Well, I don't know," argued a human. "Diamondbringer turned bright yellow from the sulphur. Well, the bits of him did, anyway. I always thought that detracted from the majesty of the occasion."

"Not at all!" an elf insisted. "Why, that just added to the uniqueness. How many *yellow* disintegrating arcs can you name? Name one other!"

"Well, there was Charles the Cowardly," a human offered with a snigger. "When he sneaked out the sally port of Castle Dangerous without noticing that the besiegers had already set a lighted petard against it."

A retainer dropped the mother shrub on the fire. Sparks and flame exploded from the tinder-dry wood. Everybody nearby had to jump away. Jancy slapped a smoldering spot on her doublet with her bare hand and cursed.

"Ah," said Sombrisio, "how I'm looking forward to the intellectual conversations I'll soon be having with dung beetles and petrified trees in Anthurus."

Jancy turned and bellowed, *"Her—"*

The hermit was settling into a squat beside her. His face had been about three inches away when Jancy twisted to bellow toward the church where she thought he was still sleeping. He yelped and fell over.

Retainers paused in their conversations. Calla Mallanik raised an eyebrow from across the fire.

"Sorry," Jancy muttered as she helped the hermit to sit up. Sombrisio tittered like a psychotic bat. The male members of the flame tableau Jancy glimpsed this time were dressed as sanitation workers, to the extent that they were dressed at all.

"Yes, well," the hermit said. "What is it, Mistress Gaine?"

He seemed humble rather than his usual madder-than-hops manner. Handled with normal decency, the fellow was unbearable. He had to be treated like dirt to behave himself. Well, Jancy was in a mood to make him behave.

"That," she said, pointing to the faint glimmer in the night. "What's that?"

When Jancy concentrated, she thought she heard a groan from the same general direction of the darkness; though that could have been wind, her imagination, or the muttering of a queue of commuters waiting for a streetcar on the Thaumidor Line. *She* didn't know what was out there.

"Oh," said the hermit. "That's just the mountain. Don't worry about that."

"A lot you know," Sombrisio chirped.

Jancy leaned forward. "What mountain?" she said, loud enough to fluff the scraggly beard. "A mountain like the one we're on?"

"Or a vale," the hermit said, bobbling his head like a chicken drinking. He wasn't being obstructive, just speaking precisely as a result of his healthy fear. "Ah, no, that's a real mountain."

He frowned. "Or it was. It's been wandering around the Desolation for centuries, looking for some guy named Mohammet, and it's pretty well worn itself down to a nubbin by now."

Jancy looked off to the east again. Probably the east. "Who in blazes—"

She shouldn't have said "blazes," because it turned her mind to the fire.

"—is Mohammet?"

The hermit shrugged. "I've no idea," he said. "Mountains don't have any brains at all, of course. I suspect this one got into entirely the wrong space-time and has been cruising around here since."

"The Desolation of Thaumidor attracts all sorts of folk who don't know their ass from a hole in the ground," Sombrisio said. She added flatulent emphasis.

"All right, but what's the . . . the glow, the light?" Jancy asked. She was emotionally convinced that the glimmer was weaving itself closer as she watched. Intellectually she knew that the light's faint waxing and waning made realistic distance calculations impossible.

"Well," said the hermit, "it's a mountain, so it's made of rock. When you stress rock, the phlogiston entrapped in the crystal matrix is first driven out, then reabsorbed. When the phlogiston content of the surrounding atmosphere increases, it causes the ether to glow."

"Ah," Jancy said, pretending that the explanation made sense to her. She had no more acquaintance with phlogiston than she did with honest politicians.

"He got through third-year alchemy before he scooted out of Quiberon ahead of the bailiffs," Sombrisio said.

"It just roves back and forth across the Desolation," the hermit said, pretending he hadn't heard the ring. "The mountain does. Quite harmless. Unless, of course, you don't get out of its way."

Now that Jancy had been told what was happening, it sounded like a mass of rock grinding its way slowly over . . . well, grinding over anything that happened to be in its way.

"Is that all, mistress?" the hermit asked humbly.

"Right," said Jancy. "Get some sleep."

If she listened hard, the growl of rock had a plaintive undertone that could have been the name Mohammet. . . .

To the (putative) east, the ridge was dry and clothed with no vegetation save glass-spiked, poisonous cacti. On the other side of the ridge was a swamp.

"Traditionalists claim a buried aquifer follows folded layers of the underlying rock strata," the hermit said. "My researchers, however, indicate that the Desolation is sweating."

Water black as a banker's heart gurgled at the base of tussocks. The reeds were gray with death, and the creatures which flitted among them were feathered skeletons instead of living birds.

"It was a place like this where I saved Princess Rissa from the Dragonspawn of Loathly Fen," Jancy said, reminiscing aloud.

"*You* saved?" said Sombrisio. "Oh, right, I suppose it was you hanging on the Princess's finger, turning dragonspawn into bullfrogs so fast your head spun for the next three days!"

"I don't believe there are any dragonspawn here," the hermit said, peering over the swamp with a look of concern. "There's been some talk of a tribe of toadmen, but I don't believe the contract details have been worked out."

"If you don't mind my asking, sir," said one of the retainers. "Mistress, that is. What sort of retainers did you have with you there? In the Loathly Fen, that is?"

"Ah," said Jancy. "We'd run into a bit of a problem earlier, you see. With the Killer Vines of Siloam."

"The truth is," Calla Mallanik admitted, "we'd expended all our retainers before we reached the Loathly Swamp."

"I blame myself for not keeping a closer eye on the supply," Jancy said.

Calla frowned. "Well, still, there'd been that recruitment problem in Sandoz when we set out."

"The Duke had marched on Tzerchingia to battle the three-headed ogre and her minions," Jancy explained. "There was a dearth of retainers in Sandoz unless we wanted to wait for the new crop of fifteen-year-olds to ripen."

"Ah," said the retainer sadly, with a nod of his hoary head. "Well, I'm sure a hero like yourself knows best, mistress. But to simple folk like us—"

He gestured with his grizzled jaw to indicate the retainers behind him.

"—it seems like a quest isn't rightly a quest lessen you have proper retainers in it."

Another retainer, an elf this time, nodded sagely. "And I do like a bit of cranberry sauce in the quest rations, too," he said.

Jancy grimaced uncomfortably. "Well, we hired a fine lot of retainers as soon as we could," she said. "At a low dive in the foreign quarter of Boroclost. Desperate men willing to murder their own grandmothers for a chance to put Princess Rissa on the throne of Caltus."

"Two of them," Sombrisio said. "Two retainers. One, two."

"Well, they *were* pretty desperate," Calla said mildly. "I know I didn't feel comfortable turning my back on either of them."

"Not a very impressive retinue," Sombrisio said.

"Well, what did you want?" Jancy shouted. "We were flat broke, weren't we? We'd been skedaddling for months from doom-ridden castle to monster-haunted mere, *not* to mention the Desolation of Thaumidor. Were we supposed to melt you down to pay for a proper mob of retainers?"

"Huh," the ring said. "I'd like to have seen you try to melt me. If you're a Third Age demigod, then I'm a soup tureen."

A sepulchral bonging sounded deep within the mist-shrouded fastnesses of the swamp. The chittering laughter of the bird skeletons ceased; reed bracts shivered with no wind to stir them.

Jancy Gaine untied the thong holding her buckler, then took Castrator into her right hand. She shrugged, loosing the powerful muscles of her shoulders so that she would be ready to react at an instant's need.

"All right," she said. "We'll enter the swamp now."

"Good lord!" said the hermit. "Why on Middle Earth would we want to do that?"

Jancy paused, feeling the noble set of her carriage slacken. "Huh?" she said. "Well, to venture boldly on our course to the Lost City of Anthurus and the accomplishment of our quest, of course."

"Yes, all that," said the hermit in barely controlled exasperation, "but we can't go through the *swamp*. Those hummocks, they wouldn't support a man."

"And what about the horses, hey?" Sombrisio chortled.

"They'd sink so far that you'd have to stack them on each other's backs to have the ears of the top one break the surface!"

Jancy shot Castrator home with a violence that she'd *really* like to have worked off on a more deserving target. "Then why," she bellowed, "did you lead us here? Is this the scenic tour of the Desolation of Thaumidor, is that it?"

"Well, no, I intended to follow the ridgeline, here," the hermit said. "It's better walking, you see, than down below."

The hermit scuffed his sandal toe at the ground. The surface was hard as concrete. Salts deposited during the swamp's periodic floods had combined with the light soil.

Jancy remembered the difficulty she'd had unpacking Sombrisio's clay jacket when the invisible giant pursued them.

"Oh," she said. "Well, let's get going, then."

"Never mind," Sombrisio said, drawing out the syllables in a nasal whine. Judging from the ring's continuing guffaws, it must have been a joke of some sort.

The sky was a bronze furnace. It should have been late afternoon, but Jancy hadn't seen the sun since her party mounted the ridgeline.

The swamp to the right gurgled and shuddered. Once Jancy happened to be looking in that direction when a thirty-foot hole gaped in the surface of the water. It could have been a bubble bursting, of course, but she was sure she saw vomerine teeth deep in the watery gullet.

The hole slapped shut. Bulging eyes the size of washtubs blinked at Jancy, then closed again.

She grimaced and looked away. The party marched on.

A spiral of fine soil curled into the air on the left. It zigzagged along on a course roughly paralleling the ridge. The funnel's spinning tip traced a broad line into the ground. A snake with scales like fire opals whirled aloft with the dust, striking in impotent fury at the air.

Jancy paused. "What's that?" she said, pointing.

"Just a dust devil," the hermit replied.

"But there's no wind," she snapped.

The initial funnel was already breaking up half a mile away, but four similar whirlwinds emerged on the left—desert—side of the ridgeline. These moved in unison, as if they were cutting tools milling away the surface of the ground.

"I didn't say it was the wind," the hermit said peevishly. "I said it was a dust devil. Obviously a number of them. Sometimes in the fall they swarm like locusts."

Each of the immediate dust devils spun out a constellation of minivortices which grew larger as they rotated. The funnels climbed only a few hundred feet in the air. Their forms, insubstantial at first, became yellow-gray and then black as the air loaded itself with soil.

"They're quite harmless, of course," the hermit added. He sounded a little doubtful. "To humans."

A prickly pear cactus beat its spiky lobes furiously. The plant was trying either to fly out of the vortex or to make the gripping funnel drop it. The dust devil spun its unintended prey lazily higher.

"Let's keep moving," Jancy ordered.

"And whose idea was it to stop an gawk in the first place?" said Sombrisio.

Logy with the dirt they had swallowed, the devils staggered farther desertward and spewed their meals in the near distance. Half a mile from Jancy's party, a new ridge began to rise from what had been flat ground.

Calla Mallanik frowned. He peered not toward the dust devils but at the ground they were sweeping in their proliferating arcs. "Say," the elf said. "There's something down there."

Then he added, "There's a lot of somethings down there!"

Where the dust devils had scoured away the soil, the remains of an army entombed standing up appeared: Pointed steel caps, some of them bearing tattered ribbons tied to the peaks. Halberds and guisarmes, their blades forged in fanciful shapes and chased with designs in gold and orichalc and rich black niello.

Within the helmets, half-rotted faces covered by veils of silvered mail.

"Run!" cried the hermit, suiting his actions to his words. "It's the buried army of Voroshek the Extremely Ill-Tempered the Fourth!"

It was an army, at least. The whole half-mile swath the dust devils were uncovering was planted with dried soldiers. Jancy couldn't estimate how far the array extended alongside the ridge on which her party traveled, but she had to assume it was a long damned way.

"But they're dead, aren't they?" Jancy asked as she broke into a run alongside the hermit.

"Not exactly!" he replied, puffing out a syllable every time his right heel slammed down. "But they don't move very fast!"

Mummified with the army were hump-shouldered mammoths. Their long hair, bleached russet during burial, fell out in handfuls as the beasts began to move. Gilded palanquins swayed on the mammoths' backs, but the bowstrings of the archers within had rotted.

As the dust devils sucked loess from the feet of Voroshek's soldiers, the army strode slowly toward the ridge along which Jancy's party was by now in full flight. The lowering menace of the mummies' advance was unmistakable.

"Are they attacking us because we're from Faltane?" Jancy asked. "*I'm* not from Faltane."

"I'm certainly not from Faltane!" agreed Calla Mallanik. The elf had nocked an arrow, but he wasn't poised to shoot. Targets were in embarrassing oversupply, and it seemed unlikely that an arrow was going to do more damage than three centuries of burial had already accomplished.

"Anyway, we weren't even born when the trouble started," Jancy said.

"Look, every member of the Voroshek dynasty was named 'the Ill-Tempered!'" the hermit shouted. "What possible excuse do you have for thinking that the last distillation of the line would need a *reason* for feeding us all our entrails?"

Since the boundary the dust devils swept was the end of the danger area—if there were soldiers buried beyond that point, that was fine: they were *buried*—Jancy thought her party ought to be able to win free. The mummies moved with slow deliberation, and the slope of the salt-compacted ridge was as sheer as a castle wall now that the vortices had excavated the soil from alongside it.

On the other hand, the mummies were trained soldiers. Already troops were forming tortoise formations by squatting with their broad, rectangular shields sloped across their backs. Further squads scrambled up the layer of their fellows and formed a second step for yet more mummies to mount.

And there was Hel's own plenty of mummies, that there was.

Jancy pulled Sombrisio from her right hand and gave the ring to Calla. "Here you go," she said. "I'm going to be busy."

She untied her buckler and drew the great ax Castrator from its belt loops. Her party was almost going to reach the edge of the danger zone before Voroshek's soldiers climbed to the top of the ridge.

Almost.

A pair of mummies stood on the backs of their fellows, clambering the rest of the way onto the ridge. They thrust pole arms toward Jancy's legs. These leaders weren't a danger to her; she could have jumped the halberds and raced ahead to safety. By the time the last of the party jounced along with the packhorses, however, the two would have become a platoon.

Castrator swept the heads from both mummies. Their necks were tinder dry. The flesh splintered despite the keenness of the ax edge.

The bodies continued to climb the ridge. Jancy kicked them sideways, tumbling the doubly dead backward.

Their fall upset the stepped array of their fellows like a house of cards. Corpses spilled like jackstraws. When they crashed into the ground, some of the bodies broke apart in a litter of limbs and powdered flesh. Even these twitched feebly as they attempted to execute Voroshek's unheard commands.

Like a tongue of water driven through a dike by the storm surge, another force of mummified soldiers climbed the ridge in front of the party. Squill and the hermit stopped short of the lethal obstruction.

A pair of retainers had thundered past Jancy while she was occupied. They rushed the mummies at the side of the Calla Mallanik.

Calla aimed his beringed fist. "Thou art dead!" he shouted.

Voroshek's soldiers needed a lot of convincing, as Jancy knew, but Sombrisio was up to the job. A mummy took the force of the ring's displeasure in the chest and folded up, disintegrating within its armor as it fell.

The only problem with Sombrisio—as a weapon, that is—was that she had an individual focus. If you wanted to blot out an army—and Jancy wanted very much to blot out an army—you had to do it one soldier at a time. That wasn't going to be fast enough.

A human retainer hurled himself against the forest of mummy-borne pole arms. This band was equipped primarily with short-bladed pikes. Groaning, "Death and glory!" the retainer managed to gather half a dozen of the points into his torso, immobilizing the weapons until they could be pulled clear.

An elven retainer leaped into the gap the human had opened, wielding a curved saber in either hand. Even before he struck his first blow, a mummy sliced through the elf's armor of grasses beaten hard by the feet of elvish maidens dancing to the Goddess on Samhain.

The mummy's guisarme stabbed deep into the retainer's belly. The blade's hook came out with a coil of intestine.

The mummy yanked back with all the supernal

strength of its preserved muscles. The elf lifted his left toe to his right knee, went up on point, and pirouetted. His sabers whickered as they spun down across a broad circle of Voroshek's army like the blades of a food processor. Edges of elf-cast dendritic steel lowered the height of nearby mummies in a sequence of delicate slices.

His solo maneuver completed, the retainer bowed gracefully and fell. He made a very flat corpse.

Calla Mallanik collapsed the ramp up which reinforcements clambered by blasting mummies at the edge of the bottom layer with Sombrisio. Boy, once a mummy was killed, he was *dead*. There wasn't so much as a bone or a patch of mold remaining within the ragged armor and accouterments.

There were still mummies standing between Jancy's party and safety, though. Jancy strode forward, shrieking, "Princess!" her war chant, to end the problem.

Three pikemen lunged toward Jancy's chest, and a fourth mummified soldier swung his guisarme down at her horned helmet. Jancy griped her buckler's two close-set handles in her left fist.

She swept the pikes aside with her chattering shield rim. One point ripped muscles-deep along eight inches of her left triceps, but in this state Jancy didn't notice the contact. She stepped inside the arc of the guisarme, swinging her bearded ax.

Castrator combined the weight and shock effect of an ax with the long cutting edge of a sword. Jancy's stroke carried the blade through the neck and shoulder of the mummy wielding the guisarme. The soldier wore a shirt of high-quality chain mail. Most of the welded, double-wired links held, but the dried flesh within exploded out the neck and armholes as powder.

The mummy continued to march forward. His guisarme fell, still in the grip of the severed arm. Because the decapitated soldier had no eyes to guide him, he plunged into the swamp a few strides on. Something swallowed him, then burped happily.

Jancy stabbed a mummy through the face with her

spiked shield boss. The creature stolidly shortened its grip on its pike in order to pierce the shield-maiden since she was too close for a normal pike thrust.

Castrator crunched through the mummy's left knee. Jancy flexed her shield arm, hurling the unbalanced semi-corpse back down the desert side of the ridge. He'd probably climb back up despite his one leg, but his presence wouldn't matter by the time he arrived.

Jancy stepped forward. There were mummies all around her. Voroshek's soldiers were clumsy and their pole arms were the wrong weapons for a close-in fight, but there were still a lot of them.

Too many of them, if she'd let herself think about it, but reflexes and bloodlust ruled Jancy Gaine in a fight.

She swung Castrator to the right and the edge of her buckler left in counterbalanced blows. The boss spike wasn't as useful as it would have been against living— fully living—opponents. She smashed the steel rim across a mummy's eyes instead, crushing the sunken orbs and the bones of their sockets. The tactic must have worked, because the soldier stopped where he was and prodded the air hesitantly with his halberd.

An elf retainer fought in a circle of the enemy on the other side of the ridge from Jancy. A guisarme blow lopped off both his feet.

"Death and glory!" the elf cried, striding forward on his ankles. He left circular pools of golden ichor behind him. His ripple-bladed kris decapitated a pair of mummies with a single stroke.

The mummy who'd cut off the retainer's feet hunched his shoulders and leaned into another whistling stroke with his guisarme. He really put his back into it this time. The broad blade, decorated with a scene of professors eating the brains of a colleague who had failed to use inclusive language, whacked the elf's legs off at the knees.

"I have not yet begun to fight!" cried the retainer, stumping another short stride onward. His kris eviscerated a mummified soldier. The mummy bent over to view the damage, thus bringing his neck within range of a following slice of the kris.

The guisarme made another enormous sweep, slinging ropes of golden droplets off its blade's hooked tip. Jancy had too much on her own plate to consider the outcome, but she'd have bet that the retainer would manage to remove at least one more mummy while teetering on his pelvis.

For her own part, Jancy howled as she spun on the ball of her right foot, whirling Castrator in a figure eight. On the high side of the arc the ax beheaded a pair of Voroshek's soldiers. When the blade dipped low, it clipped one mummy off at the knees and the next at the ankles.

The latter two were still dangerous to a degree. When the mummies hit the ground, Jancy crushed their skulls to powder with the heels of her hobnailed boots.

A guisarme clanged from her helmet and ripped a gouge down her back. Jancy's vision blurred for a moment. She spun and sliced horizontally through the mummy's brittle skull at eye-socket level.

"I got it!" a human retainer shouted. Jancy looked over her shoulder. The retainer leaped sideways, waving his arms wildly to distract the mummy who was thrusting the spike-topped blade of his halberd toward Jancy's back. "I got—"

Sklurk!

The retainer wore a cuirass of boiled leather. The spike, which was square in cross-section and so cut with four ninety-degree edges, stuck out a hand's breadth through the backplate.

"A far, far better thing I do—" said the retainer.

Jancy beheaded the mummy who was trying to withdraw the halberd from the fellow's chest.

"—than I have ever done before."

Calla and Sombrisio struck a mummified soldier dead. It collapsed to rags, rusty armor, and a whiff of cedar oils. That one was the last of those in a blocking position, though the entire ridgeline behind the party of humans now crawled with Voroshek's soldiery. Mammoths were striding toward the ridge as well. Their palanquins had fallen when the rotted leather of their cinches broke.

"Come on, come on," Jancy muttered. The rest of her party was already jogging forward at a pace mummified muscles couldn't match. Calla Mallanik offered Jancy his arm, knowing that the aftermath of berserk rage was a sleep near death—and that sleep *now* would be death for fair.

They stumbled along the hard-packed surface of the ridgeline. Everything but what was directly ahead vanished into a gray blur of fatigue. Jancy's world view was the ass of a roan packhorse whose occasional tail lift better *not* mean the beast was about to take a dump.

"Now a lot of people ..." keened Sombrisio in a voice that grated like a silver chalk-sharpener, "... when their lives had been saved by a magic ring would be saying, 'Gee, how could we reward this ring?' Others, of course, would figure, what the hell, let's dump our benefactor in the deepest lost city we can find ..."

The fallen tree had been buried in loess when the climate changed, but it wasn't petrified. In fact, judging from the way the tree groaned as the party's fire burned into the innards of the bole, the tree wasn't even really dead.

Well, it would be by morning, except maybe for the tips of some limbs.

Squill was perched on the root ball now, swaying slightly as rootlets twisted around him in agony. Dust devils, perhaps the same swarm that lighted on Voroshek's army, had cleared the tree in the recent past. That was good luck for the questing humans. There's no wind but blows ill for somebody, however: the tree wasn't in the least happy about the turn of events.

"Knowed Wyvern Two to Knowed Wyvern Base," the artio repeated. "Come in, over." Only wailing atmospherics answered him.

"Damn the man!" Jancy snarled under her breath.

"This isn't a place I want to listen to souls howling in the darkness!"

"Squill says he has to call at night," Calla Mallanik said mildly, "or they wouldn't hear him in Caltus. His spells don't propagate properly when the sun shines. The communications demons are embarrassed to make love in daylight."

"Who in Hel's house *cares* if his spells propagate?" Jancy said. "It'd be all right with me if he stuffed that twelve-foot wand of his straight up his specialized ass!"

"Don't bury me there ..." sang the four surviving retainers in good barbershop harmony, "... on the lone prairie ..."

"Sif, I wonder if we're going to run out of retainers?" Jancy muttered. Her mind was bouncing from generalized gloom to specific problems that were beyond her practical control.

"Where the coyotes howl ..." sang the retainers as lost souls keened from the comspec's receiver. "... so-o mournfully."

"Oh, I think we'll be all right," soothed Calla.

"Do you suppose there's an inn nearby where we could fill up if we need to?" Jancy said. "Hermit! Is there an inn around here with retainers? I don't care if they're off-brand."

"Well, not really very close," the hermit admitted doubtfully. "*Really* not very close, to tell the truth."

Jancy swore. She wrung her hands together as a way of working off some of her bleak anger without hurting anybody.

Almost anybody.

"Hey!" said Sombrisio. "This is the way you treat a ring that's saved your miserable life, is it?"

"Sorry," said Jancy, jerking her hands apart.

"You can't hurt her by squeezing," Calla Mallanik pointed out reasonably. "You couldn't hurt her by pounding her all day on an anvil."

"Oh, nice!" said the ring. "Sombrisio doesn't have any

feelings, is that it? Let's grind our dirty hands over her. Or better yet, we can hit her with a hammer!"

"I said I'm sorry!" Jancy said.

". . . come in, Knowed Wyvern Base, o—"

"Squill!" Jancy roared. "Will you shut the hell up, or do you want me to feed that knapsack to you, crystals and all?"

"Jancy, he's got to report back," Calla said. "Otherwise there'll be no record for future generations."

"Future generations can go bugger themselves," Jancy said, but she spoke in a low voice that indicated she was embarrassed at her outburst.

"Go ahead, Squill," Calla called. "But try to wrap the business up quickly, won't you?"

"Knowed Wyvern Two to Knowed Wyvern Base," the artio said. He spoke this time in a voice of quiet desperation. Squill's repeated call was less irritating than the fingernail squealing of the atmospherics, but he was at least doing what he could.

"There has to be a record," Calla said. He patted the back of Jancy's scarred, powerful hand. "In case in later days they have to retrace our path in order to retrieve Sombrisio against a terrible new danger."

"Or you could just keep Sombrisio in a comfortable jewelry box in Caltus," the ring said bitterly. "But no, that'd be too simple, wouldn't it?"

"Well, I don't see why," Jancy said. "I mean, a quest is a quest. If unimaginable evil breaks forth in the world again, then some hero will struggle through perils, temptations, and the foul sleights of evil wizards. That's all there is to it."

It was her grim state of mind speaking, though she hadn't said anything that she hadn't thought oftentimes before.

"Well, yes, but the quest will be guided by—"

"Oh, don't give me *that* crap again," Jancy snapped. "I don't care if the route's written on a half-charred palimpsest found in a ruined palace, stamped on a torque of unknown metal taken from the tomb of a forgotten king, or drawn in blazing letters on stone by the finger of an unseen spirit. The quest is all that matters."

"Tradition matters, Mistress Gaine," Calla Mallanik said huffily. Elves, because of their long lifespans (except for elves who took up the profession of retainer to puissant heroes, of course), were great respecters of tradition.

"It's traditional that heroes go on quests," Jancy said stubbornly. "They either triumph or they leave their bones to whiten in dire warning to those who come later. All the rest is just window dressing."

"Feckless Teuton," Calla muttered with a sigh. It obviously wasn't a conversation that was going anywhere useful, so he dropped the subject. The pair sat for a time in silence punctuated by the snores of the hermit nearby.

The retainers on the other side of the tree bole had stopped singing. They now picked at cans of sea rations with an understandable lack of enthusiasm.

"I'm really disappointed in Porthos," said a grizzled veteran. He was the unofficial leader of the human contingent, now reduced to himself and a kid who said he was from Brooklyn.

"Say, I thought he did a great job," said the senior elven retainer. "In human terms, of course. Did you see the way he spread his legs so that he stayed upright with the halberd as a brace when his body went rigid in death?"

"Sure," said the grizzled veteran, "that's fine. But he used 'A far, far better thing I do' out of context."

"An act is its own context!" said the leading elf. "You can't go importing context from outside the environment of the deed."

"And besides," said the kid from Brooklyn, "knowing Porthos, it probably was a better thing. I'm sorry now he's gone that I called him a hanging plant, though."

"*That*," said the veteran, waggling his finger in the kid's face, "is a clear example of the Autobiographical Fallacy! And—"

He returned his attention to the elf.

"—the environment of a deed is the entire universe.

Who among us can claim to have separated himself from the world?"

"Well, in absolute terms, I agree," said the retainer who had been silent until now. "But in terms of elven realities . . ."

The kid from Brooklyn got out his harmonica. He began to play "Lorena" in soft accompaniment to the groans of the burning tree.

Jancy interlaced her fingers, careful not to cover Sombrisio, and said to her hands, "You know what really frosts me? It's the injustice of it all."

"Umm?" said Calla Mallanik. He'd learned long since that if you ignored Jancy Gaine, she'd go off and do something that would *damned* well get her noticed. A passive aggressive with a big ax was nothing to joke about.

"I saved Princess Rissa's life and virtue, why, it must have been dozens of times," Jancy continued bitterly. "And here I am, out in the Desolation of Thaumidor, eating sea rations."

"Right," said Sombrisio unexpectedly. "And just when did the Princess say to you, 'Jancy, m'girl, I'm going to need a whole shitload of saving. I'm hiring you to do it in consideration of my hand in marriage when we've won through these terrible dangers.' Hey?"

"Well, that's not what happened, no," Jancy said uncomfortably. "But I *did*—"

"And as far as saving went," Sombrisio continued in a voice that would have roused dogs three miles away if there'd been any dogs in the Desolation, "I seem to recall there was about as much of that on the one side as the other. Not least because it was the Princess mostly who was wearing *me*."

"Well, I grant that," Jancy admitted. "But still, we were companions in peril, and here she's sent me—"

She waved her hands.

"—here!"

"Actually," Calla said, now that the ring had broken Jancy's icy self-absorption, "the orders came from Prince

Rango. And it seemed to me that it was more an understanding than, well, a formal order."

"Right!" Sombrisio agreed. "You know, elf, sometimes I think you might have the brains of a rutabaga after all. You. Axgirl! You're a hero, right?"

"You're bloody well told I am," Jancy said grimly. She glared at the ring in obvious contemplation of determining whether the meteoritic silver was really impervious to Castrator's edge.

"So if Princess Rissa really was your friend," Sombrisio said, "what's she going to say? 'My fiancé has a dangerous quest that'll bring eternal honor to some hero, but I told him I'd rather keep you around the palace and wrap you in angora fluff.' Is that what she's going to say, dumdum?"

"Ah," said Jancy Gaine.

"Damned right, 'Ah,'" the ring agreed. "Now, get some sleep, will you? I'm tired of looking at your ugly face."

Squill must have finally reached Caltus, because he climbed down from the root ball and wrapped himself in his cloak on the other side of the fire. Two of the retainers took station at the edge of the firelight to guard the camp. The other pair began to sing "There's a Long Long Trail A-Winding" quietly.

Neither the song, nor the ache of her bandaged arm and shoulder, kept Jancy awake. She fell into fatigued sleep like a stone wobbling down an ocean abyss.

"Hey, lover girl!" a voice squealed. "Wake up! Your dreams are disgusting me!"

"What?" said Jancy. "What—"

By the second syllable she was standing with Castrator cocked to swing. Two quick snaps had wrapped Jancy's left arm in the cape in which she'd been sleeping. Only then was she sufficiently alert to realize that Sombrisio had called her from dreams that were anything but loving.

"You and Rissa," the ring said. "Phew!"

"That's a lie!" Jancy shouted. "That's—"

"Guards!" cried Calla Mallanik. Everyone was awake now, from Jancy's shout if not from Sombrisio's shrill demand. The stalwart elf aimed his half-drawn bow toward the ground at his feet. "Where in the name of the All-Nurturing Mother-Force are you?"

Breezes parted the high overcast, allowing the moon to cast its baleful light over the landscape. The guards, an elf and a human, were a hundred yards from the fire log's sunken glow. The human waved. Nothing else moved in the night.

"We thought we heard something!" the retainer called. "But there's nothing here."

The ground shivered, a movement no less disquieting for having become familiar while the party crossed the Desolation. The hobbled packhorses were restive.

"Run!" the hermit shrieked. "It's the mountain!"

The landscape at the feet of the two retainers on guard hunched itself up like a giant inchworm.

The human turned, shouting, "Woops!" The rising cliff flowed over him, sparkling with piezoelectrical radiance. The many kilotons of rock reduced the retainer and his equipment to a molecular film.

"Save the supplies!" Calla Mallanik ordered. He knew as well as any of them that there was no time to do anything more than flee, but he also knew that depending on the bounty of the Desolation of Thaumidor was a recipe for lingering death.

Jancy shifted Castrator to her left hand. She held Sombrisio out toward the mountain in a clenched-fist salute and cried, "Thou art petrified!"

The spell had no effect on the mountain.

"Death and—" the elf on guard cried as he took two clean-limbed strides back toward the camp. A rock almost exactly the size of the retainer's head fell from the top of the advancing cliff. It precisely intersected the course of the running elf.

The helmet of boars' tusks and gold wire disintegrated, as did the retainer's skull. The elf waltzed in widening circles like those of a child's top slowing to the point it will soon fall over. In the uncertain light there was nothing unusual about the figure, though of course he'd stopped shouting when the rock brained him.

The packhorses neighed and kicked their bound forelegs high. The hobbles were of elven working, fashioned from children's mercy, maidens' constancy, and suchlike materials. The horses would never be able to break free of their mythical bonds. Even if they did, the off-loaded supplies would be lost beneath the mountain's advance.

"I said, thou art petrified!" Jancy bellowed. Telling mummified soldiers they were dead had been a striking success. Telling a rock it was rock ought to be an equally natural win.

The cliff had stopped rising. Now it began to slump forward again at increasing velocity.

"You idiot!" Sombrisio said. "The mountain doesn't have any more brains than you do, so how do you expect me to affect *its* beliefs? Blast the ground, yoyo!"

The ring's directions didn't make a lot of sense, but Jancy didn't have a better idea. Waiting for the cliff to arrive was a terrible idea.

"Thou art in pain!" she said, aiming her fist toward the soil at the base of the glittering mountain. By now the rock was moving *really* fast with gravity adding its considerable increment to force of the spell which animated the mountain.

"*Eeeeeeek!*" screamed the world, or at least as much of it as Jancy Gaine and her party were occupying at the moment. The ground drew back in agony, forming a lip of fine loess which scooted Jancy, her fellows, and the entire bouncing paraphernalia of their camp away from the mountain's line of advance.

"*The Desolation is a living entity,*" the hermit had said, or something very like that, early on in the quest. . . .

When the scarified soil drew back, it formed a huge hole. The mountain, plunging down at an enormous rate intended to carry it by inertia a thousand yards out across the moonlit wasteland, streamed into the chasm.

Crevices gaped and closed across the granite. The entire surface of the mountain glowed with expelled phlogiston.

The jiggling tail of the mountain followed the rest of the rock into the hole. There was a shuddering impact a very long way down. The Desolation of Thaumidor was a being of unsuspected depths.

Jancy got to her feet. Calla and the surviving pair of retainers had started to gather up the supplies. The mountain would probably tunnel its way to the surface again, but that wouldn't be for a while.

"Now, that," said Sombrisio in tones of exhausted satisfaction, "is the sort of spell magical implements will still be talking about well into the Fifth Age of the Middle World!"

Bushes tumbled across the landscape, dragging the tips of their branches in desperate but vain attempts to halt their progress. Occasionally one of the whirling weeds hit an unseen barrier and splattered to a stop, leaking its life juices into the dry soil.

There was no wind. Trees deformed by leprous scale stood leafless, waiting for dust to bury them. This was as doomed and barren a place as Jancy'd seen since, since the most recent time she'd opened her eyes in the Desolation of Thaumidor.

"Do you want to camp here?" Calla Mallanik suggested, obviously solicitous because of Jancy's physical state.

She grimaced. She probably looked like walking death. She certainly felt like walking death; but right now the best way to avoid Death in his real skeletal majesty was to keep on walking until they reached Anthurus.

"No," she said. "We need to keep moving as long as it's daylight. Besides, the more distance we put between ourselves and that mountain, the better I'll like it."

"The mountain isn't really hostile, you know," the hermit said. "We just happened to be in its path."

"Wrong, wrong, wrong," Sombrisio said. "You'd think

you'd have learned something about the Desolation, as many years as you've spent here."

"As big as the mountain is," Calla said, "it doesn't have to be hostile."

"That's right," said the surviving elf retainer. "I remember Elavil of the Rock and his riding brontosaur. He claimed it was the best-tempered creature alive. Maybe it was, but one cold night it decided to curl up with Elavil to stay warm. Some heroic death that was, hey?"

The kid from Brooklyn put down the harmonica on which he'd been softly playing "In the Baggage Car Ahead." His visage was sad.

"It's too bad about the old man," the kid said in a broken voice. "He was . . . he was the one we all looked up to for guidance. And then, squirt, he's gone. What kind of craftsmanship does that show, getting squirted like a tube of toothpaste?"

"Umm," Calla said. "More like a tube of red paint, from what I could see. Of course, with the moonlight you've got to extrapolate."

The elfin retainer put an arm around the kid's shoulders and said, "Don't take it so hard, kid. He didn't have a chance. It's not in our hands to choose whether we'll be Tibbalts or just so many kerns and gallowglasses."

"What I was saying," Sombrisio said, "not that any of you lot seem to be interested in something that your very lives depend on . . ."

The ring let her voice trail out in a painful whine.

Jancy looked down at her finger. "Ah, sorry, Sombrisio," she said. "I was . . ."

"Walking around in a daze," the ring said. "After all, why should today be different? What I was going to say, though, is that the mountain isn't just wandering anymore. It's following me."

"Nonsense!" said the hermit.

"Oh?" said the ring. "Like it's nonsense that the last thing you did before leaving Caltus was to rob the poor box of the Hospice of Sisters of Fallen Virtue?"

"Ah," said the hermit. "That makes sense, I was saying."

"*And,*" Sombrisio continued, never one to be turned when she scented psychic blood, "you only got three pewter buttons and a slug for your trouble."

Jancy glanced back toward the retainers. "Hey, kid?" she called.

"And when the slug crawled out of your purse that night, it wrote *thief* across the back of your robe in slime," the ring concluded triumphantly.

The kid from Brooklyn looked up. "Mistress?" he said, palming his harmonica nervously.

"Seems to me that the Old Man took worse punishment than even Hormazd the Centurion," Jancy said. "I mean, what's seventy-eight separate wounds compared to having a whole mountain fall on you, huh?"

"Gee, mistress," said the retainer. His eyes widened in dawning pleasure. "Do you really think so?"

"Anybody'd think so, kid," Jancy assured him.

"Wow," said the kid. To the elf retainer he went on, "Say, did you notice the way the Old Man threw his arms and legs wide as he fell forward? He was making sure that he'd be smashed *absolutely* flat. Now, that's craftsmanship if I ever saw it!"

Calla Mallanik looked at Jancy. "That was a good thing to do," the elf said quietly.

"I can't stand that damned song about the mother's corpse up in the baggage car," Jancy replied, also under her breath.

"Ready to learn why the mountain's chasing me, noble hero?" Sombrisio demanded.

"Yeah," said Calla. "We'd—"

"It's because I'm the closest thing it's ever found to an all-powerful prophet on his way to heaven by direct translation," Sombrisio said, deliberately interrupting the elf. "Unless one of your lot think you qualify better?"

Jancy shrugged. That motion reminded her of the cut across her shoulder. The pain disappeared behind a curtain of adrenaline when danger threatened, but it sure wasn't gone for good.

"Makes sense to me," Calla said. "What do you think, hermit?"

The hermit cleared his throat. "That's an extremely wise ring you have there," he said carefully. "I certainly wouldn't argue with any assessment it made of a situation. No, sir, not me."

The ring farted at surprising length.

Jancy Gaine raised her right fist and rubbed the corner of her mouth with her thumb knuckle. "Hey, Sombrisio?" she whispered.

"Yeah, numskull?" the ring replied.

"Thanks for waking us up last night," said Jancy.

"Huh!" Sombrisio said. "I told you—I was listening to you talk in your sleep and it turned my stomach."

"Thanks anyway," said Jancy as she lowered her hand to the head of Castrator.

She no longer worried about how long it would take them to find Anthurus. After all, the quest was the thing.

Shadows lengthened, abruptly and much sooner than sunset should have been threatening. The sudden dimness drew Jancy's mind from thoughts that were considerably darker yet.

The hermit was a few steps in the lead of the rest of the party. He stopped with his palms forward, as though he'd hit an invisible wall.

Jancy tugged Sombrisio from her finger. She held the massive silver ring out toward Calla Mallanik.

"My bow will—" the elf protested. He'd already nocked an arrow.

"Take the ring," Jancy said in a voice more terrifying than words alone could have been.

The party had entered a shallow valley. From above, the Desolation of Thaumidor would have looked as flat as a marine recruit's bunk. Swales and rises that were minute in geomorphic terms were nonetheless enough to limit the vision of humans at ground level to a few score yards.

That didn't explain the darkness. The packhorses, led in two long trains by the surviving retainers, whickered nervously. Though the beasts were only ten or a dozen yards behind the elf and humans at the head of the party, they were already lost in gloom.

"I may have made the wrong turning," said the hermit in a voice of controlled terror. "When the mountain . . . You know. I think we'd better—"

"All right," Jancy ordered in a voice trembling with hormones. "Turn the pack train. I'll wait."

Light gleamed on the shadowed hillside, faint but increasing slowly to illuminate the ruined fane from which it sprang. Pillars, most of them broken, were set in a circle. At their bases lay a rubble of blocks and tiles, remnants of the architraves and a domed roof.

The light was all the colors of the rainbow. It should have been beautiful. Instead it reminded Jancy of the shimmer of a snake's cast skin.

The hermit backed slowly around Jancy. "I'm very sorry to have brought us this way," he whispered. "We seem to have found the temple of IRiS, the rainbow goddess of evil and misfortune."

Squill's eyes rolled in fear. He formed his handset and began speaking desperately into it. Jancy doubted the artio would be able to punch a spell out of a valley with the magical resonance of this one, but at present there was almost no question on Middle Earth that she cared less about.

She held Castrator and her spiked shield out at angles before her, trying to cover as broad an area as possible. Jancy Gaine wasn't a team player, had never been that. She was a straight-ahead berserk, keep slashing so long as there's anybody else still on his feet.

That was fine when she was alone, but Jancy wasn't alone now and the people with her couldn't take care of themselves the way the old gang did. Spotty Gulick, whose idea of a good time on stand-down was to get into drunken brawls; Dominik Blaid, who saw everything on a battlefield and then fixed the problems with his own saber; even Gar Quithnick, a creep but *our* creep. You never had to worry about anybody else stabbing you in the back if Gar was there.

But now . . .

Something moved in the darkness. At first she thought it was a dog, but it was too big for that. A bear, perhaps . . .

"The minions of IRiS were once human," the hermit said. There was a singsong intonation to his voice. He spoke to keep from dissolving in panic, not because he had any necessary information to impart. "But now—"

The necessary information was the degree of fear with which this place had struck the hermit when he recognized it.

The figure rose up on its hind legs. It stepped toward Jancy, giggling loudly. The light suffusing the fane brightened. There were more of the figures, many more of them, standing now and pacing forward.

They were spotted hyenas, but they walked like men. The slavering jaws through which they laughed at their victims had teeth that could crush bones too big for a lion to devour.

"Run!" the hermit cried.

The whole valley was now bright with the rainbow radiance of IRiS and her ruthless minions. There was no escape, to the rear or in any direction.

Scores of the hyenas shrieked their joy as they pulled down the kid from Brooklyn and the stalwart elf retainer beside him. Over the monsters' laughter and the snap of crunching bones, their leaders cried, "Disallowed! Disallowed!" in nearly human voices.

Horses screamed in their final terror. The minions of IRiS wasted everything in their frenzies of slaughter.

"Princess!" Jancy called as she lunged at the leading hyena. She could focus the pack's attention on her and save the others for perhaps a few seconds. "Princess! Princess!"

The hyenas came at her from all sides, but *this* Jancy Gaine understood. The bearded ax slashed down through a minion's upper chest. Broken ribs, lengths of blood vessels, and much of the right lung spilled onto the soil as the monster's sternum flopped in two pieces.

Not only hyena jaws could crush bones.

The spike in Jancy's shield boss drove through a hyena's thin nasal bones, into the brain case or near enough. Another minion hunched to tear the tendons from Jancy's knee, met her hobnailed boot instead, and collapsed wailing as she broke its spine with a downward chop of her buckler's rim.

There was a hyena behind her. Jancy killed it with a quick, unthinking stab of Castrator's ball pommel, not even bothering to look. She thrust the ax forward again like an épée, putting the upper tip into a monster's thick throat and through the neck vertebrae behind it.

Calla Mallanik shouted something. It couldn't affect Jancy's present situation, so her ears didn't hear it. The part of her mind that processed language didn't operate at times like these.

She was drenched in blood. Some of it was her own, from her right side. She hadn't been conscious of teeth ripping along her ribs, but she'd split a hyena's skull with Castrator's edge in the same motion that smashed the pommel through the chest of the creature on her back.

She started forward. The minions were fleeing, all those that survived. They were running for their lairs, noisome holes dug into the ruins of the temple, and the rainbow light was fading.

"Sif's hair," Jancy muttered. She turned. She almost fell because the adrenaline rush had left her as suddenly as it arrived. She had very little remaining from her normal reserves of strength.

A few horses had survived the hyenas' single-minded bloodlust. They pitched and bucked in terror. Squill knelt over his pack with his handset, uninjured but blinded by fear. The hermit stood transfixed, staring at—

Jancy blinked. Staring at what looked like a much

younger edition of Jancy Gaine: herself as a young girl, just before she made the decision to go on her first war party as a shield maiden instead of staying home to marry in the village at the edge of the ice fields.

The figure, her figure, wore Sombrisio on its right hand, so it must be Calla who stood there.

The illusion trembled and vanished like a picture projected on smoke. Calla Mallanik shook himself. "Let's get out of this *damned* place," he said.

The hermit moved like an automaton until the party reached daylight again at the head of the valley, and he gave only monosyllabic directions for the remainder of the afternoon until they camped.

Jancy awakened. Every muscle hurt. Where the flesh had been severed by steel or the hyenas' teeth, it hurt more; but that was a matter of degree rather than type.

"Sif!" she muttered. Two figures were still sitting up, across the coals of the campfire. "How late is it, Calla? You should've gotten me up for my watch before now."

The constellations above the Desolation of Thaumidor weren't the familiar ones. Normally Jancy didn't see shapes in the stars, but she did see things here. Unfortunately.

"You needed the sleep," Calla Mallanik said. "You've been one of the walking dead all day. Except when it counted."

"Sif's *hair*," Jancy said; but as she moved, her muscles warmed and the pain sank to what normal people would consider bearable levels. She squinted across the fire. "Hermit, is that you?" she asked.

"Yes, Mistress Gaine," the hermit said.

"Let's throw another log on," Jancy said. She thought about the possible implications and added, "Ah, there's no ... The fire doesn't make pictures here, does it?" Calla shrugged. "Not that I've seen," he said. Instead of adding wood, he prodded the end of a thick branch from the edge into the heart of the coals. "Not a lot of heat, either, but that may be me."

"I never asked you what you did to drive off those hyenas," Jancy said. "I thought, I thought we were gone geese."

"What you thought," said Sombrisio, who was back on her finger, "was that you'd screwed up even at heroic endeavor. When you already knew you were no good at any other damn thing."

Jancy looked down at the ring. "If you want to know the real truth," she said, "I was thinking about which hyena to stick next. After things slowed down, I thought I'd blown it, yeah."

"It was what the hermit said," Calla explained. He nodded toward the man beside him, but the hermit was sunk in an open-eyed daze. Maybe he was the one seeing things in the wan firelight this time.

"That the minions of IRiS had once been men," the elf resumed. "I find it odd, but most human evil isn't done by evil humans."

"Huh?" said Jancy. It could be that she'd been whacked on the head so hard that everything she heard sounded like double-talk. And again, it could be that Calla'd been whacked on the head.

"No, I mean that," the elf said. "Most humans slip into evil deeds with the best intentions in the world. They slide down the road to destruction, thinking what they're doing is necessary or even good. If they could really see what they were doing, why, they'd stop."

"They wouldn't stop," said Sombrisio. "They'd just find some other excuse. Humans are even more despicable than elves, elf."

"And the ones who are already lost irretrievably . . ." Calla continued. They'd all learned by now that the best way to deal with the ring's gibes was to ignore them. "If you show them what they've become, they, well, they can't stand it. They'd run away. As the minions of IRiS ran away."

"I still don't get it," Jancy said. Not that that was news. *Don't worry, Jancy, we've got it all under control. Go sharpen your ax, why don't you?* How often had she heard that or a close equivalent of that? "You showed a pack of hyenas that they were hyenas?"

"No," said the elf with pardonable pride. "I showed them that they had once been men. I turned the power of Sombrisio on myself. I projected to everyone watching the image *of* the watcher before the fatal decisions that led to where they were now."

The hermit looked at Calla Mallanik with dismal, haunted eyes. "It seems to me," the hermit said, the first words he'd volunteered since the battle at the fane of IRiS, "that's using the ring on many at once. While I understood its powers were limited to one person at a time."

"So I stretched a point, buster," Sombrisio said. "Sue me! If you can find a jurisdiction this side of the Outer Sea where there aren't bad debt warrants still out for you, I mean."

"I really meant to make the money good," the hermit said. He didn't appear to be talking to anyone present, except perhaps to his younger self in judgment. "Every time. Every single time."

"You didn't look at me until after the effect had worn off, I suppose, Jancy?" Calla Mallanik said with studied nonchalance.

"Huh?" Jancy repeated. "No, I glanced back when the hyenas started running. I saw myself looking like I did when I was a kid and wondered what in Sif's name was going on. I still don't see what it has to do with the price of fox fur."

Calla looked at her sharply. "You didn't feel regret," he said, "for the choices you made, for the path you didn't follow?"

She shrugged. Damn, she needed to remember not to do that until the cut had knitted together better. "What's to regret?" she said. "I made choices, everybody makes choices. People who choose to serve an evil goddess— Sif, everybody knows IRiS is evil. People who choose to serve evil, for whatever reasons, are evil. It's just that simple."

Calla Mallanik shook his head in wonderment. "Ah, what an elf was lost in you, Mistress Gaine," he said.

"Oh, you bet," said Sombrisio. "And she'd have been a right triumph when her creche cycle was taught aesthetic appreciation, wouldn't she?"

"It's not far to Anthurus now," the hermit said. He was still speaking to himself, or at any rate to a portion of himself. "I'll guide them the rest of the way."

Either the fire or Sombrisio interjected a *BLAT/hissing* sound.

"I really meant to repay the money," the hermit added in a whisper.

The stretch of waste on which the hermit halted was unusual only in that it was so completely barren. A few gangling plants were scattered on the slope. They bent down their stems and buried their seed heads in the dirt when they saw members of Jancy's party glancing in their direction. Larger examples of the noisome vegetation which ranged the Desolation were conspicuous by their absence.

Calla Mallanik glanced back in the direction by which they'd come. There was a plume of dust on the horizon. "The mountain's after us again," he said glumly.

Jancy shrugged. "It doesn't move very fast," she said. "How much farther is it to Anthurus, hermit?"

"We've arrived," the hermit said. He pointed to the ground. "It's right here."

"Hel take you if we're here!" Jancy snarled. "I've been to Anthurus, remember? That's where I found the damned ring!"

"Where Princess Rissa found my puissant self," Sombrisio said in an arch tone. "And of course Hel, or at least some civilized equivalent of your barbaric death goddess, will take the hermit. Happens to all humans."

"I'm sure you did," the hermit said. "But unfortunately, it seems that the Desolation has covered the city again during the interim. Anthurus is down here, somewhere, under this sand dune."

He scuffed the soil. "Dirt dune, that is."

"And not nearly soon enough, in most cases," Sombrisio muttered as a coda to her previous comment.

The hermit had lost all the cranky bluster with which he'd joined the quest. It wasn't because he was afraid of what Jancy might—might very well—do to him, either. He faced her anger with what could only be described as an attitude of quiet resignation.

"Well, what are we supposed to do?" Calla demanded.

The elf looked back over his shoulder in the direction of the mountain. Sure, it didn't move *very* fast, and it wasn't even making a beeline toward the questing party. More like the line a bee really makes, jagged casts back and forth across the landscape, laboriously orienting itself.

But Calla wasn't going to forget any time soon the sight of flat ground humping itself up into a cliff a thousand feet high.

"I'm sorry," the hermit said. "I truly don't know. Perhaps you could leave the ring here and the loess would bury it eventually?"

"Or not," Sombrisio said. "Umm, you know, I could right fancy being plucked from the ground by a condor and dropped into the hands of some powerful and no doubt wicked wizard."

"Hel's bloody toenails," Jancy muttered. She was in charge of the expedition, so she had to decide what to do. Thinking through intractable problems wasn't the sort of thing she was best at, to put it mildly.

A scrawny gooseberry bush bent slowly toward her foot. The tip of a needle-sharp thorn pecked abruptly at her bootlace.

Jancy kicked the plant away with a divot of light soil. The gooseberry squawked when it landed and scurried farther away from the party.

Jancy gazed around. Her eyes lighted on the artio. "Squill!" she said.

"Mistress?" the comspec replied, wincing. He'd spent much of the past several days with his eyes closed. He

was justifiably certain that they weren't going to show
him anything he really wanted to see.

"I want you to contact Caltus," Jancy ordered. "Tell
them the city's gone—buried till who knows when. Ask
them if we ought to bring Sombrisio back with us. Got
that?"

"Yes, mistress," the artio said. He squatted down and
formed his handset. He'd closed his eyes again.

"Mistress Gaine?" the hermit said.

She looked at him again, startled that he was still
standing before her with a look of significance. "Do you
have something useful to say after all?" she demanded.

"Not the way you mean it, mistress," the hermit said.
He cleared his throat, then went on, "I have fulfilled
your request of me in the best fashion I could. There's
nothing more for me to do here. I therefore ask your
leave to, ah, leave."

"We'll be going back to Caltus as soon as . . ." said
Calla Mallanik. He glanced at the artio, speaking into his
handset. "Well, pretty quick, anyway. We'll drop you off
at your hut."

"If I may," the hermit said, "I'll go on my own. I'm
headed in the opposite direction, you see. Toward Quiberon. I have some debts to clear up there."

"There," said Sombrisio. "And debts all across the
North Coast. *And* in Caltus."

"Yes, I'm afraid that's correct," the hermit said, nib-
bling his lower lip. To Jancy, the old man looked worn
and frightened and more determined than she'd ever
imagined he could be.

"A doddering old fool like you won't ever be able to
pay off all you owe!" Sombrisio said.

Jancy waved her left palm over the ring, though without actually touching the metal. "Hush, hush," she
murmured.

"I will *not* hush," Sombrisio said. "Why, he's not even
employable. Unless maybe somebody wants a doorstop!"

"And there's my wife, of course," the hermit added.
"Well, one does what one can."

"I understood that your wife . . ." the elf said, giving Sombrisio a speculative look. "Had left you. Not the other way around."

The hermit shrugged. "Nothing happens in a vacuum," he said. "I suppose I always knew that. My wife is responsible for her actions, but that doesn't diminish my own responsibility for mine."

"There was a boyfriend?"Jancy said, looking toward the empty horizon beyond the hermit's left shoulder rather than meeting his eyes directly as she asked the question.

The hermit smiled faintly. " 'Pull your face off'n then stick your head where the sun don't shine,' I believe were his exact words," he said. "Well, he won't be as young as he was, either. And in any case, I need to apologize to her, whatever happens afterwards."

"Well, I'll be damned," said Jancy Gaine.

"Perhaps," said the hermit. "But I'm no longer sure damnation is a necessary part of the human condition."

They gave him a packhorse and more than a sufficient share of the remaining food. As the hermit said as he began trekking westward over the steep leading edge of the dune, if he had any of the sea rations left when he arrived in Quiberon, he might be able to sell the cans to a shipmaster as ballast.

The sky to the west was almost as black as Jancy Gaine's mood. Lightning flickered within the clouds. If there was thunder, it was lost against a background of the Desolation's normal rumbles and sighing.

They'd set up their exiguous camp midway on the long slope. Squill squatted at the top of the encampment that formed the dune's leading edge, the highest ground available. The artio's apparatus squealed in hopeless despair as he attempted to contact his superiors in Caltus. Every time the distant lightning flashed, a demon roared at the doomed souls.

Calla Mallanik picked grimly at a can of sea rations.

There wasn't a fire because there was nothing bigger than a gooseberry bush to burn on this bleak stretch. The best you could say for the situation was that the food in the olive drab cans was so unappetizing hot that eating it cold didn't degrade the experience significantly.

"Well," the elf said, "we could try blasting a hole in the soil, the way you did to trip up the mountain."

"Great thought!" Sombrisio said. "The first time you prod the Desolation that way, the hole will close before you can get me off your finger and throw me in. The second time, though, you'll bury me I don't want to guess how deep."

"We will?" Jancy said in surprise.

"You bet," Sombrisio said. "The second time, the Desolation'll be ready for you. It'll swallow us all down like a trout takes a fly. That'll give me some company for the next three millennia. Or however long."

"I thought it was too easy," Calla said. He took another forkful of sea ration, punishing himself for having let his hopes rise.

"Look, it's fine with me," said the ring. "I figure you both'll be about as bright after you're buried as you are now."

"The best choice," Jancy said in a loud voice, "is to take Sombrisio back to Caltus. One item won't be enough to disturb the magical balance."

She cleared her throat and added, "Besides, the ring might be useful to have around for, you know, useful things."

Jancy had spoken forcefully because she knew that whenever she had an idea which didn't involve lopping somebody to bits with Castrator, she was out of her depth. If she put enough emphasis on a statement, listeners might forget that Jancy Gaine was basically as dumb as a post.

Alternatively, they might remember Castrator, and that could be an even better way of getting them to agree with her.

She and Calla heard a gabble from the top of the dune.

They couldn't understand the words, but they could tell that the artio had made actual contact instead of flinging his spells vainly into the howling atmospherics.

"If we're going to head back," Calla said, checking the cover of his silver-strung bow, "I'd like to start before the storm hits. The rain'll come down this slope like the front of Deucalion's flood."

Squill trotted toward them. His wand, still extended, wobbled above him like the baton of a maestro conducting the sky.

"I got through!" the artio called. "They say, 'Lose it good!'"

Jancy stood with threatening deliberation. She placed her hands on her hips. "Lose it good," she repeated. "Do they say *how* in the name of Sif's blond cunt we're supposed to do that when the city's buried?"

Squill skidded to a halt so abruptly that he almost lost his footing. His cloak flapped around him and back. "Ah," he said. "No, Mistress Gaine, they didn't say that. I explained the situation clearly, *very* clearly, Mistress Gaine—"

The artio noticed the way Jancy's right hand clenched on the helve of Castrator. He closed his eyes.

"—and they just said, ah, what they said. Mistress."

"It's not his fault," said Calla Mallanik mildly. "Though of course it's traditional in many human cultures to kill the messenger, so I suppose we—if you'd like to, that is—could—"

"Put a sock in it," Jancy said grimly. She turned away from the artio before she did something she wouldn't regret but knew she ought to.

"Hel's teeth," she said. There were a variety of ways to handle frustration. The only one that worked worth a damn for her was to go berserk for a few minutes, but she supposed she'd have to make do here with being depressed.

Light glimmered in the middle distance. "Has the storm got all the way around us now?" she asked, kneading her hands together to relax the cramp threatening as a result of her grip on the bearded ax.

Calla squinted. "No," he said, "that's the mountain again. The phlogiston being expelled when the rock cracks and closes, the hermit said."

"Does a light dawn?" Sombrisio demanded.

"The mountain!" Jancy and Calla shouted together.

"You know," said the ring, "I think the intellectual dominance of this age is in the hands of the cockroaches. Or whatever cockroaches use instead of hands."

It wasn't raining yet, but when it did it was going to come down like a cow pissing on a flat rock. Not that there was a lot of rock in the Desolation of Thaumidor. Or any cows, of course, so far as Jancy could tell.

The mountain roared to the foot of the dune like an avalanche; which it basically was, though the rocks had to bootstrap themselves upward each time in order to fall.

The ground shook like a hammered drumhead. Light shot in every direction from the collapsing granite, sparkles and sheets and faintly colored balls as large as haystacks. These last hung trembling in the air, dreaming of a paradise in which ghost trains ran down phantom tracks.

The forward flow of stone exhausted itself for the moment. The silence that followed the sound was only relative, but it seemed complete because of the crashing amplitude of the cataclysm it succeeded.

Jancy Gaine and her elf companion stood at the top of the slope. They'd chosen a spot half a mile from the camp where Squill huddled with the horses. No point in leading a mountain straight over their supplies; though if things went wrong, it wouldn't make a whole lot of difference.

The dune's leading edge fell away at a sixty-degree angle behind the pair of them. The mountain's thunder shook veils of fine soil from the escarpment. The dust twisted into the shape of tortured women as it settled toward the ground three hundred feet below.

"Let's start moving apart," Calla Mallanik said. He took two steps away from Jancy, looking back over his shoulder to make sure that the ax woman intended to follow the plan they'd worked out while the mountain was still miles away.

She didn't intend to.

"Get on out of the way," Jancy ordered. Her eyes were fixed on the mountain as it inched upward again; she held Sombrisio between her cupped palms. "I think I'll take care of it myself."

"*You* think?" Sombrisio piped. "You *think*? Sure, you would think that your getting mushed into the dirt was just as good as burying me in living rock!"

"Jancy," Calla said. He spoke with the sort of controlled earnestness with which one coaxes a toddler who's managed to lock himself alone in the bathroom. "Toss me the ring, move a few steps, and I'll toss it back. We've got to keep the mountain from focusing on one point. It's got too broad a front to survive if it comes straight at one of us."

"All right," she said. "All right."

She tossed Sombrisio underhand to the elf, then walked away from him along the escarpment in seeming nonchalance. This would either work or it wouldn't. If it didn't, it was very damned unlikely that Jancy Gaine would be around to answer questions about what went wrong.

The mountain, dark and quiescent for a moment at the foot of the slope, seemed to have gotten its figurative breath. The crystalline entity humped itself taller at a steady rate, preparing for the final gravity-driven rush to the goal it sensed.

As Calla walked north along the crumbling dune edge with the ring, the rising layers of rock shifted slightly in his direction. The mountain's progress had been increasingly direct as it neared Sombrisio. If the mass of rock were a Plott hound, it would be yelping in climactic enthusiasm by now. As it was, the pop and crunch of stone sliding on itself took on a sort of tail-wagging joyousness.

"You can toss her back to me now," Jancy called, raising her voice to be heard over the background of geological preparation. She'd left her buckler and helmet in the camp, since they were obviously useless against present needs.

Castrator was useless also, but the big ax swung at Jancy's right hip. She'd always figured to be buried with Castrator. If things went wrong in the next few seconds, *mingled* would be a better word than *buried* to describe her future relationship with the ax.

"Here she comes!" Calla shouted. He was nearly a hundred feet away by now, but the mountain covered several times that width of the lower dune.

The elf put his whole body into an overhand throw. The motion was as graceful as that of a cat leaping to tear some small bird to bloody feathers. Sombrisio, spinning and lighted pastel by the discharges from the straining mountain, described a perfect catenary arc which ended in Jancy's clasping hands.

Jancy began to run along the edge of the escarpment. Castrator slapped her thigh. The base of the mountain skidded slightly toward her as the wall of rock staggered swiftly up. Friction against the loose soil wasn't sufficient to completely brake the enormous mass pouring itself into a tower from the rear forward.

As the mountain moved, it flexed beyond the elastic modulus of the crystals which comprised it. Gaps like mouths opened and shut between layers of rock. Granite teetered over Jancy in a vertical sheet. The roar echoed from the clouds in thunder beyond human imagination.

"Throw me *now*, you brainless cunt!" Sombrisio screamed.

The face of the rock wavered only twenty feet from Jancy. A momentary split appeared in the surface, like a shake in drying wood. Jancy flung Sombrisio between plates of granite. The gap slammed shut as the entire mountain plunged downward in a rush nothing could have stopped.

Jancy dived with her arms outstretched in the direction she'd been running. The friable soil lost cohesion under the impact of megatons of granite. The dune's edge exploded in a plume of dust that cloaked and preceded the river of cold stone on its dive to the flat landscape three hundred feet below. The noise continued for a quite remarkable time.

Jancy lay on the escarpment. The mountain had missed her, but her boots dangled out in the air where the cliff of dirt had collapsed when the rock slid past. Five hundred feet of the dune's face had been chiseled from sixty degrees to half that.

Well beyond the bottom of the slope, the mountain was shivering to a halt. Calla Mallanik got to his feet on the far side of the notch in the dune. He waved. Squill, barely visible in the beclouded twilight, was climbing up the slope. The artio needed high ground to report back to Caltus.

To report Jancy Gaine's success back to Caltus.

The rain fell in sheets, by buckets, and as great slashing waves. It even smelled a little like cow urine. Jancy Gaine bathed once a year, in the spring when the ice broke, so the odor wasn't a matter of great concern to her.

Despite the storm, she should have been a lot more cheerful than she was.

Calla Mallanik caught the lead of the gray mare so that Jancy could finish cinching the pack. The animal was supposed to stand drop-reined to be loaded, but the weather spooked her. Sif, the mare thought she had problems?

Under the sluicing rainfall, the soil was vanishing faster than good intentions at a bachelor party. By the time Jancy grabbed the last pack saddle, it had washed twenty feet down the slope. She hoped the damned horses liked their fodder wet and muddy, because that's the way they were gong to be eating it till they escaped the Desolation of Thaumidor.

She and Calla loaded the roan gelding. The horse came *that* close to being strangled with its own tail, but it realized its danger in time to stop sidling away from Jancy. Its breast was a froth of nervous sweat, despite the cleansing rain.

Jancy paused, then kneed the gelding in the ribs to tighten the girth another notch. "Where in Sif's name is Squill?" she shouted to Calla.

The elf pointed up the disintegrating dune. "Right where he was," he said. "I guess he's still trying to call Caltus through this storm."

The artio was silhouetted against the western sky. The clouds hid every trace of sunset, but lightning was a constant white glare across the heavens.

"Well, if he doesn't get down here *now*, we're heading back without him!" Jancy said.

Squill stood up. He took a step toward them, as if he'd heard Jancy from a quarter mile away through a chaos of deluge and thunderclaps. He waved.

A lightning bolt touched the tip of the artio's twelve-foot wand. The flash was brighter than the sum of all those the storm had flung down previously. Squill's bones stood out momentarily from a ball of actinic radiance before dissolving like the rest of him.

Jancy got to her feet again. She didn't know if electrical shock, the sky-splitting thunder, or pure surprise had knocked her on her ass.

"Let's get moving!" she said to Calla. The elf wouldn't be able to hear anything for a while after the boom that followed the lightning; but it wasn't as if he needed to be told to get out of this place, either.

The storm ended not far beyond the base of the dune covering Anthurus. The boundary between rain and not-rain was as sharp as a razor cut.

The dune that *had* covered Anthurus. Rain gouged the loess and carried it away with an enthusiasm no human public-works crew would ever show. Great rivers of silt flowed in four directions from the site, following subtle variations in topography and cutting them deeper.

Or maybe the streams were flowing uphill. This was the Desolation of Thaumidor, after all.

The packhorses whickered, congratulating one another on being alive. Calla Mallanik paused and took off his tunic to wring it. Even if they'd carried changes of clothing, nothing could have come through the downpour without being soaked.

Jancy looked back at the foaming, rain-torn lake. "I suppose we could have waited," she said. "Anthurus is going to unloose itself completely in the next twenty minutes."

"I don't think it would have worked that way," the elf said. He didn't sound particularly cheerful either.

The western sky was scarlet, though the sun should have been well below the horizon by now.

"Sombrisio's going to be all right," Jancy said in a bright voice. "Someday a guy named Mohammet is going to be seeing something on a pile of sand. When he bends over to pick it up, it'll ask if his mother brought a paternity suit against the camel."

"Yeah," Calla said. "Nothing a mountain can do is going to bother that ring."

Jancy clucked to the pair of horses she led. She began to walk on. "We really did it, didn't we?" she said. "They'll be talking about us for a long time. The heroes who got rid of Sombrisio."

"You bet," Calla agreed. "This one was a quest and a half, I'll tell the world!"

There was a small noise. Jancy spun around.

"Sorry," the elf said in embarrassment. "I had a can of beans and franks for dinner."

"Oh," said Jancy. She clucked to the horses again.

"I miss her too," said Calla Mallanik in a voice almost too soft to be heard; but then, it wasn't as if Jancy needed to be told that.

Behind them, the opal towers of Anthurus gleamed under a bloody sky.

Prelude the Third

"*How* tall are your bridesmaids, m'lady?" the seamstress said in disbelief.

Rissa gestured. "Well, I am quite tall and both are taller than me. I think I have set of Jancy's togs around here somewhere, and Domino—well, she was Dominik Blaid, so you should have no trouble seeing her tailor. She's lived here forever, at least when she wasn't in the field."

The pinched lines about the seamstress's eyes grew deeper. They had given the wedding dress a second fitting and it was stunning. Not much was left but the routine stitching on of yards of lace, hundreds of pearls, and hemming the lot—including the thirty-foot train.

Now, with Daisy's able assistance, they were designing the costumes for the wedding party. It would not be a large group, as royal weddings went. All of Rissa's family had been slaughtered by Kalaran—as had all of Rango's. This settled the difficult problem of coordinating dresses to be worn by the mothers of the bride and groom, but still left plenty of others.

"Dominik Blaid," the seamstress repeated faintly. "Very good, Your Highness. I believe I had heard something of the sort. If I recall correctly, she is dark and Jancy Gaine is fair?"

"That's right," Rissa said. "Is that a difficulty?"

"It does limit our selection of colors. Pink, for example, suits blondes quite well, but it rarely flatters brunettes."

"I don't think that Jancy would wear pink," Rissa said, flinching a bit at the thought. "What about a pale blue?"

"I considered that, but both of the ladies in question are somewhat tan." The seamstress frowned. "Pale blue might make them look sallow. How about lavender? It is quite regal and would be quite nice given that your coronation is to follow the wedding ceremony."

Rissa nodded, reflecting as they began to inspect swatches of lavender fabric that it would be nice once the new Royal House was established and had selected its royal colors. Decisions like this would become a matter of the past. No one ever worried about how suitable royal colors were to anyone's complexion.

Sketching out rough designs for the gowns drove the poor seamstress to distraction. Clothing that would suit full-figured, muscular Jancy would swallow the slimmer, more hard-bodied Domino. Dresses that flattered Domino's boyish figure would make Jancy look hulking. When she left with initial design notes in hand, the seamstress was muttering prayers to any deity who would listen.

Rissa sent Daisy to see the woman home, promising she could look after herself for a half hour. Although she meant the guild-woman a kindness, she also craved a brief moment of privacy. Daisy tended to mother her, something that Rissa would not have minded from her own nurse. However, that poor lady had been slain when Kalaran's forces looted her family castle. She had not been young or pretty enough for the slave markets. Indirectly, Nurse had saved Rissa's life, for she had insisted on dressing the Princess in servant's clothing. Thus, none of the troops had realized that the Princess had lived, instead of being slaughtered with the rest of her family.

To distract herself from these dark memories, Rissa strolled to the window and counted through the rest of the wedding party. Spotty—Stiller—Gulick was to be best man. She made a mental note to see that his outfit did not clash with red, as he was certain to be flushed and his face might blotch.

Gar Quithnick was to be the second groomsman. She shuddered a bit at the idea of an assassin at her back, chiding herself for her lack of faith. However, he could not be denied his place.

Ibble, Spotty's dwarven friend, was to be ring bearer, a role given by tradition to one of the shorter races.

That filled out the main party. Various dignitaries, religious authorities, and loyal companions would make up the guest list. The galleries of the Cathedral of Dym would be left open for the public.

Rango had insisted that tickets be sold at a token price so that there would not be mobbing. She understood his reasoning, but thought it somewhat déclassé. There was no arguing with his point that the war against Kalaran had drained the Treasury.

She sighed. He hardly seemed the same man as the dashing warrior to whom she had lost her heart. Still, he seemed a stable, responsible ruler. No doubt the people would love him. She wondered, would she?

Lemml Touday saw the silhouette of the Princess against the window curtain as he arrived at the palace for his meeting with Prince Rango. He hoped she had not put the Prince into a bad mood today. What he had to tell the Prince would not sit well even if His Highness was in the best of moods.

Prince Rango was again in his privy council chamber. Today he was moving pins around on a wall map, consulting a handful of note cards as he did so. In his simple trousers and close-fitting tunic, he looked more like a military commander than he had on other of Lemml's visits and the priest found that this made him uneasy.

"Greetings, Lemml," the Prince said. "Have a seat. I will be with you as soon as I have finished marking these position reports on the map. I've heard from my questing heroes and things seem to be going quite well."

"You seem to be marking more than four units there, Your Highness," the priest commented.

"That's right," Prince Rango said, "I've been repositioning various units around the Faltane. There are still pockets of fighting—bandit activity and such. It wouldn't do to win the Faltane from Kalaran only to lose it to Civil unrest."

"Not at all, sire," Lemml said.

Prince Rango finished with his map and bore a silver salver over the table. With a slight flourish, he uncovered a pair of fluted blue-green bottles marked with white script lettering in an unfamiliar language. They were filled with a brown liquid that Lemml suspected was identical to the beverage he had imbibed on his previous visit. The Prince removed metal caps from the bottles with a curious device and poured the foaming beverage into two iced goblets.

"Over half of the royal wine cellar has gone over to this stuff," the Prince said cheerfully. "Fortunately, I like it. Now, what is the news from the Temple?"

Lemml sipped his drink. He found that the sweet, syrupy stuff made his teeth squeak slightly. Still, it was refreshing.

"The Demon of Darkness continues to hold forth within the skull of Kalaran. The Messenger of Light has retreated so far into the right socket that it is difficult to see. Given that the more rampant manifestations of the space-time rift are beginning to disperse—Your Highness's advisors seem to have been correct on that point— I am having more difficulty reassuring the religious authorities that nothing is wrong."

Prince Rango's smile was cold. "I have paid you well to assuage their fears. Do so."

"I will," Lemml promised hastily.

He leaned forward in his chair, dropping his voice so that the Prince had to lean to hear what he said next.

"But, my lord, what if the skull is right? What if

something of Darkness *is* threatening the good of the Faltane? Shouldn't we do something?"

The Prince guffawed. "I place no faith in magical trinkets. How could the skull of an evil wizard provide us with any reliable knowledge? I swear, Lemml, you've become as superstitious as your masters! I had thought you a solid businessman."

Lemml flushed, "I am, Prince Rango. However, magic is a potent force. One who toys with it toys with dangerous matters."

The Prince slapped his sheathed sword. "Leave such concerns to me, Lemml. This sword has beaten great enemies. Keep peace within the Temple and within a handful of days all will be settled. I will be coronated and nothing will stir me or those who have served me well."

"Yes, Your Highness." Lemml smiled weakly. "I shall return to report within a few day's time."

"Very good." The Prince's chuckle was robust, but his eyes were cold. "And make certain that I like that report, Lemml."

"I will, sire. I will."

Lemml hurried from the Prince's council chamber. His belly was roiling from a combination of the sweet brew and worry. He was safely in his rooms when he recalled that the sword with which the Prince had beaten his great enemies was no longer in the capital. Mothganger, along with the other artifacts, was on its way into hiding.

Wanted: Guardian

"Baaaaa!"

Even if dragons did not have exceptional hearing, the sound would have been sufficient to rouse Schmirnov from his slumber.

Without opening his eyes or raising his head, the massive reptile reached out with his senses to confirm the noise.

"Baaa-aaa."

No. There could be no doubt about it. There was a sheep ... no, *several* sheep in his cavern.

Sheep!

What in the blazes were those idiot villagers up to now?

"Baaaa." *Clink.*

The second noise, almost obliterated by the sheep's bleating, caught Schmirnov's total attention. His eyes opened and his head came up, searching for the source of the sound.

Sheep don't wear armor. Whether four legs with fleece, or two legged with huts, sheep don't wear armor.

"Show yourself!" the dragon demanded.

"Baaaa."

He could now see the sheep, at least half a dozen

of them, milling around the entrance to his cavern. As
suspected, however, none of them were wearing armor.

"*Show yourself!*" Schmirnov called again. "State your
intent, or I shall assume the worst and act accordingly!"

A short, chunky figure emerged from behind a boulder
and stood silhouetted in the light from the entrance.

A dwarf! First sheep, and now a dwarf! Well, now.
And he had thought this was going to be just another
boring day.

"I am Ibble!" the figure said. "I come in peace!"

"In peace?" the dragon growled. "That would be a
pleasant change."

Still, the dwarf had no visible weapons . . . unless he
had some secreted behind his boulder. Then too . . .

"And what about the others?" Schmirnov sneered.

Ibble started visibly, and shot a glance back over his
shoulder.

"Others?" he said.

"Don't play games with me, little man! There are at
least a dozen more of you waiting outside. Warriors, from
the sound of them."

Now that he was more awake, Schmirnov could clearly
hear the creak of leather scabbards and other small
noises that bespoke a group of armed men. What's more,
the very sparseness of the sounds indicated not only warriors, but seasoned veterans.

This was a bit more like what the dragon had learned
to expect from humans.

The old sneak attack, eh? If he were a bit less sporting,
he would pretend that he didn't know they were there
and let them try it.

"There are others, yes," the dwarf said hastily. "But
we all mean you no harm. We seek only to talk to you.
That and, perhaps, to request a favor."

"A favor?"

This was getting interesting indeed. Searching his
memory, Schmirnov could not recall the last time, if ever,
that a human had requested a favor of him. Whether he
granted it or not, simply the asking could be amusing.

Still, one could not be too careful. The treachery and deceit of humans was their trademark.

"How do I know this isn't a trick?" he said, letting a suspicion creep into his tone.

It had the desired effect, and the dwarf began to glance nervously at the cavern entrance. If Schmirnov became angry, there was no way Ibble could reach safety before suffering the consequences . . . and they both knew it.

"I . . . we've brought you presents as a sign of our good intentions."

"Presents?"

Though much of what is said or known about dragons is exaggeration or flat-out falsehood, the reports of their avarice are accurate.

Schmirnov raised his head to the greatest extent his neck and the cavern's ceiling would allow and peered about for his promised gifts like an eager child . . . a very *large* eager child.

There was nothing readily apparent in sight.

"Baaaa."

The dragon stared at the sheep for a moment, then swiveled his head around to gaze down on the dwarf.

"When you mention 'presents,' you didn't, by any chance, mean these miserable creatures, did you?"

"Well . . . yes, actually," Ibble said, edging a bit closer to his boulder. "I . . . we thought you might be hungry."

Schmirnov lowered his head until it was nearly resting on the ground, confronting his visitor nearly face to face.

"And in return for this, you expect me to grant you a favor?" he said. "You. Personally?"

"We're emissaries from Prince Rango," the dwarf explained hastily. "The favor we seek is in his name . . . for the good of the kingdom."

"A Prince, is it?" the dragon said. "But, of course, he isn't with your party himself. Right?"

"Well . . . no."

"In fact," Schmirnov continued, "I'd be willing to

wager that you aren't even the leader of the group. Is that correct?"

Ibble drew himself up to his full, diminutive height and puffed out his chest proudly.

"I am the closest friend and confidant of the leader," he declared. "What's more, I've been his right-hand man and companion at arms for many harrowing campaigns and quests, and ..."

The dragon cut him short by throwing back his head and giving off a short bark, which was the closest Schmirnov had come to laughing in decades.

"Let me see if I have this straight," the reptile said. "Your leader wasn't sure of the reception I'd give him if he just walked into my home ... if I'd listen or simply fry him where he stood on general principles ... so he sent you in ahead to test the water. You, in turn, decided to try to maximize your chances of survival by herding a bunch of sheep in to see if I was hungry before trying to approach me yourself. Am I right so far?"

"Well ... in a manner of speaking," Ibble admitted.

"Just for the record, where did you get those sheep?"

"The sheep? Umm ..."

"From that meadow in the valley below. Right?" Schmirnov supplied.

"As a matter of fact ..."

"Quite a lot of them, aren't there?"

"Well ..."

"Ever stop to wonder where they came from, or why they were there untended?"

"That *did* puzzle me a bit," the dwarf said. "Still, there were so many we didn't think the ones we took would be missed."

"Really?" The dragon smiled. "Well, try this one on for size. What would you say if I told you that the villagers maintain that flock specifically to keep me fed ... at least, fed well enough that I leave their village alone."

"That ... would make sense."

"More sense than trying to curry my favor with sheep

from what could be called my own flock. Wouldn't you say?"

"I see your point." Ibble flushed. "Still, our intent was good."

"Ah, yes. Your intent." Schmirnov was genuinely enjoying himself now. "As I recall, we've established that your intent was to test my appetite . . . and possibly glut it if I were hungry . . . before venturing forth yourself. Tell me, do you have any idea how tired I can get of eating nothing but sheep?"

"I . . . can see where that could be a problem."

The dwarf was looking uncomfortable again.

"What I'm saying is that I have to be *really* hungry before I can bear to even *think* of indulging in another of those bleating creatures. On the other hand, I'm always up for something new to nibble on . . . especially a *small* something. Am I making myself clear?"

Ibble wavered for a moment, then squared his shoulders bravely.

"If we have offended you with our ignorance, Lord Dragon, you have our deepest regrets. If more than an apology is necessary .. well, as you have noted, I am expendable."

Now, dragons in general, and Schmirnov specifically, have little regard for humans . . . which, in their minds, includes dwarves and elves. Still, being intelligent creatures, they respect and admire courage . . . if for no other reason than the fact that particular trait might well become extinct unless actively encouraged and protected.

"Well said, Ibble." Schmirnov smiled. "You do your master proud. What's more, you can ease your mind. I have no intention of eating or otherwise harming you or any of your party."

"Thank you, Lord Dragon," the dwarf said with a bow. "I could ask no greater guarantee than your word."

"Well, don't count *too* heavily upon it," the dragon cautioned. "I reserve the right to reverse my position if anyone tries to abuse my hospitality by using it as an opportunity for an attack. Is that understood?"

"Of course," Ibble said. "I assure you, however, that my lord is an honorable warrior who would not stoop to such a low trick."

"Really?" Schmirnov's voice took on a tone of sarcasm. "You'd be surprised how many so-called 'honorable warriors' feel that their normal rules of conduct and combat do not apply when facing dragons."

"Believe me, my lord is not one such as they. I have been at his side when he has faced numerous foes, many of them nonhuman and some not living, and never have I seen him sway from his code."

"That's good enough to get him his interview," the dragon said. "But you'll forgive me if I retain my caution nonetheless. The reason there are so few of us left is that far too many trusted the words and promises of humans. Now, who is this lord of yours?"

"He is Stiller Gulick, personal friend and comrade of Prince Rango."

"Gulick?" Schmirnov frowned. "you mean Spotty Gulick? The one with the complexion problem?"

"You know him?"

"I know *of* him," the dragon said. "I didn't reach my current ripe old age by ignoring who or what might be coming up the hill at me. It pays to keep track of the current crop of heros and bravos who are building their reputations."

"I see."

"What's he doing chumming around with a Prince? Last thing I heard he was a mercenary."

"That was before the war," Ibble explained. "We aligned ourselves with the Prince to help throw down Kalaran."

"War? Kalaran?" Schmirnov shook his head. "It never ends, does it? I swear sometimes I think you humans have as much trouble living in peace with each other as you do living with my kind."

"If you'd like me to explain," the dwarf said, "I'm sure you'll agree our cause was just. Kalaran truly *was* a figure of evil."

"Of course." The reptile smiled. "He lost, didn't he?"

"I don't understand."

"The losing side is always wrong," Schmirnov said. "Especially since it's the winners who have the privilege of defining good and evil."

"But Kalaran . . ."

"Spare me." The dragon sighed. "Just go and fetch Spotty and we'll see what he has to say."

"At once, Lord Dragon."

The dwarf turned to go, then hesitated.

"Um . . . Lord Dragon?"

"Now what is it?"

"If I might suggest . . . in the interest of keeping this a peaceful meeting . . . it might be best if you refrained from calling him 'Spotty.' The nickname is due to the fact that he breaks out in pale blotches whenever danger threatens. It's a trait that has saved us on numerous occasions, but he's more than a little self-conscious about it."

"A sensitive human," the dragon muttered. "What will they think of next?"

"Excuse me?"

"Never mind. Just fetch him . . . and I'll try to remember your suggestion."

Despite his suspicions, Schmirnov studied the figure the dwarf led back into his cavern with genuine curiosity. It was rare that he had an opportunity to study a human, particularly a warrior, at leisure. Traditionally, his encounters with them were brief, and what was left could not be examined without extensive reassembling.

Stiller was an impressive specimen . . . medium height, stocky build with massive arms and legs, all topped by a shaggy head of bronze-red hair. Fierce blue eyes met the dragon's levelly and without fear, though, like his companion, the man's belt and harness were notably lacking in weapons.

Schmirnov observed that, despite reassurances given, Stiller's skin was, indeed, covered with the pale blotches of danger warning that gave the man his nickname.

Good. Maybe it would encourage Stiller to mind his manners during the interview.

Then, too, it raised an interesting point. Did the blotches forewarn actual danger, or only danger the man perceived? If the latter were the case, it didn't seem the trait would be particularly helpful. If the former, then there was something about this meeting which could prove dangerous to the man despite the guarantees of safety. The dragon resolved anew to be on his guard.

"Are you Schmirnov?" the man demanded.

The reptile regarded him for a long moment, then slowly craned his neck around to sweep the cavern with his gaze.

"Do you see any other dragons around?" he said at last.

"Well . . . no."

"Then it would be safe to assume that I am, indeed, Schmirnov, wouldn't you say? Really, Stiller, if you're going to indulge in redundant questions, this meeting could last through a change of seasons."

The man started visibly at the mention of his name.

"I told you so." Ibble murmured to him as an aside, which earned him a sharp elbow in the ribs.

"You know me?"

"Another redundant question." The Dragon sighed. "As I told your little friend there, I know *of* you. You have a fairly sizable reputation . . . mostly from your habit of reducing the population, both human and non. You're supposed to be quite good at it . . . if you take pride in that sort of thing."

Stiller's blotches paled as the skin beneath them flushed.

"I take pride in the fact that I have never drawn blood from anyone or anything that did not first mean harm to others," he said angrily. "Unlike *some* here I could name."

"*Stiller!*" the dwarf hissed in warning, but the damage was already done.

"And what's *that* supposed to mean?" Schmirnov growled.

"Warrior I may be," Gulick announced, shaking off Ibble's hand on his arm. "But I earned my reputation fighting against other arms bearers ... aye, and a few creatures as well. It is not my way, however, to lay waste to entire villages or settlements, slaying fighter and noncombatant indiscriminately as is the habit of you and your kin. If it were, then I would not have the nerve to level accusations at those who set aside their normal prejudice to visit me in peace."

The dragon regarded him levelly for a moment.

"I can see," he said at last, "that if we are to have a civilized conversation, there will first have to be some air clearing between us. Consider this, warrior."

Schmirnov paused slightly to organize his thoughts.

"If you had a home, one with good hunting and clean water, where you had dwelt contentedly most of your life, and that home was invaded by a new species which completely disrupted the lifestyle to which you had become accustomed, how would you react?"

"It would depend on the nature of the invader," Stiller said stiffly.

"Fair enough." The dragon nodded. "For the moment, envision them as a colony of wasps. Few at first, and easily ignored. They nest, however, and begin to multiply at an alarming rate. What's worse, in their new numbers, they begin to drive out the game which is your normal livelihood. In fact, you often find yourself in direct competition with them for the same food sources. What would be your course of action?"

"I'd try to drive them out or eliminate them," the man said, averting his eyes with the admission.

"Kill as many as you can, and burn their colonies." Schmirnov smiled. "Probably killing both fighter wasps and noncombatant workers indiscriminately in the process. Right?"

Neither of his visitors replied.

"Now then, to continue our scenario," the dragon said,

"let us assume that, in your own mistaken feeling of superiority, you have waited too long. There are too many of the invaders to deal with effectively. Not only that, you find that, once aroused, they are capable of harming you ... even killing you if skillful enough or in great enough numbers. With that knowledge comes the realization that you have lost. You and all your kind will be replaced by this new species ... one you might have squashed if you had taken it seriously enough when it first appeared."

Schmirnov's voice changed, becoming tinged in bitterness as memories played their scenes once more on the stage of his mind.

"All you can do then is retreat. Find some out-of-the-way place so desolate that no one will contest you for it and wait for the end as gracefully as you can. The trouble is that these 'wasps' have memories. Memories and emotions. They recall the damage you have wreaked in the past, and begin to hunt you and the scattered remains of your kind ... whether for vengeance or to eliminate a threat which no longer truly exists."

He shook his great head briefly.

"Some of my kind went mad from the pressure, launching fierce but hopeless attacks until they met the legend-inspiring deaths they sought. Others remain in hiding, and some, such as myself, have even reached a tenuous truce with small groups of humans. While I am genuinely grateful for the mutual tolerance, you'll forgive me if my view of you humans remains less than admiring."

The dragon lapsed into silence, which his visitors emulated, unable to think of anything to say.

Finally, Schmirnov heaved a great sigh and lowered his head in a slow bow.

"I fear, upon reflection, I owe you an apology. Both of you. You have come to me openly requesting a peaceful meeting, and, after granting you safe passage, I have received you with thinly veiled insults and threats. If nothing else, this violates the very spirit of hospitality, and I must beg your forgiveness. My only excuse is ill temper caused by prolonged isolation. if anything, I should welcome company, not drive it away."

Gulick returned the bow.

"Your apology is accepted, but unnecessary, Lord Dragon," he said. "Having now heard your side of the human-dragon conflict, I'll confess that I am shamed by some of the things I have done or said in the past. However our meeting goes, you have given me much food for thought in the future. What's more, you have my promise that I will pass it along to others that they might also reflect on this long-standing injustice. As to our reception, I am only grateful that it was as nonviolent as you promised. I fear you would not have been received half as graciously had you chosen to visit us at our own homes."

"That much I can testify to." Schmirnov smiled. "As can my scars. But we've agreed to leave such memories to the past. Tell me now, what brings you to my lair on a mission of peace? It must be important, as I can't imagine it was an easy journey for you."

Stiller snorted.

"Indeed it was not. If you are interested, I could tell you tales of the dangers we braved to stand where we are now."

"Spare me," the dragon said.

"First, we were set upon by . . . Excuse me?"

Stiller paused in his oration as the reptile's words sank in.

"I said 'spare me,'" Schmirnov repeated. "Not to be rude, but I'll wager I've heard it all before. I have yet to hear of a quest, campaign, or simple trip undertaken by a warrior that didn't involve ambushes by bandits, attacks by various ferocious creatures, shortages of food and water, and at last one side trip to deal with a crisis that arose along the way. Did I overlook anything?"

Stiller and Ibble exchanged glances.

"Well . . . no."

"Tell me, has it ever occurred to you that peasants,

peddlers, and merchants traverse these same lands virtu-
ally unarmed without encountering a fraction of the dangers you heroes seem to accept as daily fare?"

Again his visitors looked at each other, each waiting
for the other to answer.

"You might discuss it at leisure once this meeting is
over," the dragon said. "When you do, and if you discover I'm right, I suggest you consider two possible
explanations. First, that the mere presence of a warrior
or armed force will be perceived by whatever armed
force or creature is in residence in the land you're traveling across as an attack, and will therefore provoke a
response. That is, they will launch what they feel is a
counterattack to your attack, which you in turn perceive
as an attack and counter accordingly. What you see as a
necessary defense only confirms their fears that you mean
them harm, and the fight will continue to the death. A
fight, I might add, that was not really necessary in the
first place."

Stiller scowled thoughtfully.

"And the second possible explanation?" Ibble said.

"If your path is constantly barred by fights and chal-
lenges, you might consider your choice of routes."
Schmirnov smiled. "If someone gave you a map or suggested such a dangerous path, they might actually be
trying to engineer your deaths in the guise of assisting
you. If, on the other hand, the route is of your own
choosing, then there's a chance that you're letting your
warrior's pride outweigh your common sense. That is,
you try to bull your way through obstacles and dangers
on the strength of your sword arm that others would
simply walk around."

Stiller cleared his throat.

"Again, Lord Dragon, you give us food for thought.
Might I point out, however, that it was you who raised
the subject of our journey?"

"I did?"

"Yes. You said that you supposed it had not been an

easy journey for us, which I took as an invitation to tell you of our travels."

"Ah! I see the difficulty now. Actually, my reference to your doubtless hard trip was meant to imply that your mission would have to be important, or you wouldn't have undertaken it."

"Oh."

"Which brings us back to our original point. To wit, what mission is it that brings you to my cavern?"

Stiller blinked several times, then shook his head as if to clear it.

"My mission. Quite right," he said, almost to himself. "Simply put, Lord Dragon, I've been sent as a personal emissary from Prince Rango, to request a favor of you."

"That much your comrade here has explained to me," the dragon said patiently. "Tell me, just who is this Prince Rango?"

"He is the rightful ruler of these lands, both by bloodline and by right of conquest. He has recently succeeded in overthrowing the evil tyrant Kalaran, and will ascend the throne as King shortly at a combination marriage and coronation."

"This Kalaran you keep mentioning," Schmirnov said, "is he dead?"

"Why do you ask?"

"Before I start granting favors to any human or group of humans, it's nice to know who else might be popping up who might take offense at my taking sides."

"Kalaran is dead," Stiller said firmly. "I myself was present at the time of his demise."

"Why do I get the feeling it was not an easy death?" the dragon said wryly.

"Indeed it was not," the warrior confirmed. "Though evil, Kalaran was as powerful a foe as any I've faced or heard of. He had his followers, of course, and was no stranger to the Dark Arts. Much of our preparation for our assault involved locating and retrieving several powerful relics to assist us in our attack. As a warrior, I generally disdain the use of magick, but I must admit

that in that final confrontation I was glad we had taken
the time to gather them. No lesser items than the scroll
of Gwykander, the amulet called Anachron, and the ring
Sombrisio had to be employed before Kalaran was weakened enough to be downed by a sword stroke. Without
them, I fear our plans would have fallen to ruin."

"Impressive," Schmirnov said. "I'm not sure I understand, however. If this Kalaran has already been disposed
of, then of what assistance can I be?"

"Well, it has to do with an artifact," Stiller said,
uncomfortably.

"An artifact?"

Schmirnov's head soared up as he looked toward the
rear of his cavern where his own treasures were stored.
Determining at a glance they were undisturbed, he
returned his attention to the warrior.

"While I appreciate the originality of asking for one of
my treasures rather than trying to either steal it or kill
me to gain possession, I'll admit to being bewildered by
your request. Nothing in my trove approaches the power
of those items already in your possession. Even if I did
have something that might help, I thought you said the
battle was already over."

"You misunderstand, Lord Dragon," Stiller said hastily.
"We're not seeking any of your treasure. Quite the contrary. What we would ask is to *add* one of our items to
your undoubtedly valuable collection."

"Now, why would you want to do that?" the dragon
said suspiciously.

"Well . . . so that you could guard it for us."

"You're trying to say that you think an artifact would
be safer here in my cavern than in the kingdom capital
surrounded by legions of royal guards?" Schmirnov's
voice was tinged with incredulity. "Forgive me, but that
seems to go against everything I've heard or learned of
the arrogance of humans . . . unless there's something
you're omitting from your tale."

Stiller heaved a deep sigh.

"The truth is, Lord Dragon," he said, "we've been told

that we *have* to scatter the artifacts again. Because of that, my old comrades and I have been assigned to find new hiding places for each of them. *That* is what has brought me to you this day."

"Perhaps the years are dulling my mind after all," the dragon said, "but I still don't understand. Could you explain further why it is that you have to scatter these items?"

"Strange things have been happening in these lands since the artifacts of power have been gathered together," Stiller said darkly. "Fish and other creatures rain from the heavens when there are no clouds. Unearthly sounds ... some call it music .. issue forth from thin air with no apparent source. Flying machines have appeared and disappeared in the sky over the capital. Most frightening, ungodly creatures unknown to science or legend have begun to appear at various places around the land. Perhaps you have observed some of these phenomena yourself?"

"Not really," Schmirnov said. "But then again, I haven't been watching very closely. Usually, when something strange or unexplainable occurs, I attribute it to the latest shenanigans of your kind, and do my best to ignore it."

"Well, they are happening nonetheless," Stiller said. "The learned men of the capital have reached the conclusion that the combined power of the artifacts we gathered has somehow created a rift in the fabric between our reality and others. What's more, they predict that it will grow worse. The only solution they can suggest is that the artifacts be scattered once more. This is the task Prince Rango has assigned to my comrades and I while he makes his preparations for ascending the throne ... the task that has brought me to you today."

He drew himself up and bowed slightly.

"Hmmm. Very interesting," the dragon said thoughtfully. "And what's the rest of it?"

"The rest of it?" The warrior frowned. "I don't understand."

"There must be more," Schmirnov insisted. "There are still questions unanswered by your tale. For example, why is the Prince scattering *all* of the artifacts? If a problem is created when they are all gathered together, then why doesn't he simply order that *one* be removed for hiding? At the very least, I think he would scatter all *but* one, keeping the most powerful close at hand to ensure his continued rule."

His visitors looked at each other and shrugged.

"I really don't know," Stiller said. "The Prince gave me my orders, and I'm following them."

"Commendable loyalty," the dragon said. "But that raises another point. Couldn't he have delegated this task to others? Why is it necessary to send forth those who are closest to him and know him best at a time when it would be most reasonable to have them at his side? After helping him to win a throne, it seems a strange reward to send you forth into danger once more rather than granting you rest and honors."

"I wondered about that myself," the dwarf growled.

"Shut up, Ibble," Stiller shot back. "As to your question, Lord Dragon, I can only assume that the Prince deemed our mission to be of such importance that it could only be trusted to his most proven friends and followers. I take my honor from being included in that number."

"Hmm. If you say so," Schmirnov said doubtfully. "Oh, well, if that's all you know, then there's little point in pressing you for more details. It doesn't really concern me, anyway. All that really matters is whether or not I will accept this artifact into my keeping."

"And what is your answer to that question, Lord Dragon?" Stiller pressed.

"I suppose it all depends," the dragon said. "What's in it for me?"

"I beg your pardon?"

"Come, now, Stiller. We're all supposed to be intelligent creatures here. You want something from me, which is to say a favor. What are you offering me in return?"

"Well . . ." the warrior said, looking at Ibble for support and receiving only another shrug in return, "I hadn't really been thinking in terms of payment. I suppose if we can agree on a figure, I can get clearance from the Prince to guarantee it."

"Of course, that would take time." Schmirnov sighed.

"Not really," Stiller said. "We have with us a wizard who specializes in communication spells. Since he's been contacting the Prince's wizard on a regular basis to report our progress, I imagine we would have no difficulty obtaining approval on a payment."

"In all honesty, I hadn't been thinking in terms of payment," the dragon said. "Though I'll admit this new speedy method of communications intrigues me."

"But you said . . ."

"I inquired what you might be willing to offer me in return. I have sufficient treasure on hand already. It's actually rather easy to accumulate, since I have no place to spend it."

Schmirnov gestured negligently toward the back of his cavern with his tail.

"Well, if you aren't interested in gold or jewels, what would you like in exchange for the favor?" Stiller said, tearing his eyes away from the cavern's depths with some difficulty.

"I really hadn't given it much thought, beyond the basic instinct of not giving something for nothing. Remember, this is new to me, though you may have been thinking it for some time. Let me see . . ."

The great reptile stared thoughtfully at the cavern's ceiling for several moments.

"What I could really use," he said, almost to himself, "is something to relieve boredom."

"What was that again?"

"Hmmm? Oh. Excuse me. I was thinking out loud. You see, the biggest problem with my current existence is that it's incredibly boring. Don't tell the villagers, but there are times when I've actually contemplated breaking my truce with them, just to have something to do."

"You know, that's something *we* might give some thought to, Stiller," Ibble said. "Once this mission is over and the kingdom is at peace, things could get uncommonly dull for us as well. For years, all we've done is travel and fight."

"There's an interesting question, warrior," the dragon said. "What do humans do to wile away inactive time?"

"Different people do different things." Stiller shrugged. "Some garden, which I never cared for. Others take up hobbies."

"And what do *you* do?"

"Me? Well, whenever I get the opportunity, I like to play cards .. poker, specifically."

"Poker?" Schmirnov said. "And what, pray tell, is poker?"

"*Stiller!*" The dwarf's voice had a new note of warning in it.

"Relax, Ibble," the warrior said, waving a hand at his comrade. "I'm just answering the Lord Dragon's questions. Poker is a card game . . . one of many, actually. You might say it's a time-consuming way to redistribute wealth through the study of mathematical probability."

"It's what?" The dragon frowned.

"It's gambling," Ibble said in a flat voice. "Two or more players are each dealt several cards, and they bet on who is holding the highest-ranked combination."

"That's oversimplifying it a bit." Stiller scowled.

"And your explanation was unnecessarily obtuse." The dwarf grimaced back.

"That sounds fascinating," Schmirnov said. "Could you teach me?"

"I would be honored to teach you the basics, Lord Dragon," the warrior said. "It takes years of practice to master the game, however. Then, too, we *would* have to include wagering as part of the lesson. Much of the subtlety of the game is involved in the betting and bluffing."

"*Stiller!!*"

"Will you relax, Ibble?" Stiller hissed. "Remember, this isn't *my* idea. It's a request of the Lord Dragon. If he wishes to make this a condition for his assistance, who am I to deny it? I *did* promise the Prince that I would let no danger sway me from completing the mission."

"Danger?" the dragon said. "Excuse me, but what danger could be involved in such a lesson?"

"Forgive me, Lord Dragon," the dwarf said, "but the danger I fear would be to Stiller here, and not you. You see, when we refer to betting . . . wagering gold or jewels on the turn of a card . . . such exchanges are permanent. That is to say, the wealth is not returned to the loser after the game is over. Often, players become upset after having lost large portions of their wealth, and attack the winners out of frustration. As Stiller is extremely skillful at this particular game, he has come under attack more often than I would care to remember from ill-tempered opponents. Consequently, when I see him about to become embroiled in a game with someone as obviously formidable as yourself, especially one who, like yourself, professes little if any knowledge of the game, I find myself growing more than a little anxious."

"You needn't fear, little man," Schmirnov said. "I have sufficient treasure that I will not become angry over giving up a portion of it in exchange for knowledge."

"Excellent," Stiller said, rubbing his hands together.

"That is, of course, unless I find the mathematical probabilities you mentioned are being artificially tampered with. That would be tantamount to stealing from me, which is something I will not tolerate."

"Oh." The warrior became a bit more subdued.

"Actually, there is only one thing which troubles me in this potential arrangement," the dragon said. "You mentioned that the game requires two or more players. While the game sounds fascinating, and the lessons enjoyable, what will I do with the knowledge once you depart?"

"I could make it part of the agreement that I would return occasionally . . . say two or three times a year . . . and we could continue the game."

Stiller only let his eyes wander toward the back of the cavern once as he made this selfless offer.

"That would be splendid!" Schmirnov exclaimed. "I believe we have a bargain. Go and fetch your little trinket."

A nod from Stiller sent Ibble scrambling out of the cavern.

"I must say, Lord Dragon," the warrior said as they waited, "this method of dealing with each other has much to recommend it over the way I used to approach your kind."

"As a member of the species all but wiped out by previous encounters with your kind, I can only concur," the dragon said. "There is a lot to be said for peaceful coexistence."

"Along with the gratitude of Prince Rango, I would like to extend my personal thanks for this favor," Stiller said. "I will rest much easier knowing the artifact is guarded by one who is not only fierce, but intelligent as well."

"You're too kind," Schmirnov responded. "By the way, you never got around to saying which of the artifacts you were intrusting to my care. I hope it isn't Sombrisio. That ring can be a real—"

He broke off suddenly as a glow lit up the cavern.

Ibble had reappeared, bearing with him a sword which radiated a soft but definite light.

"No need to worry about Sombrisio," Stiller said. "Jancy has the problem of dealing with—"

"That's Mothganger!!"

The dragon's voice rang with horror and accusation.

"Well . . . yes," the warrior said, taken a bit aback by his host's reaction.

"You didn't say anything about Mothganger," Schmirnov hissed. "You spoke only of the scroll of Gwykander, the amulet Anachron, and the ring Sombrisio."

"Didn't I?" Stiller frowned. "I know I said that Kalaran was finally felled by a sword stroke. I may have neglected to mention that the sword was Mothganger. I assure you, no deception was intended on my part."

"I'm sorry. The deal's off," the dragon said stiffly.

"Off?" the warrior cried. "But why? It was an innocent mistake on my part. I mean, an artifact is an artifact. Isn't it?"

"Are you mad, Stiller Gulick" the reptile said, "or simply stupid? Under no conditions will I allow that sword anywhere near me."

"But—"

"That weapon is one of the few items known to your kind that can actually do me great damage. Why, I could be killed by a single blow from that accursed sword. You can't really expect me to keep the potential implement of my own doom in my cavern, can you? I thought we had agreed that we were both intelligent."

"But that's specifically why I thought of you for Mothganger's guardian," Stiller said, his voice edged with desperation. "If the sword were in your possession, then no one else could find it and bring it to use against you. Keeping Mothganger out of evil hands is a common goal between us."

"Hmm. An interesting point," Schmirnov said, mollified slightly. "Still, I couldn't relax, much less rest, with such a deadly threat residing in my cavern. I'm sorry, but it will have to go."

"Where would it be safer than right here?" the warrior argued. "If you won't take it, where should I go with it?"

"I really don't care," the dragon said. "Why not take it back to wherever it was you found it in the first place?"

"We can't. It's not a safe hiding place anymore."

"Why not? As I recall, Mothganger was supposed to be guarded by a rather ferocious ogre. What happened to him?"

"He . . . umm . . . we killed him," Stiller admitted uncomfortably.

"Really?" Schmirnov said. "Pity. Still, no great loss there. From what I heard, he was truly uncivilized."

"Do you have any suggestions at all as to where we could hide it?"

"Not a one," the great reptile said, shaking his head. "It's as I said earlier, you and your kind have been extremely efficient at eliminating creatures you felt were dangerous or threatening. Ironic, isn't it? After devoting so much time and energy killing off creatures, you're now unable to find one when you really need one."

"Yeah. Ironic." Stiller growled. "Forgive me if my appreciation is less than enthusiastic, but I'm the one who's stuck with the sword in the meantime."

"Too bad you don't have one of the other artifacts instead." Schmirnov observed. "I wouldn't mind watching over the scroll or the amulet. I don't suppose there's any chance you could trade missions with one of the other comrades you mentioned?"

"I doubt it," the warrior said. "We were all riding in different directions . . . the idea *was* to separate the artifacts, you'll recall. I fear by the time I caught up with one of the others, they'd have already disposed of theirs."

"Well, sorry I can't help you . . . and I mean that sincerely," the dragon said. "I was really looking forward to learning about poker. I don't suppose you'd be willing to teach me anyway?"

"We'll have to see," Stiller said, remembering briefly the dragon's treasure trove. "Perhaps sometime in the future. At the moment, I have a mission to complete."

"Good luck with that," Schmirnov said. "If no solution presents itself, remember what I said before. If the others are successful, there should be no trouble keeping *one* of the artifacts at the capital."

The two friends were silent as they trudged down the slope from the mouth of Schmirnov's cavern.

"Well, *that* got us nowhere," Stiller said at last, his voice heavy with weariness.

"I really thought we were going to pull it off that time." Ibble sighed. "I mean, he had agreed and everything. Right up until he realized it was Mothganger we were asking him to guard."

"It's the end of the battle that counts," the warrior reminded him. "However close it was during the skirmishes, the final outcome is that he said 'no'."

"Let's rest here a moment while we consider our next move," the dwarf suggested, drawing to a halt.

"Tired?" Stiller said, squatting down on his heels as was his habit when resting. "You must be getting old, Ibble. I can recall when an easy climb like this was nothing to you."

"It isn't that," Ibble said, waving off his friend's attempt at humor. "I'm just in no hurry to report our latest failure to the Prince's wizard. At the very least, it would be nice if we had our next destination in mind *before* passing the word to the Prince. It might sound a bit less hopeless and beaten if we had a positive plan to suggest at the same time as we admitted the negative results of our latest scheme."

Stiller grimaced, his earlier tight smile replaced by wrinkles of concern.

"I only hope that wizard is adding his own version of disappointment and scorn when he tells us of the Prince's reactions. I'd hate to think that Rango is really that upset with us, even allowing for our unbroken string of failures."

"Remember, it's *Prince* Rango now," Ibble said pointedly. "It wouldn't be the first time that a gold hat changed the personality of the one wearing it."

"You might be right," Stiller said. "He certainly hasn't been himself lately. I'm just hoping it's the pressure of his pending marriage and coronation that's doing it, and that he'll settle down again once all that is over."

"We can always hope." The dwarf shrugged. "In the meantime, what are we going to do with Mothganger?"

"I was hoping you'd have some ideas." The warrior sighed. "The dragon Schmirnov was my last card. I haven't even *heard* of another creature fierce enough to guard such a prize."

"If only you hadn't killed that manticore," Ibble said.

"You mean the ogre, don't you?"

"No, I mean the manticore," the dwarf insisted. "Remember, the one you chopped down *before* we could talk to it?"

"Hey. It surprised me. Okay?" Stiller said defensively, "I expected to find it on top of the hill and approach it slowly. When it burst out of the bushes right on top of us, I just swung out of reflex."

"I was there. Remember?" Ibble said. "That's most of why I thought it would be best if I made the first approach with Schmirnov."

"I've already apologized a hundred times for that. You want to hear it again? Okay. I'm sorry. I shouldn't have killed the manticore. There. Does that make things any better for us?"

"All I meant was, it left us with one less potential guardian for the sword . . . and we didn't have that big a list to start with."

"I know," the warrior said dejectedly. "Let's see, the original ogre guardian and the manticore are both dead, the merpeople refused the job, as did the dragon. Where does that leave us?"

"Sitting on a hillside talking to ourselves." Ibble sighed. "I still think we could just bury it or drop it down a ravine or something."

Stiller shook his head.

"We've been over that before," he said stubbornly. "The only way that would work is if we killed everyone in our party afterward . . . including the Prince's pet wizard and ourselves. Otherwise, someone's bound to talk and the word would get out that there was a powerful artifact just lying around waiting to be picked up. No, we need a guardian, a fierce one. Something nasty enough that even if someone finds out where Mothganger is hidden, they'll think twice about trying to fetch it."

"I don't suppose you'd consider just taking it back to the capital," the dwarf said. "As the dragon pointed out, there shouldn't be any danger if it's the only artifact there."

"That's assuming the others are successful," Stiller pointed out. "Besides, I don't like the idea of being the only one of the old fellowship that couldn't carry out my assignment."

"Then we're stuck," Ibble said, picking up a rock and throwing it at a bush. "I guess we could try talking to the merpeople again."

"They seemed pretty adamant in their refusal," the warrior said. "Besides, I'm not sure that it would do a sword any good to be kept under water."

"It's *supposed* to be indestructible," the dwarf observed drily. "That's what makes it so valuable."

"Against wear and breakage, maybe. But it's still steel, and water and steel are old enemies."

As he spoke, Stiller drew the sword and studied its glowing blade.

"It looks ordinary enough, except for that glow," he said. "I wonder if that has anything to do with its indestructible nature."

"Naw. That's just a light spell." Ibble waved.

"Excuse me?"

"The glow. It's just an elven light spell," the dwarf said. "They're fairly easy to cast, and last a couple centuries. Whoever made the sword probably tossed it in as a bonus."

"You never said anything about that before."

"You never asked before. I assumed you already knew about it."

"I never heard of such a thing. How do you know about it?"

"There's an elven sword maker in the village where I grew up. He would add a light spell to anything if you asked him."

"How far away is your village?"

"A couple day's ride from here. If we have the time when we're done with this mission, maybe we could stop there and I'll introduce you to him."

"Let's go there now." Stiller said, rising to his feet.

"Now?"

"Yes. I think I have an idea."

The elven weaponsmith looked disdainfully at his two visitors.

"Young man," he said, "if it were not for the fact that little Ibble here says you're his friend and a hero, I'd say that you were either a fool or insane."

"I assure you, sir, I'm neither," Stiller said calmly.

"Well, it certainly couldn't be told from your request. Duplicate Mothganger?"

He gestured at the glowing sword they had placed on his workbench.

"If I could do that, I wouldn't be running my shop out of a tiny village like this. Half the spells that went into the making of this sword have been lost in the march of time, and the ones that are still remembered would require years just to assemble the ingredients. You're wasting your time ... and mine!"

"Please, Anken," Ibble said. "Hear us out."

"You misunderstand me, sir," the warrior said. "I'm not asking if you can produce a second Mothganger. As you say, that is well beyond the skills and knowledge of any weapons maker known today. What I require is a sword that *looks* like Mothganger. An ordinary weapon with a light spell cast on its blade."

Anken looked back and forth at the two comrades for a moment.

"A bogus Mothganger," he said at last. "I never heard of such a thing. You two wouldn't be thinking of trying to sell the phony as the real thing, would you? Or maybe give the fake to the rightful owner, while keeping the real one for yourselves?"

"I cannot disclose the reason for our request," Stiller said stiffly. "But I give you my word that our mission and need are honorable and aboveboard."

"You've known me all my life, Anken," the dwarf put

in. "Have you ever known me to be anything other than honest?"

"That's true," the elf said thoughtfully. "The fact is, you were always a bit dull that way."

"So can you do it?" Stiller urged. "More importantly, *will* you do it?"

In answer, Anken picked up Mothganger and began studying it closely.

"Really isn't much to look at, is it?" he said, almost to himself. "Have a seat, boys. I think I've got a couple old swords in storage that will give us just the parts we need. Might have to rework the pommel, but that shouldn't take long."

"Lord Dragon? Are you here? It's Stiller Gulick and Ibble."

The great reptile turned his head toward the source of the sound.

"Stiller?" he said. "Are you back so soon? Does this mean you're ready to start my poker lessons?"

"As a matter of fact, yes," the warrior said. "But first, I have a surprise for you."

He gestured to the dwarf, who reached into the gunnysack he was carrying and withdrew a sword with a glowing blade.

"*Stiller.*" Schmirnov's voice was heavy with warning and menace. "I thought I already made my feelings on the subject of that sword *very* clear."

Stiller seemed to ignore him completely.

"Set it there, Ibble," he said, pointing to a spot a mere three paces from the cavern's entrance.

"*STILLER!*"

"Now, then, Lord Dragon," Stiller said calmly. "As I understand it, your concern is that some misguided or overconfident person will take that weapon and attempt to use it on you. Is that correct?"

"I told you before, I won't have Mothganger in my cavern. It's too dangerous."

"But Schmirnov, if someone tried to use that sword

against you, they would be in for a very rude surprise. You see, that isn't Mothganger."

"Nonsense," the dragon growled. "I'd know that accursed sword anywhere."

"That's what any interloper would think," the warrior agreed. "But they would be wrong."

He nodded again at Ibble, who withdrew a second glowing sword from the gunnysack.

"*This* is the real Mothganger," Stiller announced triumphantly. "It would be hidden safely in this sack in the depths of your cavern. The one by the door is a forgery ... powerless except for a harmless light spell. Anyone who attempted to use *that* weapon against you would be committing suicide."

Schmirnov craned his neck forward, swaying his head first one way, then the other as he examined the two weapons.

"Very clever," he said at last. "Of course, your kind always excelled at treachery. I'll admit I can't tell the two swords apart. Are you sure the one by the door is the forgery?"

The dragon was so busy with his inspection, he missed the startled glance the two comrades exchanged.

"Trust me," Stiller said smoothly, signaling Ibble to return the second sword to the sack. "So, with this added refinement, do we have a deal?"

"Well," the dragon said, "you are very persuasive and I would very much like to learn poker, but I don't feel precisely safe about having the sword laying around in my hoard. Even stashed in a gunnysack, it is still Mothganger. I am not immune to the irony of being slain by a sword the wielder believes is second-rate."

Stiller and Ibble exchanged despairing glances. Then the dwarf perked up.

"Our visited to Anken reminded me that the elves are not the only masters of magic." He let his voice drop mysteriously. "Dwarves know how to make stone!"

"That's really nice, Ibble," Stiller said, "but what does

that have to do with our finding a guardian for Mothganger?"

Ibble puffed up happily. "We imbed both swords in stone. Mothganger gets buried in a slab—I can wrap it beforehand so that it won't get gritty—and the false Mothganger gets imbedded partway in a showy pedestal."

Stiller picked up the thread of his comrade's thought. "Then you set the false Mothganger up as sort of a decoration and lure. The real Mothganger gets stowed, one more block of stone in a stony cave! That's beautiful, Ibble!"

"Thank you," the dwarf said modestly.

The dragon's voice rumbled with appreciation. "What do you need to make your magic rock?"

"Oh, just some sand, gravel, lime, and clay," the dwarf said. "The ingredients are common. The real magic is in the combination. I'll need some planks to make the form into which I'll pour the stone."

"Oh, can you make it in any form you choose?" Schmirnov asked.

"Pretty much," Ibble said proudly, hastening to add, "but making an elaborate form takes longer."

"I didn't want anything elaborate. I was just thinking that a slab of stone about this high"—he gestured with a taloned foot—"would make a perfect card table."

"I can do it," Ibble promised.

"Now," Stiller said, hiding his eagerness, "with this new added refinement, do we have a deal?"

"We do indeed," Schmirnov said. "Now we can start our poker lessons."

"Excellent!" the warrior said, rubbing his hands together. "I thought we'd start with five card draw."

"Actually, I'd prefer it if you started with stud instead."

"Excuse me?" Stiller blinked.

"I think stud would be easier for me to learn because the cards are quite small for me, and hole cards would be easier to manipulate than an entire handful of cards. Five or seven would be satisfactory."

The warrior's eyes narrowed with suspicion.

"I thought you said you didn't know how to play poker."

"Just because I don't know how to play doesn't mean I never *heard* of the game," Schmirnov explained.

"Hmmm," Stiller said thoughtfully.

"Trust me." The dragon smiled.

"It was only by the strangest sequence of coincidence that it came into my possession," Anken was saying. "But I won't bore you with that. All that's important is that it goes to a proper warrior who will put it to good use while keeping its location a secret."

His customer continued to study the glowing blade with a mixture of awe and skepticism.

"So this is really the legendary Mothganger," he said. "It's actually very ordinary looking, isn't it? You're sure there's no mistake?"

"Trust me." Anken smiled.

The elf waited for the warrior's first offer, trying to decide how hard he should haggle. He had three more copies he could sell to others, but that shouldn't affect the price of this one.

Prelude the Fourth

"We can finish the fittings when the ladies in question return from . . ." The seamstress paused. "Where did you say they were?"

"Jancy has gone into the Desolation of Thaumidor and Domino is in the farther reaches of the Lake District," Princess Rissa answered, twirling so she could see herself in her wedding gown.

Pearls glistened on the bodice, lace trimmed the plunging neckline and the floor-sweeping hem. The detachable train was trimmed with even more lace and embroidered with the crest of Regaudia, the Royal House of which she was the last survivor.

"How is work coming on the veil?" she asked anxiously.

"Well, Your Highness," the seamstress replied with a soothing smile. "Once the Prince supplied the measure of the crown with which it will need to fit, work went along swimmingly."

"Have you seen the crown?" Rissa asked curiously.

"No." A blush actually lit the seamstress's thin face. "The Prince explained that it was to be a surprise for you and that no one but the smiths and jewelers working on it were to see it before the wedding day. He said it is his gift to you."

"Have you thought about what you will give him, ducky?" Daisy asked. "And about gifts for the members of the wedding party?"

Princess Rissa frowned. "I have, but I am rather stumped. They are all so different. Finding one gift that would suit each of them would be difficult—that is, if we omit weaponry, which doesn't seem appropriate."

"No, ducky, it doesn't," Daisy said severely.

"Something with the new royal emblem would be nice," the seamstress suggested, "perhaps a crystal dish or a picture frame."

Rissa shook her head. "The emblem is a good idea, but we haven't finished designing it. In any case, I can't see what Domino or Jancy or Stiller or Gar would do with a crystal dish."

Fleetingly, she envisioned Domino watering her horse from the hypothetical piece of cut crystal or Gar using it to design some novel but poetic fashion of slaying an enemy.

"Clothing is certainly out," the seamstress said hastily. "How about a rare wine?"

"Most of the royal cellar has been transformed into this brown fizzy goo that only Rango can stand," Rissa said, sparing a wan smile at the memory of her fiancé. "We are importing wine by the barrel for the wedding feast, but I don't count on it staying wine."

"Do the members of your wedding party have any hobbies?" the seamstress asked.

"Domino used to raise horses, but I'm not certain if she still does. Spotty—I mean Stiller—gambles." She frowned. "I never did learn if Jancy had any hobbies. She's a warrior by training and most of what we did was fight."

"And this Gar?" the seamstress said hesitantly. "Does he have any hobbies?"

Princess Rissa nodded. "He kills people. Elegantly."

"Perhaps weapons would be best." Daisy sighed.

"Something like a ceremonial dagger with a place for the new royal crest to be mounted once you have one."

"I'll speak to Rango," Rissa said, although that was the last thing she really wanted to do. "Certainly he will know a smith who can do the work quickly."

"You should change first, ducky," Daisy admonished. "He shouldn't see the gown until the wedding day!"

In his council chamber, the impending bridegroom was in conference with Lemml Touday. He frowned as the priest finished his report.

"And so, Your Highness, I have diverted discussion from the skull repeatedly. Now that the Temple is in festive upheaval with plans for the wedding and coronation the question should be moot until afterwards."

"Afterwards?" The Prince raised his elegant eyebrows. "Afterwards everything will be happy. The artifacts will be returned, the magical phenomena will cease, and we will settle down to an era of peace and justice."

Lemml frowned. "I sincerely hope so, Your Highness. However, I have been researching the history of prognosticatory devices like the skull and they are rarely wrong. Their portents have been misunderstood and their warnings ignored, but if they consistently warn of impending Evil, then that Evil is impending."

"I see," the Prince said, sipping his brown, frothy drink with urbane relish, "and you think that I am being overly casual in regard to these portents."

Lemml took a deep breath. "In a word, sire, yes."

He reached into the sleeve of his robe and removed the small pouch he had received from the Prince on his last visit. It jingled, slightly fuller even than before.

"I have meditated at length," he said, "and have decided to return some of your donations to my favorite charity. I will not speak of anything that has passed between us, but I am a priest and I find that I cannot forget my duty."

The Prince studied Lemml, then his gaze came to rest

on the map on the wall. He rose, studied the position of some of his pins, and then returned to his seat.

"Lemml, on that map I have been tracing the progress of several things. The blue pins mark the last known positions of my questing heroes."

Lemml turned so that he could look. Behind him, he heard the Prince take the cap off one of the bottles and refresh their drinks.

"The red pins mark bandit incursions and monster sightings," the Prince continued, "the green pins mark natural disasters—floods, earthquakes, tornados. The yellow pins mark unnatural disasters."

"There seem to be a good number of those in Caltus," the priest commented, accepting the freshened goblet from the Prince's hand.

"There do, but there are fewer than there were before," the Prince said. "Several of my heroes are on their return journeys and the number of disastrous occurrences—natural and unnatural—has been falling off steadily. To be brief, I have been looking for any evidence of the Evil that you and the skull have been fussing about and have seen no trace."

Lemml sipped his drink. It seemed a trace bitter this time—perhaps the magical sweet stuff had begun to spoil. He rather hoped so. He didn't share the Prince's fondness for the drink and longed for a cool goblet of wine or a mug of beer.

"I am relieved that you are being so careful, sire," he said, "but my position stands. I can no longer serve as your eyes and ears within the Temple. Also, I must warn you that I will be alert to foil those who might be tempted to do so now that I am not."

Rango shook his head sadly. "You misjudge me, priest. Do you not recall that you came with this offer to me, not me to you? You think that because you were corrupt that others will be or that I would seek to ask other priests to serve both Crown and Temple? No, when you came to me, I took it as an omen that the Deities of Light wished for me to have eyes and ears within their holdings. Now that you depart my service, I will end that phase of my rulership."

"I hope so." Lemml rose unsteadily, the strain of the conversation having frayed his nerves. "Then I bid you good day, my lord, and offer my blessings on your impending nuptials."

"Good-bye, Lemml Touday," the Prince said with a curious smile. "I shall not see you again."

Dismissed, the priest made his way down stone corridors that suddenly seemed infinite. His head spun. One stone wall looked much like another. He passed the same tapestry three times without coming to the side door which he had used to come to his meetings with the Prince.

Calling out was out of the question. He did not know what type of reception he would get from the Prince's Guard, some of whom were tough soldiers, hardened by service in the wars against the Fallen Sunbird. Staggering on, he froze as he heard light footsteps tripping down a stone stairway. Then the Princess Rissa came into view.

"Oh, my!" she cried, kneeling beside him. "What has happened to you?"

He tried to reply and vomited on her shoes.

When next he knew himself, he was lying on a pallet in a cool, shadowy room. The Princess knelt beside him, putting aside a basin of cool water and a rag.

"Am I in the dungeon?" he whispered.

"It depends on how you see it," the Princess said. "This is the room reserved for my lady companion. Daisy prefers to go home to her husband, so it is empty. After what I've been through, no one is terribly worried about guarding my virtue."

"Ah," he moaned.

"Now, what happened to you?" Rissa asked. "As best as I can tell, you were poisoned. I administered purgatives then fed you activated charcoal to absorb the residue."

Lemml Touday gaped. "I was in conference with Prince Rango. I . ."

He stopped. This lovely woman was the Prince's fiancé. She had just saved his life and hidden him away, but could he trust her? She studied him and he remembered the steel within that lovely breast.

"Princess, I have been the Prince's spy within the Temple. . . ."

He told her the whole story, not even omitting the monies he had received or those he had kept. He told her his suspicions that Evil was looming and that somehow the Prince had an interest in hiding the rise of that Evil. Princess Rissa listened, a frown furrowing her brow.

"I, too, have worried about the Prince," she confided when Lemml finished his tale. "He has not been acting like himself. He takes pleasure in bookkeeping, accounting, and meetings. When he rides or does sword practice he does it as one would a duty, not a pleasure. I do not know what ails him, but I dread this wedding as no bride should dread her wedding and dread this coronation as no Queen-to-be ever has."

Lemml sipped the cool, clear water she poured for him from an earthenware pitcher. His mouth still tasted like the sour remnants of a dog's dinner, but his head was clearing.

"What should we do, my lady?" he asked.

"You said that the Prince said that some of the heroes are already returning?"

"Yes, he did not specify which, but he seemed pleased."

Rissa nodded "The day for the wedding and coronation will be set soon. You shall become my eyes and ears in the city. There is no way you can return to the Temple, for the Prince clearly meant to have you dead."

Lemml nodded. "I fear leaving the skull untended. What if the Prince sends someone to steal it or damage it? It is a powerful magical device and the last remnant of the Fallen Sunbird."

"A good point," Rissa said. "As soon as darkness falls, you must steal over to the Temple and bring it here. I will rinse the worst of the filth from your robes."

"What if the Prince sees me leaving?" Lemml asked. "He must wonder that my body has not been found."

"A good point," Rissa agreed. "I shall give him a plausible story to cover for the absence of your body—the palace has been fraught with magical phenomena lately—and you shall leave the palace dressed in a gown belonging to a member of Rango's late family. You can change into your own robes when you are safely away."

Lemml began to protest at this slight to his dignity, but his words died unspoken. The Princess was right and her expression brooked no argument. This was a lady who knew her own mind, not a palace-bred royal pet.

For a moment, he almost pitied the Prince, but only for a moment.

Domino's Tale

Domino stretched to her full height, her fingertips brushing the tent's canvas roof, the last soreness easing from her muscles with the motion. Outside, she could hear the early risers in her Company stirring awake in response to the pink glow to the east.

Damn, but it was good to be out on the road again! It was even worth sleeping on the ground. Of course, as General, she was entitled to a cot, but a cot was rather crowded for two. She smiled, her gaze resting fondly on Jord, still asleep in the crumpled heap of blankets and pillows. His dark blond hair tousled around his heart-shaped face made him look more like an angel than ever. For a weak moment, she considered leaving Rafe to rouse the Company while she tended to Jord, but she shook off the impulse with quick effort.

She'd been worried about Jord's safety when he insisted on coming along, not her reputation with the men she commanded. Only after she'd given in to her poet's request had she wondered about the men's response. Fortunately, most of them were still in shock from learning that their Colonel Dominik was a Domino. In this state of affairs, they weren't inclined to quibble any more than if any other commander had picked up a camp follower. Only if she gave Jord any more attention than he was due would there be trouble.

Still, she wondered as she left her sleeping poet to his dreams, how would Jord feel if he knew that the men regarded him largely as the General's floozy?

"Morning, Seth," she greeted the boy tending the fire just downhill from her tent. "All quiet?"

Seth flipped a lock of straw-colored hair out of his eyes in a half salute, his main attention on the potatoes he was easing from the fire coals. In the year since she had found him as a starveling waif in the ruins of a village destroyed by Kalaran's forces he had grown amazingly, but he was still scrawny for a nine-year-old. Scrawny or not, he was ferociously loyal to her and thus an ideal personal servant, especially in the days of her masquerade. Unlike a "properly trained" orderly, he had never insisted on dressing or arming her and she suspected that even had he learned her secret he would have carried that knowledge to the grave.

Of course, there was no need for that anymore, but she kept him on. Seth was trustworthy, loyal, kind, obedient, and all the rest. And besides, Spite tolerated him, which was something right there.

"All's quiet, sir," Seth said, blowing on his fingertips to cool them. "Colonel Rafe sends word that we can move within the hour."

Domino nodded absently. "Very good. Break down my gear at your convenience, Seth."

Taking a potato in one hand and a tin mug of hot, bitter tea in the other, she went to review her troops.

The Company was rather small, a mere two dozen soldiers, a few orderlies, pot scrubbers, grooms, wagon drivers, forty horses, assorted dogs, and Spite. In all, about eighty souls, if dogs and horses had souls (which she was sure they did), and Spite. Most of them were in motion now, an almost festive swirling of the green-and-black uniforms, the dark brown of leather armor, and the occasional flash of metal as a sword was polished or sharpened.

The wave of conversation muted as she passed through, a path appeared as if by magic, but she hardly noticed. This was the way things had been for her from the start, first in the shadow of her illustrious father, Kerman Blaid, and then more and more for her own merits. She paused by each fire, accepting a freshener for her tea, a hunk of bread or a haunch of roasted rabbit. By the time she had reached the camp bottom, she'd greeted just about everyone and finished breakfast.

"Sun-cursed, marsh-mouthed, horse-assed son of a sea hag!" came a familiar bellow from where the Company's mounts were pastured.

"Right on schedule," sniggered Rafe, Domino's rusty-haired second-in-command.

Domino grinned at her friend. "Seems so."

A wiry saddle veteran so windburnt that even his freckles had worn away, Rafe could have claimed his own command. In fact, he'd been promoted to Colonel when Domino had made General. But when he'd caught wind of her going into the field, he'd requested a chance to accompany her "rather than wear out my welcome on some parade ground."

Prince Rango had agreed readily and Domino was glad for Rafe's experience and companionship. Of all her command, he alone had taken her sex change as a matter of course, as if the wonders and weirds of Kalaran's defeat had needed this as their final garnish. She could trust him to run the Company when Rango's business pulled her away.

Together they laughed as the staccato curses of the senior groom, farrier, and horse doctor, Yor Chase, drifted up.

"He'll never learn, will he?" Domino asked.

"The day Chase admits there's a horse he can't befriend will be the day water runs uphill," Rafe agreed. "Doesn't help that Seth can lead Spite around like a lamb on a ribbon—I think the horse does it to spite Yor."

"Maybe." Domino rose. "I'll go save Chase in spite of himself and we can move out within the half hour."

Yor Chase was a big, solid Northman of the same people as Jancy Gaine. Like his countrywoman, he was loyal and dependable—and solidly determined once he made up his mind. The heavy-framed blond had long boasted that there wasn't a horse he couldn't get to like him—and that boast, rather than the more conventional "couldn't ride" had singled him out as someone special. He'd kept his boast, too, until Domino had acquired Spite and though Chase insisted that Spite wasn't a horse, this didn't keep him from trying various ploys to befriend it.

These all ended the same way, with Chase bitten, kicked, or tossed on his ass in the mud. Still, looking just beyond where Chase sat in a watering trough, Domino thought that she could understand why the groom kept trying.

Although as large a horse as any in the Company, grace flowed from Spite like water over polished granite. The stallion's coat was pale green; his long mane and tail were sea-foam white. As if this was not startling enough, his hooves were translucent green, like heavy glass somehow devoid of bubbles. His eyes were the same glinting green, without pupil or iris, though Domino had noted that their inner light seemed to increase with the maliciousness of the horse's mood.

Right now they positively sparkled as the stallion pranced over to Domino, kneeling like a camel so that she could mount. She took the hint, swinging herself on bareback and twisting a handhold in the frothy mane—even for her, Spite would tolerate no tack.

"Good morning, sir," Chase said, awkwardly rising.

"Good morning, Sergeant," she acknowledged, most of her attention for Spite, who was dancing with his shadow. "Are Nightsky and Dove ready?"

"Yes, sir! Of course, sir!" Chase whistled and two horses trotted up, fully equipped. "You'll be taking them with you?"

"I think they'll follow," she replied, "but if you'll hand me the lead ropes we'll make certain."

Chase complied and with Spite strutting as if he were on parade, she set off for her pitch. Seth would have things struck by now and this would save him the trouble of running for the horses as well. Dove was the boy's mount, a silvery gray gelding, just a half hand away from the indignity of being classified a pony—a steady, reliable horse, perfect for a boy who hadn't ridden until a year ago.

Nightsky was another matter. The black Appaloosa mare was nearly as remarkable as Spite and had been Domino's own favorite until Spite had made any other steed unthinkable. Giving Nightsky to Jord was as much a gift to the horse as to the rider, for it took the horse out of the battle lines where too many good horses were crippled or killed.

Swinging around the fringes of the camp, she quickly came to her pitch. Nothing remained but a small heap of gear they would carry on their own persons, and the fire pit which Seth began to smother with sand as soon as he saw her.

As Jord looked up from the scroll of Gwykander, his warm smile could not distract her from the scarlet bruise that marked his right cheekbone. Domino leaped down from Spite before the stallion could come to a full halt.

"Jord! What happened to you?"

The poet smiled ruefully, his free hand moving to cover the bruise, his almost violet eyes round with feigned ignorance.

"This?" his voice was a measured baritone, schooled through hours of reading aloud. "Why, it was there when I woke up. I thought you might know where it came from, honey."

Horrified, Domino felt herself blush.

"You mean I might have . . . last night?"

She searched her memory slightly frantically. Had she gotten too rough again? After years of training to pass as a man, she was just learning how fragile people were.

Jord laughed. "No, Domino, don't worry. I just was clumsy this morning."

Seth jerked his head up suddenly.

"I did it, sir. You told me I could take down the tent and I forgot about him being in there. So I pulled up the stakes . . ."

"And it all came tumbling down," Jord finished. "Seth, I told you not to worry. I should have been awake. The canvas just stung my skin some, Domino. It'll be fine."

Domino leaned to inspect it. "You'll see Sergeant Chase. He has an ointment that'll soothe the bruise to nothing by afternoon."

"I'll be fine, really . . ." Jord began.

"That's an order, soldier," she snapped, looping her hands in Spite's mane and leaping astride.

Jord stared at her, then his easy good temper took the fore.

"Aye-aye, General. Say, isn't Sergeant Chase the horse doctor?"

Domino nodded. "Yes, but he's also a natural healer and his charms and potions have been collected from every corner of the Realm. I wouldn't have you see a lesser doctor than the one who treats our horses."

The silvery trumpeting of the call to assemble saved her from an inappropriate—and awkward—apology. With a nod to Seth and a smile for Jord, she wheeled Spite to take her place in the front center of the Company. Jord either rode with her or dropped back to the supply wagons where he could work on his translations.

Prince Rango had not protested when Jord had petitioned to finish his work, but he had insisted that when the Lakes were reached that Gwykander be sent to its grotto without delay. However, he had never said that they had to proceed with all haste and so, knowing that Jord had a fair amount left to cover, Domino wasn't pushing the Company overquickly.

To Rafe she merely noted that the Lake regions could be dangerous and exhausting the men and horses made no sense. If the Colonel had reason to think her motives were otherwise, he wisely decided not to say. Fate, however, chose not to make a liar of her.

They were slowly climbing a rise so as not to outdistance the wagons toiling behind, when one of the scouts galloped up.

"General Blaid!" he panted. "Fire and destruction! Bandits! A man . . ."

"Report, solider!" she barked.

"Yes, sir." The rider straightened and managed a salute. "We've encountered evidence of bandit activity ahead. A small village has been plundered and torched. We found an old man who'd escaped and he's being brought along more slowly."

"Any evidence that the bandits are still in the immediate area?" she asked.

"No, sir."

"Colonel Rafe, take five soldiers and range for any sign of these bandits. Kerran," she said, turning to the scout, "you go and meet up with the survivor. Unless he's hurt, have him brought directly to me."

"Yes, General."

Not bothering to see which riders Rafe picked, Domino sent word for guard to be tightened around the wagons and for the pace to be accelerated so that they would be out from under this rise before nightfall. Seth materialized beside her and she sent him to make tea as raised voices heralded the return of Kerran and the old man.

"General Blaid," Kerran hailed her, something like relief in his voice, "here's the old . . . Here's Farmer Dennis."

The man who rode behind Kerran certainly deserved the epithet "old." What hair remained to him was more like a wispy memory of hair and his skin was so wrinkled that even his wrinkles bore wrinkles. But his face pruned up with indignation as Kerran started to say "old man" and his scrawny arms tightened around Kerran's waist so that the solider nearly choked out his introduction.

"General Blaid," Dennis began in a cracked voice, then he stopped, staring at Domino through narrowed eyes. "You're not General Blaid. I served with General Blaid in the wars thirty years ago."

Domino directed Kerran to bring his horse so that Dennis was alongside her.

"That General Blaid was my father, Kerman Blaid," she explained as she had repeatedly over the course of her career.

Dennis continued to peer at her. "You're a wench!"

"I am pleased that your eyesight hasn't failed," she replied dryly, "I am General Domino Blaid. Now, tell me about these bandits or I swear that I'll reactivate your commission and then have you flogged for insubordination."

"Sounds like Blaid," Dennis muttered, "lass or no. Here's how it is, Blaid. Two days ago my hamlet—a thriving, taxpaying community of nearly four farming families—was stormed into by some thugs. They demanded gold and goods that we didn't have—nor would we have given them if we'd had 'em. They threatened us, but we stood firm. The next day they came back, took what we had and torched what they couldn't take."

" 'Nearly four families'?" Domino commented.

Dennis suppressed a sniffle. "Aye, my granddaughter, Ami, was to be wed to Gus of Hillville. We had a nice cottage built and a field all turned for them. Now she's taken and Gus is in Hillville trying to raise an army."

Rafe rode up just then, his weathered face troubled. "General, a word, please."

Domino waved Kerran and Dennis back.

"Yes?"

Rafe reached into a saddlebag and pulled out a swatch of familiar-looking green fabric trimmed in black.

"The old man's people didn't go without a struggle," he said, "I cut this from a bandit's corpse. Cavalry uniform."

"One of ours," Domino breathed. "Turncoat or at least someone clad in our colors. I think that these bandits have become our problem."

Rafe nodded stiff military agreement.

"There's a secure place to camp a few miles down if we continue to push the wagons. Shall I give the word?"

"Yes," Domino found that Seth had returned with the tea. "Good, lad. Take the old . . . Take Dennis back to the wagons with you and make him comfortable. I'll send someone presently to take a full report from him."

Jord rode up to join them, Gwykander at his side like a sword, pen case strapped to Nightsky's saddle.

"May I volunteer, General? It will free up your soldiers."

"Do it," she ordered. "I'll take the full report over dinner."

She softened for a moment, smiled. "You *will* join me?"

"As you command, lady," he said with an almost correct salute, "as ever you command."

The next afternoon, they came upon the first troop of bandits camped in a hollow near Hillville. Leaving eight of the soldiers with the wagons and other gear, Domino lead the rest after the bandits.

"They've been terrorizing the Hillvilleans in the same way that the old . . . Dennis said that they did his hamlet," Rafe reported. "I sent Chase and Kerran into town garbed as a smith and his oaf and they brought back the gossip soon enough. That almost grandson of the old . . . Dennis. What's his name?"

"Dennis?" Domino asked, puzzled.

"No, the young man," Rafe thumped himself on the forehead a couple of times, "I've got it! Gus—that's the name. This Gus is quite a firebrand. As he sees it, the bandits have either killed or kidnapped his sweetheart and he's not for backing down."

"Good for him," Domino said approvingly. "After seeing what they did to the old . . . Dennis's hamlet during my tour yesterday I can sympathize with his position. How did the old . . . Dennis survive anyhow?"

Rafe sniggered. "Apparently, he was asleep on a cot and they took him for a corpse all laid out for burial. He only woke up when they were setting fire to the place and he caught some comments about it 'being a good deed, cremating the old stiff for the family.'"

Domino suppressed a giggle. "I'm surprised that the old ... Dennis even admitted as much. I thought that he'd bluster by anything that humiliating."

"That poet of yours got the story from him," Rafe admitted, "I didn't hear anything wrong in the old ... Dennis's tale, but Jord caught it right off."

Looking away so that Rafe would not see how unaccountably pleased she was by the praise to Jord, she caught motion off to the north.

"What the blazes is that!" she cried, kneeling on Spite's broad back for a better view. "It looks like a band of men with torches and spears! Those can't be the bandits. Kerran's report placed them to the south and west of Hillville."

" 'Tis a band of men, sir," Rafe said, passing her his field glasses, "but those aren't spears, at least not most of them. Those are hoes and pitchforks and a few garden rakes, if I don't miss my guess. And I'd bet that the stout lad with the florid skin and the determined expression is the old ... Dennis's almost grandson, Gus."

Domino studied the vigilante leader before returning the glasses to Rafe.

"He wouldn't be a relative of Spotty, would he?" she said, sparing a fond thought for Prince Rango's ever-reliable companion. "No matter. Rafe, take five of the men and stop those villagers—by force if you must. We can't have civilians doing our job. It's bad for our image with the taxpayers, especially in peacetime."

"Will that leave enough soldiers for you, sir?" Rafe asked, even as he signaled his five.

"Of course," Domino said, as Spite reared around like a cresting wave. "The day that ten of my cavalry aren't a match for any number of bandits is the day we go into the dog-food business. Now, follow my orders, Colonel!"

Gesturing for the rest of the Company to follow her, Domino had Kerran lead them to the bandit's hollow at a steady canter. The bandits might have had spies in Hillville and, if they had, the Company would need every advantage that time could give them.

What they found as they thundered up to surround the camp with drawn bows and ready blades was far worse than anything that Domino had expected. She had known that she would be dealing with renegade military, some from her own army, even from her own branch, but this went far beyond her ability to imagine.

The bandits had been taking advantage of the pleasant weather to camp in the open. The one structure they had taken time to construct was a loose holding pen made from saplings lashed with rope. In this cage captive women and children languished, wild-eyed and haggard, bound no doubt for some distant slave market like the one in which Princess Rissa had been sold. Domino pitied them, but her horror was reserved for the bandits themselves.

There were nearly a score of them, all armed and armored. Clearly, word had gotten to them that Hillville was attacking. Many were in uniform, but the condition of those uniforms set Domino's blood to boiling. Boots were scuffed and mud caked; caps were askew. One fellow actually wore a nonregulation jacket over his shirt and trousers.

Trembling at the indignity of it all, Domino jerked Spite to a halt at the edge of the hollow.

"You are surrounded and outnumbered," she announced, blithely ignoring that neither was precisely true. "Throw down your weapons and we may deal more gently with you."

There was an astonished silence as the bandits traded glances. A few seemed to be counting heads and figuring the odds. Then a thin, balding man in a disreputable foot soldier's uniform stepped forward.

"You have us outnumbered?" he said.

Domino stared back, her hazel eyes steely. "We do. Now throw down your weapons or I will order my archers to fire. I assure you—I would prefer to take prisoners."

In the silence that followed a man's voice could be

heard saying, "Is that horse green? Damn, I've got to give up drinking."

The bandits' spokesman shouted derisively, "You wouldn't dare fire. We have prisoners here—you won't risk them. It's a stalemate."

"Oh, no, it's not," Domino shouted back, signaling her men and raising her own bow. "I am General Blaid and my men don't dare to miss."

The first volley took out ten bandits, including the speaker. The others surrendered with complimentary haste. Rafe rode up as Domino's troops were binding the bandits and freeing the prisoners.

"We've secured the villagers a quarter mile out," he reported. "Two had to be forcibly subdued, but Chase says that they will survive."

"Very good," Domino replied. "Have you ever seen such a nasty-looking lot, Rafe? Of the survivors, two thirds were in some form of uniform—many our own people gone wrong. I'm going down to speak to them. Do you want to come?"

"I'd be pleased to, sir."

Kerran had lined the captured bandits up along one edge of the hollow, as far from the angry huddle of their former victims as possible. Domino noted with approval that the Company's Quartermaster was already going through the captured loot with the vocal assistance of two women.

"I'll take over here, Captain Kerran," she said, sneering down at the sloppily clad captives. "Ride out and check the status of the main Company. We should rejoin them within two hours. You also might tell the old ... Dennis that at least some of his family is safe."

"My eyes, it *is* green," came the same thin voice.

Spite snorted and Domino chuckled dryly.

"You three," she said, gesturing to the bandits in civvies, "go with Private Arlen and assist the Quartermaster. I have words for these seven that don't apply to you."

Unable to contain herself, she vaulted down from Spite's back and stalked over to the first man in line. He wore the remnants of a foot soldier's uniform with a pikeman's insignia hanging raggedly from one sleeve.

"What do you have to say for yourself, soldier?" she barked.

"Say?" He shuffled nervously. "Well, we were hungry and the crofters wouldn't share and . . ."

Domino snapped her riding crop against her boot top. The pikeman jumped and stopped talking.

"I don't care why you turned to robbery, man. I want to know why you chose to wear your uniform to go about it."

The man looked sheepishly at his tattered trousers. "Didn't much think about it."

"Didn't much think about it, what?" Rafe said, his voice a silken garotte.

"Didn't much think about it . . . sir?" The pikeman paused, looking closely at Domino for the first time.

"Better," Rafe said. "Address the General with respect, rat. If you're in uniform, you can be expected to observe the courtesies."

"One moment," came a voice from the other end of the line, "I have a question of procedure."

"Step forward," Domino commanded.

The man who slouched out of line was a thickset, unshaven young fellow in the cavalry's green and black. Studying him, Domino decided that he'd never been under her command.

"I was wondering," he said calmly, thumbs in his belt, "why you're talking to us like we're still in the army. I, for one, was honorably discarded after the last cataclysmic battle against the forces of Evil and, best as I know, none of these here is any more army than I am."

Domino's expression was grim and merciless. "You're in the uniform—disgraced as it is—that my father taught me to revere. If that wasn't enough to set honest blood boiling, you and your fellows misrepresent the army by performing your perfidious acts in what a civilian might mistake as army colors. However, if you insist—Colonel Rafe, according to my orders from Prince Rango, we are on a Crown Mission. Remind me, what powers does that grant me?"

"The power to exact due cooperation from any and all servants of the Crown. The power to raise an army for said Crown. The power to reactivate any member of the Crown's forces." He grinned wickedly at the now-trembling bedroll lawyer. "And the power to exact the Crown's justice as you see fit. Among other powers, sir."

"Very well, Colonel, witness that I've just reactivated these seven sorry souls. And now," she said, her voice getting husky with suppressed passion, "I'm going to review their uniforms. Somehow, I don't think they'll pass inspection."

Some time later, she sat astride Spite watching a bandit kick out his life from the makeshift scaffold Gus and his posse had built from the timbers of the prisoners' holding pen. The scaffold had been a bit short, so the bandits tended to strangle rather than break their necks. Still, for such short notice, it had been a workmanlike job.

"That's the last?" she asked.

"Yes, sir," Captain Kerran answered, "Private Hob Tanger, charges included unpolished boots, buttons and brass; torn and dirty uniform; hair untidy, face unshaven, robbery, banditry, conspiracy to enslave others, rape, and murder."

"Very good, Captain. I've promised to have a meal with the old . . . Dennis and his reunited family. Apparently, there will be a wedding as well. Carry on here."

"Yes, sir!"

There was indeed a wedding, a country wedding replete with a variety of customs that Domino found everything from baffling to downright distasteful. The service itself was pleasant enough, but when after a slew of toasts Ami perched on a chair and the older women started herding all the young women over to her, Domino balked.

"What's this?" she asked Jord, who had escorted her to the wedding.

"Ami's going to scatter her bouquet over the women," Jord explained. "It's a country charm for fertility."

"Like hell," Domino said, twisting away from the biddies. "Do you have any idea how much I pay a wise woman in the city just to stay infertile? They must be kidding!"

"No," Jord said, "they just figure that a woman's goal in life is to have lots of kids and Ami's passing on her luck as a new bride to all the rest."

Domino grabbed her beer mug and headed outside. Jord trailed her.

"You're upset, Domi," he said, not bothering to make his words a question.

"Yes, I am," she snapped. "That whole routine is disgusting!"

"Well," Jord said, cradling her hand in his, "the other women don't seem to mind. In fact, they seem pleased."

"They're idiots!" Domino said flatly, draining most of her beer. "To have breeding as your only goal is crazy."

"It's not that bad a choice, Domino," Jord said softly, "especially for a farm family. Ami's luckier than most. Gus loves her and would have fought twenty bandits to save her. She could do worse than letting him care for her and having a mess of kids."

"She could," Domino replied acridly, "take care of herself without letting him start running her life. Look at Rissa—perfectly competent on her own, doing just fine, bringing back Sombrisio with Jancy, and now she's lurking back at the palace waiting for other people to do things while she waits for wedding bells and coronation."

"Well, the wedding at least should be fun," Jord said, steering the conversation to more neutral ground. "You're in the bridal party, aren't you?"

Domino nodded, "Yes, Rissa asked both me and Jancy. I wonder what she expects us to wear? All I have are uniforms."

"I believe that the bride normally selects gowns for her attendants," Jord answered, "so you don't need to worry."

"Worry?" Domino shrugged. "I'm not worried. It's just

that the last three weddings I was in I was in the groom's party—I was Rafe's best man."

Jord suppressed a chuckle. "Were you? Well, I think you'll make a lovely bridesmaid. I can see you all done up in something orchidy with lots of lace."

"You don't think that my hair is too short, do you?" she asked with an anxious stroke over the close-cropped nape of her neck. "I never let it grow out. Long hair seemed like such a bother on the road and just as we were getting settled in the capital, Prince Rango sent us out again."

"No, it's not too short," Jord said, trailing a finger down her throat, "I find it very soft and very sexy."

"Oh." Domino glowed. "Orchidy, you think, with lace? You really think that would look nice?"

"Beautiful," Jord replied, slipping his arm around her waist. "They've started the music again. Would you care to dance?"

Domino paused awkwardly. "I only know how to lead."

"No matter, my dear. You can learn new tactics." He took her arm. "Think of it as a field exercise."

"I can do that," she said, "but I'm afraid we have to leave fairly early. No dancing until dawn, this wedding."

"Of course," Jord agreed. "We have to hit the trail again early tomorrow morning."

Domino twinkled. "I was thinking more about hitting the hay with a certain poet. If you're interested, of course."

"As the General commands." He smiled. "As she commands."

The Company departed Hillville before noon the next day. Gus and Ami had been given the villagers' full support in rebuilding Dennis's hamlet as a wedding gift and Domino left them most of the cumbersome loot as the Company's gift.

"Is there anything that you will take as a sign of our thanks, General?" Gus asked. "We all owe you so much."

"Just one thing," Domino replied. "Rope."

'Rope?" chimed Gus and Ami.

"Rope," she repeated. "If things are as bad farther north as we have heard, I suspect that we will be doing lots of hangings."

And she proved a prophet. The very day the Company left Hillville, Captain Kerran's outriders captured six bandits, these in Kalaran's colors. Domino reviewed the complaints of the local farmers, the contents of the bandit's camp, and their tattered uniforms, then ordered all six hanged.

Two days later, they encountered ten more and again Domino passed the death sentence. As she was supervising the mass burial a natty figure on a light riding horse rode to join her. When he drew rein, Domino was tempted to ignore him. With a sigh, she reminded herself of her loyalties and motioned for him to join her.

"Hello, Piggon," she said, with an effort at politeness. "Fine day for a hanging, wouldn't you say?"

"General," he said, without returning her pleasantry, "I am preparing my magical communiqué to Prince Rango and I was wondering how I should explain our slow progress towards the Lakes."

Domino studied the small red-haired and goateed sorcerer, wondering, not for the first time, how he managed to ride a horse while wearing full skirts.

"I fail to understand your question, Piggon," she said in the steely soft tones that made even her bravest men reassess the status of their wills. "What is there for you to explain?"

"Well," he said, unrolling a map with a bossy flourish of his deep sleeves, "according to my travel estimates, we are making very limited progress. This dallying with the bandits has slowed us further. I believe that we are behind schedule and I wish to be able to explain why to the Prince."

"What is there for you to explain?" Domino repeated in the same soft tones. "I understood that your job was to report. Report then, but don't believe for a moment that this gives you the right to tell me to explain anything."

Spite stomped one hoof and green diamonds of light flew from the turf. Piggon hesitated as if for a moment he would protest, then kicked his roan and rode back into camp.

Domino waited to regain her temper before following, but the episode rankled and that night she rolled over and elbowed Jord, who was half-asleep.

"I don't like Piggon," she announced.

Jord sleepily propped himself up on one elbow. "Why?"

Domino fidgeted with a corner of the pillow. "He's so bossy—trying to give *me* orders! And I don't like his name."

"His name?" Jord grinned. "Piggon—yeah, it is an ugly name. I have a theory about that, Domino."

"What?"

"Can you imagine any mother naming her son Piggon?"

Domino shook her head.

"Me either. Therefore, Piggon must be a nickname and although most nicknames come from your peers, only your superiors can force you to keep one. Right?"

"Like Dominik for Domino?" she said, her deep voice suddenly husky. "Yes, I know. Go on."

"Well, the only group which fits both of those criteria are the sorcerers. Prince Rango assured us that Piggon is a sorcellet—a one-trick pony—so he's a bit of a failure as a sorcerer." Jord shrugged. "So he's stuck with an ugly name and probably a bunch of other problems. Sorcellets must be a lot like critics or reviewers—they can't quite make it, so they spend all their time on the edges of the business, telling everyone else how to do it right."

"Poor poet." Domino chuckled, running her fingers through the curly hair on his chest. "You have the oddest ways of looking at things. I'll be more patient with Piggon—as long as he doesn't tell me how to run my Company."

"Good. Now," he said, reaching out to extinguish the last candle, "I have a sonnet I've been saving for you."

"I'm not much of a critic," she murmured, pulling him to her.

"Good."

The next morning as Domino waited for Seth to bring her fresh tea, Jord sauntered from the tent clad only in a long tunic.

"Going to review the troops, General?" he yawned.

"Yes," she answered, self-consciously aware of the contrast between his bed-warm near nudity and her own crisp uniform.

"The job must take longer these days," he said, accepting tea and trousers from Seth.

"Why should it?" she asked.

"The lot trailing the Company's gotten bigger," he answered. "I wonder where they're coming from?"

Domino followed his gesture, her initial confusion turning rapidly into comprehension. The Company remained its tidy self, but trailing on the southern edge was a ragtag cluster of tents and brightly colored wagons. Quite a collection of strange beasts moved among the structures. She was certain that she saw a camel and possibly a llama among the horses, mules, donkeys, and oxen.

"Who on earth are they?"

Seth piped up from where he was feeding Spite a handful of salted sardines. "Word has it that they're Magical Folk, General, and that they've been drawn here by you."

"What childish nonsense . . ." Domino began, catching herself when she saw the boy's crestfallen expression. "Thank you, Seth. That's valuable information. Excuse me. I'm going to see Colonel Rafe."

She found Rafe briefing the outriders on the bandit rumors garnered from the last village they had passed.

"They're dressing better now," he was saying, "and are less likely to be in uniform, but don't let that make you careless. Many of them still have military experience and as the General's policies put the fear of hanging in them, we can expect them to be pretty cunning. Dismissed!"

Rafe nodded to Domino. "Good morning, General. The Company's just about ready to move."

"Very good." She twirled her riding crop between her fingers. "Colonel, why didn't you inform me about our camp followers?"

"Camp followers? You never minded before . . ." His expression changed. "Oh . . . those. Yeah, strange, isn't it?"

"How long have they been trailing us?"

"The first ones showed up after our second or third tangle with the bandits," Rafe said, "about the time that your policy regarding those who break the peace was getting obvious. When I suggested that they weren't wanted, the answer I got was that they were within their rights and we had no cause to stop them traveling through public lands."

"Have they been bothering the Company?" Domino demanded.

"No, they've even been helpful. A couple are healers and have helped Chase patch up our men. They may have done some trading with Supply as well. Certainly the food has been fresher than we have reason to expect."

"I see. Carry on, Rafe, and keep this discussion between us for now." Domino scratched her chin thoughtfully. "After we are moving, I believe I will check in with the Quartermaster."

The approach of the General on her pale green horse sent the occupants of the supply wagons into something of a tizzy. Said General on said horse smiled somewhat sardonically. Early in her career, Kerman Blaid had given her advice never to fix something that wasn't broken. Supply had benefited under her benign neglect, but it never hurt to remind them that she was in charge.

Although the Quartermaster technically was Colum Vrame, actually the operation was a joint effort between him and his wife, Bysha. In the old military, Bysha could not hold a commission, but Domino had plans to make some changes and Bysha, whether she wanted it or not, would be one of the first women to receive a retroactive commission.

Bysha rather than Colum intercepted the General as Spite trotted up before the first wagon. Thin, almost angular, features and oversized ears gave some credence to the rumors that Bysha had elven blood, but both her large eyes and straight hair were a matter-of-fact brown and her manners were anything but eldritch.

"General Blaid, good of you to drop back and see us!" she trilled in a voice just shy of shrill. "I'll wager you're here to check on Seth. He's back on the head wagon, doing his lessons."

Domino shook her head. "No, Bysha, I have no need to check on Seth. He is always admirable. I have come to consult with Colum. Where can I find him?"

"Colum? He's around here somewhere," Bysha was saying when Domino felt Spite stir between her knees.

The green horse trotted lightly to the back of a covered wagon and stretched his nose inside. There was a noise, half yelp, half shout, and Spite took a few steps backward, ears flat but eyes sparkling with malicious mischief.

Domino was not surprised to see that Spite's prey was the missing Quartermaster.

"Sergeant Colum," she said dryly as the horse dropped him in the dirt.

"General Blaid," he answered, stumbling to his feet, edging away from Spite's teeth, and trying to salute all at once. "A pleasure, sir."

"At ease, Colum," she answered.

Colum was a tall man gone soft with good eating and too many wagon rides. His skin was fair and rosy from the wind and his neatly cropped hair was the soft shade of candlelit silver.

"Hop back in the wagon so that we don't fall behind. We can have our conference informally."

"Yes, sir," he said, scrabbling onto the tailgate. Spite stretched his neck as if to give the man a boost and suddenly the portly sergeant found wings.

Domino suppressed a grin and moved in for her attack.

"You've been trading with that ragtag band that's trailing us, Colum. Given that we don't know what their intentions are, you could be in considerable trouble."

Colum blanched, "Sir! You know that I wouldn't be part of anything that could hurt the Company. What they wanted was so harmless that I couldn't see any harm in dealing with them."

"What did they want, soldier?" Domino said with more patience than she felt.

"Rope, sir, just rope."

"Rope? Any special rope?"

"No, sir," he began, but Bysha interrupted, jumping from her wagon to join him.

"Yes, General, there was something special. They wanted pieces of the rope that we retrieved after the hangings, the parts that were made into the noose."

"Now what use would they have for that?" Domino mused. "That's the most twisty part of the rope, the hardest to reuse."

"That's what I thought," Colum said hastily, "and since they were offering to turn bad rope into good meat and beer, I didn't think that the General would mind."

"No, Colum," she said thoughtfully, "consider me convinced for now, but I believe that I will ride back and have a visit with our colorful train."

"Bide, General," Bysha advised. "They're a touchy lot, like greased hedgehogs, slippery and prickly all at once. Let me have a chance to pass the word on to them so they'll have time to think about being polite."

"Very well," Domino agreed, "but ready or not, at dusk I'm going in."

That evening after the Company had camped and Domino had supervised the routine hangings of a half dozen bandits, she washed her hands, combed her hair, and rode to meet the Magical Folk. Both Jord and Rafe offered to accompany her, but she refused.

"If I can get into difficulty scarcely twenty yards from

my own camp, I deserve what I get." She laughed. "If I'm not home by dawn, call out the cavalry."

Riding in, Domino estimated that the camp followers numbered somewhere around a dozen, if one did not include the assorted—and often very odd—livestock.

But she had less time for surveying the peculiar village of tents, pavilions, yurts, and gypsy wagons than she would have liked, for she had to give her full attention to the welcoming committee.

One was a hunchbacked man with not one but two humps on his back, broad lips, and a sour expression on the long face just visible beneath an untidy mop of brown hair. The other was a woman who was the archetypal crone. Her white hair was the only attractive thing about her. Her nose was hooked and her skin blotched and leathery; gnarled hands grasped a polished staff the same light brown as her faded eyes.

"You!" the crone shrilled, "Domino! Dominik! You who have made me sick . . ."

The hunchback spat into the road, effectively interrupting the crone. Then he straightened as best he could, spread his fabric-shrouded arms wide, and began to intone in a voice as harsh as sand against a wind-scoured eye.

"Trouble us at your own woe, General Blaid! This is a public road and we have as much right on it as your Company does. We are a potent force for sorcery, I warn you . . ."

The crone stomped on his boot toe with the silver-shod heel of her staff, "Oh, shut up, Mel. Domino doesn't fear us. Why should she? She has defied the Fallen Sunbird himself. She has made mysterious compacts with the Sea Hag. She has no reason to fear such pathetic, piss-poor hangers-on as we."

Domino stared at them with as much amazement as she ever permitted herself. Between her knees, Spite seemed to be laughing, a sensation she found more disturbing than reassuring.

"You have stolen the march on me," she managed

finally, "for you know my name and I have not yet been introduced. Mayhap you could assist me."

"I am Mel," the man said, "from the far East. Ignore this old fool and tremble, for I am a force to be reckoned with!"

"He's a hedge wizard," the crone said calmly, "or a sand dune one, anyhow. I am known as Cranky Granny, but I suggest that you call me simply Granny. My art is telling the future."

"Poorly," Mel added acridly, spitting again, "but we are remiss. General Blaid has come to meet our merry band."

"I," said Granny, with a sprightly skip, "already know what she wants and you don't!"

"Oh, nonsense," Mel hissed, "you don't even know what's for dinner."

"Do so," she said, "oatmeal and honey and peppermint tea. Hah!"

"That's all you ever eat," Mel groused. "That's hardly a fair test."

"You're just jealous."

"I am not!"

"Are so!"

"Am not!"

"So!"

They continued bickering as they stomped up the road. Shaking her head, Domino nudged Spite into a walk and followed the Magical Folk into their camp.

The varied structures were arranged haphazardly around a central bonfire that leaped and crackled, casting odd shadows on the people clustered around it. After a few moments, Domino was not so certain that the shadows were what was so odd, for as her eyes adjusted she realized that Seth's naive terminology might be more accurate than she had believed.

This was no gathering of guilded mages such as had aided Prince Rango during the battles against Kalaran. These were people in whom magical power lurked and who had been warped by it in much the same fashion—

she realized with a spark of insight—as the area around the capital had been warped by the excessive magic contained in the artifacts.

Swinging down from Spite, she accepted a folded camp stool from an emaciatedly delicate elven woman. Mel and Granny settled onto seats and the rest of the Magical Folk drew near.

"Now, General, my sight tells me that you came calling to sniff out what interest we have in your Company." Granny cackled. "And to learn why we're buying your hangman's rope."

"Any eavesdropper could have figured that," Mel muttered, "or anyone with anything other than oatmeal between her ears."

Domino ignored him. "Yes, that is why I am here. I am on a mission from Prince Rango and I cannot let anything interfere with its success. If you plan trouble for my mission, I will be forced to act against you as I have against the bandits."

Granny grinned a gap-toothed grin. "No, we wouldn't impede your mission, General. It doesn't take my powers to tell that the Prince wouldn't send four of his favorites into the wilds without serious reason."

"Your powers!" Mel spat into the fire, causing it to flash with green and purple sparks. "Get on with it, crone."

"Simply put, General Blaid," Granny continued, "we want your rope because it's useful for our charms and spells. Usually, one must search carefully to find a hanging, but you are a stormy petrel indeed."

"I see," Domino considered. "Reasonable, as long as you don't deplete our stores overmuch. It might even prove useful to have your band trailing my own—the Lakes are a dangerous and magical region."

"Yes," Mel agreed, "they are, but you have braved them before and are traveling at a—cautious—pace."

Domino glared at him. "What are you saying, Sorcerer? If you are implying that I am derelict in my duties I will have you hanged."

An excited whispering rose like a sudden wind around the fire circle. Domino caught fragments: "Ooh, finger bones! "The skull for me!" "Hair! Hair and fingernails!" "I want his robes."

Mel blanched then growled, spitting into the fire so violently that a rainbow of sparks erupted.

"Tut-tut, children," Granny soothed. "Now, General, I am certain that Mel was implying nothing of the sort. Here, as a token of our good faith, let me read your future."

She tottered to her feet. Leaning heavily on her staff, she began drawing circles in the dust and sprinkling them with powders shaken from sacks she plucked from her braided rope girdle.

"Sugar and spice and everything nice," she crooned with a surprisingly gentle smile for Domino. "That's because you're a girl, sweetling. Must have thrown Kalaran's precognitors all off when they were working with frogs and snails and puppy dog tails—that's what boys are made of, you see."

Domino smiled wryly. "Nice to have been of help, even if that is all over now."

"Hush," Granny said, twisting her gnarled fingers over the pattern. "Let us see what the future holds for you."

Half doubting, half fascinated, Domino held her breath as the brown sugar and cinnamon began to glitter and steam, shedding an aroma of baking cookies.

"I see a long road and trees swinging with bandits," she began.

"Some foresight," Mel sniggered.

Domino stretched slightly, thumped him once behind one ear, then caught him as he crumpled. Spite snorted. No one else seemed to notice.

"The trail ends thrice," Granny muttered, struggling for each word, choking over each syllable. "Once on the road, once in the Lake, once in a high-vaulted room. I see you both succeed and fail. You will keep what you should lose and lose what you hold to be most true."

Mel moaned, flopping on the dirt by the bonfire.

When his hand brushed a bit of hot ash, he yelped and sprang to his feet with surprising agility. As his foot scattered Granny's magical drawing, the crone collapsed unconscious over the ruins.

"Granny!"

Domino lifted the old lady like a rag doll (although she'd never had a rag doll, except for target practice) and set her gently on a pallet that had appeared as if by magic by the fire. The crone was already stirring. Domino settled her and the crone sipped with brave intensity on the cup of honey sweetened tea that a bright green goblin brought.

"Necrotica would have words with you," Granny whispered, "a warning for you—a gift to go with my prophesy."

Domino refrained from commenting on the value of Granny's prophesy. She had little faith that anything so contradictory could be significant except in the most general sense.

"Where is this Necrotica?" Domino replied. "I will listen to her warning, but do not expect me to heed some feeble attempt to turn me from doing as Prince Rango has commanded."

"Brave words, General," came a raspy, whispery voice from the darkness, "but my warning has naught to do with your mission from the Prince. Rather it concerns the consequences of your own actions."

"Speak," Domino said, gritting her teeth against yet another admonition about the Company's pace.

"I am a necromancer," the voice continued, "a specialist in enchantments concerned with the dead. Your Company's actions profit me in many ways, therefore I believe you are owed fair warning about the danger that you are releasing on the very countryside you seek to protect."

"Riddles." Domino snorted. "All your type speaks in riddles—I suspect to cover ignorance. I am a plain-speaking soldier, Necromancer. I have fought creatures both natural and unnatural so am not easily cowed. Speak your piece without this skulking or I shall go my way!"

"So rudely is it said that Colonel Dominik Blaid spoke to the Sea Hag," piped the green goblin from where it was refilling Granny's cup. "More balls than brains they said then, but I think that the Hag knows."

"Yes." There was a motion in the darkness and the emaciated elven woman Domino had glimpsed before stepped into the light.

"So I recall."

Domino quirked an eyebrow at Necrotica. "An elf who deals with the dead? I thought that your people were interested in natural things like weather, animals, and flowers."

"So we are." Necrotica's smile threatened to split her taut skin over her high cheekbones. "And it was in trying to raise the ghost of a flower that I first discovered my talent and power. It's a living. Answer me a question, General Blaid. Do you know why most hangings are done at crossroads?"

"No, I never considered it."

Necrotica fingered the circlet of tiny carved skulls that dangled from one enormous ear. "I had thought so. The reason for the custom is so that the ghosts of those executed will have difficulty picking the route taken by their killers. Since most haunts become bound to the location of their death, this mixing of routes traps them."

"And these hangings that I have been ordering," Domino said, "have been out in the open and we have been traveling slowly."

"Yes," Necrotica whispered. "I have trapped some of the ghosts and ripe eating they were indeed, but there will be more than I can handle if you do not cease your executions."

Domino leaped to her feet, whistling for Spite.

"Never! justice will be done, Necrotica." She grasped Spite's mane and vaulted astride without waiting for the horse to kneel. "We will simply build crossroads."

The elf gaped and the other Magical Folk chattered and twittered in amazement, all but the green goblin, who rolled on the ground, nearly sick with laughter.

"She would! She would!" it peeped.

Domino waved her farewells. "Thank you for your warnings and prophesies—and for the tea. As long as you abide by our agreement, my Company's protection is extended to you all. Defy me and we will find rope enough to have you."

Seth had dinner waiting when she returned to her tent.

"I fed him," the boy said with a toss of his head toward Jord, whose silhouette was visible within the lamplit tent, "so that he could study more."

"Very good, Seth," Domino said, sparing him a pat on the shoulder. "How are your studies?"

"Fine, I guess," he said, scuffing the dirt with one foot, "but I'd rather have a sword and a bow and a horse than learn to be a clerk."

"Am I a clerk?" Domino asked, ripping into her roast pheasant with teeth and hands.

"No, sir!" the boy said with shock and admiration. "You're too much of a man for that!"

"But I can read and write and cipher," Domino said, wiping her greasy hands on her trouser legs, "and my father, General Blaid, insisted on this as part of my training as a soldier."

"Am I training to be a soldier?" the boy asked, something suspiciously like joy in his level voice.

"You might be," Domino replied, "and you might find yourself getting at least a bow to go with your horse if I hear from Bysha and Colum that your lessons are going well."

"Really?" Seth's grin suddenly turned serious. "Thank you, General, I'll clear now, if you permit."

"Carry on, Seth," she said, "I'll be turning in as soon as I wash."

When Domino entered the tent, Jord held up one hand, indicating that she should not interrupt him. She unstrapped her armor, putting the pieces outside for Seth to oil. Jord continued scribbling for so long that she was nearly asleep when he finally turned down the lamp and came to join her.

"Domi! Domi!" He poked her softly. "Wake up, honey."

"Urm," she said, rolling cooperatively into his arms. "Finally done studying for tonight? How much work do you have left, anyhow?"

He let her go. "Don't be petty, Domino. The scroll of Gwykander is a cranky old artifact written in archaic script by some older sorcerer."

"No, don't get me wrong," Domino said, squeezing him close. "I appreciate how difficult what you are doing is, but people have been commenting about how slowly we've been traveling. I'm going to need to pick up the pace."

"Uruck!" Jord gasped. "Domino, ease up! You're breaking my ribs!"

She let him go all at once and he fell back, alternatingly gasping and chuckling. When he had his breath back, he snuggled her again.

A few minutes later, he paused long enough to comment, "I should be done in a couple of days."

"Jord, I knew you were good, but," Domino blushed. "Oh. The scroll. Forget it and attend to your General."

"I am at attention, my lady."

The next morning, Domino met with Rafe and divided up the Company.

"We've been taking things too easily," she said. "I believe that we can count on the Magical Folk to help with the defense of the wagons, so we'll leave a minimal force here under Chase's command. If I recall, Kerran did some work on fortifications during the war."

"That's right, sir," Rafe said. "He's actually a fine carpenter, though he doesn't care to admit it."

"Very good. I want him to select a small group who will ride ahead of the day's travel and set up gallows for us where the wagons should camp at day's end."

"They'll be ready for us then," Rafe said with a wolfish grin, "but hangings don't take that long to set up."

"Ah, but that's not all they'll be doing," Domino replied. "I have been warned that we are releasing 'haunts' and that the best way to entrap them is to perform our hangings at crossroads. So . . ."

"You're going to have them build crossroads?" Rafe said. "To where?"

Domino took a stick and drew two intersecting lines, "Crossroads." She surrounded them with a circle. "And the road that they feed into."

Rafe studied the quartered circle. "Very clever, a ghost trap. I'll brief Kerran at once."

As the Company advanced into the mountainous Lake District, Domino and Rafe found excellent hunting. The hilly, isolated area offered good land for grapes, beef and dairy cattle, and a tourist industry that was beginning to thrive again now that the epic battles with Kalaran were fading into history. The bandits did not treasure the area for its limited wealth alone, but for the culverts, gullies, ravines, and caves that gave them shelter after a long day of theft and pillaging.

The two leaders urged their men to think like men on the run—not a difficult task since during the darkest days of the war against the Fallen Sunbird many of them had been men on the run. Competition between the teams was fierce and those soldiers relegated to guard duty soothed their savaged egos by betting on everything from how many bandits would be captured on a given day to how long each would take to hang.

Jord continued his private competition with the scroll, his usually casual manner vanishing when he set to work. Yet, although he was nearly finished, the expression with which he regarded the artifact did not reflect pleasure or accomplishment, but something far more grim.

"Look at that, Domino," he said to her one night, "really look. The average, run-of-the-mill artifact—like the ring or the sword or the amulet—reaches out and grabs you with its power. They're made of precious metals, lavished with gems, and hold in themselves the power to actively shake reality. But this is so plain."

"Plain?" Domino pointed to an elaborate illuminated

tracery that curled down and became a border. "This isn't plain."

"Plain may be the wrong word," Jord agreed, "subtle would be closer to what I mean. The power both is and is not in the scroll. It's in the words, in the knowledge. It's in the choosing of one word over a synonym or a certain meter over one equally good, but somehow not right. The power of the scroll of Gwykander is in the written word that holds in its curves and angles the thoughts and dreams and aspirations of some long-ago writer. I tell you, Domi, sometimes the power of those words just overwhelms me."

Domino squeezed his hand. "Poet, you are beyond this simple soldier, but I think I understand. Keep the scroll safe until we get to the Lake; that's all I ask."

She hugged him. "I've got to go. Want to come and see some people hanged? Kerran has made a really pretty circle this time and I think you need some entertainment. You've been working too hard."

"You're good to me, Domino," he said, slipping the scroll into its case. "I could use a break."

"Come on, then. They won't start without me, but we'd better hurry." She tousled his hair. "It'll be nice having you there. I'm just sorry I can't hold your hand while I'm on duty."

"I'll make up for it later," he promised.

Two nights and two dozen hangings later, Domino cat-napped while Jord worked on his translation. Earlier that evening, the officers had dined within the ghost trap— something of a consolation for the engineer when neither of the teams had brought in any bandits.

"Kerran did himself in tonight," she commented sleepily. "I felt terrible that we didn't have anyone for him to hang after his Corp went to the trouble of building the ghost trap out of stone, complete with lintels to use for gallows."

"I thought it was especially nice when they ignited the straw dummies to give us corpse light to dine by," Jord added without looking up from his work.

"Lovely and eerie," Domino agreed. "What are you scowling at? You're going to put lines on your face if you keep on."

He didn't smile at her joke, but gestured for her.

"Domino, come and look at this, please. I need you to check my memory, not that either of us is likely to forget the night that Kalaran was slain."

"No," Domino said, kneeling next to him. "There we were—I was one of those delegated to guard Agonamerince and I was champing at the bit while Rango and Rissa used their toys to strip Kalaran of his magic and beat at him. I hate to speak ill of the Prince, but I don't think the duel would have taken as long if he'd let me have the sword."

"Braggart," Jord chided. "Now, after they got Kalaran down you brought Agonamerince forward and he started reading off the exorcism from the scroll of Gwykander. I had my eyes shut—listening to the roll of the Thermaean as Agonamerince did his reading. I seem to recall that things stopped rather suddenly."

"Yes." Domino nodded. "Agonamerince was having a bit of trouble; the entire situation was a strain on the old man, but he kept on reading. Finally, Kalaran sighed, rolled his eyes, seemed to smile faintly, choked, and went limp. I was rather distracted, however, because Agonamerince grabbed his chest as soon as he'd finished reading and crumpled. Poor fellow's heart gave out on him."

"As soon as he'd finished," Jord mused. "Are you sure he finished the scroll?"

"Well, Kalaran was dead, but I think that the ring and sword did that. The exorcism was supposed to banish his spirit once the body was dead—we didn't want a zombie demigod." She smiled. "Anyhow, they finished by burning the body. And, after the head was displayed for an entire moon in the Temple's central tower, they flensed it and turned it into some complex magical early warning system against the return of the Dark. So, even if Agonamerince didn't finish, the spirit wouldn't have had a very pleasant refuge left."

"Hmm, humor me, General. I have a bad feeling about this." Jord held up the scroll. "There's a pair of funny depressions on the scroll toward the bottom, right about where Agonamerince's thumbs would have rested as he unrolled and read. Now, if he was holding it at this point and these marks are from his hands convulsing as he had his fatal heart attack . . ."

Domino looked. "I don't read Ancient Thermaean, Jord, but I can see that there are a bunch more lines here below the marks."

"If I were to read it aloud," Jord asked, "might you recognize the sounds from where he broke off?"

"Maybe. Try and I'll tell you."

He began, his voice soft and eerily like that of the ancient priest. Domino stood to listen, her eyes shut and her hand resting where her sword would hang.

"That's it," she said, after Jord had read for several minutes. "I remember the ending clearly, *'Quatendo erbud, altonfuss dermain aah!'* "

Jord squinted at the scroll. "The last word isn't *'aah,'* Domino."

"It was, the way Agonamerince read it," she said. "He collapsed right after that and those words were seared into my memory."

"I think we have trouble, then. If I have my translation right, the exorcism was never completed."

"A formality certainly," Domino protested. "The body was destroyed. Where would Kalaran go?"

"Remember the warnings that Necrotica gave us about the ghosts?" Jord asked, carefully rerolling the scroll. "Dead bodies don't mean dead spirits and Kalaran was a demigod."

"Jord, I don't like this. If you're right, the last place that scroll should be is tucked in a grotto at the bottom of a lake. We should turn around immediately."

"Domino." Jord grabbed her as she turned to rouse the camp. "The spirit had to go somewhere. Since we didn't hear any stories about hauntings at the palace—at least beyond the usual—we can guess that the spirit has found a new refuge."

"You mean that it has possessed someone." She nodded. "Who would be likely?"

Jord nibbled on his knuckle. "Well, I'm not really a student of the arcane arts, but I have been talking with Necrotica on the subject of ghosts and I'd guess that most of the same rules would apply."

"Report, soldier!" Domino snapped, her exasperation melting instantly into a blush. "I mean . . ."

"Don't worry, Domino." He squeezed her hand. "I was going on a bit much. Basically, ghosts find possession easier if the person is ill, injured, or weakened. We have two good candidates there."

"Rissa and Rango," Domino said. "Not only were they injured, but they were weak. Either would be tempting vessels—they're both powerful people."

"Rango has been acting rather strangely," Jord offered, "now that I think about it. He's sent everyone off with those sorcellets you love so much and scattered the magic that defeated Kalaran to distant and difficult to reach places."

"There were all those phenomena," Domino said doubtfully, "but if Rango is Kalaran, then perhaps he created the special effects as staging for his plan."

"Or augmented them," Jord agreed. "I think we'd better not give Rango the benefit of the doubt."

"I agree. We'll continue on and plant a dummy scroll so that we have the scroll of Gwykander to deal with a possible possession," Domino said slowly, the decision to distrust her Prince coming with difficulty. "If we're wrong, we can apologize to Rango later."

"And if he's Rango," Jord said with a reassuring smile, "he'll understand and probably pin a medal on your chest for it."

"I don't think that Rissa would much appreciate that," Domino answered. "Maybe we can get the Prince to delegate someone."

"I'd be happy to volunteer." Jord grinned wickedly. "But I'd need some practice first."

"Oh, so you're finally done with the scroll for now and have time for me?"

"If you'll give me a chance," he promised.

For the next several days they rode on through rain that turned the road into a gluey morass. Finally, the wagons stuck and could not be unstuck.

"We're close," Domino said, shoving her streaming hair from her eyes. "Can't you see how happy Spite is? I don't think I should wait any longer. Rafe, have the men set camp here and I'll take a small group ahead."

"Yes, General. I request permission to accompany you."

"Request granted, old friend."

She rode back to the wagon in which Jord had taken shelter.

"It is time," she announced. "Give the scroll to me."

"I'm coming with you, Domino," he said. "Nightsky is saddled and ready."

Before Domino could speak, Piggon waded up.

"I will accompany you, General, so that I may report to the Prince when the deed is done."

"I . . ."

"I want to come too, General," Seth piped. "Please?"

Domino sighed and Spite sniggered.

"Is anyone staying?" she finally managed.

"Most of us," Bysha said, stomping over with a canteen of steaming wine. "Some people have the sense to stay out of the rain."

Yet, it hardly mattered. As soon as they left the outskirts of the Company, Spite surged into a gallop so rough and choppy that Domino felt as if she were being tossed on a stormy sea.

"Damn it, Spite! You know I get seasick!" she yelped, clamping her jaws against her roiling stomach and looking to leap free.

At the pace Spite was moving even Nightsky was soon left behind. She heard Jord yelling, "Domino, the scroll!"

Then the metal tube was sparkling through the rain-streaked air. One hand firmly locked in Spite's mane, she reached for the cylinder with her free hand. Without slowing, Spite plunged into the icy Lake waters. She snagged the tube just as the waters closed over her head.

The water tasted strongly of trout, but Domino sucked it in, grateful for Spite's ability to let her breathe easily underwater. In her first such descent, she had carried an enchanted trident that allowed her the same ability in a more limited fashion. Astride Spite she felt like a sea creature, seeing everything clearly, aware of the unnatural montage of sounds the water bore.

Spite laughed as they glided toward the bottom—not a snort or an equine chuckle, but a nearly human-sounding laugh. Domino gripped the snowy mane more tightly, shocked to feel the figure between her knees shifting, melting, melding into another form. As they landed solidly on the sandy lake bottom, Domino found that she was straddling the very trim waist of a humanoid figure.

Blushing, she loosened her grip and, trusting the magic that had protected her thus far to continue to do so, stepped back for a better look. The sea-foam white hair and pale green skin were the same, as were the clear, pupil-less glass eyes. Nothing else was and Domino gaped as she studied the graceful, nude sea-elf who had drifted to face her.

"You . . . Spite, you're a girl!"

Spite smiled, revealing strong, if somewhat horsy, white teeth. "So I am."

"But you were a stallion." Domino felt herself blushing again. "I mean, I looked."

Spite snorted. "You think you're the only one who can cross-dress? The sea is, if nothing else, changeable. But you have more urgent concerns than what is—or is not—between my legs."

"Right." Domino hefted the scroll tube. "I need to return this to its grotto."

The glass green eyes studied her. "The grotto is guarded, Domino."

"Yes, I expect that it is. It was before."

"You did not wonder at how swiftly the guardian fled from you last time?" Spite needled, twirling a white lock about a fingernail embossed with a tiny horseshoe charm.

"No." Domino grimaced at the memory. "I plummeted into the depths and then kicked my way into the grotto bearing with me the enchanted trident forged for the purpose by the dwarves. Despite the enchantment that let me breathe underwater, my head was pounding and red sparks danced before my eyes. Yet, like a hero, I bore myself with courage and defeated the creature who had been set to guard the scroll of Gwykander."

"You also," Spite said, "had a cute little ass and a trim figure under your soaking clothes. Mama thought you were a real charmer and she's gonna be real sour now that she's aware that you made a fool of her."

"I?" Domino floundered, "I didn't try to . . ."

"Doesn't matter," Spite carped. "Last time, the Hydra fled after a few token snaps and you found a crystal-caparisoned steed waiting to bear you and your prize to the surface."

"Crystal," Domino muttered, "ice. It melted."

"Tell your boyfriend," Spite said. "I'm just quoting the official epic. Last time things went comparatively easily for you. This time, you're going to have a fight."

"Great," Domino said, fingering the scroll of Gwykander and considering just dropping it where she stood. "Look, Spite, are you still with me?"

The elf maiden spread her dainty hands. "But of course, Domino. If I wasn't, you would have drowned long since."

"Great." Domino crossed her legs and drifted to sit on the sand. "Last time the layout was something like this."

She picked up a razor-edged clamshell and began to sketch a diagram.

"The lake bottom sloped off here and narrowed to run into a channel. The grotto we want is off that channel and—of course—I expect the guardian to be there. Last time, I beat it off."

"Yes, you charged in with your magical trident, it took a few snaps, and swam off. Right?"

"The thing had seven heads," Domino protested, "and they took more than a few snaps. One even tore my sleeve."

"Forget it, General," Spite retorted, "you won't be dealing with a snap dragon this time. The Sea Hag is serious—you'll have a real fire Hydra this time."

"Fire?" Domino said doubtfully. "In the water? Don't you know? Fire and water don't mix."

"I've also heard that the best way to fight fire is with fire," Spite said, "and that's the stupidest thing I've ever heard. All you get is more fire."

"All right, I'll concede that sometimes stupid things work. Even with your help I'm not certain that I'm up to a seven-headed, fire-breathing dragon."

"Hydra," Spite corrected. "They're worse, since if you cut off one head a new one will grow unless the stump of the neck is cauterized. I don't suppose you brought the trident with you, did you?"

"Well, sort of," Domino said. "You see, I left it here last time. I had thrown it at the creature and so I was running out of air. All I could manage was to grab the scroll and swim."

"Then it's probably still there," Spite said. "Mama's a lousy housekeeper. Now, I have a plan."

"Hey, Hydra!" Spite shouted into the inky channel mouth, "You've got halitosis times seven!"

Crouched to the right side of the opening, Domino groaned silent disapproval. Apparently, Spite wasn't any more subtle as an elf. However, her ploy seemed to be working. Something even more solidly black than the lightless waters of the subterranean, subaquean channel was swimming forward. She could feel the warm currents that emanated from its vicinity and taste a sulphurous tang in the waters.

The Hydra burst from the channel, a stream of pearlescent bubbles in its wake. Domino had a vague impression of dragonlike heads, finned necks. lots of malachite scales, and a filmy, fishy tail. Though something struck her as not quite right, she didn't pause.

Diving into the newly vacated channel, she bounced between ceiling and floor. Head reeling from this unaccustomed form of locomotion, she nearly missed the grotto. Doubling back, she ducked into the coral-lined alcove. Tiny white tongues only an inch long curled out of the living wall to reach for her.

Claustrophobia came from nowhere, urging her to flee this cave within a cave before she was sealed in. She felt as if her breath were becoming thin and that water rather than air were swirling into her lungs, preparing to drown her. Shuddering, she shoved the scroll tube into a curving opening just large enough to conceal it.

Backing away, only stopped from running by the fear of what would most assuredly chase her, she stumbled against something that rolled beneath her boot. It looked rather like a broom handle encased in coral, but where her foot had struck it, some of the coral had broken and a pale red light leaked like blood into the water.

Despite panic she remembered and bent to pick up the magical trident from the grotto's floor. Two or three sharp blows against the cave mouth freed it of its calcified cerements and with each one, more of the red light brightened her way and clarity swam back into her thoughts.

Something had tried to frighten her into fleeing and only to herself would she admit how close that it had come. Now she was in control again and in possession of a weapon made for this element. Baring her teeth grimly, she launched into the channel. As a brother in arms, she knew that she should hope that Spite had defeated the Hydra; as a warrior, she knew she was spoiling for a fight.

Once out in the glimmering blue waters, she saw an astonishing sight—Spite fleeing from the Hydra!

The pale green elf maiden was swimming as rapidly as she could, deftly twisting and dodging to avoid the multiple gouts of flame the Hydra spat after her. But even though Spite was a minnow for grace and celerity, she could not match the sheer strength of the pursuing monster which thrashed through the water with powerful strokes of its fishy tail.

Domino doubted that she could reach Spite in time. The elf maiden was slowing, clearly exhausted by the furious chase. The best the General could hope for was to avenge her steed.

Then intervention came, not divine or miraculous, but in the form of a large rock that plummeted down from the surface and neatly pinned the Hydra's tail to the sandy bottom. Spite shot away in a burst of gleeful speed and before Domino's wondering eyes began to shift shape again.

The human qualities vanished completely to be replaced by the familiar sea-foam-and-green horse. Familiar from the shoulders up, that is, for from the torso down Spite now wore a fishtail, covered in glassy green scales the same shade as its mocking eyes and ending in a filmy white fin.

Shaking her head, Domino gritted her teeth and looked across what must have been the battlefield. The white sand, pale pink under the light of her trident, was strewn with boulders. Clearly the shot that had pinned the Hydra's tail had been as much a matter of luck as of finding range. Once the monster won free, they could not hope for more help from above.

Although much of the Hydra's attention was on Spite and more on freeing itself, it still had a spare head to note Domino's approach. Breathing a burst of almost liquid fire at her, it craned several of its necks to prepare for her.

Coolly assessing the situation, Domino leaped from the top of a boulder with all the strength of her cavalry-bred thighs. Making herself into a torpedo with the trident at its tip, she pinned one of the Hydra's heads to the lake bottom. Whipping out her saber, she ducked under more flames and took a swipe at the next-closest head.

Behind her, Spite had joined the fray, pummeling the Hydra with powerful forehooves. The unshod edges were as sharp as razors and where they hit blood welled up through the Hydra's heavy green scales from crescent-shaped cuts.

The water was red now from more than the trident's light. Yet, as Spite had warned, the Hydra was rapidly healing the wounds that they had inflicted upon it. Knowing that they could not truly harm it, the Hydra could fight until exhaustion made one of them careless.

Brandishing her saber, Domino sprang upward. At the height of her arc she took an unorthodox two-handed swipe at the centermost of the heads she was fighting. The blade swiped cleanly through scales and flesh, grated on bone, and when she gave an added, savage tug it cut cleanly through the neck.

Blubbering like a manic teakettle, the Hydra focused two heads on her, furiously blowing flame. Twisting with an agility of which a true seaborn could be proud, Domino avoided most of the flames. Even so, the back of her tunic was burnt into ash, but the freshly sheered neck stump was solidly cauterized.

Spite's trumpet of delight suddenly died into a few embarrassed coughs. The flailing hooves fell still and more amazingly, the Hydra ceased its attack. Poised to behead another neck, Domino broke off her swing and slowly turned to face whatever new enemy had appeared.

A female figure stomped across the sea bottom toward them. The skin of her face was fine and delicate—like seaweed that has crisped to tissue paper in the sun. Unlike Spite's skin, which was a healthy, uniform green, this creature's was mottled olive. Nor did her hair, stringy and matted, hung with a variety of sea detritus, add to any overall impression of health. Yet, despite this, the angular female thumping across the lake bottom radiated a vitality and fecundity that was as tangible as the cold caress of the water that eddied around her.

Recalling Spite's words, Domino thanked her patron deities that she was a woman, for the mere thought of what service the Sea Hag might have otherwise demanded of her was enough to shrivel into impotency what she didn't have.

From the corner of her eye, Domino could see Spite shifting shape again, the upper part of its/his/her body becoming a female form, the bottom remaining fishy, so that the hippocampus became a mermaid.

"Mom had revamped the Hydra," Spite whispered as soon as she had a human mouth. "Originally all it had were stocky legs. I worried that you had drowned when I had to swim out of range to share my water breathing magic with you."

The Sea Hag cupped her hand behind an ear that was truly shell-like: the irregular, lumpy shell of an over-sized oyster.

"Whispering isn't polite, child," she said, bulging eyes like luminous pearls orienting on Spite. "You were raised with better manners."

Grasping the trident, the Sea Hag wrenched it from both the sand and the Hydra's neck without apparent effort. Holding it, she surveyed Domino, who realized somewhat uncomfortably that she was still standing on the Hydra's back.

"Domino Blaid," the Hag said, drawing out the "o" unreasonably, "we can't have this, you know."

"Ma'am?"

"You charging down here and assaulting my creature. Poor baby was only doing its job and you come down here and hack its head off and burn it and frighten it beyond belief."

She stroked the nearest head which flicked a forked tongue at her in a gesture that would have been kittenish except for the eight-inch fangs through which the tongue glided.

"It was attacking Spite," Domino explained, jumping down next to her erstwhile horse. "I didn't have any choice."

The Sea Hag stared coldly at the mermaid. "Spite

taunted the Hydra unreasonably. It's powerful, but not very bright and rather short-tempered."

Domino reflected silently that short tempers seemed to run in the Sea Hag's family.

"No matter," she said aloud, "Spite is an ally and I stand by my actions."

"You have gone to a great deal of trouble just to put something useless in an inaccessible place," the Sea Hag mused. "I could overlook it for the amusement value if you hadn't permanently damaged the Hydra."

"You can't punish us for attacking a guardian, Mother," Spite retorted. "That's why you put it there."

"Well," the Sea Hag considered, "actually, I did expect it to stay unharmed. That's why I selected a Hydra, a creature that not only regenerated but could grow new heads as needed. I don't like having my creations hurt. Now, as to the matter of your punishment . . ."

"Wait!" Domino commanded, "I believe that I can set this right, but I need your permission to return briefly to the surface."

"Oh, no," the Sea Hag actually chuckled, "what kind of guppy do you think I am? Your purpose here has been served. You would only use the opportunity to flee."

"I am not stupid," Domino retorted coldly. "Even if I escaped now, your reach is greater than this lake. I would rather die honorably than exist in fear of your eventual revenge. Secondly, you have already hinted that you know that the scroll I planted here was a dummy. A simple messenger with that news and I would be as efficiently undone as you could wish. Thirdly, Spite is within your power and, as I have stated, I will not abandon an ally—even a cantankerous one."

"Pretty speech," the Hag replied, "and I admit that I am curious. You may go but no farther than the glass-bottomed boat within which even now your men watch from the surface."

"There will be delay," Domino said, "while they send for what I request."

"You will return here," the Hag stated. "They can drop you a weighted parcel."

Domino wasted none of the Hag's patience when she got to the surface, but dictated a list to Rafe.

"Make certain that Chase realizes that I'll need powders or pills, not liquids," she said. "Now, I must return."

"Domino," Jord said, reaching to clasp her hand, "please be careful. What you're doing is dangerous."

"That's a soldier's job, sweetheart." She said, "I'm just glad that you're safe. I'd be happier if you would stay ashore. Who knows what the Sea Hag may do?"

"My place is with you," he insisted stubbornly, "and you can't have Rafe put me ashore. I rented the boat."

Accepting defeat, Domino kissed Jord's hand and saluted Rafe. As she sank back to the depths, she could see the boat skittering toward shore like a crippled water bug.

The Sea Hag pursed her lips approvingly as Domino rejoined them. Spite had retaken the hippocampus form, Domino suspected as much as to avoid talking to its mother as to be ready for fight or flight.

The Hag fanned a deck of scrimshaw cards. "I realize that you're not Spotty Gulik, but would you care for a game to pass the time?"

Several hands of Go Fish and Old Maid later, a canvas-wrapped package was lowered on a line from above.

"Nice rope," the Sea Hag commented as Domino untied the package. "You've been busy."

Domino grunted as she undid her bundle, but she did remember her manners enough to cut several feet of rope off and present it to her hostess.

"Now," Domino said, "if you will request that the Hydra swallow these pills, we can get under way."

"What's in them? The hag said, squinting at the large tablets.

"Mostly poppy syrup," Domino replied. "Chase uses them to dose the horses when they need surgery. I had him send a half dozen—one for each head."

"You don't plan on doing surgery on the Hydra, do

you?" The Hag's bulging eyes were wider than Domino would have thought possible and even Spite looked astonished.

"Yes, after a fashion."

"Crazy human," the Hag muttered, but she fed the Hydra the pills.

As soon as the Hydra had collapsed into a slumber so deep that its gills barely fluttered, Domino hefted a heavy, curve-bladed, two-headed ax. Experimentally, she held it to a flimsy stalk of seaweed that was being aimlessly carried by the slight current and the stem parted so easily that the pieces continued to float side by side as if still the same plant.

"Sharp," the Sea Hag said admiringly.

"Yes," Domino replied, and in the same breath brought the ax down in her best woodcutter's stroke down onto the Hydra's damaged neck, just above where the neck joined the stocky body.

The Hag's wail of surprise ringing in her ears, Domino dodged the Hag's long-nailed hands easily and knelt by the now-bleeding Hydra.

"Won't be needing this," she said, dropping the ax and reaching for the neck. "Spite, calm your mother. I'm not hurting her monster."

She felt the waters swirl as the hippocampus swam to intercept the Sea Hag. Her attention was for the newly wounded neck. The blood was flowing less freely now. Rocking back on her heels, she watched carefully as not one, but two heads budded from the stump and sprouted forth, each on its own skinny neck. Quickly, she stepped back so that the Sea Hag could see.

"There," she said, proud despite herself, "I've fixed your Hydra for you. It's even better than before."

"Well," the Hag weaseled, "those heads are awfully scrawny and the necks look like eels rather than dragons, but, yes, you've done well."

"Are we quits then?" Domino asked. "You'll let me go free unharmed and will keep the news of what I suspect about Prince Rango to yourself?"

"On one condition," the Hag said, stroking the sleepy baby heads. "You take Spite with you. I can't stand its sass."

"Gladly."

Domino swung onto Spite's back, feeling the odd curve where the horse's back merged into fishtail. Without prompting, Spite carried her to the surface. As they ascended, Domino felt the hippocampus's gait become choppy and lose some of its power. The glass-bottomed boat paced them until they emerged in the shallows, Spite once again a powerful horse.

Domino snuck a glance down and under as she was dismounting. Yes, most definitely a stallion. The horse's glass green eyes glittered wickedly at her as she hurried to greet Jord, Rafe, and the others.

"It is done," she said, mostly for Piggon's benefit.

"We saw," Jord replied, a bit pale about the gills. "You went back and cut the Hydra's neck off! It's a wonder the Sea Hag didn't destroy you then."

"She had given me her word that I could attempt to cure the monster," Domino said simply, "for some creatures that is still enough."

Rafe meanwhile was studying Spite with an amused expression on his weathered features.

"You got to keep the horse, I see." He grinned. "Good thing that only a handful of us saw what we did. It made quite a fetching maid."

Spite snorted and stomped one hoof, slicing away a deep divot of turf.

"I wouldn't mention it if I were you," Domino interpreted. "Might be bad for morale. Will the Company be ready to move come morning?"

"Aye, General."

"Good, speak with Colum about lightening up the wagons. We're going to move double-time."

"Trouble, General?"

"No, Rafe, but we took some time getting here and I want to make it up on the way back."

"Anything else, General?"

Domino looked at the puddles around her feet and the still-rainy sky. "I know it seems hopeless, but how about a towel?"

Despite dry towels, spiced possets, and hot teas, Domino caught a cold so severe that for several days she rode in a daze. Seth tended her by day and Jord by night. Both the Magical Folk and Yor Chase sent remedies, but they were slow to work—perhaps because she refused to rest.

"I hate having a cold," Domino announced, giving Seth a grateful squeeze and accepting the hot, sweetened peppermint tea. "It makes me feel less than human."

"Ride in the wagons," Jord suggested. "Rafe can lead the Company for a few days."

"You must be jesting," Domino said, sneezing repeatedly. "I am Domino Blaid!"

"You," Jord replied, "are a crazy lady, but I know better than to argue with you when you get that look."

Domino merely looked haughty—and sneezed.

When Kerran gave her his report that afternoon, she was almost too busy being miserable to wonder why he was making his report to her rather than to Rafe. Not wanting to embarrass Rafe, she waited until Seth appeared with a fresh cup of hot tea.

"Find Rafe for me and I don't care where you look, even if you roust him out of some lover's bed." She stifled a particularly violent sneeze. "If you can't find him, at least find out who saw him last."

The Company was settling into night camp when Seth finally came to report.

"No sign of the Colonel anywhere, sir," the boy said, "and best as I can tell, the last time he was seen he was heading toward the caravan of the Magical Folk."

Domino tried hard to think. The Magical Folk had stayed with them even after they had departed the Lake. They had sent some complaints at the increased pace, but Domino had considered this beneath her notice. Otherwise, her only contact had been a gift of herbal teas and comfits from Granny and a warm lap robe from Mel.

She sipped her tea wearily. "I must go and look for him. Just let me finish this. Seth, can you find me some dry socks and a fresh tunic?"

"Yes, sir."

She didn't miss the worried look he shared with Jord, but chose to overlook it. For now, all she wanted was to lean back and feel the warmth of the tea on her throat and breathe the fragrant steam.

When she awoke, the tent was dark except for a small figure huddled over a lamp turned down low. Outside, the first birds were giving a querulous welcome to false dawn. Significantly, Jord was nowhere near.

"Seth? What are you doing here and awake?" She sat up, her head feeling miraculously clear. "And where is Jord?"

The boy turned to face her, misery etched in each angle of his face. "He went there last night, General, to ask the Magical Folk about Colonel Rafe and he hasn't come back. When I went to look for him I found that the Magical Folk have moved out!"

Domino did not stop to be angry that Jord had acted as he had. He was a poet, not even military, and certainly he couldn't be expected to follow orders. Nor did she yell at the boy. His first duty was to look out for her and, as he saw it, that's what he'd been doing.

"Get me Captain Kerran and Sergeant Colum," she ordered. "Tell Spite to get his green ass up here—don't worry about leading him. Then report back here."

"Yes, sir!" The boy vanished at a run.

Domino strapped herself into her armor, refusing to let her residually aching muscles stop her. Kerman Blaid had insisted that she be ready in any condition and there were times she had hated him for it. Now, especially as a terrible suspicion surfaced within her mind, she was grateful to the old horseman.

"Seth," she said when the boy ducked back into the tent,,"did Jord have his scroll tube with him when he went to look for Colonel Rafe?"

The boy chewed his rosy lip as he struggled to recall.

"Yes, sir, I'm certain that he did because I suggested that he take a larger blade than his hunting knife and he made a joke about the pen being mightier than the sword. He tapped his pencase then and I'm sure that he had some scroll tubes with him."

Buckling on her saber, she strode outside to meet her officers. She quickly filled them in on what Seth had discovered, only omitting the significance of what Jord was carrying.

"I'm going to find them. Kerran, you will have command of the main Company. Colum, I want you to deal with the wagons and with Piggon—the sorcellet."

"That little bastard?" the Quartermaster questioned. "May I inquire why, sir?"

"If Jord and Rafe were undone by the Magical Folk," she explained only half truthfully, "Piggon may be in league with them, especially since his magical talent is communication. He should still be asleep—how about keeping him that way?"

"Yes, sir!" Colum sucked in his gut and looked fierce. A quartermaster didn't often have hazardous duty and everyone knew that you should let sleeping wizards lie.

"General, do you plan on going alone?" Kerran asked.

On cue, the sound of hooves against the damp turf was heard. Spite came up the slope, driving Dove, Nightsky, and Rafe's Blaze in front of him. Dewdrops sparkled from their glossy coats; those that fell from Spite glittered like diamonds.

"No," Domino answered, "Spite will be with me and I'm bringing mounts for Jord and Rafe. I should be fine and I'll move more quickly alone."

"General?" a small voice came from the tent. "May I come with you, sir? To help—I can watch the horses."

Seth stood holding the tent flap in a white-knuckled fist. The stiffness of his skinny frame said with wordless eloquence that he expected to be refused.

"I pity the horse thief who tries to steal any of these horses," she answered, "as you should. No, Seth."

"Yes, sir." He stood straighter, if possible. "May I speak with you? Privately, sir?"

Concern for Jord and Rafe pulled her, but something made her follow the lad into the tent.

"General," Seth pleaded, "I should go with you. You'll need me. I promise I have things to offer you."

"Seth," she tried hard not to patronize him, "I need to leave."

The boy sucked in his breath, "General, I was listening when Cranky Granny told your fortune. I was out in the dark. She said that Kalaran couldn't have his sorcerers read you because you were a girl, not a man. General, don't be mad at me, but I'm a girl."

Domino wondered if anybody was the gender they seemed, but skipped all the usual questions. It was obvious why Seth hadn't told Dominik Blaid that she was a girl when the Colonel had pulled her from the ashes and protected her. Equally, it was obvious why the little girl had been dressed as a boy when the armies of Kalaran and the Prince had swept through. Instead, she jumped to the most immediate problem.

"Do you want to continue as a boy?"

"Yes, sir, for now at least." Seth squared his/her shoulders. "May I come with you?"

"I surrender," Domino said, "but stay out of any fights. You don't have any armor except that no one will expect you."

"Yes, sir!" Seth tried not to bounce. "I'm ready."

Finding the direction in which the Magical Folk had gone was easily done, but Spite set a pace that would stagger the ordinary horses in a few hours.

"Slow," Domino hissed, "this is too important to risk because you insist on showing off. Not only are Jord's and Rafe's lives in danger, but Jord has the scroll of Gwykander with him."

When Spite slowed to a pace that was only rapid, not breaking, Domino did not chide him again. She knew that the horse could be sensitive to forces of which she was unaware. When night fell, they could see the flickering bonfires of the Magical Folk's encampment in a hollow some distance off the road. Pausing on a tree-sheltered hillock, Domino scanned through her spy glass.

"They have the wagons and tents drawn into a rough double defensive circle with a bonfire in the center. There is no way that I can tell from here where Jord and Rafe are being held. However, they aren't being roasted for dinner, so that's something."

"Let me go in and scout, sir," Seth said. "They can't help but be expecting you."

Domino nodded permission reluctantly and Seth slipped away. The night sounds played counterpoint to the breathing of the horses and the occasional snap as one or the other grazed on the shrubs around them. An hour passed without untoward activity from the Magical Folk encampment.

When Seth emerged from the underbrush, her eyes were wide and wild, but she pulled herself up and snapped off a passable salute.

"General, I found them and they're alive." She paused to calm herself. "I didn't talk with them though. They were pretty tightly tied up in one of Mel's tents."

"Did Jord . . . have the scroll with him?" Domino asked, biting back a flurry of undignified questions.

"No, sir," Seth answered, incongruously blushing. "They were pretty much down to their underclothes— no weapons or gear of any type."

Domino scuffed a space clear with the side of her boot. "Come and sketch the layout of the camp for me. Don't leave anything out."

Seth hunkered down and drew her dagger, using the edge to shape the dirt into lines and lumps.

"The double circles are pretty tight. The wagons have trip ropes strung between and there is a patrol—not just humans, some of those critters they have are helping."

"That's not good," Domino said.

"Then they have magical wards. I think that Mel may have set them up—they're kind of wet and sparkly. I saw a raven go through one and it dripped glittery slime for a few feet."

"That's not good."

"I'm not sure that all of the Magical Folk are in favor of the plot," Seth continued. "There were some little knots of people grumbling."

Domino brightened.

"But they seemed scared stiff of the ringleaders—Mel, Granny, and Necrotica. From what I've overheard, even those who don't like being pushed around are afraid of being hurt or of missing out on any payoff. So I don't see us getting much help."

"That's not good."

"I didn't notice at first," Seth confessed, "but they've set up camp near to one of our ghost traps. It may be just coincidence, but I overheard a scout reporting to Colonel Rafe as we came down from the Lake District that many of the circles had been disturbed."

"That's not good."

Domino chewed her thumbnail for several minutes, weighing the information. Then she turned to Seth.

"We're going to have to move tonight, while they won't expect the Company. First, we need to get the prisoners out. Second, we need to find the scroll or, failing that"— she swallowed hard—"destroy it. Thirdly, we need to punish the Magical Folk."

Seth nodded, so eager to serve that Domino felt like a bastard for what she was going to say.

"You are going to have to take care of freeing Rafe and Jord and then do what you can about the scroll." Domino watched Seth gulp as she realized that the crucial tasks were up to her. "I will provide you with a distraction by riding in the main gate as it were."

"Oh." Seth slumped forward, the thatch of strawy bangs hiding her eyes. "I can do it, I think."

"You must." Domino refused to soften. "There is no one else who is so well suited. When we separate, I want you to take all the horses except Spite and leave them in a convenient spot. Once you have the men out and have dealt with the scroll, you are to get clear."

"What about you, General?"

"I have Spite," she reminded him, "and I'm just going in to bluster and leave. We'll meet up with you."

When the irritated bleat of a camel alerted them to the proximity of the Magical Folk's camp, Domino signaled a halt.

"Now," she whispered, her throat oddly tight at what she was sending the kid into. "Good luck, Seth."

"Yes, sir. You too, sir."

When they were away, she squeezed Spite with her knees.

"Let's go, horse. There's a kid counting on us—a kid, two men, and, bright heavens, possibly an entire kingdom." She ran her hand through her hair. "Why did my daddy want me to be a soldier?"

Spite flickered an ear back, but was apparently too busy concentrating on the most graceful canter possible to spare a sarcastic snort. His mane and tail frothed in the pale moonlight and his hooves and eyes mirrored the stars. Despite Domino's concern for her men, she allowed herself a moment of awe at her steed's unholy beauty.

Alerted by Seth's report, she could see the magical wards about the camp. The woven lines of force shone like snail tracks in our morning sun. Spite slowed to a trot and carried her through the gap between two wagons, leaping the trip line as if it didn't exist.

Trailing rainbows, they came to a halt by the central bonfire. Shadowy figures resolved into men and women, elves and goblins, cats, dogs, hedgehogs, and camels. Domino resisted the impulse to look toward the prison tent, but instead sat straighter on Spite's back and scanned the throng with a consciously haughty sneer.

In the silence, she became aware of two familiar figures in a fiercely whispered quarrel.

"She wasn't supposed to be awake yet!"

"She certainly shouldn't have! That cold combined with my tea should have kept her groggy."

"Your teas! My wrap was ensorcelled to keep her from healthy sleep but too tired to think clearly."

"No, I told you. Magical teas are the best way to do the job so I sent some nice peppermint and chamomile ones."

"You weren't supposed to send the tea! My wrap was charm enough."

"No, we agreed that she was a tea drinker and would surely be more likely to drink tea than wrap in some ugly blanket."

"Ugly!"

As Granny and Mel degenerated into name calling, Domino repressed a desire to laugh.

"You outdid yourselves, did you?" she said coolly.

Mel and Granny were jolted from their argument and looked at her guiltily.

"You did," Domino repeated, "one or the other would have knocked me out, but together you healed me. Well, it's too late now. I'm here and you're going to have to deal with me."

"Oh, we will," came a dry voice. "These fools may have brought you to us sooner than I had planned, but I have power enough to handle you."

Necrotica minced out from the brightness of the fire. Her scraggly gray hair blew lank and greasy from her bony skull. The pointed ears that were exotically beautiful on most elves became demonic horns in the firelight.

Domino swallowed hard.

"Well, hello, Necrotica," she said, trying hard to sound smooth. "This isn't a surprise."

"It is," Necrotica said, "for you, Domino."

"General Blaid," Domino corrected. "I don't believe we're on a first-name basis."

"Very well." Necrotica dismissed the comment with a shrug. "I don't care what you want to be called. I only care how you die."

"I'm not going to die," Domino said, squeezing Spite into a walk.

Oddly, the horse did not respond to the signal.

"I hope you don't expect to ride out of here." Necrotica cackled. "I think your strange horse has dozed off. Why don't you get down and walk?"

Domino was prepared to stay put, but to her horror she felt herself dismounting.

"Oh, very good, General Blaid," Necrotica crooned. "Now come on by the hanging tree. I have some friends who would meet with thee."

Domino shuffled along in the direction the elf necromancer indicated. Surreptitiously, she tested her fingers and toes and knees and ankles. Nothing worked at her command. Somehow, Necrotica gathered what she was doing.

"Give it up, General," she shrilled. "You won't even be able to wiggle your ears if I don't want you to."

"I can't wiggle my ears anyhow," Domino retorted, "and I can talk!"

"Oh, I know." Necrotica's grin was pure evil. "I've left your voice alive because I want to hear you scream."

As Necrotica marched her to the gallows tree, Domino decided that there was an advantage to having one's muscles controlled by another: no one could see that she was trembling. Mel and Granny bound her hands behind her back, apparently less certain than Necrotica of the necromancer's power.

"For how long did you think that we would be content to grovel for your leavings, General?" Necrotica hissed. "Making us trade herbs and bread, sausages and tea for the very tools of our craft. That's restricting the development of industry and I understand that Prince Rango is very opposed to that. Yet, you're very useful, General, and I plan to make you more so."

She raised her hands, elbows akimbo, hands clawed, and, to Domino's startlement, began to sing. Her skinny lips rounded into an O and a noise like mating alley cats issued therefrom. Most in the surrounding circle cringed, hands over ears. Domino was not permitted this luxury and so watched in horrified fascination as a slender tail of white issued forth from Necrotica's lips.

From a wisp of white smoke it solidified into an elastic goo that resolved into elongated human forms, barely wider than a straw where they left the necromancer's lips, broadening to twice that as they swirled up around her outstretched arms.

Mesmerized, Domino realized that she recognized some of the faces and mismatched uniforms as belonging to the bandits that she had ordered executed.

Twisting the ectoplasm into a noose, Necrotica tossed one end over the tree branch.

"We're going to hang you, General," she said somewhat unnecessarily, "and then I'll have control of your body. Your soul is of no use to me, but some of my associates have been bidding for you, the Colonel, and your pretty boyfriend."

"Remember, I get the horse," Mel interrupted.

Domino's skin broke into goose bumps as the noose was lowered around her throat with the caress of tiny, clammy hands. Under Necrotica's direction, her feet marched up stairs her own men had built. Within moments, she would be swinging from her own gallows.

She wondered if Jord would appreciate the poetic justice.

"General Blaid!" a high voice called.

At the same instant, the feathered butt of an arrow protruded from Necrotica's throat and the elf began to crumple.

Domi!"

Jord raced from the shadows, impulsively intent on freeing her when a scraggly warlock and his equally moth-eaten black cat sprang upon him. At the edge of her vision, Domino could see Rafe working his way toward her, but the cavalry officer was clearly handicapped by having to fight on foot. A wild flight of arrows hinted at Seth's presence.

When Necrotica fell, Domino's own limbs returned to

her control, but bound as she was, there was no way for her to join the fray. Nor did the ectoplasmic noose loosen its strength. Indeed, Domino became aware that it was steadily tightening, the clammy fingers drumming an agitated tattoo on her throat. If the spell that gave them life was not broken soon, she would be strangled by this noose of her own making—whether or not anyone kicked away the stair.

Frustrated by the specter of such an ignominious death, Domino focused her hatred and despair on Necrotica's corpse. They had been so close to winning. Now, not only would she die, but her troops would die, and Kalaran would continue unchecked.

Her vision tunneled as the strangling hands cut off more of her air. Blood pounding in her ears muffled the sounds of the melee. Domino knew death was near when the hallucinations began. Necrotica's corpse rose from the ground, the arrow butt unbloodied, the fiery eyes brighter than before, her clawed hands grasping.

"Being killed is only an inconvenience when you're already dead," Necrotica gasped, "but you'll know soon enough, General Blaid."

Necrotica staggered toward Domino, apparently unwilling to wait for strangulation to kill her prey. Seeing the clawed hands reaching for her, Domino drew in the deepest breath she could manage. Cording the muscles in her neck and flexing for some faint purchase against the stair, she leaped at her tormentor. The ectoplasmic rope caught her in midswing, but she was too stiff-necked for it to break her. Instead, she swung enough to get purchase against something solid behind her—a person, she suspected, as it crunched against her bootheels and screamed—and launched forward with greater velocity.

This time she impacted solidly with Necrotica. One foot thrust the imbedded arrow deeper, slicing between neck vertebrae. The other caught her in the face, smashing the hatchetlike nose up and between the eyes.

The strain of resisting strangulation had nearly driven Domino unconscious so that she almost missed the sensation when her bound hands were freed. Lifting her numbed arms with a strength only the nearness of death could have granted her, Domino grabbed the rope above the noose and hung from her arms.

Her breath came easier and even the sensation of strangling hands diminished slightly, but a new torment awaited. Those same tiny hands were now focused on breaking her tenuous grasp on the rope, joined by myriad blunt-toothed mouths that nipped and nibbled with painful slowness.

Domino resisted even when driblets of her own blood tricked down into her underarms, tickling mercilessly. Hand over hand, she climbed the vengeful rope until she was astride the tree limb. Her confident captors had not removed her weapons, so she drew her hunting knife in bloodied fingers and slashed at the rope. At first, there was no effect, then gradually a shower of miniature, elongated corpses began to fall beneath her. Gasping her first free breath in an eternity, she looked down to see how she could help.

Her people were doing her proud. Jord was laying about him with his pen case, holding it two-handed and clubbing the hedge wizard, who was trying to return the favor with his staff. Jord wisely remained inside the staff's effective range and was certainly getting the best of the battle.

Rafe had found a camel somewhere and from its height was subduing any who came near and many who did not. Seth had given up on archery, but Domino glimpsed her among the tents and wagons, cutting lines and removing cotter pins from wheels.

Some of the Magical Folk had changed sides, but after a brief inspection Domino wasn't certain that this was intentional. One lanky man clad in varicolored rags was spinning wild circles, effectively toppling whatever he touched. Seven swirling whirlwinds spun like tiny tornadoes in his vicinity, crashing into friends and foes alike.

Grasping the remnants of the ectoplasmic rope, Domino slid to the ground. Unsheathing her saber, she dashed happily across the battlefield to where Spite still stood frozen. Lesser combatants got out of her way with flattering alacrity, but Mel maintained his proprietary seat on the green horse right until Domino leaped astride behind him and put her blade to his throat.

"I don't suppose you would believe that I was protecting him for you, would you?" he said.

"No," Domino growled. "Release him from your sorcery."

"Spite is encased in a formfitting shell," Mel replied, "and it is not of my making, so I cannot break it. If I could I would have stolen the horse already."

Domino had her doubts, but kept them to herself as she slid to the ground, forcing Mel down with her.

"Did you hear that, Spite?" she asked. "Formfitting."

The response was immediate and gratifying. Spite's hindquarters became amorphous and then reshaped into a fishtail. Now the force-bubble that had held the horse was obvious as its glittering confines shifted to accommodate the new form.

Next, Spite shifted his upper body. The stallion's heavy head and muscular upper body became the torso of a very buxom mermaid. Her white hair was styled in a cute pixie cut and her waist was trim, for Spite had shifted all available mass into the mermaid's enormous breasts so that the magical field broke under pressure. Spite tumbled to the ground, her tail flapping in the dirt.

"Very creative," Domino commented. "Now, if you would kindly change back."

"Envious?" the mermaid queried with a flutter of her long, snowy eyelashes.

"Nope," Domino replied, "but I can't ride a mermaid and too many of my men would lose sleep trying to figure out how."

Spite's provocative smile vanished and hastily she shifted back into the green stallion.

When Mel would have run, Domino snapped, "Hold it right there, sorcerer. I have questions for you."

Mel sneered at her. "Why should I answer them?

"Well," she said, "one of my men is standing right behind you."

Jord tilted his battered pen case so that ink splattered blue blood across Mel's shoulders.

"I'm right here, General," he said cheerfully, "and the fight is about won. Rafe and Seth are rounding up captives with the help of a little green guy."

"And?" Domino prompted.

"We haven't found it yet, Domi," he answered, his violet eyes troubled.

"Mel," Domino said with a calm she didn't feel, "any advice you have would be useful—now."

The sorcerer trembled, hearing the gravel that seeped into her tone despite her control, studying the ink coursing down his arm with singular fascination.

"I won't let you dye me, General," he said, "not to further Necrotica's plans, but I don't know what you want."

"General!" Rafe came hurrying over, the camel padding along behind. "We've secured the field and imprisoned those who opposed us. Necrotica still appears to be dead, but without her control, the ghosts have been sucked into the ghost trap."

Domino spared a warm smile for him. "Very good. We'll release with a warning those who fought with us."

"Shall we set up gallows for the rest?" Rafe asked.

Domino felt a sudden, acute distaste for hangings.

"No," she considered, "we'll behead them instead— set up the block within the ghost trap. See if you can commission an axman from the Magical Folk. He can take his pay in body parts."

Domino returned her attention to Mel. "What I want to know is where is the scroll tube that Jord was carrying when you took him prisoner?"

Mel stared back in stubborn silence. Domino was considering trying Granny when Seth came running up.

"Colonel Rafe says to tell you that the spinning guy will handle the ax and he'll work for first choice on fingers and a couple of hands. He wanted to know if he could harvest some while the victim was still alive—they're more potent that way."

Domino slowly unsheathed her saber. "Normally, I'd say no, but I have a possible exception here."

Mel's eyes widened and then he started babbling. "Necrotica wouldn't let anyone have anything until it could be checked for value. She heaped the booty in a tent and put Herb on guard."

"Which one is Herb?"

"The goblin," Mel replied, his gaze fixed on the saber. "He's an herbalist."

"Got a green thumb, huh?" Domino chuckled.

Seth cleared her throat. "Herb has been helping us, General. He swears he hasn't seen the scroll and I believe him."

"Fine, but I'll tear limb from limb any who cross me on this matter . . ." Domino's words trailed off. "What the hell?"

Beneath the gallows tree a motley puppy worried a cylindrical object. The puppy's floppy ears kept getting underfoot and his brown-and-white spotted hindquarters were stuck in the air, his tail wagging furiously.

"That's one of Vernon's animals," Mel offered, "very cute, but hardly . . ."

Domino ignored him, striding over to the puppy. Seeing her, the puppy yipped playfully, wagging, if possible, even harder. When Domino stooped to retrieve the scroll case, he snatched it up and ran a few steps before putting it down. Domino hurried after him and again the puppy grabbed the case and ran.

"The little bastard is playing with me!" she said incredulously. "Call his owner."

"Ah, he's dead," Seth answered, "the camel sat on him."

"It was his camel," Mel said mournfully, "but she never liked him."

"Great." Domino hunkered down, trying hard to be unthreatening. "Here, puppy! Here, boy! Give me the stick."

The puppy yapped, growling playfully. Crawling on her hands and knees, Domino got almost into grabbing range before the puppy seized the scroll and ran yet again.

"Damn it!" she cursed, sitting back on her heels. "Give that to me!"

The puppy ignored her command and her face grew hot as she heard smothered titters from behind her. She scowled back over her shoulder and the tittering stopped.

"Sir," Seth said, "if I can get the scroll for you, can I keep the puppy?"

Domino glowered. "Soldiers do not barter for their services, Seth. You are in my Company, are you not?"

"Yes, sir," Seth held her ground, "but they do get booty and I've never asked you for gold or horses or wenches or anything."

"True." Domino hid a satisfied smile. "Get me that scroll case and the puppy is yours, but you walk it and feed it and all the rest."

"Yes, sir!"

The puppy watched her, tail wagging faster and faster as Seth skipped over, but when Seth closed in to grabbing range, it took the case and ran a few paces. Seth feigned indifference and picked up a stick which she tossed into the air and caught again.

After a few tosses, the puppy was watching in fascination. Seth ignored it until it was whining at her feet, then she threw the stick. The puppy ran after, tripping over its own ears and yelping in delight. Before it could turn around, Seth had scooped up the scroll tube and tossed it to Domino.

"Puppy spit!" Domino swore. "Well, the puppy is yours, Seth, but if it wets on my bedrolls, I'll court-martial you."

"Yes, sir! Thank you, sir!" Seth took off her belt and made a leash for the puppy. "What next, sir?"

"Well, we have executions to deal with and by then the Company should have rejoined us. So, let's get away from this mess and start setting up camp."

"Yes, sir." Seth looked less happy than any kid with a new puppy should.

Domino studied her. "Do you have something to say?"

"Yes, sir," She glanced over at Mel. "But not here."

Domino sighed and motioned for Mel to go to the prison tent. When he was out of earshot, she looked at the kid.

"Speak, soldier."

"Do you have to kill them, General? I mean, we know them and I think that they're sorry."

"War often means killing people you know, Seth," Domino answered, "and being sorry isn't enough."

"Still, General," Seth pleaded, "I really don't like this."

Domino bit back a growl. "I'll take your advice under consideration. Now, get to your tasks. On the way, send the Colonel to me."

Domino shoved the scroll case into her belt, annoyed that she should feel so untriumphant. Rafe arrived, the camel trailing him. This time the beast was hung with a variety of camp implements, including several items of Rafe's personal gear.

"Damn, Rafe, can't you go anywhere without that thing?"

"She follows me, so she might as well be useful, and I get seasick riding for too long." He shrugged. "If I may say so, General, you look in a foul mood."

"I am not in a foul mood," she retorted sharply.

"As the General wishes," Rafe said respectfully. Surely it was the camel that said "Humph," but Domino gave the Colonel a narrow-eyed stare just in case.

"What are the General's orders?"

"How many prisoners do we have?"

"Eight, if you don't count assorted livestock. Four others assisted us including Herb, the goblin, and I've granted them conditional amnesty. The rest are dead— even Necrotica seems to be still dead, but Jord passed on a warning about her and we've been keeping a watch for anything strange."

"The eight are well secured?" Domino asked, more hesitantly than she had intended.

"Yes, sir, and I've a chopping block and axman ready for your orders." He studied her. "What are your orders?"

Domino ruffled her hands through her hair, disliking her indecision immensely.

"Rafe, should we execute them? They did act against us, but they're so motley that they're pathetic. I don't feel right about killing them."

Rafe tilted his head and considered. "I know what you mean. They didn't even know what they had captured. Don't worry, I won't say anything, Domino, but you wouldn't have been that worried about the scroll if Jord had just lost his poetry."

She smiled gratefully. "We can't just let them go unpunished. What can we do?"

"Punishment for eight freelance mages," Rafe mused. "We could send them on a quest, I suppose."

"Or," Domino said, a wicked glint greening her eyes, "we could enlist them into the Company with the responsibilities and restrictions attendant thereupon."

Rafe grinned. "Yes, freelancers should hate that. I'll go and offer them the opportunity to enlist—with your permission, sir."

Domino stretched. "Yes, I like that solution. When Sergeant Colum arrives have the enlistees issued uniforms."

That evening, when she and Jord were resting, Domino allowed herself to admit her final worries.

"Preserving the scroll of Gwykander isn't enough," she explained to Jord, "we need an opportunity to use it on Kalaran and somehow I don't think it likely that he's going to hold still while you incant over him."

"You could pin him down," Jord suggested, demonstrating, "and then I could read off the scroll."

"I could," Domino agreed, wriggling free, "Rango isn't that strong. I doubt that we could get close enough to him when he's alone. He usually has a guard or two in the vicinity these days."

"We need an occasion when my reading aloud wouldn't seem strange," Jord said, "I could do a poetry reading."

"In Ancient Thermaean?" Domino shook her head. "I don't think so. Kalaran was never stupid."

"Ancient Thermaean isn't used very often, Domi, only for ceremonies and the like."

"Ceremonies," Domino said, "like weddings and coronations."

"Smart idea, Domi." He kissed her nose. "But I'm not likely to be asked to say the wedding. The Chief Priest is old, but he's not so senile that he'd fail to notice if we switched texts on him. Do we dare take him into our confidence?"

"No," Domino said decisively, "there may be corruption in the Temple. There are very few people I'd trust with this information—unfortunately, they've been scattered to the far corners of the Realm."

"Probably not by accident," Jord said, "and it's going to be hard to reach them."

"Hard," she said with a smile, "but not impossible. Kalaran may have outdone himself by sending Piggon with us. We should be able to get him to pass the message for us. We'll make it sound innocuous, like we're setting up a surprise for the bride and bridegroom."

Jord shook his head admiringly. "I love it, Domino. Speaking of 'love,' don't you think it's a bit late to do anything?"

"About Kalaran," she agreed, pulling him close.

"Domi," he gasped, "you're breaking my ribs."

The next morning, Domino made a point of hunting out Piggon.

"What do you think of our new recruits?" she asked with a friendly smile. "I must admit that your service with us gave me the idea of adding a bit of arcane power to the Company."

Piggon preened. "I think that you have chosen wisely.

We are even moving more efficiently now that you have them marshaled. I've notified the Prince of our projected arrival date and I believe that plans for the coronation are proceeding accordingly."

Domino held her smile. "Wonderful! Of course, since Jancy and I are in the bridal party, so much of the final detail has to wait for our return."

"Indeed." Piggon nodded. "I was talking with Squill the other day and he said that Jancy had expressed some small concern on being separated from the Princess at such a critical time. Spotty, of course, is to be best man. I suspect that even that very strange Gar Quithnick will have his part."

"Maybe he'll handle the sacrifices," Domino suggested. "He does have a certain odd perspective towards death."

"Artistic," Piggon agreed with a delicate shudder, "I've spoken with Spido on the matter."

"Hmm," Domino said, trying to stay casual, "so you speak with the others?"

"Somewhat," Piggon said, "we have much more in common with each other than, for example, I do with most of your soldiers."

Domino made her expression even warmer and inched Spite over so that they were riding quite cozily.

"Piggon, can you keep a secret?"

The sorcellet's expression warred between curiosity and a shred of his usual supercilious arrogance.

"If it does not violate my loyalties to Prince Rango," he said, "but you certainly would not wish to harm the Prince."

"Never," Domino said. "My loyalty to Prince Rango has never been questioned. But I need your oath that you will tell neither Rissa nor Rango what I am sharing with you now."

"Well . . . Since you say that no harm is intended to the Prince, I agree."

"Wonderful!" Domino leaned closer. "As I mentioned, Jancy and I are in Rissa's bridal party. Traditionally, we are supposed to have a surprise party for her."

"How can tradition be a surprise?" Piggon asked.

"Don't ask me," Domino said, "I'm still trying to figure women out."

"You and every man ever born," Piggon agreed.

"Well, this party is my responsibility and I've been torturing myself over how to reach Jancy and set up a meeting to plan this."

"You want me to contact Squill and give him your message," Piggon said with a satisfied nod.

"Exactly, and while we're at it, we should remind Spotty and Gar of their similar duties." She shrugged. "When I was Dominik I tended to direct such responsibilities. They may have forgotten that I'm on the other side now."

"Very wise, General," Piggon agreed stuffily. "Draft your messages and I will be happy to pass them along for you."

"Can you make the contact directly?" Domino asked. "Since the other sorcellets may not share your discretion?"

Piggon considered. "It will take more power, but I can do it."

"Very good." Domino sat up straight and gave him a snappy salute. "I'll have the messages drafted this evening."

The message that she and Jord worked out read: "We need to meet privately to make plans for the wedding and coronation. I suggest that the Onyx Eagle would be an appropriate spot. Can you send me an estimate of your return date? Please do not tell Rissa or Rango as surprise is essential."

"I'm not completely happy," Domino said, reviewing the completed text, "but it has the essentials and the Onyx Eagle as a meeting point should offer some warning, since we used it during the Wars for planning sessions and kept the Tipsy Cherub for play."

"More detail would be a risk," Jord reminded her, "since we need one of Kalaran's creatures to be our go-between."

"I know, sweet, I know."

Piggon sent the messages that evening and reported to Domino's tent immediately thereafter.

"I have replies for you," he said, his proud bow not completely covering his embarrassment at Jord's and her state of undress. "Jancy Gaine and Stiller Gulik will meet you at the appointed place and will notify you of their arrivals in advance. I was unable to reach either Gar or Spido. However, if they are still in Gelfait, my magic would be unable to reach them."

Domino nodded. "Thank you, Piggon. You have served Prince Rango well. Now all we can do is wait and hope that we'll have sufficient time to plan when we return to Caltus."

Postlude

The day of the wedding and coronation dawned bright green and gold. The gold came from the risen sun, the green from the trio of comets that arched in slow, spectacular passage across the blue sky. In the palace chambers, surrounded by twittering maids who were dressing her for the festivities, General Domino Blaid reflected that thus far nothing had gone quite according to plan.

On her return to Caltus, she had settled her troops, reported to Prince Rango, and checked the Onyx Eagle to see who else was back. Jancy had left word—and in any case they saw each other at the interminable fittings for the bridesmaids' dresses.

Spotty was late. When he did arrive in the capital, he admitted that he'd gotten caught up in a poker game with the dragon Schmirnov from which he had been dragged bodily by his dwarven companion, Ibble. Gar Quithnick had not shown up at all and, from what Domino had been able to pry from Prince Rango, neither he nor Spido had been heard from for some time.

The only good thing was that Princess Rissa had been receptive to their suspicions. Jancy had sounded her out with the blunt delicacy of her fine-honed ax and the

Princess had confessed that she had developed her own suspicions during the weeks they had been apart.

Domino obediently sat so that a woman could try to do something artistic with her short-cropped hair. From the adjoining room, she could hear Jancy thoroughly cursing someone who was removing curlers from her blond locks. The phrasing was particularly good—Sombrisio's influence no doubt.

Wishing that she had the resources of both Sombrisio and Mothganger, Domino let her thoughts drift to Jord. He and Spotty should be carrying out the first stages of their plan just about now. They had the help of the renegade priest, Lemml Touday, so she was little worried. How much trouble could subduing one elderly Chief Priest be?

Waiting outside the sacristy of the Cathedral of Dym, Stiller Gulick and Jord Inder listened for Lemml Touday to give them the all clear.

"The blessings of all the Gods, Goddesses, and Demideities of Light be upon you, your Reverend Grace," they heard him greet the Chief Priest.

Fenelais, the new Chief Priest, was known for his idiosyncracies—one of which was his desire to garb himself in privacy and have some moments of meditation before any religious service at which he was officiating. Despite knowing of his eccentricities, the comrades in arms were startled by his response.

"A good day, perhaps for me, foolish intruder," growled a controlled voice, "but for you it means your death!"

They burst into the sacristy to find an elderly man with a freshly shaven head standing over Lemml's crumpled body. Blood leaked from the priest's nostrils. The elderly man was partially garbed in the ceremonial robes of the Chief Priest and a sand-cast gold sunburst with a starburst of diamonds at its heart rested upon his breast.

"Udan Kann!" Stiller swore, his complexion immediately blossoming with pale blotches.

"You know me, ill-favored one," Udan Kann hissed. "No matter, this knowledge will only hasten your demise."

Stiller unsheathed his sword and dove at the *hingu* master. Udan Kann twisted his torso with the suppleness of a high-priced prostitute and avoided the blow. Then he tapped Stiller lightly on the arm and sent the warrior reeling.

Jord was about to charge into the fray when the grating voice of Calla Mallanik sounded in his ears.

"Move, poet," the elf said. "Domino would never forgive us if we got you slaughtered."

The elf raised his silver-strung bow and let fly with the arrows of fiery elf-wrought gold that never failed to find the life of evildoers at whom they were shot. Two arrows raced toward their target—overkill by a hundred percent—yet Udan Kann plucked both arrows from the air.

He tossed them like darts back at the astonished elf. One sliced the silver bowstring into glittering twine, the second pinned the elf's floppy-toed boot to the floor.

"I will tend to you in a moment." He laughed.

"Not if I have my say!" Stiller Gulick cried, charging back, his sword angled to give the assassin a new spinal column.

Udan Kann didn't even turn as he twisted to poke Spotty in the eyes.

"Snake eyes!" He giggled. "Or don't you play dice?"

"That piece of jewelry you're wearing," Jord Inder said, "it's Anachron, the amulet that Gar Quithnick was supposed to return to Gelfait!"

Udan Kann lurched as if struck, then he grasped the amulet in one hand, sparing the other to pluck a flight of arrows from Calla's newly strung bow from before his breast.

"Yes, it is Anachron. The Pariah has failed you as he failed me. In both cases, his obsession with the perfection of his art made him less than the demands of his task!"

"Damn Gar Quithnick!" Spotty Gulick cursed, struggling to his feet.

"I never trusted Gar Quithnick," Calla agreed, reaching for another arrow.

Udan Kann lurched twice more, his supple hands pawing at his chest. His humorless eyes bulged from his head. Falling to his knees, he moaned.

"Gar, my son, I did you ill to call you Pariah," he gasped, his voice coming thinner. "What a beautiful use of the delayed death touch! Truly, I should have named you *hingu-Grashanshao!*"

With a final moan of chest-crushing pain, Udan Kann crumpled to the ground, embracing at last the death that had been his best student's final exam.

"Well, I guess Gar did come through for us after all," Stiller Gulick said, looking at the dead assassin with respect, the blotches on his countenance fading slightly. "Is the priest still alive?"

Jord checked the body, "Yes, thank the Gods of Light. I guess that Udan Kann planned to play with him first."

"I wonder why Gar let him get away with the amulet?" Calla mused as he wiped the blood from the priest's face and began to administer first aid. "Clearly, he could have slain him."

Jord knelt by Udan Kann and began to remove the ceremonial robes. "I think that he had grown suspicious and let Udan Kann return as a warning to us."

"He could have come himself," Stiller commented. "It would have been a hell of a lot safer."

"True," Jord agreed, "but I don't think he knew that Kalaran had possessed Prince Rango, only that the Fallen Sunbird was somehow still active. Gar did not dare risk that Udan Kann's failure to return would warn his master."

"I guess it makes sense—for a *hingu* master," Stiller said. "I hope that Gar's alive, wherever he is."

"I wonder," Jord replied. "Legend says that Anachron will return to its previous bearer when the first is slain. It rests yet upon Udan Kann's chest."

"I guess that means Gar is dead, then, though I would

have given odds on him," Stiller said sadly. "He was a creep, but he was our creep."

Calla Mallanik cleared some litter from a bench and lifted Lemml up, then he started back in surprise.

"Spring's bouncing balls!" he exclaimed, "I've found the Chief Priest and he's breathing!"

"I guess that Kalaran didn't want any more problems with the religious establishment than he could help," Stiller said. "Now let me tend him. I've a dangerous job for you."

"Do you want me to climb into the eaves and serve as a sniper?" the elf asked.

"No."

"Go and see if any other *hingu* assassins are lurking in the bushes?"

"No."

"Carry a secret message to the Princess?"

"No."

"Then what?"

"I want you to put on Gar's outfit and get ready to take his place in the wedding party."

"How is that dangerous?"

"Have you thought about how Gar would feel if he hurried back here all the way from Gelfait and finds that you've taken his place?"

"Oh." Somberly Calla began to put on the grooms-man's uniform. "Wait, I thought you said he was dead, so why are you worried?"

"I also said that I'd give odds on him," Stiller said. "Hurry, they're starting to play the music."

Trumpets blared the opening of the triumphal march of the Royal House of Regaudia as Princess Rissa's carriage drew up in front of the Cathedral of Dym. Daisy, elegantly garbed and inordinately proud in her new role as Dame of Protocol, ordered the footmen to open the carriage doors.

"I've been going into battle since I was a child,"

Domino mused, "and I never was afraid. Why am I scared now?"

"Maybe because you don't have a horse between your legs." Jancy chuckled, then she softened. "Sif, I went into my first battle before I was born—my mother was a warrior woman like me—and I'm nervous, too. How are you doing, Rissa?"

The Princess looked up from the enormous bouquet of white roses, baby's breath, apple blossoms, and tulips in her lap.

"I'm nervous. Who wouldn't be, knowing what we know, suspecting what we suspect? I only wish we didn't have to do this so publicly."

"You know why we must," Domino reminded her. "Kalaran would not sit through the exorcism. Our only hope is that he will fail to notice that Jord is reading not the wedding text but the exorcism from the scroll of Gwykander. Jord has been memorizing as much as he can, so that he will not need to make obvious what he is doing, but ..."

"There are lots of buts," Jancy interrupted. "We can do no more planning. Now is the time for battle and praying for the blessings of both your Gods of Light and those of my battle-loving Northern Gods."

"Amen," Rissa breathed. "Amen."

They processed into the Cathedral of Dym amid a cheering throng of the citizenry who pressed against the uniformed guards to bombard the bride and her attendants with flowers, birdseed, sugared almonds, small coins, and light wheaten cakes.

"Fertility charms," Jancy explained to the puzzled Princess.

"Damn," Domino swore.

When they entered the Cathedral, Prince Rango, Stiller Gulick, and Calla Mallanik strode from the sacristy. Stiller bore a broad tray with the newly minted crowns of the Faltane. Calla bore a slightly smaller tray holding four beautiful daggers. The Chief Priest followed them more slowly, bearing in his arms the heavy, leather-bound Book of the Service.

"Is that Jord?" Jancy whispered.

"I don't know," Domino answered.

"Hush," Princess Rissa said.

The first one to process down the aisle was Seth. The little girl was crowned with a diadem of pink rosebuds and bore a basket with dried rose petals that she scattered along the aisle.

"Walk slowly, slowly, ducky," Daisy coached her. "Now you, Captain Ibble."

The dwarf wore a set of knee britches and matching vest with a white shirt. His feet were in open-toed sandals and he puffed a large pipe of the finest tobacco. He carried the wedding rings carefully balanced on a satin pillow.

"Behold the bearer of the rings!" Daisy said reverently. "Isn't he just precious?"

Ibble shot her a dirty look before heading down the aisle, a measured distance behind Seth.

"Now you, General Blaid," Daisy said, "and Jancy just a few paces behind."

The march swelled to a triumphal crescendo as the bride finally advanced down the aisle. From above, the ticket holders sprinkled the wedding party with more flower petals. From the aisle seats the guests smiled and waved, bursting with the peculiar somber pride that only comes when one is part of a wedding of someone very special indeed.

Spite, in its guise as a green elf maid, stood beside Rafe and his wife in the pew reserved for comrades, along with Piggon and Rolfus, the surviving sorcellets. A few other members of Domino's Company filled out the row. The quests had been singularly hard on the other companions.

When Rissa had reached the sanctuary and stepped to stand beside Rango, the congregation turned as one to face the front. The orchestra finished the last few bars of the march and fell silent.

"Dear people of the Faltane," came a rusty voice from beneath the Chief Priest's veiled shawl, "we come here to join two people in holy matrimony and to celebrate the coronation of our new King and Queen."

The congregation burst into enthusiastic applause. Jancy glanced at Domino as if to say "Is that Jord?" Domino shrugged.

She tried to catch Stiller's eye, figuring that he would give her some signal, and found that he was studying the Prince's Guard with a faintly quizzical expression marring his poker face. He had the advantage of her in that he could see the ones lining the side aisles and the back of the Cathedral. Domino, at least, could see the ones in the sanctuary without craning around in an undignified fashion.

Initially, nothing seemed out of order. The armed men stood ranked, wearing a variation of the same black-and-green uniform that was her habitual attire. Some looked bored—which was understandable as the Chief Priest had now begun intoning the ritual in Ancient Thermaean. Some stood square shouldered and alert, proud to be the honor guard for their Prince's most important day. Still others rested their hands on their sword hilts, ready for action.

Domino paused, her gaze scanning the faces of the men, rather than their uniforms and stance. She realized that she did not recognize a one. True, she had been a cavalry commander, not an infantry commander, but engagements had overlapped. Surely she would recognize at least one face among this chosen elite.

She glanced back at Spotty. His complexion was blotched. Their eyes met and she dipped her head in a slight nod. Unfortunately, neither Jancy nor Calla Mallanik were enlisted in the Faltane's military, so to them one grunt would look much like another. When the trouble started, as she knew now it would, they would not realize that the odds were stacked against them.

The Chief Priest droned on. The congregation waited in an attentive hush. The wedding party also stood attentive.

Then, shockingly, Prince Rango fidgeted. He shifted from foot to foot. He cleared his throat. The Chief Priest droned on, perhaps at a slightly faster rate.

Prince Rango's unrest migrated to his Guard. The bored ones straightened; the alert ones grasped their sword hilts. In the special section reserved for members of the clergy, a few of the older priests were leaning forward, listening now to the words that tumbled from the Chief Priest's mouth. Confusion crinkled their shaved heads as they realized that what they were hearing was not the wedding ceremony.

"Sif!" Jancy whispered. "It's gonna hit and my ax isn't close!"

"Daggers," Domino muttered, glancing toward the pillow that Calla held.

"Wait!" Prince Rango announced, his voice at its noble best. "What nonsense is this? Who has substituted this drivel for the wedding ceremony?"

"Why, darling," Princess Rissa drawled, "I didn't know you knew Ancient Thermaean. . . . "

Rango/Kalaran stiffened as he realized that he had been caught out of character. It was barely believable that the warrior Prince had become the ardent administrator, but completely impossible that he had suddenly acquired fluency in a long-dead tongue.

"My love," he said in honeyed tones, "I have been reviewing the ceremony in anticipation of this glorious day. I merely thought I heard some discrepancies. By whose right has the ceremony been altered?"

Rissa drew the skull of Kalaran from beneath her bouquet with a grim flourish. Stiller drew his sword. Setting down the satin pillow, Calla produced his bow from under the altar cloth. Domino and Jancy stepped to guard the Princess.

"The ceremony has been altered by my right," Princess Rissa said, and dashed the skull to the marble floor. "We had some questions . . ."

The skull shattered into flinders of sun-bleached bone, the small figures of the Demon of Darkness and the

Messenger of Light bouncing clear. A mist rose from the
Messenger of Light, becoming a pale, insubstantial form
with the features of Prince Rango. The Prince of mist
glowered at the Prince of substance. His eyes glowed
blue.

"You have my bride and my body, Kalaran," his voice
rang out. "The process is about to be reversed!"

"Deception! Black arts!" yelled Kalaran, "Guards!"

Turmoil erupted in the Cathedral. Wedding guests
screamed as Guards drew swords and advanced on the
sanctuary. From the row reserved for companions, Rafe
and Spite rushed to help. Rafe bore a sword, Spite an
oddly shaped wedding gift.

Knowing where the real threat lay, Kalaran lurched
toward Jord. Princess Rissa grabbed his arm to slow him.

"Wench!" he scowled.

"Demon!" she returned.

Ibble set down the rings and slid a dagger each to
Jancy and Domino. Together, shield maid and cavalry
general turned to face the advancing members of the
Prince's Guard. Spotty leaped to engage those coming
from behind him.

"Do you mean to attack members of your own military," Kalaran shouted, "to slay men who are only doing
their job?"

Stiller paused, indecisive. From her post at the Princess's back, Domino also paused.

The same thought was in both their minds: Could they
slay men who were only doing their sworn duty to defend
their Prince?"

Jancy Gaine didn't pause.

"Fuck that!" she said, thrusting her bridesmaid's bouquet into one guard's face and knifing a second. "I'm
a mercenary!"

"Cash and carry!" The ancient elven mercenary's cry
rasped from Calla Mallanik's throat as he began firing
arrows with near impossible rapidity from his newly
repaired silver-strung bow. "Die beautifully, you dumb
punks!"

A pair of the Prince's Guard obliged him by reeling forward, plucking at the arrows in their right eye sockets before collapsing over the rail into the clergy section and spattering the entire front row with blood.

"Beautiful!" Jancy cried. "Come on, Domino, get with the program! Aren't you in the uniform of the Princess's Guard?"

Domino glanced down at her lavender-and-lace bridesmaid's dress. A slow smile spread over her face as she tore the sword from a Guardsman's hand.

"For Rissa!" she yelled, stabbing the sword's former owner through the gut. "For Rissa!"

From his place, Stiller Gulick dove into a Guard who was racing to behead Jord.

"It was self-defense," he explained as he beat the man's head against the floor and relieved him of his sword. "Do you have any idea what Domino would do to me if I let Jord get hurt?"

Tossing Rissa to the floor in a sudden burst of cruel strength, Kalaran reached for Jord, only to find Prince Rango blocking his way. Kalaran sought to push him aside, finding to his dismay that his usurped body's arm was merging with the shade of its rightful owner and that Rango had control.

"Disarmed you, have I?" Prince Rango chuckled.

From the floor, Princess Rissa moaned in pain. "Rango, that was terrible!"

"Thank you, darling," the misty Prince replied.

Jancy had few smiles to spare for puns. Her dagger had been wrested from her and she was unfamiliar with the sword she had taken from one of her slain. Three Guards had forced her a few steps away from the Princess and were determinedly wearing her down.

Spite fought her way to Domino's side. She had shapeshifted into a buxom pale green centaur. Without hesitation, Domino grabbed the centaur's shapely soft shoulders and mounted. As she did so, Spite tossed the wedding gift to Jancy.

"Warrior maid," the centaur called, "Castrator!"

The Guard fell back for a moment, their hands falling to cover their privates, believing that the title was one that Jancy claimed. She caught the package neatly and tore away the wrapping from her bearded ax.

"By Hel's black-and-white hair," she gloated, "now this is going to be fucking great!"

Even Ibble and Seth joined the battle that ensued—ring bearer and flower girl back to back, daggers in hand. The slaughter was enormous. The wedding guests froze in terror, knowing that if they fled they might become the next victims.

Through it all, Jord kept reading, though his voice was growing hoarse as he strove to be heard over the turmoil. Joined at the arm with Prince Rango, Kalaran spat at Jord and his spittle became a ball of fire that flew at the poet, growing enormously so that it threatened to engulf both reader and text.

Rissa screamed and struck Kalaran a fierce blow in the kidneys, but she could do nothing for Jord. The fire crisped both the Book of the Service and the robes of the Chief Priest. Then a flash of light burst from Jord's breast. The fire vanished completely, leaving the poet nude and grasping the ancient scroll of Gwykander.

"The amulet Anachron!" Kalaran gasped, "and the scroll! Don't any of you do what you are told?"

Stiller chortled from where he had felled yet another of the Prince's Guard.

" 'Tis a good thing that Domino had initiative, but you have none but yourself to blame for Anachron's presence. It was brought to Caltus by Udan Kann."

"Udan Kann!" the Fallen Sunbird brightened.

"Don't get your hopes up, godlet," Calla Mallanik added, "Udan Kann was slain by Gar Quithnick by means of a delayed death touch. You are alone here."

"Damn Gar Quithnick!" Kalaran cursed. "And damn you! Anachron cannot protect you all!"

Again he spat, this time directing his spittle toward Calla Mallanik. The elf stepped nimbly aside, but Ibble and Seth who had fought to his lee were not so fortunate.

The dwarf took the brunt of the fireball. What remained spilled over onto the girl.

"You bastard!" Prince Rango yelled as the two small forms toppled to the floor. "I have had enough!"

He grabbed the demigod, shaking him as if to wrest him from the body he had stolen. With an aplomb that only poetry reading could have trained him for, nude and singed, Jord continued to read.

"*Quatendo erbud, altonfuss dermain! Akanetendo, ranma! Tendo soon, pan gen da ma! Royu gah haf!*"

The Prince's shaking effectively kept the demigod from effecting another spell as the final words of the ancient exorcism split Kalaran's immortal soul from Prince Rango's body.

On the sanctuary floor, the tiny figurine of the Demon of Darkness glowed with the blackness between the stars. Then, as once Kalaran had captured the Prince, the figurine captured the demigod's immortal essence.

Battle ceased as Jord's chanting finished and all the combatants realized that the true fight was won. Prince Rango swept Rissa to her feet just as she was about to land another punch in his kidneys. She looked into his eyes and smiled.

"This is my Prince!" she declaimed in a loud, clear voice.

Spontaneous applause rose from where the guests sat—though everyone was too polite to wonder aloud whether the intensity was due to the return of the Prince or to the fact that the guests now knew they would not be slaughtered as a wedding sacrifice.

Domino swung down from Spite's back and hurried into the sanctuary, but she didn't spare even an appreciative glance for Jord. Instead she rushed to the two charred heaps on the marble floor by the altar. Calla Mallanik shook his aristocratic head sorrowfully and tried to stop her.

"They're gone," he said. "You can do nothing more."

"Maybe," Domino said, pushing past him. "Jord, bring that damned amulet here."

The poet hurried over, his shapely ass drawing appreciative comments from the audience. He pulled Anachron over his head and held it to Seth's breast.

"That's right," he said softly, "it has the power to heal."

"But not to resurrect," Domino added anxiously, "I only hope that we're not too late!"

A glow far purer than the fires of the Fallen Sunbird rose from the amulet and suffused the burnt child. Absolute silence fell within the Cathedral of Dym, broken by wild cheering as Seth shook off the charred remnants of her flower girl's frock and sat up.

Domino clasped the girl to her heart and Rissa knelt and slashed off ten feet of her lace-embroidered train to cover her.

"Thank you, Your Highness," the girl whispered, looking down in wonder at the amulet, "and thank you, Anachron."

"Ibble!" Stiller cried. "Use the amulet on Ibble, Domino."

But as Domino reached for the glowing amulet, it shimmered, faded, and was gone.

"It's vanished!" the Princess cried. "But where has it gone?"

"Back to Gelfait, I'd wager," Stiller said, looking down at the corpse of his companion. "Gar Quithnick must not be dead after all, but Gelfait's position out of time delayed the amulet's return to him."

"What an irony," Jord declaimed from where he was stripping a set of pants and a uniform jacket from a recently slain Guard. "Gar lives but is lost to us forever and the amulet's flight to him has robbed us of Ibble as well."

"Well, not really," came a familiar voice from the small charred heap on the floor, "we dwarves are pretty tough, you know. We're particularly well-protected from fire. Wouldn't be worth much as smiths if we weren't."

A second spate of applause, this one flavored with hearty laughter followed the dwarf's announcement. Stiller bent and embraced his friend.

"Brush yourself off and find some pants," he said. "We have a wedding and a coronation to complete!"

"Wait!" twittered a female voice as Daisy hurried from the rear of the Cathedral. "You can't mean to continue the ceremony with bodies all about and half of the wedding party soaked with blood and gore!"

Rissa looked at Rango and the Prince nodded, embracing her about the waist. Then the Princess spoke.

"We do and we will! After all we have been through, the wedding must not be delayed." She looked at the older woman and relented slightly. "Very well, there will be a brief intermission to clear away the bodies."

"What shall we do with this, Rissa?" Jancy asked, picking the figurine of Darkness from the floor.

"Can you hold on to it for now?" Rissa asked. "Disposing of that is going to take some thought."

As the bodies were cleared away, Lemml Touday and Fenelais were roused from their bench in the sacristy. Clad in his second-best robes, the Chief Priest came forth and officiated, Lemml in the place of honor at his side. The Book of the Service was gone, but the memory of the ritual remained and if it was a bit shorter, that was all for the best.

Newly wed, the Prince and Princess knelt before the Chief Priest to be coronated the new King and Queen of the Faltane. Their trusted comrades stood in a half circle behind them, battered and bloodied faces glowing with pride.

Only Ibble stood apart, the cushion with the crowns in his broad dwarvish hands. He studied the crowns as the Chief Priest intoned a prayer requesting that the new rulers be just and wise and brave in the rulership of their kingdom. When the Chief Priest reached for the King's crown to set it on Rango's head, the dwarf interrupted.

"Uh, do you really mean what you just said there in that prayer?"

The Chief Priest stared at him in puzzlement, "Of course I do, Ibble. Do you think we want a ruler like Kalaran for the Faltane?"

The dwarf shrugged. "I just wanted to make certain it wasn't one of those pro forma things. I never know with humans. I remember when Stiller was teaching the dragon poker—"

"Ibble," Stiller interrupted, "do you have a point?"

"Sure, Stiller," Ibble said, "I was studying these crowns here and you know that dwarves are great craftsmen, right?"

"Right."

"Well, I'd like a second opinion from Calla, but I'd say that these crowns have been enchanted to make them control devices. No points for guessing who would be doing the controlling."

"Kalaran!" Prince Rango gasped.

Calla Mallanik rose from his inspection of the crowns and nodded agreement.

"Yes, Your Highness, I would guess that the Fallen Sunbird, being immortal, had designs on your kingdom far exceeding a human life span. Through these crowns he could control the new King, after your death."

"And the Queen while she was yet alive!" Jancy said in horror. "Sif's shining hair, that's ugly!"

A faint cursing could be heard from the sash of her gown where she had stowed the figurine containing the imprisoned demigod.

"If these crowns are cursed," Prince Rango said, "then let the coronation be continued but let us be coronated without crowns!"

"That's fine with me," Rissa said, with a faint shudder as she looked at the crown destined for her and contemplated what Kalaran might have intended, "I've never like crowns. They're terribly uncomfortable."

The coronation was concluded without further incident. As the congregation rose to cheer their new King and Queen the Cathedral of Dym shook and shimmered. The vision of each person within blurred and when it cleared, they found that they were standing within a rounded building as large as the vanished Cathedral but without a roof so that it was open to the sky.

Across that sky, three green comets looped in increasingly erratic patterns.

"What is this?" King Rango asked.

"An arena of sorts," Stiller offered, "or a stadium."

They looked about. The congregation was now seated in the round, those who had been on the ground floor in small, hard seats, those who had been in the balconies on wooden bleachers. The royal wedding party stood on a mound amid a broad, grassy field that had been marked into a diamond with solid lines of white paint. Small shelters stood where the sacristies had been.

"I think I know what has happened," Jord Inder said. "Kalaran did not lie when he said that the presence of so many magical artifacts could cause a rift between time and space. The strange phenomena faded somewhat after we left on our quests, but Caltus remained fraught with them. Now we have gathered again several magical artifacts of great power in one place."

"The scroll!" Domino said, picking it up from the grass.

"The crowns!" Ibble added, looking down at them.

"The Demon of Darkness," Jancy said, pulling it from her girdle, "or the Imprisoned Fallen Sunbird, if you'd prefer."

"The weakened fabric of reality cannot tolerate their presence," Calla Mallanik agreed, "and I really dread telling you what the solution is."

"A quest!" groaned Stiller, the blotches rising on his face.

"Three quests," Calla corrected.

"I guess we could take the scroll back to the Lakes," Domino said. "For real this time. It shouldn't be that bad. There aren't many bandits left."

"If the crowns are not as powerful as the other artifacts, I could lose them in a game of poker," Stiller said. "I promised Schmirnov I'd come back after the wedding."

"The Demon of Darkness is a harder call," Queen Rissa said. "Jancy?"

"I'd love to get rid of the old bastard," Jancy replied, "and I didn't much fancy going along on your honeymoon. Calla, are you with me?"

"As long as I don't have to enlist," the elf promised. "The kingdom rewards its heroes a lot better than it pays their soldiers."

"Let me join you," Ibble said, "I'd feel much safer if we encase that damn thing in some of my magic dwarven rock when we ditch it. A figurine could be tempting, but who'd want a chunk of ugly rock?"

"Then it is agreed," King Rango declaimed, "but reality will have to bear the strain long enough for you all to attend the wedding reception. Look, the stewards are bringing in the refreshments, even now."

Dressed in white trousers and shirts, with trays slung suspended from their necks, stewards were moving through the seats and the stands handing paper cups of drink and bags of peanuts and popcorn to the gathered guests.

Daisy led a few stewards over to the royal party.

"The weather's so lovely that I've ordered tables be set for you here on the lawn," she said. "But I fear I must report that the wine has spoiled—all we have is that sweet, frothy brown drink and plenty of ice."

The wedding party groaned, but the new King took a tentative sip from his cup.

"Sweet," he said, "but I rather like it."

Rissa laughed and held him close. "I guess that Kalaran got that awful habit from you. I should have known!"

Minstrels struck up drums and flutes in light dance tunes and the military band spelled them with merry marches. Occasional rifts of the amplified strings and bass were heard from the unseen world beyond. The new King and Queen held out their hands to their comrades.

"Come," Queen Rissa said, "join us in a circle dance to celebrate new beginnings."

As they spun on the flat, grassy lawn, overhead the three comets finished their twisting course and exploded into each other, sprinkling the heavens with a dusting of stars, bright against even the daytime sky. Not even the giant lizard that snapped at the trailing sparks could dim their brilliance.

Forever Afterword

by David Drake

I've been a fan of Roger Zelazny since I read "A Rose for Ecclesiastes" on its original publication in 1963. I went to my first SF convention in 1974 (the worldcon) in part because Roger was Guest of Honor and I wanted to meet him and tell him how good he was.

And finally, just before the early and unexpected end of Roger's life, I had the pleasure of working with him on this project. Baen Books has asked me to describe how this came about. Roger's work is his monument; he needs nothing from me. But as it's traditional for friends and family of the deceased to each toss a pinch of dust on the grave site, you can think of this as my offering.

Less business gets transacted at SF conventions than I was solemnly assured was the case when I was a young writer, but sometimes it does happen. One of those occasions occurred when Jim Baen gave a quite wonderful dinner for a dozen or so friends and authors who were attending World Fantasy Con.

Jim had been publishing Roger since the early '70s when Jim was editor of *If* and *Galaxy* magazines. I was delighted to see Roger at the dinner, but I assumed we were both there as old friends of Jim.

True . . . but as Roger explained during the meal, there

was also a project. He'd planned a shared universe involving a series of reverse quests: returning four magical talismans to their hiding places now that the Forces of Good have defeated the Evil Wizard.

Roger would write the opening and closing segments and had plotted the quests in some detail. He'd enlisted his friends Jane Lindskold (present at the dinner), Mike Stackpole, and Bob Asprin to write three of the four stories. He'd arranged for Bill Fawcett (my friend and Jim's, also present at the dinner) to handle the business side; no one could be more trustworthy. And before dinner, he'd sold Jim on publishing the volume.

That left one obvious hole in the project. As everybody at the dinner stared, Bill said loudly to me, "Gee, David. Who do you think we could get to do the other story?"

I immediately suggested the writer sitting across the table from me. She just as quickly turned it down, noting that she was too busy.

Me too, but the real trouble with *Forever After* for me was that it called for whimsically funny fantasy with a serious core—the sort of thing that Roger Zelazny did better than anybody else in the field, and I didn't do at all. I wasn't sure that I could handle the job. Normally that's all right—I learn by trying new things, which means sometimes I fall on my face. But I didn't want to fall on my face in front of Roger Zelazny, a writer I'd idolized for decades, even if it was his idea that I try.

I tried anyway. Roger sent me the opening segments (which I thought were hilarious) and the pages of plot for my portion. I used Roger's own "The Furies" as my stylistic model. It's an extremely funny story on the surface and gut-wrenching just below that surface. To my mind it's one of the best SF stories ever written.

I did my story; the other people did their stories; and Roger wrapped up the project to his own enthusiastic satisfaction. He phoned me at the beginning of May to see if I'd join him and other *Forever After* writers on a panel at WFC '95 in Baltimore (the city in which he started his writing career). In the course of the conversation he told me he thought my segment was funny and added that he was delighted with what all the writers had done with his concept, especially Jane.

I wish Roger was writing this afterword.

I wish I was going to see Roger again in Baltimore.

I wish I was going to read more wonderful Roger Zelazny fiction.

He gave me and the field so much that it isn't right to complain that he isn't around to give us more. I miss him anyway.